GUY GARCIA

SWARM

Cover art: Emil Alzamora
Cover design: CirceCorp
Photo credit: Kenneth Willardt

ISBN: 978-0-9974398-0-9 (sc)
ISBN: 978-0-9974398-1-6 (hc)
ISBN: 978-0-9974398-2-3 (e)

Library of Congress Control Number: 2016913601

Publisher info:
Name: Morphic Books
Address: 450 West 42nd St. 40M New York, NY 10036
Phone number: 9174064132
Legal name: GDG Inc.

rev. date: 03/27/2017

Even the most harmful man may really be the most useful when it comes to the preservation of the species; for he nurtures either in himself or in others, through his effects, instincts without which humanity would long have become feeble or rotten.

—Friedrich Nietzsche

It is not the strongest of the species that survives, nor the most intelligent, but the one most responsive to change.

—Charles Darwin

For a minute there, I lost myself, I lost myself.

—Radiohead

PREFACE

In the beginning, it was all fun and games. Long before the barricades fell and the pyres were lit, before the dream became a cold sweat in these dis-United States of imperiled possibilities and perpetual discount plans, before the stars strayed from the stripes and the iTribes gathered their dismay and forged it into something different, before they became something different, before everything was different, it all still seemed the same. Nobody noticed, nobody knew, nobody cared. There were signals, hints of the yawning abyss, of course, in the nattering re-tweets and bloodshot blink of LEDs, in the predator drone of bilious blogs, and the dopamine drip of the next text alert. It could be glimpsed in the slingshot shrapnel of Asteroid apps, the fuming funnel clouds and insistent hacker's cough, the warm-weather kudzu vines creeping up our forests and our spines. It was there in the *Oprah* revelations and *Jackass* stunts, in the grim smile of the alligator hanging by its teeth from Steve-O's underpants. It was right under our noses, in the video clips of IEDs and the collateral damage of *Deal or No Deal*. Maybe it had always been in the cards, a DNA Dear John waiting for its moment to reshuffle the deck and up the ante. It was in the fading strokes of a quill pen—invisible and indelible—written into that sacred space between the lines, tabula rasa, a palimpsest plain as day for all the blind to see. And even before that, in ritual chants and mossy tombs, pyramids lined up like landing lights, pointing not to the past nor to the future but to the ever-impending present, the imminent now. In any case, it was already a foregone conclusion—even in those gasping last days of denial, when the foundations foundered and the heavens heaved, when the prayers of trampled hope were finally answered and the levies broke and the water rushed in, carrying everything and everybody along with it. And for the first time in a long time, the table was cleared and the tab was paid, gifts were given and taken, all was lost, and everything was gained.

Part I

EMBRYO

It was true that Air Force Airman Donald Westlake was even more withdrawn than usual that morning, hunkered over a low row of benches that bordered his bunk, oblivious to everything except the sounds from the compact MP3 player clipped to his sleeve. Westlake's barracks were situated away from the bustle of center base, an unadorned concrete box near the perimeter gate supervised by a lackadaisical contingent of Afghan government troops. Westlake was wearing high-fidelity headphones that covered his ears, but the crunching chords and booming beats were faintly audible over the rattle of the communal air conditioner. The singer sounded angry, livid, his voice ripping into the lyrics.

> *You gotta load the ammo and cock the gun*
> *You gotta point the barrel and make them run*
> *Don't give them time to pray*
> *The maggots won't forget this day*

In the base commander's report, after the government launched its official investigation and the global media fanned the flames of mutual distrust and recrimination, nobody remembered exactly when Westlake had become obsessed with skinhead metal music. It wasn't unusual for the whipsaw cocktail of chronic stress and numbing routine to warp the habits and tastes of the most mild-mannered recruits, suddenly pumping iron around the clock until their bodies bulged like G.I. Joe action dolls, tattooing themselves with the names of dead relatives in Morse code, muttering lewd and sarcastic comments in the showers. Idiosyncratic behavior was the norm, tolerated as long as the strangeness never boiled over into a bona fide situation. Exiled in this color-leached land of blinding heat and giant biting spiders, nobody felt like himself, so how could he expect it of anybody else?

The pieces of Westlake's improvised battle set were laid out before him on a neatly folded blanket. He had cleaned and reassembled his M16 rifle at least twice since dawn, carefully loading the magazine and laying it next to his Beretta M9 pistol, which was designed to withstand temperatures of up to 140 degrees Fahrenheit and function after exposure to saltwater, mud, or sand. Westlake pulled on his camouflage flak jacket, stowed the pistol in his Bianchi side holster, and counted out four M67 fragmentation grenades. He gently hooked the grenades onto his utility belt, making sure not to accidentally snag the pins, grabbed his rifle, and headed for the door.

> *These days demand guts*
> *No ifs ands or buts*
> *A million miles high and looking down*
> *It's time to run amok*
> *It's time to give a fuck*

Some of Westlake's fellow soldiers peered up from their cots as he passed, hardly seeing him through the groggy haze of their own preoccupations. They didn't ask him where he was going or why he was suited up for combat. As far as any of them knew, he was following orders, just one more flyboy trying to get through his tour without succumbing to the ache of distant wives and girlfriends raising kids without their fathers. Men who were just doing their jobs defending democracy or at least defending each other from the dread of being a living target, not just for bullets and body bombs but also for the serrated stares of children and old women who saw Allah knows what in the speckled camouflage and expensive battle accessories. Men who felt not just the weight of their ammo and dehydrated rations but also the psychic baggage of soldiers sent to regulate wars on foreign soil, protecting moist green lawns in the summertime, or at least the idea of moist green lawns in a place where no such thing existed and never would.

Airman Westlake pushed through the door and paused, squinting as his eyes adjusted to the blare of the parched terrain. Less than a hundred yards away, a half dozen or so Afghan commandos were on sentry duty at the base checkpoint, Ray-Bans glinting and rifles propped against the whitewashed perimeter hut as they gregariously recounted the previous evening's escapades. Westlake held his M16 by its middle grip as he sauntered toward them, just another early bird American coming to shoot the shit and share a smoke. As Westlake approached the checkpoint, a couple of the Afghan soldiers recognized him and smiled. Even when he leveled his weapon in their direction and clicked off the safety, their comprehension of what was happening lagged behind the dry clatter of the gun and the impact of the first bullets on flesh and bone. The few rounds that missed their marks chipped dark holes in the wall, which was soon splattered red in Jackson Pollock patterns. Without breaking stride, he unclipped a frag grenade and lobbed it toward the far end of the group, its dull thud and shock wave knocking two of the men to the ground as they scrambled to return fire. Westlake took his time, his eyes cold and unblinking as he picked off his targets with brutal efficiency.

This isn't Iraq
There's no turning back
Don't be a nigger
Pull the goddamn trigger!

Most of the men at the checkpoint were already dead by the time Westlake's fellow airmen began pouring out of the barracks, horrified by their comrade's confounding carnage, their shouts and commands no match for the grinding guitars in his head. Westlake kept advancing and firing even after his hapless victims were all dispatched, pausing only to load another clip, when an American hand grabbed his shoulder and swung him around. He didn't hear the report that would end his remorseless rampage, a bullet to the head at close range, to be later classified, for PR purposes, as an unfortunate case of friendly fire. Westlake died in the dirt, surrounded by twitching corpses and speechless half-clothed US servicemen, the music in his headphones still blasting.

> *Don't hesitate—attack!*
> *Don't negotiate—attack!*
> *We reap what they sow, bro.*
> *Send them down below!*

The singer's scream was guttural, primal, insistent, inhuman.

1

Tom Ayana entered the glass facade of Austin's Frost Bank Tower and took the high-speed elevator to the top floor. He was dressed in his customary uniform of plaid shirt, jeans, and black cotton hoodie, a padded backpack slung over his shoulder. The receptionist for the Texas headquarters of Free Range Energy Industries was on the phone as he walked in, and he waited for her ersatz eyelashes to flutter in his direction.

"Hang on a sec, Sheryl." Her metallic blue nails flashed as she moved the phone away from her mouth. "I'm sorry, young man, but all deliveries have to go through the service desk down in the lobby."

"I'm here to see Frank Reston."

"Do you have an appointment with Mr. Reston?"

"Yes, I do."

"Sheryl, I'll call you back." She punched a button on the office intercom. "Mr. Reston, a Mr. ..."

"Ayana."

"Mr. Ayana is here to see you. He's not on your calendar, so ... I see. Yes, of course, sir."

The woman rewarded him with a brittle smile. "You can go right in."

Reston was a hale fifty-something in khakis, a wrinkle-free blue dress shirt, and a tightly knotted silk tie. He rose from his desk with the easy confidence of a self-made millionaire and trapped Tom's hand in a bear paw grip.

"Thanks for dropping by," he said, waving to a sturdy lacquered chair. "Tom, I don't usually answer unsolicited e-mails, but I was intrigued by your pitch about cybersecurity threats." Reston sat in his Aeron ergonomic chair and leaned forward. "So what can I do for you?"

"Well, Mr. Reston, it's really about what I can do for you."

On the shelf behind Reston's sprawling hardwood desk, college football trophies shared space with a photo of him wearing a yellow hard hat and stepping jauntily onto a gas-rig elevator. The actual hard hat was on the shelf too, conveying the message that Free Range Energy's CEO was a man of action, a man who didn't mind getting his hands dirty, a man who didn't like to waste time.

Reston looked at his watch and interlaced his thick fingers. "Okay, you've got ten minutes."

"That should be plenty," Tom said.

"But before you start, I have to warn you that I've got lots of smart guys working for me who know plenty about that." He pointed to the computer next to his desk. "And we're doing just fine without any outside cybersecurity experts. That's what people like you call yourselves, right?"

"Actually, we like to think of ourselves as cyber ass protectors."

"No kidding." Reston smiled and glanced at his watch. "How's that?"

"Because once someone penetrates your back door, you're fucked."

Reston guffawed. "That's nice, Mr. Ayana. I really do appreciate your, ah, metaphor. But I think our back door is just fine. I've got an extremely busy day, so if you don't mind …"

"Mr. Reston, if you have an operations dashboard on your desktop, you're probably already in trouble."

Reston glanced at his computer screen. "I'm listening."

"Well, you can't have a dashboard unless your IT and OT are linked, and we all know what happened to Talvent after it was

8

breached by Comment Group, or the ATG network hack, a while back. They thought they had all the security they needed too." Tom was referring to a case where a Chinese hacker group successfully broke into the remote administration tools that monitored the status of gas and oil pipelines stretching across the United States, Canada, and Mexico, including the widespread disabling of the software that measures the levels of gasoline station fuel tanks across America.

"Well, Mr. Ayana, that's scary stuff, to be sure," Reston said. "And the government is going after the people who are responsible, as they should. But I don't see what that has to do with Free Range."

"What if I told you that your entire OT smart grid was vulnerable to online intrusion? I'm talking up, down, and midstream—in real time."

"In *real time*?" Reston chuckled amiably. "I'd say prove it to me."

Tom removed his laptop from the backpack, flipped it open and spent the next fifty seconds typing in a series of commands. When Tom put the laptop aside, Reston looked bemused. "I thought you were going to show me something."

"Your operational technology and hydrocarbon supply chain switches at your main processing plant in Colorado, and all three of your Texas gas rigs have emergency surge cutoffs that are triggered by pressure gauge controls," Tom said. "Once the master grid server is compromised ..."

Reston shook his head. "You can't change the pressure in the storage tanks without setting off the emergency compression shutdown alarm."

"I don't need to change the pressure if I can use your own OT grid to control the pressure gauge monitors. Think of what could happen if your plant managers kept raising the pressure in the storage tanks when they're already full."

Reston's office intercom buzzed. He raised his finger. "Hold that thought."

"Hank Lakusta is on line one, sir," Tom heard the receptionist say. "He's says it's urgent."

Reston punched a button on his phone. As he listened, his jaw clenched and his complexion reddened. "Yeah, I heard what you said. Don't do anything yet, Hank. Just sit tight. I think I might have the fix right here in front of me."

Reston hung up and glowered threateningly at Tom. "I could have you arrested, you know."

"You told me to prove it to you, Mr. Reston. The main thing, what should matter to you, is that if I can do it, then so can someone in China or Russia—or a hacker working for one of your competitors. And when it happens, and sooner or later it will, I guarantee that the people behind the attack won't be sitting in your office."

"This isn't a joke, son," Reston said with something akin to contempt. "Unlike your little virtual scenarios, the things we do here are real. The gas we harvest from the earth helps people cook their food and heat their homes. The country depends on it, and the men who work for me have families to feed. This isn't some kind of friggin' video game."

"Cyber intrusion is definitely not a joke or a game, sir. The hackers who can get inside your system and shut it down or even blow it up are real too. Just ask Hank."

Tom watched Reston's expression morph from anger to comprehension and finally resignation. "Okay, you're hired," he said sourly. "Now will you please turn my damn company back on?"

The savanna bristled under the equatorial sun, its grassy shoulders hunched over the banks of a squiggly ravine. Off to the west, the inflorescence fanned out to the horizon, welded to the sky by molten bands of mercury. The shadow of the single-engine chartered aircraft flickered across a caravan of giraffes gliding toward the mountains like a fleet of tall ships. Lions, cheetahs, and leopards lurked in the undergrowth, and hippos and crocodiles patrolled the lakes and rivers. Under the flat-topped acacia trees, baboons kept a wary lookout for hyenas and snakes as they groomed one another. In this sublimely raw and rugged terrain, it wouldn't be that surprising to spot a grazing triceratops or a velociraptor poised to pounce on its prey—just two more genetic wild cards in the primordial contest for water and blood.

It was during moments like this, soaring above the savage paradise of the African bush, that Cara Park was glad she had fended off her parents' entreaties to be a doctor and instead pursued her passion to become an evolutionary biologist. This was the payoff for those countless hours in the lab, toiling to grow insects under fluorescent lights, keeping diaries of their miniscule dramas, cataloging and combing through the busy regimens of beehives and ant colonies. Why, she wanted to know, did the locust swarms that had ravaged the western and southern parts of the continent for centuries suddenly shift eastward to the famed wildlife parklands of Kenya and Tanzania? And would the battery-powered contraption in the back of the plane, secured in place by bungee cords and hemp straps, have the same effect in the field that it had in the lab?

In the back of the plane, Eric Wightman was fiddling with the tangle of wires and duct tape linking the device to its power source and the cluster of loudspeakers bolted to the aircraft's belly. With his swimmer's frame, unruly bangs, and reddish stubble, Cara's assistant looked more like an indie rock guitarist than a scientist, which was appropriate for a gifted egghead who moonlighted as a keyboardist in a band called Rubik's Kewb. Of all the graduate students enrolled in the biological sciences PhD program at the University of California, Berkeley, he had most impressed Cara with his empathic smile, inquiring mind, and burning enthusiasm to explore the convergence of traditional biology and cutting-edge technology. In an era in which living organisms were increasingly viewed as complex machines, and vice versa, it made sense to have a student with a grasp of biomimicry and an MS in computer programming on her research team.

"Almost ready," Eric announced. "This baby's gonna rage!"

"I hope so," Cara said. "Did you decide on a name for it?"

"Poly-harmonic audio-redactive omnidirectional hardware," he replied. "But you can call it PHAROH."

"As in ancient Egyptians?"

"As in biblical plagues."

"We're in East Africa, not the Nile Valley," Cara said, without letting him see her smile.

Eric grunted and turned his attention back to the glowing radar bands on his scanner. "We're getting close—not more than a couple of miles away. Looks like a big one."

Flying over the treetops, Cara, her long black hair shoved under a UC Berkeley baseball cap, felt unfettered and filled with a sense of purpose. She was here to help the local government study a sudden rash of locust swarms with the aim of fending off an agricultural catastrophe, not to mention the economic downside of scaring off the lucrative tourist trade. But Cara was motivated to understand not just why the swarms had suddenly appeared but also what they revealed about the ineffable impulse of living things to organize and assemble into something larger than themselves. Darwin's biological imperative was apparent everywhere she looked—in the disorienting patterns zebras made when they huddled close and rested their heads on each others' backs, in the flocking instinct of birds and the skittish herds of Thomson's gazelles, even in the majestic processions of Cape buffalo and wildebeests, flowing to and fro with the seasons like some ancient sentient tide. The truth was that unraveling the puzzle of life on the planet, delving into the micro and macro machinations of existence itself, was more than a profession or intellectual calling. It was Cara's religion.

"There it is!" Eric shouted. He was pointing to a dense brown cloud drifting over the grasslands. Cara motioned to the pilot to take them lower and closer to their target. She'd seen videos of locusts on the move in the American Midwest, Australia, and northern Africa, but there was no preparation for the sight of billions of insects moving en masse, driven by a bioenvironmental trigger that caused otherwise harmless grasshoppers to morph into a ravenous scourge. A large swarm could blacken the sky as it consumed everything in its path for hundreds of miles before dissipating. Locust plagues had occurred for millennia, appearing in the Koran and the Bible. Moses summoned them to devour all the crops of Egypt after the pharaoh refused to release the Jews. But Cara knew they were not just the stuff of religious fables and ancient history. Locusts had decimated large swaths of the US plains during the 1930s, magnifying the misery of the Great Depression. Even after American farmers started fighting back with modern pesticides, locust outbreaks continued to occur in the United States and around the world to the present day.

The insects were dead ahead, flying in a fluidly consistent formation, a shape with no edges. "I'm initiating PHAROH software!" Eric shouted above the engine noise, and Cara involuntarily clenched her fists. There was so much time and money riding on the next few moments. The swarm was thick enough to blot out the sun, and its shadow was like a stain on the defenseless vegetation below. Cara could understand why people from any century who saw the airborne eclipse coming would flee in horror.

Cara's interest in locusts had intensified after recent breakthroughs in understanding how they happened in the first place. For most of human history, it was assumed that the solitary and normally benign common grasshopper and its voracious Mr. Hyde–like brother were two separate species. Then, in 1921, entomologists discovered that crowding and proximity to other grasshoppers were all it took to trigger a phase change during which the grasshoppers' bodies become darker and more muscular. The bugs also become sexually animated and aggressive, moving forward and taking flight to avoid being eaten by the cannibalized locusts swarming behind them.

In 2009, researchers from the universities of Sydney, Cambridge, and Oxford pinpointed serotonin, a monoamine neurotransmitter also found in the brains of humans, as the agent that caused docile grasshoppers to morph into a gregarious, uninhibited state and mass into a frenzied collective of flying monsters.

Cara was already a noted authority on biocollectivism and had published several papers on the emergent behaviors exhibited by ants and bees when she got wind of the new research and started musing over how it could be leveraged to prevent or disrupt locust swarms. She knew that locusts, which affected one-tenth of the world's population, could cause famine and economic calamity and that the powerful pesticides keeping the insects at bay were too expensive for the poor, undeveloped nations of Africa. She had applied for a grant from the United Nations Food and Agriculture Organization. With the funds, she began working on a method to deter locust swarms by using sound waves to disrupt their communication system.

Cara had recruited Eric to help her design PHAROH on campus, and they succeeded in using it to disperse a simulated swarm in the lab, but this was the first time the device would be tested in the field. They spent two days in Nairobi prepping the plane, mounting the speakers and loading the digital equipment. Then, with the help of UN officials and meteorologists from Kenya and Tanzania, they set out to intercept a swarm last seen heading southeast over Lake Victoria. With their fluttering target finally in sight, Cara and Eric were about to find out if the PHAROH would live up to its imposing name.

The pilot descended to under a thousand feet, close enough for the uppermost fliers to hit the plane's windshield with a sickening splatter. Eric was poised over his contraption, recording the event with the video camera in one hand. "Here, put this deflector on," he said, handing Cara a headset that clipped to her ears and wrapped around the back of her skull. "It'll shield you from any PHAROH beam radiation." He put a set on himself and indicated with a nod that PHAROH was booted up and ready.

"Not yet," Cara instructed as she donned the deflector and handed one to the pilot. "Wait until we're in the middle of it."

The swarm was all around them now, obscuring the horizon as the cloud of wings shimmered and roiled. The heaving storm of bugs washed over the plane, coating the propeller and wings in a milky sludge. The pilot gripped the controls nervously, and Cara knew it was only a matter of seconds before he'd be forced to pull out.

She turned to Eric. "Do it," she said.

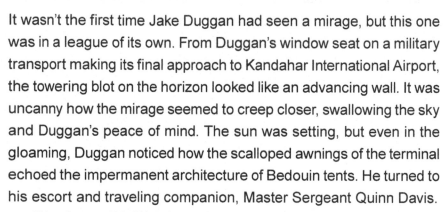

It wasn't the first time Jake Duggan had seen a mirage, but this one was in a league of its own. From Duggan's window seat on a military transport making its final approach to Kandahar International Airport, the towering blot on the horizon looked like an advancing wall. It was uncanny how the mirage seemed to creep closer, swallowing the sky and Duggan's peace of mind. The sun was setting, but even in the gloaming, Duggan noticed how the scalloped awnings of the terminal echoed the impermanent architecture of Bedouin tents. He turned to his escort and traveling companion, Master Sergeant Quinn Davis.

"You know, if I didn't know better, I'd say that big mountain over there is moving toward us," Duggan said casually.

Davis craned his neck to look out the window and nodded grimly. "You don't know better, and that, my friend, is what the hajjis call a haboob." Duggan ignored the slur. Davis handed him a pair of goggles, a dust mask, and a bandana. "You're going to need these. The dust storms in Afghanistan are savage mothers. They can last for days, and I'll tell you that this one looks like a real dick twister. We got here just in time before they close the base."

"How come I don't feel so lucky?" Duggan muttered, fastening his seatbelt and returning his attention to the open file in his lap.

Davis had been there to greet Duggan on the tarmac at Riyadh. After introducing himself with a firm handshake, he led Duggan to the US Air Force transport waiting to fly them to Kandahar. It was only after they were in the air and drifting above the dagger-like postmodern skyline of the Saudi capital that Davis handed Duggan a folder containing the details of his mission. Duggan broke the tamperproof security seal and settled in to read the documents that would explain what had brought him so far outside his normal jurisdiction. He immediately recognized the picture of a young soldier that was stapled to the inside corner of the briefing file. Donald Westlake, an otherwise unremarkable air force recruit from Ontario, California, had shaken the US military and generated an international diplomatic crisis by shooting half a dozen Afghan military personnel in cold blood for no apparent reason at the allied base in Kandahar. The official story was that Westlake had a history of psychological problems, which the air force had somehow overlooked, resulting in a formal apology from the secretary of defense to the government of Afghanistan and a promise to do a better job of screening military personnel assigned to politically delicate duties on foreign soil.

It wasn't until Duggan read through a detailed description of the shooting and got to a summary of interviews with Westlake's barrack mates that he finally understood why his boss had sent him halfway across the world to investigate an incident that would otherwise have been handled by the Air Force's own internal security corps. Westlake, according to several of his fellow airmen, had not only been complaining about headaches before the shooting but also claimed that he was hearing voices with a foreign accent. Even odder was the fact that Westlake told at least one other soldier that the voices were coming from his laptop. The US military intranet was one of the best-encrypted systems in the world. It would have taken the cyber equivalent of a howitzer to break the firewall, and the fallout from such an attack would be relatively easy to detect. But the internal report described evidence of any intrusion as "inconclusive."

When Duggan looked up from the folder, Davis was already waiting with an answer. "We need to be able to rule out a breach in the internal allied network," he explained, "a breach that could have been used to communicate with enemy agents who would like nothing more than to drive a wedge between the States and our

Afghan allies. On the other hand, if the messages to Westlake came from someone inside the air force, we can't be sure that they haven't infiltrated internal security."

"So why didn't you call in the CIA?"

Davis grinned and shook his head. "You know what it's like around here. I mean, between the services, with everybody looking for the slightest excuse to grab more turf. The consensus was that you could be trusted to stick to the game plan."

"Which is to tell you whether Westlake was compromised and, if so, whether the messages being sent to him came from outside the base or from embedded sources. And you're worried that your military cyber ops might be dirty too, so you can't trust your own people to do the job."

Davis tipped his head and shrugged.

Duggan had been an agent of the National Cyber Security Division of the Department of Homeland Security long enough to know that silence from a fellow operative was an implicit yes. It was even better than a yes because it eliminated the need to delve into the nuances of why Duggan's statement might be partially, or even slightly, under certain circumstances, less than completely accurate. Plus, if the mission went unexpectedly awry, there would be no need to confirm or deny that Duggan's assumption had been endorsed by someone who lacked the authority to do such a thing. Never saying more than necessary was a mutually understood occupational guideline that itself was better left unsaid.

"We'll be on the ground in a few minutes," Davis said finally. "We can talk on the ride to base."

The wind was already picking up as they descended from the plane to a cordoned-off section of the runway. The tsunami of sand loomed menacingly as men in fatigues hastily loaded their bags into a waiting jeep and scurried to batten down the base. Then, as Duggan watched, the control tower half a mile away disappeared into the roiling murk.

"Holy cow."

"Get in," Davis instructed. "The sooner we get away from the airport and flying debris, the better."

Duggan put on the goggles and mask and tried not to focus on the countless tons of dirt coming toward them at near-hurricane speeds.

"Look on the bright side," Davis noted cheerfully. "If nobody can see us, they can't shoot at us either."

Duggan tried to look appreciative. His job at the NCSD was to "assess and mitigate" threats to the cyber infrastructure of the United States. But as the US government had quickly discovered, the line between cyberspace and real space was more than a little fuzzy, meaning that Duggan's beat sometimes took him into territory normally patrolled by the FBI, the CIA, and in this case, the Department of Defense, and the National Security Agency, whose penchant for secrecy had provoked speculation that its acronym actually stood for "No Such Agency." Adding to the bureaucratic imbroglio was the creation in 2009 of an entity called Cyber Command, overseen by the Pentagon, which had instantly ignited an interagency debate over the governmental distinction between "defensive" and "offensive" cyber weapons. With so many landmines on the playing field, the NCSD was obligated to tread lightly and cooperate with the bigger players, which partly explained why Duggan had been dispatched with only the disturbingly opaque instruction to grab his passport and meet with a Defense Department liaison in Saudi Arabia. Duggan was pretty sure that his cover would include an identity designed to ruffle the fewest number of feathers among his counterintelligence counterparts in the military and probably the CIA as well, which was undoubtedly why Davis made no effort to continue the conversation that had started on the plane. That Duggan was now trapped in a sandstorm inside a moving vehicle with almost zero visibility, heading into a highly charged environment he knew nearly nothing about, only added to his discomfort.

"So do the men in Westlake's barracks know I'm coming?"

Davis veered sharply to avoid an object that Duggan didn't recognize. "They know *someone* is coming to inspect Westlake's computer, which is still right where he left it. As you know from reading the file, they've already been interviewed several times, and as you might imagine, the whole incident is kind of a sore subject. That's why I'm putting you up in the officers' quarters. There's no point in throwing you to the wolves. As far as they know, you're just a DOD tech wonk here from Washington to check out the hard drive for computer bugs."

Duggan smiled mirthlessly. The best false identity, he knew, was one that hewed closely to the truth, and this was a classic case of warping reality by simply withholding certain pieces of information. In fact, it was not that long ago that Duggan actually had been a private sector cyber wonk, an idealistic entrepreneur with dreams of changing the world and getting rich in the process. Back in the early nineties, fresh out of the University of Chicago with a degree in computer programming and the idea for an online TV network, Duggan had seen the Internet as a fresh start for civilization, full of possibility and promise, a place where digital visionaries could stake a claim and roll the dice, a place where anything and everything was possible. Duggan and a few college chums collected seed money from friends and family, rented a former women's underwear factory with bad ventilation in New York's Silicon Alley, and incorporated under the name NexTube Technologies. Everybody wore T-shirts and jeans to the office and worked twenty-hour days in exchange for free Cokes and sweat equity in a company with a T1 Internet connection and no proven revenue model. Arriving for work each morning, Duggan would look across the open-plan office—with its exposed brick walls, protruding water pipes, and dangling wires, clots of young people hunched over boxy CPUs and monochrome monitors—and feel the adrenaline jolt of an explorer who had reached the summit of an unnamed mountain. He was gazing out across an untracked panorama to be claimed, mapped, and populated, except that cyberspace had no physical boundaries or limits and its power grew exponentially with each person who logged on, an infinite parallel universe that would transform the material world and everything in it.

The day came when their hard-wired baby was ready to be born. Film crews from Japan and France flew in to cover the launch party, which featured live video chats with people in other cities via grainy black-and-white feeds that were hailed at the time as miraculous. By the third case of champagne, the user base was over twenty thousand and climbing. There was alchemy in the way that electrical pulses and glowing pixels could be almost instantly transformed into product, and some pals with a shared vision of watching movies and sports on their computers were suddenly actually in business.

A year later, Duggan married a reporter who had come to interview the budding entrepreneur for his hometown daily, the *Chicago Tribune*. Duggan was a freshly-minted millionaire, on paper at least, which in those days was as good as the real thing. He bought a loft in Soho on easy credit and a black BMW with custom plates that spelled DOT COM. NexTube seemed to be at the top of every heavy hitter's acquisitions list, and Duggan's platinum payday was just a few notarized signatures away. Then the Internet bubble went pop and wiped it all away. Suddenly, all the partners in his company had their own personal lawyer, but Duggan still didn't see it coming. A new CEO was installed, and the board stopped returning Duggan's phone calls. His marriage lost its valuation too.

Duggan retreated to Chicago in a self-righteous exile of indignation and denial. Then an acquaintance asked him out for a drink. Did he know, his friend asked, that the US government was looking for experienced programmers and paying top dollar for their services? There was even a fast-track training program that would give him the equivalent of a PhD in computer science and an FBI security clearance to boot. That night, well into his third Jack and soda, he laughed away the offer. But after a few more weeks of glimpsing his future through the bottom of a shot glass, he called his friend back.

At first, Duggan welcomed the rigor and distraction of his federally funded re-tooling. He sincerely believed that freedom and creativity on the Net couldn't exist without justice, and that justice required that certain basic rules of cyber conduct be enforced. Then came 9/11, and Duggan once again felt the window for a better world slam shut. At the same time, the rampant lawlessness of the Net and the hideous virility of the latest viruses were demoralizing. Even in the tight-lipped corridors of the NCSD, he heard rumors that the United States and its allies were collaborating on a more powerful follow-up to Flame, Olympic Games and Stuxnet, early-generation cyber weapons that had penetrated the vital industries of enemy nations, collected information and delivered it back for analysis and further manipulation without the targets ever knowing. Murderous apps that had slipped their leashes and renegade strings of computer software were roaming the Internet like packs of wild dogs, or festering like sociopathic orphans that had somehow developed a need and ability to evade destruction or capture.

Were government-commissioned cyber-attacks acts of war? Sure. Was it a problem that military viruses had gotten loose by accident or been intentionally released by hotheaded allies, thereby accelerating a cyber cold war, an arms race of killer computer viruses, each more destructive and insidious than the last? Of course. But what, Duggan had finally concluded, was the option? Was this better or worse than guns, bombs, or bio weapons that rotted people's organs from the inside? Was there an online equivalent of a suicide bomber? Meanwhile, there was always the possibility of newer, stronger malware, like Conficker, a program that had already infected an estimated five million computers in thirty-five countries, turning them into unwitting slaves and linking them together into a turbo-charged botnet, a massive web of processing power that rivaled the world's fastest and strongest supercomputers and seemed chillingly capable of defending itself against all attempts to stamp it out.

These days, patrolling the Web for enemy hackers and anarchists made Duggan feel like a sheriff trying to keep order in a once booming town that had degenerated into a sprawling slum of misguided nerds, amoral swindlers, anarchists, and paranoid autocrats. Decent folk were cowering behind their firewalls, ducking to avoid getting splattered by spammers, praying that justice and parental controls would prevail and make cyberspace safe again for women and children. It pained Duggan to see the Eden-esque promise of the Web's early years defiled by doubt and distrust, the dark pools gathering behind the high-resolution display of a billion handheld devices. Everything and everybody was for sale, whether aware of it or not. Everybody's opinion mattered, whether it made sense or not.

Duggan was trained and licensed to carry a sidearm, but most of the bad guys he was after did their dirty work with a trackpad or a mouse. He knew that a shadow war was already being fought by blackhat battalions that used attachments instead of guns, aiming not to kill the enemy so much as to delete it. The next Pearl Harbor would not be delivered by a naval fleet or a massive air strike; it would produce no riveting images of flaming ships and wounded men leaping into the Pacific; there would be no day of infamy to rouse the population. No, it would come silently through the same wireless conduits that powered your dishwasher, brewed your coffee, and brought you the evening news. First the air conditioner would turn against you—and then the fridge, the lights, and your car. You'd fumble in the dark to find your phone so you could call for help, but the device would be useless because the satellites and radio towers that power such things would have been disabled. Since mass communication as we know it would be nonexistent, it would take hours, maybe days or weeks, before the true scope of the disaster was known. Airlines, railroads, utilities, and financial networks would all be crippled or destroyed by camouflaged code aimed at the same machines that make modern life possible and tolerable. And if all that weren't enough, it was also conceivable that the true source of the catastrophe would be impossible to trace, that those responsible for so much suffering and destruction would remain faceless, nameless, and, in their own minds at least, blameless.

It rankled Duggan that even those who knew better, the corporations and agencies whose systems had been repeatedly infected and hacked, chose to cloak their losses in willful denial, like rape victims who couldn't bear the shame of going public. But what really worried Duggan wasn't the mounting evidence that individuals, groups, and entire nations were plotting a black swan event, a cyber-attack on the United States that would dwarf 9/11 and usher in a new Dark Ages. What kept him drinking after last call and staring at the ceiling in the predawn hours was the disconcerting prospect of scanning a crowd of people glued to their phones without knowing which one was about to enter the five-digit passcode that could bring a government to its knees.

3

....

Tom took a deep breath as his fingers hovered over a computer keyboard and pressed ENTER. Amazing how the same simple command that he used to freeze the blood of his corporate clients could also be configured to unleash artful mayhem on a perfect summer day. One by one, a half dozen micro video cams switched to record mode, the glowing RECs indicating that the operation was being dutifully collected and cataloged for future reference and recruitment purposes. Tom knew that there would be Fourth of July fireworks at San Antonio's Woodland Park, but his mission at this moment was to initiate shock and awe during the bright procession of the red, white, and blue children's parade.

Tom surveyed the live feeds on his computer screen, each one focused on a different part of the parade route. They even had one set up on the promenade at River Walk, which would be packed with shopping-fatigued families and tourists gobbling their lunches as they took surreptitious snapshots of twenty-first century Texans: sinewy, bronzed couples flaunting their youth by the lake; soda-amped kids clenching bouquets of helium balloons; cart vendors hawking tacos and freedom dogs—while actual canines strained on their leashes to get a sniff of each other. None of them had the slightest inkling that dozens of subversives lurked in the trees and in the restrooms, behind the concession stands and in plain sight, waiting for the moment to step forward and reveal their true colors. A crowd was beginning to coalesce along the parade path: buzz-cut jocks in cargo shorts and flip-flops; suburban moms in droopy hats and sensible shoes; retired servicemen rolling up in their wheelchairs for a better view. And most importantly, TV crews from KSAT, WOAI, and KABB, overdressed and looking bored as they sipped bottled water and waited to tape a holiday spot for the five o'clock news.

On video cam one, the vanguard of the caravan came into focus: two clowns, a huge US flag stretched between them, skipping down the path, surrounded by squealing children and barking canines. Papier mâché busts of former US Presidents lumbered along on bunting-draped flatbeds. Not far behind, a high school marching band took its best shot at "America the Beautiful."

Eighty miles away, in a nondescript residential section of Austin, Tom's mother appeared in his room holding a tray with a turkey sandwich and potato chips. "I made you lunch, *m'ijo,*" she said.

Tom nodded without taking his eyes off the monitors. "Thanks, Mom. Just leave it on the table, okay?"

Sonia Ayana put the food down and shook her head disapprovingly. Tom's lair was in the back of the house, separated from the rest of the dwelling by a long hallway with a bathroom that he had also claimed for himself. His walls were lined with several rows of bookshelves crammed with audio and computer equipment; outdated CDs, DVDs, vinyl records, and video games; assorted swag from free networking events; software programming textbooks; stacks of back issues of *Wired;* and dog-eared paperbacks of *Cat's Cradle, Neuromancer,* and *The Catcher in the Rye.* In the center of the room, elevated on a plywood platform concealing power strips and cables, was a U-shaped command module of metal worktables piled high with CPUs, laptops, and high-definition LCD monitors. A doorless closet, an unmade bed, blackout shades over the windows, and a Steelcase mesh swivel chair completed the cyber-geek decor.

Sonia started to say something but checked herself. What was the point? When he was online, she didn't exist; nothing existed except the computer. She worried that Tom's obsession would rob him of a real life. How would he ever meet a girl if he didn't have a job that took him outside the house? How could a grown man be content to sit indoors by himself all day and most of the night, unshaven and wearing the same clothes, the pale light from the screen commanding his attention like a demonic blue flame. She had managed well enough without a husband, supporting herself as a seamstress at a local clothing store, raising Tom as best she could, but the growing likelihood that she would never see a daughter-in-law, let alone grandchildren, wounded her with guilt that she had failed him as a mother. If only she had understood what was happening sooner, if she had been able to recognize the signs, she might have steered him onto a different path before losing him to the toxic attraction of that *maldita* machine.

Tom looked up from his cyber command center, alarmed to see his mother holding a sheet of paper, her eyes brimming.

"Mom, what is it?"

"It's your *tía*, Lupe." Sonia blotted her tears with an embroidered handkerchief. "I told you she was sick, so I sent her to the doctor like you told me. Now the bill came. And it's twelve thousand dollars."

"I thought she had insurance."

"She does, but the insurance company won't cover it. They sent Lupe a letter, but she couldn't read it. I'm trying to help her, but they say the policy is no good." Sonia took a step forward and held out the letter. "She's a widow, all alone. She can't pay this. *Necesita ayuda*."

"Why didn't you tell me sooner, Ma?"

"I don't like to bother you when you're in your room doing your electrical work." Tom winced at her choice of words. To this day, when friends or relatives asked Sonia what Tom did for a living, she told them her son was an electrician. He had stopped trying to correct her. "If Chevo were here," she lamented, "he would know what to do."

Tom could feel a familiar pressure expanding in his chest. Chevayo Ayana was his father, the pneumatic engineer who disappeared in

Alaska when Tom was five, who knew how to drill for oil through frozen mountains, and whose loss had torn a gaping hole in the lives of his wife and son, a vacancy so deep that sometimes Tom felt that his mother would be devoured by it. Just hearing the way she uttered his father's name was like a poke from a sharp stick. He took the letter from his mother's hands.

"Don't worry. Tell Lupe I'll take care of it."

"How M'ijo?" Her expression was equal parts curiosity and concern. "Promise me you won't do anything dumb."

"Don't worry, Mom. They're the ones who just did something stupid. But right now you've got to let me work."

Tom shut the door and turned his attention back to his computer. The shock troops for Operation Uncle Sam were standing by, waiting for his signal.

"Team leaders, hold positions," Tom texted to the video cam operators. "Wait till they get a little closer."

It had all started just a few months ago as a dare: an online acquaintance bet that Tom couldn't get a hundred people to show up for a naked car wash fundraiser for the women's track team at the University of Texas at Austin. Tom hacked into a dozen college sports chat rooms, posting an invitation for "filthy boys and dirty girls to drop their pants and show some skin for the team" by downloading an app that would use lewd humor and suggestive icons to point the way to their ultimate destination. The queue of scantily clad coeds that showed up the next day stretched for two blocks and made it onto the local news. It dawned on Tom that he had a gift for group activation. He knew how to rally the troops; he knew where to find them and how to entice them with clever clues and prizes; he could organize and orchestrate a mob like a maestro, conducting the crowd not with a wand but with software commands and augmented reality mobile apps that merged the real world with treasure maps and fantastical images.

There was a degree of danger in all this. Local law enforcement, getting its cues from the federal government, was taking a dim view of flash mobs and any other online mischief that suggested a terrorist threat, and new statutes against encrypted digital transgressions were being passed every day. Tom decided he needed a secure handle, a fake identity that would insulate him from snooping surveillance sentinels and rival hackers, both of whom he knew plenty about from his freelance duties for the Austin-based Internet security firm. No one, not even his top flash mob lieutenants, had ever met him or seen his face, and he would keep it that way. Even his voice was digitally filtered into a low-pitched snarl. The key was the collective, the spontaneous combustion of individuals joining for a common cause, working together as a single entity to make an indelible social statement. There could be only one name for the elusive alpha that controlled the hive mind, a moniker that succinctly captured the ephemeral spirit of chaotic cohesion: Swarm.

A message scrolled across the text window of his control dashboard.

Mobile 1: Swarm, the patriots are in position. Waiting for your signal.

Tom scanned the monitor one last time. "Okay, people," he said. "Let's show them what the land of the free really looks like!"

As the aircraft flew into the heart of the locust storm, Cara held on to her seat straps, hoping for a miracle. At first, PHAROH's electric song was indistinguishable from the din of the propeller engine—then its frequency broke through the mechanical noise, pulsing with the deep sonority of a distressed cello fused with a piercing wail that made Cara hold her hands over her headset. Almost immediately, the thick curtain of locusts opened up and the crunching hail of buzzing bodies diminished.

"It's working!" Eric shouted. "Professor Park, we freaking did it!"

Cara peered through the muck on the windows to get a better view, and what she saw lifted her heart. A bug-free bubble had opened up around the plane as the locusts lurched in tandem to evade PHAROH's angry whine. The splattering had diminished to a few isolated pops, yet the mass of insects still surrounded them in every direction. It was like flying into the eye of a fluttering hurricane, the eerily calm center of a swirling vortex with walls made of insects. Cara was gripped with speechless wonder. The swarm was defending itself from PHAROH by creating an insulating pocket of space around the plane. The swarm had instantly adapted to minimize the disruption without changing course. Cara was incredulous, exhilarated, and disappointed all at once. What had just happened didn't seem possible, yet ...

"Holy shit," Eric blurted. "The swarm is protecting itself by avoiding us!"

"Where are we, exactly?" Cara asked the pilot.

"We're in Tanzania. Just south of the border with Kenya, in the Serengeti."

"No, I mean *exactly*. I need to come back to this place on foot."

The pilot grinned at Cara's naïveté. "You can't walk around the Serengeti, ma'am. The lions are not in a zoo."

"I'm not a fool," Cara said tartly. "I need the coordinates for where we encountered the swarm so I can examine specimens. Where's the closest airstrip?"

"We're a bit northeast of Ikorongo Game Reserve, ma'am. The closest airstrip is half a day's drive from here, not far from a nice travel sanctuary."

"Can we stay there tonight and hire a driver to bring us back to this spot in the morning?"

"I'll radio them now, ma'am."

She looked at Eric. "You can turn PHAROH off. We're done for today."

The Serengeti airstrip was a mile-long clearing of ragged grass, and the landing was more than a little bumpy. When they emerged from the six-seat aircraft, a blond man in pressed khaki shorts was waiting to greet them with cold drinks and biscuits arranged safari style on a folding table. The man introduced himself as Malcolm. He and his wife were the managers of Rawana Sanctuary, a high-end tented camp that catered to well-heeled tourists. During the ride to the camp, Malcolm gave them brightly patterned Masai blankets and horsehair swatters to keep the tsetse flies at bay, telling them that they were lucky to be in East Africa during the great migration.

"Watching the animals march north to Kenya is one of the world's great blessings," he told them before leaning solicitously toward Cara. "It's a deeply emotional experience for me, and it would be my pleasure to personally take you out for a closer look before sunset."

"No, thanks," Cara answered, glancing at the gold band on his left ring finger. "I've seen it before. Anyway, we're here for the locusts." Noticing the look of dismay on the man's face, she added, "We're researchers from the United States, working with the United Nations. We came to help the farmers."

"Ah, I see. Very good. Though I have to say I think you are way too attractive to be into bugs, miss."

"Well, thanks, but I have to say that you look exactly right to get emotional with a wildebeest," Cara replied, whipping a tsetse fly that had the audacity to land on her bare leg. In the backseat, Eric pulled the blanket up around his head to stifle a guffaw and fend off the buzzing pests.

Malcolm sat rigidly for a while, then turned to them and said, "The driver you requested will be here in the morning. Cocktails are at six, and dinner is at seven thirty." He added that camp rules required them to be accompanied by a Masai warrior guard anywhere outside their tent after dark. When Cara asked Malcolm if he was serious, he didn't answer.

The creature comforts of the camp, which included permanent tents with verandas, hardwood floors, electric lights, and hot running water, pleasantly surprised Cara. The place seemed a tad extravagant for a nonprofit researcher's budget, but there was no other lodging available on such short notice. Taking advantage of the unscheduled break, Cara rebooked their flight out of Arusha for the next day, made some notes in her journal, showered, and dressed for dinner. A few minutes later, she was lounging on the domed top of a giant boulder near the main building with Eric and Laura, Malcolm's wife. When Laura told them that her husband was feeling ill and would take his dinner alone in their tent, Cara and Eric exchanged a knowing glance.

An African waiter served them gin and tonics from a portable bar and offered them salted cashews as the sun ballooned into a giant red disk over the plains. Cara watched as Eric recorded the scene with his phone and uploaded it to the cloud.

"Eric told me about your experiment with the locusts today," Laura said pleasantly. "I've never seen these horrible creatures before. If they eat all the grass, the animals will starve, and this"—she held her hands up to indicate the estate—"will be all gone. I've been praying that someone would come and help us stop this plague."

Cara sighed. "I'm afraid we're a long way from being able to do that."

"I've been told the locust migration is a result of global warming," Laura said, offering them sweet seed cakes.

"Could be," Eric answered. "It's happening in other places, too. Australia and even Argentina."

A Masai man appeared at the top of the rock lookout. "Dinner is being served, madam," he announced.

The food was delicious, and Laura proved to be an entertaining hostess, amusing them with stories about monkeys sneaking into the gift shop and giving the tourists a scare when they went in to try on hats. Malcolm, she informed them, was a South African whose parents had left the country when Nelson Mandela was elected to the presidency. Laura had met her future husband when she was studying at the London School of Economics. "My dream was to work in international development, but my persuasive spouse had other plans," she said wistfully. "It gets a little lonely sometimes, but to be able to live here so close to the animals is a real privilege."

On cue, their plates were whisked away and their glasses refilled with Cape Town pinot noir. The occasionally sluggish Wi-Fi notwithstanding, the whole place had a sumptuous lost-empire atmosphere. Laura wiped her mouth with a napkin and peered at a large black shape lurking near the driveway.

"What's that?" Eric asked.

"Oh, that's Joe."

"Joe?"

"We made the mistake of feeding him some leftovers, and now he thinks he's part of the family," Laura explained. "Just make sure you don't get too close. Cape buffaloes can be unpredictable."

It must be nice, Cara wanted to say, to live in this oasis of colonial accoutrements, graciously holding court over an ever-changing guest list of intriguing strangers. Out there, beyond the bronze hills and the big game parks, the continent was reeling from epidemics, famine, and civil war. But here, within the mahogany gates of the sanctuary, even dangerous beasts were treated like house pets.

After dessert, Eric, who had been exchanging glances with a pair of young women at another table, excused himself and took his coffee into the lounge, where the diehards were gathering for a nightcap.

Laura tiled her head in Eric's direction. "Your protégé' is rather adorable—and smart too. Our wireless was acting up, and he was able to fix it in about five minutes." She propped her hand under her chin. "It must be nice to have such a handy young man around to help you with your work."

"Yes, it is."

Cara rose to leave, and Laura repeated Malcolm's warning about never going anywhere on the property unescorted. Sure enough, when Cara got to the door that led to the grounds, a uniformed guard was waiting with a spear in one hand and a flashlight in the other. As she followed her protector down the gravel path under a blazing canopy of stars, she was grateful to know that the Masai were famously fierce hunters, fully capable of taking down a big cat if necessary.

Back in her tent, Cara undressed and climbed under the mosquito net. On the nightstand next to the bed, she found a wrapped candy and a single page of text mounted on handmade paper: a fable by Lala Salama, "How the Zebra Got Its Stripes." It was a fanciful tale about how the Creator had originally made all animals with the same black skin. Deciding this monochromatic scheme was not lively enough, the Creator held a kind of costume party at which the animals could choose their own patterns and colors. But a voracious zebra stopped en route to gorge on grass, making him plump. When he arrived at the costume party, all that was left was a white suit, which he gladly put on. But the suit ripped to ribbons on his fattened body, letting his black skin show through. Since the suit was now too tight to take off, the zebra was forced to wear it forever, so his hide bears the black-and-white stripes of his gluttony to this very day.

Cara put the story aside. She knew that the zebra's suit had nothing to do with grass or greed. It was part of a protective camouflage that kept predators at bay. It allowed them to merge and disappear into the herd behind the interlocking patterns. The reason the zebra still wore his black-and-white suit was that it had enabled his ancestors to survive and mate and pass their genes on to the next generation of striped zebras, and so on and on for millions of years. Cara knew it was natural selection, not the Creator, who had given the zebra its stripes—and also the hippo's ebony skin that merged with the water and mud, the leopard's spots that helped him

34

hide under leafy trees, and the cheetah's pale fur, perfectly matched to the boundless fields of golden grass.

The mind-boggling diversity of wildlife in Africa, the kaleidoscopic spectrum of patterns, shapes, and sizes, was both astounding and reassuring. After all, it was the genetic diversity required by evolution that had persuaded Cara to become a biologist in the first place. Growing up as the daughter of Korean immigrants in the San Francisco Bay Area, she had wondered why people looked different, why some people had black hair and others had blond, why some were short and others tall, why some eyes were slanted and others round. Even if she had been raised Christian instead of Buddhist, she would have wanted to know why the Creator had decided that one color of skin for all the animals wasn't good enough. What was his reason for giving the animals different clothes? And why was nature's actual wardrobe so extravagantly varied and unpredictable?

It was a conundrum that dogged Cara until the day she sat in an introductory biology class at UC Berkeley and discovered—in an epiphany that was akin to a professor's pulling a rabbit out of his hat—that evolution requires genetic variation. Nature's fashion show, she was fascinated to learn, has the widest range of choices possible, the better to adapt to a constantly changing environment. Being different isn't a flaw—it is a requirement for the survival of the species, for the only way to make sure that the fittest survive is to make sure that there are as many different kinds of potential winners as possible. In the great gamble of evolution, it turns out that Mother Nature likes to hedge her bets.

It was then and there, with her pen poised above her ruled spiral notebook in a dumbstruck haze of revelation, that Cara knew she had found her life's work. She immersed herself in Charles Darwin's seminal texts and H.B.D. Kettlewell's nineteenth-century studies of black-and-white English moths. It wasn't long before she was following in the hallowed footsteps of behavioral ecologists like Deborah Gordon, whose work with harvester ants at Stanford showed that experiments with insect colonies in the field and in the lab could provide material evidence of emergent collective behavior in ordinary insects. By carefully documenting the activities of colonies and how the actions of individual ants produce elaborate communities and physical structures, Gordon had begun to bridge the gap between mathematical models of complexity theory and of the self-organizing abilities of living things, unveiling an entire new paradigm for understanding the genetic machinery behind the development and growth of social networks, cities, and even human brains.

For Cara, this groundbreaking fusion of mathematics and biology was much more than a powerful lens through which to view and understand all of nature. It was also an exhilarating source of hope. If intelligence was distributed across groups of insects, people and programs in ways that we had only begun to understand, then why couldn't it be harnessed to fight disease, poverty, and war? If the intrinsic wisdom of crowds included and transcended any single intention or piece of information, if civilizations were the product of collective awareness expressed and amplified by the genetic fabric of human society, why couldn't it be harnessed and directed to do something good?

Cara's drowsy ruminations were momentarily interrupted by a guttural groan emanating from just outside her tent. It reminded her of the sound a cat makes when it's trying to cough up a hairball, but much lower and louder. A Cape buffalo? Or an elephant? Impalas didn't sound like that, did they? There it was again: a mournful, heavy huffing of air moving though spacious lungs. Trying to communicate what? A cry for attention or a warning? Should she be worried? Didn't the Masai guards sleep outside the guest tents at night? Cara turned off the light and shut her eyes.

Cara's mind resisted her body's need for rest. In the morning, she would know if the experiment was a valid contribution to the study of emergent behavior in locusts or if it had fallen short of her primary objective, which was to help African farmers stave off famine and protect the habitats of some of Earth's most incredible creatures. The proto-physician in her still wanted to help people, especially those who had no one else to protect them. How many farmers had lost their crops today? How many animals had lost their favorite grazing pastures? How could the zebras get fat and earn their stripes if there were no more luscious pastures of grass? Once the vegetation that nourished the herbivores was gone and the food chain broken, even the predators at the top of the ladder would eventually falter and starve. But why was some part of her alarmed by the way the swarm had evaded their sonic trap? What was the deeper significance of the day's events that still somehow escaped her, like the dodging, startlingly intelligent blizzard of insects whirring in her thoughts?

The next time the lion's roar rang out across the camp, Cara was fast asleep.

Operation Uncle Sam didn't unfold without a few battlefield glitches. Not that there was any shortage of people willing to "fully embrace one's right to bare arms—and a whole lot more!" as Tom put it in his encrypted call to action. By following the virtual arrows and clues that they could see on their phones, the participants had arrived on the scene with paint and other patriotic paraphernalia, ready for a time-bending skirmish with the Red Coats. Before anybody could react or stop them, the nudists began to organize on an imaginary ten-by-twenty-foot rectangular grid: the ones painted blue with white stars in one corner and those covered in all red or white lining up and then lying down lengthwise in alternate rows.

The unfurled human flag was compelling but not perfect. In the rush to remove their clothing and reveal their hued bodies, several of the freedom streakers tripped on their shorts and tumbled over one another on the lawn, their tangled limbs forging improbable sculpture. The ensuing screams of panicked picnickers alerted police sooner than expected, resulting in at least three arrests. Several yelping pranksters sprinted across the parade path and continued into the woods, never to be seen again.

As one TV commentator later noted, there were six more stars than an actual Old Glory, and several of the red stripes kept blurring the lines by groping their white stripe neighbors. In any case, the anonymously e-mailed communiqué to news media explained that Operation Uncle Sam was "a spontaneous public action against the recent arrests of nude swimmers at Lady Bird Lake by police officers who should have better things to do than tackle unclothed teenagers and wrestle them to the ground without cause or condoms."

"Good job, guys," Tom said, congratulating his team leaders. "Let's wrap it up before more cops show up." But before logging off, something on the screen caught his eye. He leaned closer to the monitor and typed out a message. "Mobile 3, zoom in, three stars right from the left-hand corner, two stars down." The field of view narrowed to a girl with a gorgeous grin on her face. It was impossible not to notice the beckoning blue field of her chest, a white star strategically spangled on each nipple, a virtual tri-cornered hat tilted jauntily on her head. But it was the way she held herself, exuding commendable composure under the circumstances, that had attracted his attention. She wasn't just beaming back at the camera but *into* it, as if somehow able to see through the lens and follow the electrical particles back to their source. Did she know who was watching her? Impossible, yet …

"Mobile 3."

"Yes, Swarm."

"Who is that?"

"Twinkle Tits?"

"Yeah."

"That's Lucy."

"Do we have her contact info?"

"Hang on. She's a newbie."

The camera's orientation jerked toward the grass for a moment, then righted itself. "Lucyinthesky2025, aka Susan Oliver. Whoa!"

Lucy was rising to her feet, leaning toward the camera, shamelessly filling the entire frame with her pixilated body. She lavishly kissed the lens, smudging it with a fog of crimson lipstick. And then she winked.

"Gotta go, gotta go," Mobile 3 barked. "The heat's moving in!"

Tom glimpsed disconnected body parts of nude patriots scattering in all directions, then nothing. All the cams had gone dark.

It was over. Tom rewound the file to the image of Lucy kissing the camera lens and stored it as a JPEG on his desktop. The girl's easy familiarity, the suggestiveness of the kiss, and the way she winked at the camera made an impression. They had never met before, and there was absolutely no way that she could know the identity of the actual person behind the scenes. Still, Tom was intrigued. Was the trickster being teased? There was only one way to find out.

The password generator Tom had purchased for a couple of hundred dollars coughed up the pass codes for Lucy's Facebook, Instagram, snapchat, and mail accounts, which led him to her street address and phone number, personal documents, and Internet provider for her computer, which Tom could now control and peruse as he pleased. Even without actually seeing her room, he had no problem imagining how it looked: low lighting and beige curtains, bookshelves filled with archeological textbooks and classics from her American lit and poetry courses, a Gerhard Richter print on the wall, and a stuffed koala bear perched on the bedspread.

It took Tom only minutes to assemble Susan Oliver's entire life story, right down to the source of her desire to become a nurse: growing up as the only daughter of a mother of three who succumbed to cirrhosis not long after Susan was born. She was twenty-eight, held a bachelor's degree in sociology from the University of Texas, had two older brothers, and lived with her widowed dad in a two-bedroom apartment on the south side of town, not far from the one-story stucco where Tom lived with Sonia. Preferring to be called Lucy, even by her friends, she had an endearing habit of crossing her eyes as if to undermine her comely features, as if saying, *Don't pay attention to that.* Lucy was an ardent ecologist, a defender of innocent victims, and an outspoken crusader for socially progressive causes, which at least partially explained why she would join a troupe of exhibitionists chiding the police for pushing unclothed kids around in the park after dark. She loved the music of Joni Mitchell and an Austin heavy rock band called Dog Spelled Backward, and she adored the works of the poet T. S. Eliot, particularly "*The Love Song of J. Alfred Prufrock.*" How could a girl so nubile and sweet-tempered be drawn to a desolate hymnal of regret and squandered love? What did she know about old men who would walk alone on the beach with their trousers rolled up? A mystery that begged to be unraveled. Her favorite things about being born and raised in Austin: "Coyotes and wildcats still run wild in the hills, anyone with a guitar and an amp is a star, and the tallest building in town looks like an owl." She was talking about the Frost Bank Tower, which many Austinites believed was intentionally created to look like a hooting bird of prey. Not true, Tom knew, because a client had informed him that the bank logo circles that looked like eyes were added only after the building was finished. But Tom also knew that owls were nocturnal, solitary, and smart, which he related to and took as an encouraging sign.

Tom needed just a few more moments to hack into the soundboard of Lucy's laptop, allowing him to surreptitiously monitor every word and sound. She was talking to a girlfriend on her cell phone, a loquacious acquaintance apparently, for Lucy hardly spoke at all, but when she did talk, her thoughts were delivered in an impetuous, slightly imperious purr. They were discussing whether depictions of women warriors in video games and movies like *Kill Bill, Kickass,* and *Mad Max:Fury Road* were overcompensating for centuries of female subordination. Or were they doing women a disservice by making ordinary females feel inferior if they couldn't wield a sword, shoot a gun, or physically demolish any man who made the mistake of messing with them? "No, no, no, it's not about *actual* violence," Lucy demurred. "It's a metaphor for female empowerment—jobs, education, financial independence; those are the real weapons. But what man wants to make a movie about that?"

Tom was completely and irrevocably smitten. With a few more keystrokes he could have activated her laptop camera, but he resisted. The next time he saw her naked, he wanted it to be her idea.

Tom's surreptitious snooping was interrupted by the familiar sound of a pedicab downshifting on the street outside his bedroom. He closed the computer screen, launched iTunes, pulled up the shade on the window and unlatched it. Xander Smith stepped across the sill and plopped down in a battered leather armchair with a duct-taped gash in its side, a hand-me-down from Tom's maternal grandfather.

"Un-fucking-believable!" Xander was saying as he pulled off his bike gloves and produced a joint from his breast pocket. He cocked his head and nodded in approval of the Moderat mix oozing from the speakers. The smeared coat of red and white body paint made him look like a slacker soccer fan, which in fact, he was. "Dude, is your TV on? Go to Channel 5. You should have been there. Fifty naked people painted in stars and stripes running around collecting revolutionary war relics on their AR app. We made *a frigging flag* in the middle of the park in broad daylight! It was epic Swarm!"

"Swarm," Tom repeated. "Isn't that the same guy who put on the porno flash mob at Whole Foods?"

"Yeah, after some homophobic clerk refused to ring up a couple of gay guys from San Francisco," Xander said, lighting the joint. "I mean, five hundred people wearing 'Straight Friendly' T-shirts and looking at AR porn though their phones in the checkout lines. That was a good one, but today—oh my God—pure genius." Xander offered Tom the joint. He took a hit and handed it back.

"How did you find out about it? The flash mob, I mean."

"Tommy, like I told you, man, it's by invitation only. Somebody who's already done a Swarm has to submit your name and mobile number. And then you get a text with instructions at the last minute. A girl I know hooked me up. I offered to vouch for you."

"Yeah, I know. Thanks," Tom said. "I don't like the idea of being tracked, my every move dictated and recorded by somebody I don't even know."

Xander took another hit and blew the smoke toward the ceiling. "Right, and social media sucks out your brain so it can sell it back to you. Man, you've gotta stop being so paranoid." Xander knew his friend had an aversion to being liked, poked, friended, and followed, but it would be some time before he fully grasped why. "I just don't understand how a techie like you could be such a Luddite when it comes to social media."

"Social and media aren't necessarily compatible," Tom said.

"Actually, it's funny you'd say that." Xander took another lungful of pot and rose to his feet. "I just gave a ride to this aerospace engineer at UT Austin who told me that he saw that documentary, *The Spirit Molecule,* and it inspired him to take a vacation in the Amazon and partake in a shamanic ayahausca ceremony. I think this guy probably did DMT in a dorm, or who knows, maybe it was actually ayahuasca. Anyway, I was inclined to give him the benefit of the doubt, given our shared interests. But then he says that during the ceremony he saw his own death and rose through the clouds and into deep space, where he was befriended by an alien."

Xander paused for dramatic affect. "Did I mention that this guy was a PhD candidate in aerospace at UT?"

"Yeah, so what did you tell him?"

"I said, 'Listen, pal, you of all people should know that when the universe was born and all there was in the cosmos was helium, which over millions of years gathered into giant clouds of molecules that collapsed into a ball that become so dense it triggered a nuclear reaction and was reborn as a star, basically a giant galactic furnace that cooked and fused the atoms, creating bigger, heavier molecules, forging all the elements in the periodic table down to iron, until the star exploded, a supernova, and this cosmic debris fanned out across the empty universe and cooled and clumped into galaxies and solar systems and planets, and one of those planets was Earth, where volcanoes and coagulating gases created the oceans, and single-celled organisms were born when lightning struck—like

Frankenstein's monster—and fish hung out in the oceans for a few million years before they got up on their fins and grew feathers and hair and came out of the sea—not necessarily in that order ..."

A few months earlier, channel surfing on a THC-infused evening, Xander had come across *The Cosmos,* a formative encounter that led to his binging on the entire TV series and devouring every movie and book he could find on wormholes and black holes, interstellar travel, and the origins and predicted demise of the universe. Tom watched as Xander paused to reentact the iconic scene from *2001: A Space Odyssey*, vocalizing simian grunts, and waddling in a circle, arms and knuckles dangling below his knees, pretending to gape in wonder at the black obelisk before gingerly touching it and lurching backward.

"So for reasons that only Stanley Kubrick and Christopher Nolan can fully appreciate," Xander continued, "our monkey ancestors climbed into the trees and onto the savannah, and humans were spawned, people, bipedal conscious beings. And we, you and me, my overeducated friend, are basically living dust balls of cosmic debris. We are interstellar immigrants born from the splattered guts of quasars, the orphaned offspring of black holes, the cremated ashes of deflated dead stars. You, my friend, are the fucking *alien!*'"

"And what did he say?"

"He goes, 'Well, of course. That was my whole point. But if you're going to get technical about it, then we are actually made of empty space because the distance between the nucleus of an atom and the electrons circling around it is, relatively speaking, like the distance from here to the moon, so if it weren't for the negative charge of the electrons in our bodies repelling each other, I'd be able to put my finger right through you.'"

Tom raised his eyebrows. "Cheeky monkey."

"Right?!" Xander waved the joint in the air like a stylus on an invisible chalkboard. "I considered pointing out that most of the known universe is made of dark energy, not to mention the parallel dimensions in string theory, and the Boson Higgs, but instead I just said, 'Hey, that's great, buddy, but your molecules just arrived at Second and Congress, and you owe me twenty bucks extra for the pot.'"

Tom frowned in mock disapproval. "You shouldn't do drugs with your fares."

"But, *actually* ..." Xander offered Tom the end of the joint, but he passed. "On the other hand," Xander continued, "you and I got stoned when we met and it didn't turn out so bad."

This was true. Tom had been outside the Frank Erwin Center that night, trying in vain to score an extra ticket to a Radiohead concert. He was loitering dejectedly near the entrance, anguished over the stirring spectacle he was missing, when he heard someone say, "What if you could see Thom Yorke spin after the show on Sixth Street tonight?"

Tom had turned to see a lanky fellow in shorts, T-shirt, and a trucker's cap perched on a dark green pedicab jackknifed at the curb. A deal was cut: Tom would pay the pedicab fare to the club and Xander's cover charge in exchange for the chance to see Radiohead's lead singer perform an after-hours DJ set. Since the band hadn't finished yet, there was no particular rush, so Xander took his time meandering across downtown Austin, pointing out which of the myriad bars and clubs specialized in illicit commerce of one sort or another. When the Frost Bank Tower wheeled into view, Tom showed off his knowledge, debunking the building's owl-inspired legend, which seemed to impress his garrulous chauffer.

"How do you know that?"

"I spend a lot of time on my computer."

Xander lit up a joint and held it out to Tom. "Well, tonight you're going offline, pal."

Tom sat in the back of the pedicab that balmy night as Xander glided through the artsy enclaves of East Austin, mixing outrageous anecdotes with keen observations about the psychology and economics of the hippest town in Texas. Eventually, Xander rolled to a stop outside one of the countless clubs on Sixth Street, secured the pedicab with a chain, and motioned Tom to follow him inside. As Xander had promised, the doorman waved them in without even charging them, and a couple of beers later, Yorke sauntered through the door and took his place at the turntables. The music that throbbed from the speakers for the next few hours was dark and edgy but also thrillingly percussive, and before long Tom and Xander had joined the crowd in an ecstatic convocation of motion and rhythm, dancing themselves into a sweaty state of blissful abandon, exchanging sloppy grins, tequila shots, and back-slapping bouts of solidarity.

When Tom tried to pay Xander for getting him into the club, Xander wouldn't take the money. "Many more to come," he said, pushing away the cash and offering his new friend a free ride home. Tom talked about his job protecting companies from online theft and how most people were absolutely clueless about the cyber battles raging in a parallel universe right under their noses. Xander, for his part, revealed his aspiration to become a professional DJ, conjuring a vision of ecstatic throngs stomping to his beats without a trace of doubt that it would happen.

That night, Tom and Xander formed a bond that went beyond a shared appreciation for *Fight Club,* cosmology, and the latest electro beats. It was unsaid but mutually understood that in a world that seemed indifferent to the tribulations of the modern male, it was crucial to have a trusted ally, someone who would make sure that you got home on nights when you got too drunk, who would convince you that your best moment was waiting right around the corner, who would be your wing man on a date, take your side in a street scuffle, and share your estrangement from the traditional duties of manhood with no compelling alternative in sight.

Xander's post-Nirvana slacker shtick, Tom eventually learned, was just another anti-designer outfit, insouciant camouflage for the bright, ambitious music wonk who tirelessly pursued his passion.

When he wasn't pedaling rides or complicating his life with girls, Xander befriended visiting DJs, landing an occasional gig behind the turntables or pinch-hitting for talent that got sick, flaked out, or just wanted a few free minutes to chat up a woman at the bar. On those nights, Tom would show up late and watch his buddy rehearse his mega star aspirations, swathed in a shirt that showed off his taut torso, nodding and rocking to the beat with supreme confidence, even when his entire audience consisted of just a few blotto college kids and middle-age tourists who wouldn't know Radiohead from Motörhead. But even then Tom noticed the way the crowd watched Xander's every move, thirsting for his slightest glance or acknowledgment. And so the incipient seed of where this could all lead, an untrammeled path of opportunity and possibility that Tom was barely beginning to fathom, was planted.

Xander's musical proclivities leaned toward deep house and the throbbing minimalist techno of the Berlin School, but Austin was hardly a mecca for electro dance aesthetes. Mainstream ravers wanted bombast and a steady beat, predictable lulls and swelling crescendos that mimicked the rhythms of rough sex. Every now and then, Xander would stoop to the gravitational wallop of dubstep just to keep everyone awake, but playing it safe bored him. He told Tom that he was working on a new sound, a neo-techno hybrid that fused rock and dance with galactic ululations that he imagined emanating from comets, quasars, and black holes. "When I spin," Xander told Tom, "I want people to turn off their ears and dance to the electrons spinning inside."

A week after the Operation Uncle Sam flash mob, they were having happy hour specials at their favorite dive when Xander had an epiphany. "Warhol was wrong," he blurted out. "He said that in the future, everybody would be famous for fifteen minutes. What he should have said was that in the future, everybody would be famous for fifteen gigabytes.'"

"Right," Tom said wearily. "Social media."

"No, shut up. Not just social media—I'm talking about virtual reality, augmented reality, everything, everybody."

"What about Swarm? Tom asked. "Are his fifteen gigs used up?"

Xander swirled his drink before answering. "Swarm is different. Nobody knows who he is or even where he lives. Some people say he's a bot, a program playing people like chess pieces, but that doesn't explain his social awareness or his sense of humor. He uses AR to mix reality and cyber clues to what's going to happen next and where. It makes everything like a game where you can meet people and have fun while you're changing the world. The guys who talk to him online say he seems like a normal dude, except for his voice, which is, you know, disguised." Xander shrugged. "Then again, maybe Swarm is a fifty-year-old woman who taught herself how to program C++ when the kids left home."

"Yup," Tom agreed. "She could be that old lady sitting at the end of the bar."

Xander shrugged. "Entirely possible."

Tom felt bad about intentionally misleading his best friend. But his public distance from Swarm had become progressively necessary as his flash mobbing alter ego had become a minor Internet celebrity and Tom had discovered shady ways to supplement his regular income as a security programmer. Fending off the hacker hoards for his clients, feeling unseen minds and fingers prying around the edges of their firewalls, probing for the slightest weakness, had a way of blurring the boundary between what was acceptable and unacceptable, possible and impossible, right and wrong. Data— names, credit cards, bank accounts, passwords—was like chum being chewed and digested by hungry hackers, which in turn became bait for something bigger, which itself was eventually swallowed. Many of the predators were legal businesses, the same ones that paid Tom's salary. But others were rogue sharks, ready to take a byte for profit or just the sheer sport of it. In the invisible war for proprietary information, it was impossible to know the motives of your adversaries, impossible to tell if you were squaring off with a seventeen-year-old boy in Iowa or a forty-year-old colonel in the Chinese government, let alone anticipate which one was smarter, faster, or more ruthless. All you could know for sure was whether you had survived the hit. Pieces of raw data floated where the attacker had sunk his teeth. Then came the hasty job of cleaning up the mess and patching the gashes of compromised code so there wouldn't be a next time—although, naturally, sooner or later, there was always a next time, from the same intruder or from a new contender who smelled blood in the water.

But as scary as the Internet's porous underbelly could be, Tom had gradually become aware of a bigger, darker menace that dwarfed all the rest. Thanks to a client who had given him his platinum pass to the SXSW Interactive conference, Tom spent the better part of a week gorging on high-minded technology talks and panels, soaking in every possible aspect of the fast-forward future, including a disconcerting scenario where the same giant companies that were supposedly ushering in a gleaming bright tomorrow were putting people out of jobs as algorithms and robots inevitably replaced their human masters. How could all these people be smiling when it was just a matter of time before the machines they worshiped rendered them obsolete? Tom was shocked by the audacity of Silicon Valley unicorns that espoused transparency and social responsibility even as they fleeced their customers by harvesting their intellectual property and reselling it to third parties behind their backs. Couldn't the young techies see that the digital utopia they were so enamored of was just another scam? Worst of all, Tom realized, the rigged gig ecology that he so disdained depended on people like him to keep its mega-servers free of bugs and running smoothly. He was an accessory to the crime, and that shadow passing over his beloved Net was the digital economy itself, a crowd-sourced leviathan siphoning up every scrap of plankton without having to do much more than open its gaping mouth.

True to his Catholic upbringing, Tom told himself that he would never cross the line, that stealing was bad, simple as that. But what was right about getting two hundred dollars an hour when you had saved your client from losing ten thousand or ten million? Not to mention the billions that Big Tech was slurping up right under his nose. It was like being a money sorter at the Federal Reserve, a trove of unmarked of dollars flowing through your hands, none of it yours. Except that in cyberspace, there were no armed guards glaring at you as you worked; no cameras zoomed in on your fingers as you counted and bundled the frayed fives, tens, and twenties. As it was, your own bosses barely understood what you were doing. The only reliable measure of your competence was the fact that they were still in business. So naturally, inevitably, Tom got tired of keeping his hands to himself, acting like a choirboy in a candy store while looters, lunatics, and robber barons ran rampant all around him.

Tom obsessively followed the fanfare and brinksmanship of the notorious online hacker forum 4chan.org, keeping track of the dispersal of classified documents by various hack-tivist individuals and groups, and DOS attacks on corporations that triggered their ire. He was fascinated by the specter of an invisible organization commanding thousands of slave computers to overwhelm an adversary's websites. He also knew that Julian Assange, the combative WikiLeaks founder and editor in chief, had become a persecuted target of international extradition and that half a dozen Anonymous hackers were in jail after one of their own turned into a double agent for the FBI. And he knew that Edward Snowden became a hunted man after releasing classified documents he had obtained while working as an analyst at the NSA. The members of Anonymous claimed to be "everything and nothing." Their defiant motto: "We are Anonymous. We are Legion. We do not forgive. We do not forget. Expect us—always."

Tom was transported by the notion of cyber Robin Hoods stealing from the rich and powerful and giving to the poor and powerless, or at least shaking up the system of privilege and patronage that to him no longer seemed to guarantee life, liberty, and the equitable pursuit of happiness. He had invented himself from nothing, working odd jobs and taking online computer programming classes, sensing that if there was any way for a Latino-Native American nobody to make a mark, to level the playing field, it was in an arena where what you looked like and where you came from didn't matter, where the only numbers that counted were ones and zeros. If you knew what you were doing, it was enticingly easy to turn those integers into hard cash. Tom was past the point of trying to justify his intentions; he was simply the product of a society that had given him no alternative, no other option than to join the enterprising rogues who roamed the back alleys of the cyberverse. To those with guts and the right skills, ruminations about night and day, black and gray, and legal and illegal were extraneous or subject to interpretation. Why wait for an actual bank to open when the digital back doors to its loot were always on and waiting to be pried open? Or even better, who needed keys when you were the one helping to install the locks?

The trick was to figure out a filch that would never leave a trail back to home base, something that blended in so well with the scenery that even the victims had no clue that they'd been punked. Tom had taken up the habit of visiting 4chan chat rooms in which hackers traded tips on what they quaintly referred to as "social engineering." Torrents of pilfered data, some of it proprietary, some of it not, streamed constantly through the Net like an underground river. And there were packs of hungry predators always watching from the sidelines, waiting for a scrap of information that caught their attention.

The idea came to Tom when someone posted a list of mailing addresses from a major magazine publisher. It took him about twenty minutes to duplicate the subscription renewal form and set up a secure proxy on a blind server in Singapore. The algorithm required to operate the con took him much longer, and the morning sun was seeping around the window shades by the time he was finished. Tom's code added five dollars to the actual price of each subscription and spammed his phony e-mail to the publisher's pilfered customer base—all 275,000 of them. When a subscription was renewed, the program would shave off the extra five dollars and send it to a proxy bank account in the Cayman Islands before forwarding the correct balance due to the fulfillment company. The publisher would get paid, the subscribers would get their magazines, and no one would be the wiser that an extra five dollars from each transaction had been collected by Tom. All he had to do was sit tight and watch the Web do its wondrous work.

5

The jeep shuddered and lurched as the curtain of sand closed around them like a malevolent fog. A fine powder had seeped into the passenger compartment, clinging to everything inside, including the air. Duggan pulled the dust mask tighter over his mouth and nose to keep from inhaling it.

"When a haboob like this kicks up," Davis announced with apparent relish, "you can't even see the damned base from the air!"

Duggan wasn't worried about the weather. If he was spooked by anything in this unhinged no man's land, it was the Afghanistan camel spider, a fist-sized venomous, demon-faced arachnid that could supposedly chase a person at a pace of ten miles an hour. He'd seen pictures of US soldiers holding them up between their hands like lobsters. Duggan could imagine the damned things out there in the dark, scurrying around, hiding under rocks and in the eaves of local houses. He knew it was wimpy for a grown man to be spooked by bugs, even big ones, but as a child, he'd been stung by a bee, his whole arm swelling up like a sausage from the allergic reaction, and ever since, he'd been skittish about any insect that pierced skin or craved blood.

"There was a haboob the night before the Westlake incident," Davis said.

"You think that had something to do with it?"

"Dunno. But storms like this can definitely mess with your head."

Davis rattled off more facts as he drove: Since the nominal end of the war, the allied base in Kandahar was technically under the jurisdiction of the Afghan army, and the US personnel assigned there were mainly tasked with training and technical support. "Since the official withdrawal, we are here at the pleasure of the Afghan government, such as it is," Davis said with a smirk. They were out in the open now, zipping past a complex of low buildings that were noticeably unlit. Duggan couldn't help wondering if Davis's speedy pace was because of the haboob or because driving slowly was unwise.

"I'm here to make you as comfortable as possible and help you with your mission," Davis said. "I also got you clearance for a bunk at the officers' quarters. Not the Four Seasons, but tolerable."

"I'd rather stay with the men, if that's all right."

Davis shrugged. "Suit yourself."

Duggan tied the bandanna around his neck and pulled up his collar. The mountains around them were shapeless blotches, but he could feel their presence. "How many of the Americans are here on combat duty?"

Davis grimaced. "We don't use that term anymore. Just a few hundred or so special advisors to watch our backs. Like I said, we're here primarily for training and logistics."

"What was Westlake doing here, training or logistics?"

"Communications."

"Meaning?"

"His job was to assist the Afghans with building and maintaining their own wireless networks."

"But he was trained for combat obviously."

"Everybody here is trained for staying alive, if that's what you mean," Davis replied. "It goes with the territory. Westlake's job on the base was to assist the locals with communications logistics. That's all I can tell you."

The jeep slowed as it approached a gate manned by American troops. A high-powered floodlight glared in their direction, until the guards recognized Davis and waved them through.

"Where exactly did the shootings take place?"

"We just passed it—between the gate and the basketball courts. I'll show you tomorrow."

"What about the Afghan checkpoint?"

Davis downshifted. "We moved the internal perimeter back to increase the buffer zone after the killings," he said. "The American and Afghan troops are now kept in non-intersecting areas—which is probably for the best since, technically speaking, we're not even supposed to be here. This way everybody keeps his dick clean."

"Meaning?"

"Listen, I've seen my share of green-on-blue casualties," Davis said, his voice rising over the wind. "Locals come into our bases dressed in NATO uniforms and open fire and blow themselves up and nobody ever opens an investigation or flies in on business class." Davis looked askance at his passenger. "No offense."

"None taken."

The jeep halted in front of a single-story tin-roofed structure with screened windows along one side. There were lights on inside, but the canvas flaps were pulled down. "This is your stop," Davis announced. "You can use Westlake's old bunk. It's the last one along the wall to the left, just before the showers. Breakfast is at six sharp."

"I'll be there."

Duggan put on the goggles, got out of the jeep, and grabbed his duffel.

"Here, take this." Davis held out a gun. Even in the dark, Duggan recognized it as an Austrian Glock 23 with a tritium night sight, the same .40-caliber pistol he had used at weapons training camp. "You know how to use it, don't you?"

"I have one back home," Duggan said. "I'll see you tomorrow."

"Hang on," Davis said, cutting the engine. "On second thought, I'd better introduce you. The guys have been a little jumpy lately." He handed Duggan a bundle of camouflage clothing. "I guessed your size from your picture. You'll fit in better if you wear them."

As they approached the barracks, Duggan could hear the muffled throb of house music and male conversation. When Davis swung the door open, a dozen faces turned in their direction. The soldiers, most of them in T-shirts and regulation pants, jumped to attention. Davis told them to be at ease. They had interrupted a card game, with one of the bunks serving as a makeshift table. The other GIs had been reading or playing games on their phones. There was an open bottle of Jack Daniels, several empty beer cans on the floor, and a whiff of marijuana in the air.

"Men, this is Jake Duggan from the State Department," Davis announced, ignoring the signs of alcohol and pot. "He'll be staying with us while he does due diligence on Westlake's personal electronics. Please make him feel at home. He's here to help us get to the bottom of what happened to Donny. As you were. Good night."

Davis closed the door on his way out, and the men immediately shifted to clean-up mode, dumping the cans and stowing the bottle and cards and plastic casino chips, displaying obedience without fealty. It was clear that Duggan had violated their personal space, which was already reason enough to hate him. The fact that he was there for some sort of official probe made him virtually radioactive. He looked into the eyes of the men who had watched one of their own massacre allies in cold blood with no warning or provocation, and he saw the residue of shock and disbelief in their vacant stares. Nothing would ever be the same after that day, and Duggan's presence in their midst was just a reminder of the stigma they would endure for the rest of their lives, a kind of guilt by association that no investigation or explanation could ever undo.

"Nice to meet you," Duggan said, trying to break the icy silence. No dice. "Okay, well, please go back to what you were doing. I'm looking forward to meeting you all, but right now I'm tired and I'm going to bed." Duggan walked to the end of the room and put down his duffel.

"Not that one."

The men were looking at him as if he'd lowered himself into Donald Westlake's grave.

"You can use Fisk's bunk." One of the men pointed. "It's that one over there."

Duggan picked up his duffel and moved it to the empty bunk across the aisle from Westlake's. He grabbed his shaving kit and went to the bathroom, careful to check for anything crawling around the toilet or under the sink. Splashing water on his face helped, but he was still rattled. Duggan took an antacid from his kit and washed it down with water from the dispenser. When he came back, the lights were out and all conversation had ceased. This wasn't going to be easy. He hadn't expected the warmest reception, but he might as well have been a venomous snake dropped into their quarters without warning and curled up in their dead friend's bed. *Goddamn Davis—the son of a bitch set me up.* He should have seen it coming, but it was too late to back down now.

The haboob was still hissing outside, but not as fiercely as before. As Duggan's eyes adjusted to the nocturnal gloom, he couldn't help noticing a laptop on the long wooden bench near Westlake's bunk. It was the reason he was in Afghanistan, and the sooner he got to it, the sooner he could leave. But it would have to wait until morning.

Duggan broke the oppressive silence with a question. "Is that Airman Westlake's computer?"

"Yes, it is." The voice came from the bunk to his left. It was calm and comprehending, almost cordial. Duggan figured that at least it was unlikely that he'd get strangled in the middle of the night. Nonetheless, he kept the Glock that Davis had given him cozy under his pillow.

"Good night, guys," he said to the soldiers in the darkness.

Nobody answered.

It was just a trickle at first, five hundred dollars in the first week, twelve hundred in the second. Then the trickle turned into a gusher.

He hauled in more than sixty thousand dollars over the following three weeks, and the money kept coming. It was around this time that Tom decided that the best way to protect his anonymity was to open source his online identity as Swarm. He did this by using a random number generator to append numbers between one and ten thousand to the end of each of his messages, in effect cloning himself into a swarm of Swarm permutations, none of which could be traceable to his actual IP address or physical location. As an added precaution, Tom's online interactions as Swarm were disconnected into separate packets that took their own routes to a proxy server, where they were reassembled and automatically erased as soon as they were completed, leaving only a trail of thousands of discarded bits of information distributed across an ocean of disconnected dead ends with no discernible content, sender, or receiver.

Tom opened the encrypted Cayman account to check on his latest balance, which had climbed to $129,000. He celebrated by punching the air with his fists and grabbing a Red Bull from his mini-fridge. He was wondering how long his illicit payday could last when an instant message popped up on his screen, inviting him to enter a contest in which the winner would be awarded a piece of software worth millions or possibly billions of dollars. It also said that anyone capable of solving the puzzle would be considered for membership in a "an elite confederacy of like-minded individuals who have no boundaries in their abilities, resources, or ambitions." All he had to do was solve a puzzle that would certify his programming skills. The answer to the puzzle was embedded inside the security firewall of a major commercial corporation. He had one hour to solve the puzzle, and he would receive only one clue: blue.

Tom stared at the message, calculating the pros and cons of answering the dare. He knew that federal agencies often used cypher ploys to attract and recruit talented programmers. But that didn't rule out the possibility that the same tactic could be used as bait to lure black hat hackers who were wanted by the authorities for breaking the law. On the other hand, Tom also knew that covert hacker collectives looking for new conscripts used the same method to locate and harvest allies with the skills needed to crack the defenses of corporations and government agencies. Was this enticing invitation a once-in-a-lifetime opportunity or a trap? Tom figured the odds of winning the contest were slim, but as long as he participated as Swarm, the risk seemed minimal compared to the potential payoff. It was probably a hoax anyway. What was the harm in giving it a shot?

Tom looked at his watch and opened a browser to the Fortune 500 list. One company immediately caught his attention: Spectrum Bio Industries. SBI was an umbrella corporation for a constellation of firms engaged in everything from sustainable energy to human genome research. It took him about forty minutes to pierce the company's firewall and another ten to find what he was looking for: a buried file in the SBI database labeled Code Blue. The only problem was that Code Blue required a separate password for entry. With less than nine minutes left, he decided to go with his gut. Tom opened the Wikipedia entry on the visible light spectrum and looked up the electromagnetic wavelengths for the color blue, which are between 450 and 495 nanometers and 670 and 610 terahertz. He typed 450495nm670610THz in the password box and pressed enter. A link to an anonymous chat room appeared on the screen, along with this salutation: "Welcome to the MM. Your life is about to change forever."

"Bingo!" Tom said, clicking the link.

macktheknife247: hey, Swarm. nice work on the riddle. We had faith in your abilities, but we had to be sure. The revolving IP address is a nice touch. We enjoyed your magazine scam too.

swarm9020: excuse me?

macktheknife247: don't be coy. we have no interest in your lunch money, and covering your tracks is always a good move.

swarm2008: who is this? how did you find me?

macktheknife247: you can call me mack, as in the knife. all you need to know is that you've been on the illuminati's radar

swarm6630: are you web security?

macktheknife247: ha-ha, do I sound like a cop? it's your talent for smart mobs and programming chops that we appreciate. your skills are more valuable than you can imagine

swarm9828: so I've heard. What happens now?

macktheknife247: nothing yet. consider yourself a top-level recruit.

swarm1875: I thought I was a member of your group

macktheknife247: not quite, but you've definitely passed the first hurdle

Swarm4898: what's the second one?

macktheknife247: you'll find out soon enough

swarm5158: what do you mean by recruit? it sounds like you're building an army

macktheknife247: something like that

swarm3220: how will I find you?

macktheknife247: mack has been known to hang at 4chan/b/. but you already know that. just be ready

swarm4283: for what?

macktheknife247: for the wind that wipes the slate clean

macktheknife247 has logged off

6

Duggan awoke with the Afghan sun in his eyes. He looked at his watch and cursed. He was already ten minutes late for breakfast with Davis, and he hadn't even touched Westlake's laptop yet. A few of the men were already gone, and the rest were still cradled in the bunks with pillows over their heads. To avoid eye contact with the intruder? Duggan showered, dressed, and hurried out for a look at his new surroundings. The wind was still gusting, but the haboob seemed to have lost its breath. The landscape around him was flat and nearly treeless, almost every building in sight a drab tin-roofed structure. Power lines and barbed wire completed the bleak far-flung outpost motif. Off to the opposite side of the barracks, Duggan could see a couple of recreational sports fields, including the infamous basketball courts.

On the horizon, across an expanse of ragged bushes, loomed the dark brown silhouettes of overlapping mountain ranges, the terrain of countless infiltrations, skirmishes, and atrocities. A US flag flapped resolutely in the arid breeze. The chain-link barrier surrounding the base was supposed to keep the turmoil at bay, defining an orderly oasis amid the sectarian madness. But somehow, like the blond dust that rode the air and seeped into everything in sight, the chaos had found a way through the fence and into Westlake's head. Duggan had no trouble imagining how a howling sandstorm might fray a soldier's nerves and wipe away all vestiges of human restraint, leaving nothing but debris and unanswered questions in its wake.

Davis was halfway through his bacon and egg burrito when Duggan arrived at the mess hall. Duggan loaded up his plate with basic breakfast grub and sat down across from his official guardian and guide. Davis took a sip of his coffee and grinned.

"I'm guessing you didn't get tucked in with a kiss last night."

"It's all right. I don't mind one way or the other.

"Really. So then why'd you force yourself on them?"

Duggan finished chewing a bite of his omelet. "The barracks is where Westlake lived. I need to see where he slept, find out who he was spending time with in the days and weeks before the incident. I need to know why he broke routine. It's possible that one of those men can tell me, intentionally or not."

Davis arched his eyebrows. "You consider Westlake's bunkmates suspects? I thought your mission was to do a tech sweep."

Duggan ignored the question. "I'd like you to take you up on that tour of the base. Show me where Westlake worked, where he went to relax and blow off steam. Everything. But first give me a couple hours at the barracks."

Davis took his napkin and wiped his mouth. "Anything you want. I'll pick you up at ten hundred."

Most of the men had cleared out when Duggan got back. But his bunk neighbor was still there, bent over some sort of military manual. The stencil on his jacket identified him as M. Wasson.

Duggan sat at the bench and booted up Westlake's computer. It took a few seconds for the screen to blink on, but within a few strokes, he knew that, appearances notwithstanding, the computer was not untouched. There was no password prompt, and the mailbox and the trash had both been emptied. There was one other thing that bothered him.

"Pretty weird, right?" Wasson was looking at Westlake's computer. "I mean, why did they leave it there like some museum exhibit. Kinda obvious, I'd say." Wasson was wry and wiry, athletic in an unassuming way, with dark cropped hair. Duggan sensed that he wasn't hanging around the barracks by accident. He'd been waiting to watch Duggan check the computer, and his curiosity had gotten the better of him. This could be an asset or an obstacle. Duggan wasn't sure which yet.

"What's the *M* for?"

"Mitch."

"Nice to meet you, Mitch. Where's Fisk?"

"He's not here."

"I thought we were having a friendly conversation."

"I'm not your friend," Wasson said. "You have to do more than wear camouflage to fit in around here."

"In that case, I'm going to do my job now."

Wasson rose from the bunk and pulled on his jacket. "Me too."

Duggan turned his attention back to Westlake's machine. He downloaded a couple of industrial-strength virus scans and checked the e-mail folder and drive. No files or messages in or out. He already knew that the only fingerprints on the machine were Westlake's, but he went through the motions anyway. The network was secure as far as he could tell, no history of wireless networks beside the base log-on. The hardware was working perfectly, and there was no evidence of an outside intrusion. Case closed. But the anger was rising in him like hot lava. Why would the air force call in a cybersecurity specialist from NCSD to check a machine that had already been wiped clean? Surely the military had better things to do than waste taxpayers' money and his time. Duggan tipped the laptop over to inspect its underside. The Post-it was lime green, three-by-three-quarter inches square. The words were written in pencil, crudely scrawled but legible: *Look for what's not there.* A joke? A taunt? A warning? Everything in Kandahar, Duggan mused, was either hiding in plain sight or conspicuously absent.

Davis was waiting outside when Duggan emerged from the barracks. "Nice day for a ride around the base." Davis's tone was so casual that they might have been two buddies about to head off on a fishing trip. "Any luck?"

"Well," Duggan replied as he climbed into the jeep, "that depends on how you define luck. No signs of exterior foul play, as far as I can tell."

"What about the other kind?"

In that instant, Duggan realized that the DOD had brought him in to see if he could find something they had missed. Or maybe Davis was just fishing to make sure that Duggan hadn't stumbled on something they wanted him to overlook. Either way, Duggan was positive that Davis didn't know about the Post-it crumpled up in his pocket.

"Westlake's machine is free of any known virus—no prints or signs of tampering," Duggan said. He sat in the jeep for a few seconds, letting Davis study his face. "Are you giving me a tour or what?"

"Yeah, absolutely!" Davis said, regaining his affability as he started the engine. "I thought I'd take us around the perimeter and then over by the personnel rec area. Westlake liked to work out when he wasn't playing soccer." Davis was tracing a vague half circle with his arm as he drove. "Then I'll bring you back to the scene of the incident."

"Sounds good," Duggan said absently. He was thinking about the soft-cover military manual that Wasson had left behind on his bunk. He'd stared at it for a good while, wondering what would be inside a book with a title like *Enemy Archetypes and Cultural Profiles.* No harm in taking a peek. Duggan picked it up and flipped through pages of drawings and photos of various al Qaeda and Mujahedin guerrillas, some packing suicide belts, others in camouflage or tribal garb. The largest section was made up of long-distance and aerial photographs of hostile operatives, vehicles, weapons and tented camps. Unlike the crisp Post-it, the manual was dusty and dog-eared. And inside the front cover, in neatly penned letters: D. Westlake.

Their first stop on Davis's tour was the base recreation facility, aka "the rec." They entered a large building that reminded Duggan of an airport terminal food court—TGI Friday's, KFC and Mama Mia's pizzeria outlets surrounding tables packed with men and women of various ages and ranks in identical T-shirts and fatigues. Davis and Duggan moved on past grocery stores filled with American staples, gift shops with racy postcards and souvenir teddy bears, a gym offering yoga and spinning classes, and other familiar comforts designed to banish the harsh reality outside the gates.

Duggan's attention was drawn to a room filled with cubicles equipped with computer terminals. "Yeah, I figured you'd find that interesting," Davis said. "This is where people can send e-mails to their girlfriends and families, if they have any."

"Anybody can use these?"

"Anybody with a base ID."

Duggan watched as troops pecked at keyboards and stared intently at computer displays under framed photos of desert vistas in the American Southwest. "Did Westlake ever come here?"

"I honestly don't know," Davis answered. "Probably. But as you know, Westlake had his own laptop."

"Did he need special clearance for that?"

"Westlake was an instructor," Davis replied. "So, yeah, I imagine he did."

On their way to the "incident venue," Duggan noticed a shadow flitting over the shrubs and craned his neck to see a Predator drone hovering above them. He had always expected the unmanned weapon to look like a toy up close, but as it drifted overhead, its sleek profile glinted with menacing authority. Duggan could almost feel the thing scanning the ground and everything and everyone on it.

"You never said anything about Predators," Duggan said.

Davis didn't bother to look up. "What about them?"

"What happened to the man in the bunk across from Westlake's?"

"You mean Fisk? Lemme think." Davis massaged his jaw as if trying to remember. "Fisk was honorably discharged. He completed his tour, and he got to go home, lucky bastard."

The jeep halted in front of a cluster of outdoor sports fields featuring a running track, baseball diamonds, and even an ice hockey rink. Duggan could see that Westlake's barracks were just a few hundred yards away. He regarded the open space near the basketball courts.

"So, just in case you were wondering," Davis said dryly, "Donald Westlake wakes up one morning and loads his gun and walks over to where some Afghan soldiers are posted—US allies, people he probably knew—and mows them down, kills them all without a word. No note, no explanation, not a sound from his mouth as he blows them all away. Westlake had been acting up, with symptoms of PTSD. They only way anyone could stop him was to shoot him dead at blank range. End of story."

It was Duggan's turn to study Davis's face. "And you don't find that even a little bit odd?"

"The guy snapped—that's all," Davis said. "Psych-outs like Westlake's happen all the time around here."

"Where's the checkpoint where the Afghans were shot?"

"Over behind the basketball courts, but it's long gone," Davis replied. "Bad for morale."

"I'm getting out here," Duggan announced. "I can walk back."

"If you're going to be walking around alone, you should take my rifle."

"No, thanks."

"Whatever, man." Davis waited for Duggan to get out of the jeep and drove off without saying good-bye.

The foundation of the razed checkpoint jutted from the mangled earth like overgrown molars. Duggan strode out to the bulldozed area adjacent to the basketball courts and visually traced Westlake's route from the barracks. The path from point A to point B was almost a straight line, hardly the trajectory of a demented psychopath. Westlake knew exactly where he was going, and he knew what he was going to do when he got there.

A chorus of boisterous shouts broke Duggan's concentration. On the other side of the basketball courts, on a flat open space bookended by regulation goals, a group of guys were having a soccer match. Some of the faces looked familiar, and Duggan walked closer to confirm that it was the airmen from Westlake's barracks.

Duggan was no stranger to the adrenaline kick of what fans like to call "the beautiful game." During his salad days, soccer had already started making inroads across the empty lots and urban streets of Chicago, its popularity fueled by globally savvy youths and immigrants from Europe and Japan. In the barrios of Mexico and Central America, where the first rubber balls appeared, the game was revered as the sport of gods and warriors who challenged defeated enemies on the sacred court before detaching their heads and kicking them into the sky, where they continued rising until they joined the sun and the moon.

The ball skittered and bounced between the men, absorbing energy from the clash of limbs, daring and defying any single player to claim and command its kinetic essence. Duggan watched from the sidelines, and the men did their best to ignore him. But when one of them missed a kick and the object of their attention careened in Duggan's direction, they were forced to acknowledge his presence. He stopped the black and white sphere and balanced it, still spinning, on the tip of his foot.

"Mind if I join you?" Duggan asked amiably.

Before anyone could respond, he took possession of the ball and charged onto the field, maneuvering toward the opposite goal. The stunning audacity of Duggan's move gave him a window to advance fifteen or so yards before the defenders overcame their incredulity and closed in. The first interceptor was so unprepared for Duggan's deft dodge and pivot that he was sent sprawling and cursing on a collision course with two other players. He fended off two more attempts to cleave the ball from his control and was about to take a shot at the goal when a sharp blow to his ankle threw him off balance. A well-aimed elbow in the face, and what might have been an accidental scrape of cleats across his thigh as he was going down, completed the message. Flat on his back and tasting blood, Duggan raised his arms in surrender. No broken bones as far as he could tell, but his jaw and leg would stay tender for a while. As would the oozing contusions on his elbows and knees.

Duggan became aware of a hand outstretched to help him up. It was Wasson.

"You should probably get off the field before your ass gets kicked again."

Duggan nodded, still catching his breath as Wasson helped him to a bench on the sidelines. Wasson stamped his feet and stretched without looking at him. "Where the hell did you learn to play soccer like that?"

"South Side," Duggan answered. The abrasion on his thigh looked particularly nasty, but it wasn't deep.

"You crazy motherfucker," Wasson said. "You think you can just waltz in here and everybody's gonna drop their pants? Who the hell do you think you are?"

Duggan said, "I'm on your side, remember?"

"Yeah, so are the Afghans."

"You left Westlake's manual behind on purpose, didn't you?"

Wasson shrugged. "It's a free country."

"And the Post-it?"

Wasson shook his head almost imperceptibly.

"What happened to Fisk?"

"He went home."

"Davis told me he was discharged."

"That's one way to put it." Wasson seemed to hesitate before adding, "There's usually a party at the rec on Friday nights. I bet you could use a drink." He ambled toward the field and signaled for the ball. "He'll live," Wasson announced.

"Too bad," someone said, as sneakers resumed their aggressive shuffle on the baked brown dirt.

Duggan limped back to the barracks alone, trying not to wallow in self-pity. This whole assignment had been a sham and a set-up, an orchestrated farce to simulate an actual investigation. But there was nothing to investigate and nothing to find because the evidence had long since been erased or carted away. He might as well have written his report before he ever got here because nobody was interested in finding out what had actually happened, and those that knew were already doing their best to bury it or forget. Duggan didn't blame the soldiers one bit. They had come to the gates of hell to risk their life for their country and watched one of their own go berserk right under their noses. And just when things had started to settle down and seem halfway normal again, Duggan appeared out of nowhere like the grim reaper, resurrecting Westlake's ghost, asking questions and rattling chains, reminding them that no matter how much they rationalized their situation, how much they pushed the nightmares away, their continued presence at the scene of the crime contaminated them. They were all implicated, all guilty of mindless murder, all, to one degree or another, crazed assassins.

The barracks were blessedly empty when Duggan got there. He gingerly removed his bloody clothes and took a long shower, running different scenarios and outcomes through his head as the water trickled over his wounds and the steam fogged the mirrors over the sinks.

Swarm3524: hi, lucy
LucyintheSky: who's this?
Swarm296: a friend
LucyintheSky: do i know you?
Swarm6481: in a way
LucyintheSky: who is this, really?
Swarm2970: it's Swarm, from the flash mob on the 4th of July

LucyintheSky: is this a joke?

Swarm9432: no joke

LucyintheSky: u can't be

Swarm4405: why not?

LucyintheSky: because Swarm doesn't really exist

Swarm9460: are you trying to hurt my feelings? I should have been a pair of ragged claws/Scuttling across the floors of silent seas

LucyintheSky: you just quoted my favorite poet.

Swarm2215: really? You like T. S. Eliot? Looks like we've got something in common after all.

LucyintheSky: And I'm supposed to believe you're actually Swarm, *the* Swarm

Swarm3337: I am no prophet ... I have seen the moment of my greatness flicker ...

LucyintheSky: ha—okay, then prove it to me

Swarm609: remember Operation Uncle Sam? You had white stars on your body. Two of them were, well, strategically placed

LucyintheSky: nice try. lots of people watched it on TV

Swarm7626: not what I saw on camera 3. Do you remember kissing the camera lens?

LucyintheSky: ...

Swarm1389: you still there?

LucyintheSky: omg—it can't be

Swarm5896: why not?

LucyintheSky: how did you find me?

Swarm2586: that's a silly question. You wanted me to find you. admit it.

LucyintheSky: sorry, I just ...

Swarm2852: just what?

LucyintheSky: why?

Swarm534: you mean what do I want?

LucyintheSky: yes

Swarm6892: watching you that day, I felt you could see me, yet I knew you couldn't. I'd never felt that before ... from anybody. I had to find out if you were real

LucyintheSky: Do I dare/Disturb the Universe?/In a minute there is time.

Swarm249: exactly. It can get pretty lonely here in the silent seas of cyberspace.

LucyintheSky: I'm not an idiot, you know

Swarm250: ?

LucyintheSky: you can't be lonely when you've got thousands of followers. everybody knows you.

Swarm9643: do they? i can get people to collaborate. they follow my tweets and augmented reality breadcrumb trails, but that's different from personally connecting.

LucyintheSky: so what's stopping you?

Swarm012: growing up without a dad, you're not always exactly sure who you are, so it's hard to reveal yourself to others. you seemed so natural, so free, so real—I had to trust my instincts, risk my feelings

LucyintheSky: ...

Swarm608: still there? sorry if i scared you.

LucyintheSky: sorry about your dad. i like what you said

Swarm: 6922: the things I do as Swarm, they're not me, at least not all of me. the flash mobs are performances

LucyintheSky: political theater

Swarm7537: I'm a little blown away. I mean the odds that I could be attracted to you and then find out that you're even more amazing inside, even more beautiful ...

LucyintheSky: no fair

Swarm3042: why?

LucyintheSky: you know what I look like but I can't see you. a little one-sided, wouldn't you agree?

Swarm1958: cant argue with that. but I have to be careful—some people think I've broken laws. maybe I have, technically, but I'm trying to make people look around and think … People get threatened when their assumptions are challenged … Make sense?

Lucyinthesky: it makes perfect sense. I get so frustrated sometimes because I see people just lurching forward, without thinking about the consequences of their actions or the consequences of their inaction

Swarm112: i wish I could be more normal about this …

LucyintheSky: how's that?

Swarm2550: you know, get a friend to introduce us online, follow each other, join the same groups, go on a date in public …

LucyintheSky: sounds like a relationship

Swarm7578: sorry, I'm being pretty presumptuous

LucyintheSky: slightly. But u don't have to apologize

Swarm3258: yes, i do. it really sucks that I have to be so stealthy and just barge in on you like this.

LucyintheSky: im glad u did

Swarm4200: really? Can I talk to you again?

LucyintheSky: sure

Swarm3354: awesome. I'll find a place online for us to meet and we'll take it from there.

LucyintheSky: that sounds good ☺

Swarm3585: do you know the avatar world called Luminescence?

LucyintheSky: yeah, of course. I love that place! I like to take walks by the river and watch the sunsets

Swarm2204: meet me there next Thursday at midnight, at the castle under the drawbridge.

LucyintheSky: how will I find u?

Swarm1876: just look for Mr. Aws

It was salsa night at the base, and the lifestyle committee had set up a DJ deck under the awning outside the mess hall. A GI wearing a Mexican sombrero, Hawaiian shirt, cut-off shorts, and combat boots stood behind a card table dispensing beer and hard liquor. Duggan asked for a Jack Daniels on the rocks and edged closer to the fray. The men outnumbered the women by about four to one, which the females seemed to be using to their advantage. Someone had wrapped a string of plastic chili pepper lights around a lamppost. Out on the crowded dance floor, couples formed, collided, broke apart, recombined.

"We recycle the party favors."

Mitch Wasson was standing a couple of feet away to Duggan's side, a sweating can of Budweiser clenched in his fist. There was no sign of Davis, not yet anyway.

Duggan nodded. "I can see that."

They watched the dance floor maneuvers for a few seconds. "You know," Wasson said, keeping his voice below the music, "trying to get us to like you only makes us more suspicious."

"Oh yeah? How suspicious are you?"

"Very."

"That's the nicest thing anyone's said to me all week."

The corners of Wasson's mouth twitched in the direction of a smile. "If I had half a brain, I wouldn't tell you a fucking thing."

"I'm listening."

"Ha—that's a good one." Wasson tipped his head toward the dancers. "See that blonde in the white top?" Duggan indicated that he did. "Keep watching her while we talk."

Duggan took a swig of bourbon and obligingly ogled. Wasson was right—they only had a few minutes before their conversation would start to attract attention.

"Westlake was a UAV driver, and Marty Fisk was his sensor."

"What kind of driver?"

"Man, I thought you spooks were supposed to be smart. A drone pilot. UAV, unmanned aerial vehicle, or RPA, remotely piloted aircraft. The pilot flies the drone, and the sensor controls the cameras. The pilot and the sensor are a team, like salt and pepper. They go through the same training. They live in the same barracks. They do everything together. They are a two-headed killing machine. The sensor finds the target, and the pilot fires the missiles. But it's not unusual for both to press the button together. If anyone can tell you what really happened to Donny, it would be Marty."

"I thought all the Middle East drone operators were based in the States."

"Congratulations," Wasson said. "You finally asked an intelligent question. Westlake and Fisk were training RPA operators. Now I'm going to make this one easy for you—what country are we in?"

"You're telling me Westlake and Fisk were stealth training Afghans to fly their own drones," Duggan said, forcing himself to keep his voice low. "The CIA couldn't take Afghans to the United States without attracting attention, so the RPA training had to be local, a clandestine operation."

"Bingo."

"So you've got a couple of UAV operators who have no official business being here on a secret mission. One of them goes off the reservation, but nobody wants anyone to know what they were actually doing, so they cover it all up and write Westlake off as a wacko. I'm betting Fisk didn't take too kindly to that."

"They awarded Marty a Distinguished Warfare Medal, and he gave it back. Ballsy son of a bitch."

"Is that why Fisk got discharged?"

"Duh," Wasson said. The blonde had registered their attention and was wending her way in their direction.

"Was this an inside job or an outside job?"

Wasson drained his beer before answering. "Are you talking about the base operations or Westlake's head?"

74

Duggan said nothing, digesting the comment.

"What you're looking for isn't here, not anymore," Wasson said. "But I think you already knew that."

The blonde was within striking range, her hips undulating to "La Bamba."

"Peace, bro." Wasson took a couple of steps forward and started to dance. He and the girl faced off and jostled into the middle of the crowd, provoking hoots and hollers of fervid camaraderie. Jello shots were deployed.

Duggan looked at his watch; he had to be packed and ready for his ride to the airport in five hours. He went over to the bar and got himself another drink.

7

....

J. T. Nutley was standing in the doorframe of Duggan's office, arms crossed, lips pursed to convey urgency without commentary. His designer suit was custom fitted, and his shoes gleamed in the fluorescent light.

Duggan put aside the file he was reading. "What?"

Nutley cocked his head down the hallway, indicating that Duggan should follow. They'd been friends since meeting at cybersecurity training camp, where JT had teamed up with Duggan on several assignments. Beside also being from Illinois and sharing a rabid devotion to the Cubs, JT had impressed Duggan with his incisive logic and knack for ferreting out the political motives behind even the most mundane organizational directives.

"Are you going to tell me where we're going?" Duggan asked, even though he had a pretty good idea.

Like most government agencies devoted to conducting covert operations on a large scale, the NCSD frowned on unnecessary communication of any kind. Only the most trivial or most important information was ever rendered onto paper or transferred verbally. Everything else was implied, inferred, committed to memory, and/ or immediately destroyed. Doodling in a notebook during a meeting, for instance, was grounds for a reprimand, or so JT had once told him. Nutley was an encryption expert, which he liked to describe as "making sure that nobody knows what nobody knows." Like everybody else at the Department of Homeland Security, it was hard to tell when he was joking or serious because even the most lighthearted quip could contain a coded insinuation or warning, which was probably why the summons by Duggan's boss, Section Chief Simon Gupta, was delivered by his colleague and friend without a single word being uttered.

Two minutes later, Duggan was standing in front of Gupta's desk, waiting for him to finish typing on his computer. Nutley stared into his phone for a moment before leaving them alone. Duggan liked Gupta, who shared his background in software engineering and his distaste for supercilious superiors.

"Jake, sit."

Duggan did.

"How was your trip to Afghanistan?"

"I filed my report yesterday, sir."

"I don't want to read your report," Gupta said. "I want to know what you think."

Duggan told him that the whole assignment was a wild goose chase and a waste of time and that the last thing the Defense Department wanted was for anyone to know what had actually happened to Donald Westlake in Kandahar. "They left a laptop that had already been sanitized and showed me the base bowling alley," Duggan said.

Gupta made a sympathetic face. "Well, so the case is closed."

"I guess that's one interpretation of the facts."

"Exactly." Gupta leaned back in his chair, indicating that they were moving on to a new topic. "I need you to think about something else, Jake. We're conducting another round of sim games, this time with the Russians."

Gupta was referring to a series of cyber-warfare simulations that the United States conducted jointly with foreign powers to preempt the real thing. Cyber war games were intended to provide a common framework for both countries to deal with large-scale cyber-attacks before they escalated into full-blown confrontations. The last one had been with China, but it didn't take long for the Americans to suspect that the Chinese were using the event to understand how to repel or disable US cyber weapons. In response, the United States had begun a parallel program overseen by the Defense Advanced Research Projects Agency to build a national cyber test range at which American programmers could fight mock cyber wars in a more controlled environment. The joke around the NCSD was that the games were a thinly disguised rehearsal for a digital skirmish that both sides knew had already begun, or, as JT liked to say, "a game within a game within a game."

"I want you to go to NetOps in Colorado," Gupta continued, "and brief the participants on backdoor worms."

"To keep them from planting any?"

"In a perfect world, yes."

"Always more than happy to take another bullet for the Pentagon Cyber Command," Duggan said cheerfully.

"Objection noted," Gupta replied. "JT will assist with logistics as usual. I'd like you to leave today."

When Duggan got back to his office, JT was there to greet him with an I-told-you-so shrug.

"You knew I was going to get drafted for NetOps."

"Yep."

"And you're smiling because you're going too."

JT shook his head gravely. "I'm smiling because I'm not. But how about you let me buy you a welcome back and bon voyage lunch at Outback."

"As wonderful as that sounds," Duggan said, "Outback will have to wait until after Colorado."

"Is Gupta up your ass?"

"That's not it," Duggan said. "It's the trip I just took to Kandahar."

"The Westlake shit show."

"Yeah, Donald Westlake. A soldier goes berserk for no apparent reason and the Pentagon responds by using the NCSD for a fresh coat of whitewash. Doesn't make sense. They were hiding something, but I can't figure out why. Especially since ..."

"Since what?"

"There was definitely a breach, but I think it came from inside."

"Whoa. You mean a worm inside Cyber Command?"

"I don't know, but the CO at the base couldn't get rid of me fast enough."

JT was pensively studying the carpet. Duggan could almost see the dots connecting.

"Maybe I can cheer you up," JT said finally. "There's a guy I know at the NSA, Jordan Sharpe. I'm pretty sure he'll be at NetOps. He's a sniffer, with a particular interest in Cyber Command shenanigans. I bet he'd love to hear your story. Off the clock, naturally."

"What's to stop him from ratting me out to his bosses?"

"He's a player who keeps his cards pretty close, especially when the stakes are high." JT made a church steeple with his fingers. "How lucky are you feeling?"

"Not very," Duggan said.

"In that case," JT said jovially, "you've got nothing to lose by shuffling the deck with Agent Sharpe."

Tom could usually hear Xander before he saw him. It started with boisterous dings from the bell on his pedicab, followed by squealing brakes and, in the case of this particular night, a ceremonial howl of animal exuberance. Once he actually arrived, Xander was in perpetual motion, flipping a random piece of paper between his fingers, making electric drum noises with his mouth. Evoking sound from inanimate objects and his own body was how Xander perceived and internalized his environment. Chairs, cars, walls, books, empty cereal boxes, dining utensils, pencils and pens, pots and pans, chest, hands, elbows, and feet—all were potential instruments to express a mood or texture or to simply confirm an object's *thingness*. In Xander's universe, until something made a noise, until it was coaxed to release an audible presence, it didn't completely exist.

An almost preternatural obsession with the timbre of a drum or the buzzing chatter of electronic instruments was only the most obvious manifestation of Xander's aural compulsion. He was instinctively attuned to the cadence in a person's breathing, speech, and stride; the swaying of trees; the asymmetric arias of traffic, the swooning waltz of the moon and sun; the way shadows of passing streetlights kept time inside a moving vehicle. He was even sensitive to the way a sentence could be orchestrated and scored with staccato starts and stops, sub clauses, hyphens, and commas, pausing abruptly to make a point or unspooling into rolling legato ribbons of words that pooled and cascaded on their leisurely journey to illustrate an idea or make a larger statement about human sensitivity to the metronomic intervals between letters, spaces, events, and ideas before finally punctuating its finale with a single conclusive period.

"What," Xander shouted, his fists battering the sill of Tom's window, "is happening!"

"*Where*," Tom shot back, "is happening?"

"*Why* is happening!"

"*Who* is happening!"

Xander vaulted over the threshold and planted himself directly in front of Tom's chair. He beamed and pointed both thumbs at this chest. "*This guy!*" he boasted. "Because I just signed a deal with Mash Machine Records. And we, my friend, are going to Vegas!"

"You're spinning on the Strip?"

"Yeah, man. I just got a paying gig at the freaking ARK Festival!"

Tom tried to look surprised. During the months since Operation Uncle Sam had reinforced Swarm's standing as a social media sensation, Tom had surreptitiously dedicated himself to boosting Xander's career. By anonymously hacking into every electronic music webzine, chat room, and message board, in addition to posting ersatz reviews along with Xander's photo and a sample of one of his best mixes, Tom managed to nudge his buddy from a total unknown into a budding phenomenon. The master stroke that pushed Xander over the edge came during the Austin City Limits Music Festival, where many of the top musicians in the world, and most of the top music executives in the country, gathered for a three-day marathon of parties and showcases by hundreds of performers of every stripe. As Tom guessed, it wasn't very hard, given Xander's genetic gifts and musical proclivities, to tilt the media machine in Xander's direction by inciting a flash mob of more than a thousand instant fans to gather for his ACL gig, vaulting him into one of the festival's fast-track discoveries and getting him a "New DJs to watch" clip on Turntable.com. Tom stood on the sidelines and observed proudly as Xander mesmerized the crowd with a thudding tattoo, building an interlocking matrix of bass lines anchored to layers of gritty synth; turning the knobs of the mixing board with kinetic flair; looking up from the decks and raising his palms toward the writhing crowd like a high priest giving his benediction; and blessing the jumping, pumping throngs that came to worship the beat and give themselves up, if only for a few hours, to a higher audible power.

Tom had clinched the Vegas gig for Xander by secretly instigating a grassroots campaign among the trendsetters who drew their power from sniffing out the next cool thing and serving it up to the ARK bookers on a digital platter. Xander's sound system and lighting were still relatively rudimentary, but that would change now that he had Mash Machine Records to back him. Mash Machine's marketing whiz, Fabian Beres, who already represented several of the world's biggest DJs, was taking Xander to the next level as his new pet project. Tom could help with that too since Xander had asked him to join his crew to "deal with the technical stuff." Tom agreed, on a conditional, part-time basis, to contribute code for the audiocontrol system and supervise some of the visual effects.

"Tom, I'm going to be spinning on the same stage as fucking Tiesto and Deadmou5?" Xander's statement was uttered as a question, as if saying it aloud to Tom would somehow make it more tangible.

"That's great, Xan. You've worked hard for this. You deserve it."

Xander's blooming confidence filled the room like a rise in barometric pressure. He was on the brink of breaking into the big leagues, and Vegas would be the flashpoint. There was no way Tom could miss his buddy's coronation at one of the biggest EDM events in the world. Besides, Tom had never been to Las Vegas, and he couldn't imagine a better reason to get his own chips.

"It's gonna be like the Rat Pack on ecstasy," Xander quipped.

"Yeah, and you'll be chairman of the mixing board."

Xander took a breath, suddenly serious. "You know, I never doubted that this would happen, but now I can feel all that space between the molecules, invisible forces, electrons, and billboards flashing. Everything connecting across platforms in multiple dimensions." He looked at Tom as if for the first time. "Nothing will ever be the same again, will it?"

"Probably not."

Xander put his hand on Tom's shoulder. "But you and me, Tommy, I mean it—we will stay brothers no matter what, right?"

"Absolutely."

They exchanged a heartfelt hug. "I want you to know I consider you a part of what's happened to me," Xander said. "You listened to my tracks and told me they were good, you told me to keep going when nobody else gave a shit, you loaned me money when I was broke and let me crash on your floor till I was back on my feet. You've been with me all the way, mano a mano, brother to brother. We did this together."

"Yeah, Xan, we did."

"C'mon, then. Let us go forth and inebriate!"

"Sorry, man. We shall go forth, but not tonight. I've got a date."

"Really? Where?"

"Luminescence."

"Wait, let me get this straight: you're taking a girl on a date in a fantasy world video game." Xander shrugged. "I guess it beats stuffing bitcoins into a virtual stripper's thong."

"You would know."

"Yep," Xander affirmed before exiting through the window.

A moment later, he telegraphed his adieu with the pedicab bell—a single exuberant ding.

Tom checked the time. He had a few minutes before his date with Lucy, just long enough to scan the posts on 4chan/b/. Helping Xander become an EDM star wasn't the only thing Tom had been up to during the past few months. After a series of sporadic, occasionally disturbing chats, macktheknife and his friends invited Swarm into their inner circle, tutoring him on the ins and outs of the 4chan underworld. The site's structure was deceptively straightforward—forty-nine different multimedia message boards, each with its own subject and abbreviation bracketed by slashes, ranging from 4chan.org/an/ (for animals and nature) to /x/ (for paranormal). Tom's new chums were denizens of /b/ (for "random"), an image board that served as a playground and online hangout for an unruly aggregation of self-proclaimed "b-tards"—hackers, anarchists, and social malcontents, some of them harmless, some not, all of them resourceful, opinionated, and stridently anonymous, which Tom soon learned was not at all the same thing as unknown. Macktheknife, quasar539, toke, bbreath, and the rest of the gang were alt-J celebrities in their own right, online lords of mayhem who patrolled the posts and lashed out at those deemed unduly dense or unworthy.

At first, Tom found himself intimidated and rattled by the scabrous stew of midget porn, cartoons, snuff-joke video clips, and non sequiturs, but gradually certain personalities had emerged, distinct themes and voices bubbling up out of the piquant cyber soup. The underlying assumption was that society was broken and corrupted, which demanded a radical intervention and reboot of the American experiment. The Internet, with its unmarked boundaries and dark crannies, was a safe haven for the neo-patriots who would save democracy by keeping it honest, by taking carefully aimed potshots at the corporate gentry and the military-industrial plutocracy. It eventually dawned on Tom that "random" was anything but. The constant barrage of queries, invectives, miscellaneous facts, and outrageous accusations was all part of a vetting process guided by contrarian stipulations and unreasonable expectations. Those found lacking in skill, wit, zeal or bravado were quickly hounded out, marginalized, or ignored. To be called a fag, for instance, had nothing to do with sexual preference. While hetero lewdness generally ruled, nobody cared what anyone did with his or her own body or anyone else's, for that matter. Alacrity, audacity, and programming pluck were the valued commodities of this geek-ruled realm. Before long, Tom was giving as good as he got, solidifying the respect and trust of the b-tards, who were intrigued by his uncanny ability to fire up flash mobs at a moment's notice. Except that it wasn't really Tom that the mobbers were following anymore—it was Swarm. Swarm was the one who communicated an authority that transcended ego, his confidence emanating from a deepening awareness of allied forces, not just his 4chan cronies but also the minions who acted out his wildest fantasies with fanatical verve, storming shopping malls in rabbit suits, converging at busy intersections for instantaneous pillow fights, assembling for candlelit Edwardian dinner parties in a parking lot at dusk. It was Swarm, not Tom, who was beginning to regard the flash mobsters as a physical extension of his will, a congregation of connected brains and limbs reaching out across the city, materializing out of nowhere and then melting away, leaving no trace. It was Swarm as much as Tom who was drafting a message, a manifesto that would speak to the masses, which would make them understand that they were part of something that had never existed before, something that could fulfill and even transcend the lofty ideals sketched out by the b-tard bros and every soul who felt a sea change coming but didn't know what to call it or how to help make it happen. Tom had created Swarm as a protective alias, a disembodied alter ego invented to crystallize and lead social media disruptions without revealing who was behind them. Gradually, though, Swarm had begun to embody something beyond flash mobs and mere weapons of mass distraction, a possibility that demanded a new language and a new definition of the here and now, where it was going, and what was coming next.

But tonight Tom was focused on more mundane concerns. After Sonia came to Tom for help with his aunt's predicament with the Munificent Life Insurance Company, he had spent weeks corresponding with the adjuster, patiently explaining that the forms should have been sent to Tom's aunt in Spanish, to no avail. An appeal directly to the CEO, Wallace F. Brown, went unanswered, phone calls deflected. At that point, Tom decided to take a different tack. Thanks to tips from his 4chan pals on how to launder the cash from the magazine subscription scam, Tom had more than enough money to cover his aunt's medical bills. The b-tards also agreed to help Tom teach the company, particularly its callous CEO, a lesson in community relations.

Tom's war on Munificent Life was waged on multiple fronts. The first volley was in the form of a DOS attack on Muni-life.com, followed by a corresponding flurry of negative instant messaging that triggered a hail of bad publicity and shut down the company's website. Meanwhile, macktheknife and a few other b-tards focused their ire on Brown. It didn't take long for them to unearth and publish an e-mail string between the CEO and his underage mistress, a University of Texas junior, which did not sit well with Brown's wife—or the conservative church congregation of which he was a prominent, and soon to be former, member. In an effort to stem the damage, the company reimbursed Sonia for her sister's denied coverage, but not before Munificent's stock plummeted by 15 percent.

The coup de grâce had come just a week ago, when one of Swarm's hacktivist confidants passed him a tip that Munificent Life had engaged former NSA data analysts to help them sift through social media sites to preemptively identify and freeze out customers with higher than average health risks. Details of Munificent's malfeasance were leaked to strategically chosen industry bloggers, eventually flowing upstream to major media and progressive pundits, who in turn demanded a federal investigation. The final touch was an AR image that appeared from nowhere and instantly went viral. It showed Brown as the Grim Reaper, smiling as he entered the Munificent headquarters building made to resemble a tombstone. The caption: "Business is good." Within days, Brown announced his resignation, taking most of the company's board of directors down with him.

Tom logged on to 4chan/b/ and checked a forum he had authored under the heading "Cancers in the Munificent C-Suite." All the comments on Tom's C-suite message string were verbal high fives; one had even attached an animated gif of a triumphantly fluttering pirate flag. "This one goes out to Jeremy Hammond!" announced Toke, referring to a hacker who had been sentenced to ten years in prison for breaking into databases of corporate and security firms. "The geek shall inherit the Earth," crowed macktheknife. "And meanwhile, they will beat the shit out of mendacious Munificent fucks who try to withhold medical coverage from helpless widows! Bravo, b-tards. It's been a good day in the good fight. The cloud has spoken! Long live Swarm!"

8

The damage was already catastrophic and getting worse by the second. Several hundred dead, power stations and electrical towers in six states leveled by explosions, police and medical teams delayed by malfunctioning GPS systems, online defensive response and coordination efforts paralyzed by DOS attack viruses and worms, millions of Americans left in the dark without power or phone service. The offensive was being carried out simultaneously in major cities across the country, all with the same goal, which was to destroy the nation's power grid and emergency response abilities and foment chaos and panic in the civilian population.

In a windowless room filled with wall-size screens, Duggan watched the disaster unfold on a map of the United States as dozens of technicians and cyber-defense strategists struggled to fight back. Nearby, a young man in a white shirt was calmly humming to himself and pressing buttons on a tablet computer. He spoke to Duggan without looking up from his screen. "Having fun yet?"

"Nothing fun about losing a cyber war."

The man looked up at the situation map. "We're not losing," he said. "We have auxiliary backup systems on the eastern grid and satellite offensive options that the Russians can't match. This is just the beginning. You wait and see."

A text popped up on Duggan's phone. It was from Jordan Sharpe, asking for a meeting, just as JT had predicted. They agreed to coffee at a Denny's not far from the operations facility. Sharpe was slightly pudgy, balding, and visibly stressed—classic NSA. Duggan was pretty sure there would be no official record of anybody named Sharpe attending the cy-ops games. Sharpe had the drooping posture of a man who carried the weight of the earth's atmosphere on his sloped shoulders.

"JT tells me you're discreet," Sharpe said wearily, "which is the only reason I'm here." Sharpe emptied a pack of sweetener into his coffee and slowly stirred it. "I hear you got fed a pile of crap in Kandahar."

Duggan gave Sharpe a brief description of his trip to Afghanistan. As Duggan told his story, Sharpe's foot started to jiggle slightly. It made Duggan nervous to see Sharpe getting excited.

"Have you heard from Mr. Post-it?" Sharpe asked.

"You think I will?"

Sharpe shrugged. "It's possible. But that's not the part I find interesting."

"Go on."

"No offense, but NCSD is small potatoes for Cyber Command. If they were serious, they never would have outsourced an investigation for something this juicy. From what you just told me, I'd guess that your visit was a pro forma Band-Aid designed to stop anyone else from kicking the tires."

"I've come to the same conclusion."

"Did you tell your boss?"

"He declared the case closed and sent me here to watch the cyber games."

"Ouch." Sharpe's condolence was genuine. "Look, you can do what you want, but your boss might be right. There's no upside in getting your tit caught in a tiff between NSA and Cyber Command. Plus, whatever happened is probably outside your jurisdiction anyway. My advice would be to enjoy the games and double down on room service."

"Maybe, but I don't like getting on airplanes for no discernable reason. Twice."

Sharpe sighed. "Only amateurs take this stuff personally."

Duggan started to get up.

"Hang on," Sharpe said. For the first time during the entire conversation, he looked Duggan straight in the eye. "There's a DOD research wonk who turned up MIA just a few days after your buddy Westlake went apeshit. The only reason we know about it is because DOD wanted to make sure we didn't have him. The inquiry came from the Cyber Command office in Afghanistan. There might be a connection. Or maybe it's just wishful thinking."

Duggan put a ten-dollar bill on the table and rose to leave. "Thanks for the coffee," he said.

Back at his hotel room, Duggan ordered a cheeseburger, fries, and two rye whiskey and sodas before noticing the blinking red message light on the phone. It was Sharpe's voice, uttering a single sentence: "My missing friend was studying electromagnetic effects on the human brain."

Duggan erased Sharpe's message and opened his laptop. For the next few hours, he trolled the Internet, delving into something he had always known bits and pieces about but had never really paid much attention to until now. Duggan was surprised, intrigued, and finally alarmed by the mountain of verified information he encountered, some of it published by various departments of the US government itself. The origin of mind control as a weapon, Duggan learned, dated back at least to the 1950s, when a Chicago-born MD of Yugoslavian descent named Andrija Puharich discovered that electromagnetic pulses of extremely low frequency, or ELF waves, had dramatic—and potentially destructive—effects on people and the environment. Puharich was influenced by Nikola Tesla, the turn-of-the-century mathematician who had already explored the concept of using radio waves to transmit electrical energy through the Earth and its atmosphere, even filing a number of US patents based on that idea. Puharich found that a person's emotional state and health could be modified by exposing him or her to signals that corresponded to particular points on the electromagnetic spectrum, literally "tuning" a person's mind like a radio set. In tests conducted in conjunction with Robert C. Beck, Puharich reported that human reactions to various ELF frequencies ranged from headaches, nausea, and anxiety to a sense of well-being, as well as aggression and riotous behavior. Tesla himself had foreseen a form of future warfare that would be "conducted by direct application of electrical waves." In 1908, Tesla predicted that the greatest achievement of science would be to master the universe by manipulating the invisible ether, a "tenuous fluid" of matter that encapsulated the earth, and usher in a new reality in which "old worlds would vanish and new ones would spring into being" and man would "fulfill his ultimate destiny."

Duggan's fingers drummed on the imitation wood veneer desk as he scrolled down a list of news reports and documents that cataloged a zigzagging trail of mind-control weapon experiments conducted by the CIA and the DOD, beginning in the 1940s and continuing right up to the present day. Was this why Sharpe had gotten so excited at Denny's? And why the delay before telling him about the DOD researcher who'd gone AWOL?

A related news link took him to an article published the same day in the *New York Times* under the headline "Agency Initiative Will Focus on Advancing Deep Brain Stimulation." The article mentioned that one hundred thousand people with Parkinson's disease had already received electrical implants to help them control involuntary movements. Then it got to the point of the story, which was that DARPA had announced that it was spending more than seventy million dollars to develop technology that would help scientists "acquire signals that can tell them precisely what is going on with the brain." DARPA's project, the article continued, was "partly inspired by the needs of combat veterans who suffer from mental and physical conditions," which by definition included PTSD.

Duggan thought about what the Post-it had told him: *Look for what's not there.*

He rubbed his eyes and took a gulp of his second whiskey. He had read enough to know what he was going to do next. It was Thursday. Duggan e-mailed the office to say he was taking a personal day and spending the weekend with friends on the West Coast. Then he logged on to Expedia and booked a flight to Spokane, Washington.

Tom was still exhilarated from the endorsement of his victory over Munificent Life when he logged onto Luminescence and made his way to their usual trysting place near the castle. In the magical mythical reality where Tom and Lucy courted and flirted as 3-D avatars, Mr. Aws was a dashing young wizard, powerful enough to unleash lightning bolts from his hands and repel attacks from trolls, zombies, and dragons. Lucy always looked lovely, her long blond hair cascading over a white gown studded with glowing stars and planets, a crown of diamonds floating above her head. Her hidden power was an ability to control the weather. Her freezing rainstorm could immobilize large animals and paralyze stout knights who found themselves trapped inside their own icy armor.

The key attraction of Luminescence was the way any group of players could pool their power to create new areas of the game, ranging from Jurassic jungles and futuristic clone colonies to medieval kingdoms, like the one Lucy and Tom had chosen as the pastoral setting for their amorous trysts. The very real politics of how and why different players came together to create—and sometimes destroy—virtual realizations of their wildest communal desires and dreams was what gave the game its addictive charm.

It didn't take Tom long to cross the meadow, making sure to avoid the testy winged lizards that lurked in the weeping willows, and climb the hilly path that skirted the battlefield. He could hear the clinks and zaps of swords and wands, grunts and screams, and the whooshing sound of a fighter using earned credits to increase his powers. Deaths in Luminescence were always temporary, but in order to buy back one's soul, it was necessary to earn regeneration crystals by doing good deeds. The key to survival, besides being courteous and kind to everything and everybody, was to stay in the brightly lighted parts of the kingdom, where unicorns roamed and butterflies floated over the ferns. Those who wished to indulge their darker fantasies could seek out like-minded adventurers in the Dionysian caves and crannies of Pan's forest.

When Tom approached their special spot, he immediately knew something was amiss. A steady rain was falling, and the flowers were drooping dejectedly. He couldn't be sure, but the drops streaming down Lucy's face looked like diamond tears. Tom raised his staff and scanned the area for troublemakers.

Lucy, what happened?

Nothing. I mean, there's nobody here but us.

So then why the bad weather?

I'm starting to get a little freaked out. I don't even know who you are.

I told you already that it's for our own safety.

Yours or mine?

Both.

Yeah, I know, you keep saying that, but somehow it doesn't make me feel any safer. If you really love me, then why don't you trust me?

Tom made a flower appear and held it out to her.

That won't work anymore.

The flower dissolved into a yellow puddle on the forest floor.

The make-believe dimension of their relationship had started out as a playful tease, a way to get to know each other with no strings or limbs attached. At first, the strangeness of dating a mysterious cyber legend in an artificial paradise had appealed to Lucy's imagination. They could talk about anything, do anything, be anything. They could fly over the hills or swim with weird fishes in the crystalline river. Once they had even made friends with a lute player and a unicorn and joined them for ersatz tea in a treehouse made of feathers on the shores of a purple lake. But Lucy's emotions were becoming stronger, and she was growing tired of the charade.

I thought we agreed that it's perfect like this. Why mess it up?

It's not perfect, Mr. Aws, or Swarm, or whoever the hell you actually are.

You promised …

I know, I'm not supposed to use that word. An enchanted chipmunk might overhear us and call the FBI. How do I know that's not bullshit too?

Lucy, please don't

Don't what? Type my actual feelings? Sometimes I think you just love me for my name. Not the real one, of course. I mean the fake one.

They had been virtually seeing each other for about a month when Tom asked what had led her to choose lucyinthesky as her online moniker. She told him the inspiration had come from an anthropology class where she learned about the paleoanthropologist Donald C. Johanson, who in 1974 discovered a 3.2 million-year-old fossil of a female skeleton in Ethiopia. The scientific name for the missing link was *Australopithecus afarensis*, but Johanson had decided to name her after the title character in the Beatles song "Lucy in the Sky with Diamonds."

Intrigued, Tom decided to do some online research on Johanson's Lucy. It turned out that a cassette recorder in the camp had been playing *Sgt. Pepper's Lonely Hearts Club Band* while they were celebrating their historic find. A woman Johanson was dating at the time had suggested that he call the fossil Lucy. Afterward, Johanson's students started asking him when they were going back to the Lucy site. Decades later, he told a reporter, "Initially I was opposed to giving her a cute little name, but that name stuck."

The Lucy discovery catapulted Johanson into one of the world's foremost paleoanthropologists, but that wasn't why Tom was thunderstruck by the scientist's story. The connection between Lucyinthesky of Austin, a ravishing soldier in the flash mob rebellion, and Lucy of Ethiopia, a female fossil that proved protohumans once walked the earth, was more than just an interesting tidbit of kismet in the history of their relationship. The alignment of collective action with an unexpected acceleration in the calendar of human evolution was too significant to be random or inconsequential. It touched directly on theories that Tom had been kicking around in relation to Swarm, a growing conviction that quantum social change was coming, that the species was about to take another leap, like when the first prehumans left the forest and set out together on the savannas, their enlarged brains conjoining through touch and sounds and a germinating recognition of shared destiny. Tom couldn't foresee the next level of human evolution, but he sensed that Lucy and Swarm were interlocking pieces of a bigger puzzle, two enigmas conjoined into the contours of an answer, like fragments of bone dug up in a dusty ravine suddenly fitting together.

I want to hear your voice. I want to see your body. Flesh and blood. I've got to know that you're not a creep or a bot, or some algorithm in a box running an auto-seduction program.

The rain stopped, replaced by a fine mist that made the atmosphere murky and drained the color from the plants. A veil fell between them, and Tom was suddenly worried that Lucy might disappear altogether.

Okay, we can Skype, but no faces.

The fog lifted, and the flowers regained their brilliance.

When?

Next week.

I don't suppose you're going to give me your Skype name.

I'll come to you Wednesday, 9 p.m.

How will I know it's you?

That's a silly question.

I'm worried.

I promise you it'll be different.

No, not about us.

Then what?

The animals have been acting even stranger than usual, and the witches in the netheregion are babbling about omens.

What sorts of omens?

They say a great darkness is coming, that all the flowers and trees will be pulled up from their roots. They say the Great Eraser will reclaim his domain and the dead will rise from their catacombs to suck out the souls of the living, and the alt-world as we know it will end.

Do you believe that?

Of course not, but it's still creepy. Everybody is on edge, and you don't hear as much laughter as you used to.

Nothing will happen as long as I'm here to protect you.

But what if you're not? Can I trust you?

There will be time for you and time for me.

Then prove it.

The wizard of Aws took Lucy's hand and kissed it. She moved closer, but before she could embrace the man of her dreams, he disappeared in a puff of blue smoke.

9

The house where Marty Fisk lived was located on a leafy suburban street in Millwood, just a short drive east of downtown Spokane. Duggan had rented a car and a room in a hotel with a gilded Wild West decor that evoked the town's nineteenth-century-roots as a hub for miners, loggers, and farmers. Perched on the eastern edge of Washington State, between the Pacific range and the stern expanse of the central plains, Spokane retained a scrappy outpost aura that even the shiny new malls and snazzified saloons on Main Street couldn't gentrify or tame. It was a good place for a man to hole up and hide.

Duggan walked up to the plain stucco facade and knocked on the door long enough to get the small dog inside barking. He waited a few seconds and knocked again. When there was still no response, he slid his card under the door. A moment later, a comely young woman warily opened the door and asked him what he wanted.

"Hi. I'm looking for Laura Fisk." The woman didn't respond. "My name is Jake Duggan, and I'm an agent with the Department of Homeland Security. I'm investigating an incident that your husband was involved in before he was discharged. I'd like to have a word with him."

The woman's tight smile hardened. "He isn't here."

"I see—then could you please tell me where I can find him?"

"See those mountains over there?" She tipped her head to the end of the street where the city succumbed to grassy green fields and, beyond that, a snow-streaked range of jagged peaks. "He goes fishing every other weekend. He always goes alone, just him and the trees and the fish. There are a thousand miles of river in those mountains. He probably stands a better chance of finding trout than you do of finding him. He's usually back in a week or two."

"I can't wait that long," Duggan said.

When she saw that he wasn't going to budge, Laura Fisk added, "Maybe you should talk to his shrink."

"His psychiatrist?"

Laura Fisk nodded. "Peter Palladino. His office is downtown on Sprague. You should have gone there first."

Palladino's assistant seemed annoyed that Duggan had shown up without an appointment, but when Duggan identified himself, she grudgingly ushered him into a reception area furnished with two Shaker-style armchairs and a large leather sofa. Duggan lowered himself into one of the chairs and regarded a framed reproduction of miners panning for gold in a mountain stream. Duggan felt himself being scrutinized by a trim, youngish man with piercing blue eyes and long dark hair tied back into a knotted stump.

"They didn't tell me that anyone from Homeland Security was coming," Palladino said. He held out his hand, and Duggan shook it.

"They?"

"The people at the Fairchild Air Force Base Hospital. Almost all my referrals come from there. But it's unusual to get a visit from Washington, even in a case like this."

"What kind of case would that be?"

"Would you mind," Palladino asked, "telling me why you're here?"

"I got your name from Martin Fisk's wife."

Palladino blinked. "You know Marty?"

"No," Duggan admitted. "But I'd like to ask him some questions about his drone pilot, Donald Westlake. I thought maybe you could give me some insight into their relationship."

Palladino's eyes flickered toward his receptionist. "Let's go into my office."

Duggan followed him into a small, spotless chamber decorated with framed awards from various psychiatric associations and a PhD certificate of philosophy from Gonzaga University. Palladino waved Duggan to a chair, and there was a prolonged silence as the young doctor studied his uninvited guest, his limpid eyes probing, evaluating.

Still standing, Palladino said, "I really don't mean to be rude or uncooperative, Agent Duggan, but there are certain privacy issues at stake, not to mention doctor-patient confidentiality. I mean, is this an official investigation?"

Duggan made a quick decision. There was only one way to get Fisk's psychiatrist to talk, and that was by telling him the truth. It was risky but unavoidable. As Duggan spoke, Palladino became visibly tense. Duggan had wagered correctly; the doctor was smart enough to know that he could never repeat what he had just heard without getting Fisk and himself into trouble.

Palladino sat down behind his desk and looked at Duggan. "You think the government is hiding something? Something about Marty?"

"I don't know—maybe. Not Marty, though. Westlake, his drone pilot. A few weeks ago, in Afghanistan, he—"

"Yes, I know. A psychotic episode ending in bloodshed, caused by battle fatigue. Plus the additional stress of being in the kill zone."

"How so?"

"Well, I'm sure you know most drone pilots almost never leave the United States. Marty and Donald were actually in Afghanistan, which is unusual." He looked at Duggan for confirmation.

"Go on, Doctor."

"Well, I treat a lot of F-16 fighter pilots. They look down on the drone operators."

"Why's that?"

"The main reason is that they're generally perceived as not being in any physical danger," Palladino explained. "The airmen who fly jets in battle zones think the drone pilots don't deserve their respect. They call them 'Nintendo fliers.'"

"But Fisk and Westlake were near the front lines in Afghanistan," Duggan observed, "so they were in harm's way."

"Yes, of course." Palladino was nodding. "That makes sense. It explains a lot."

"It explains what?"

"In my practice, the men I treat are all suffering from different degrees of PTSD. The symptoms include nightmares, depression, withdrawal, antisocial behavior, and, in the worst cases, self-destructive tendencies."

"Suicide?"

"Sometimes."

"Are you saying that Marty Fisk is a danger to himself?"

"No, no, I don't think so." Palladino crossed his arms. "The fact is that Marty is a very special case."

"How so?"

"You see, there are a number of treatments for PTSD. One is called CPT, for cognitive processing therapy. You take the patient through the story; you get him to talk about the event that caused the trauma in detail so it can be neutralized. You knew that Fisk was the one who shot Westlake, right?"

Duggan grimaced. "No, I didn't."

Palladino was on his feet again, pacing as he spoke. "The thing is, when I had him reenact that moment, which would have been highly emotional for anybody … I mean, imagine putting a bullet through your best friend's head. Anyway, his neural indicators barely moved. I thought it must be blockage, yet he had no trouble talking about it. And that's not all of it. Another type of treatment is EMDR, or eye movement desensitization and reprocessing. In this approach, the patient talks about the trauma while we expose him to visual and audio stimuli. The idea is to use flashing lights and sounds to jog or detach the trauma from the memory at the root of the problem. I thought maybe he was being haunted by the guilt of killing people by remote control—bad guys and good guys all look the same on a video monitor, right? We get a lot of this type of thing from drone operators, particularly the sensors, who pick out the targets. But that didn't seem to be the problem with Marty."

"So in Marty's case, you're saying none of the standard PTSD therapies worked."

"I've been giving him Prozosin, an alpha blocker, to stop the nightmares so he can sleep at night. That certainly helps. But here's the weird part: when we do the EMDR, like I told you, we use flashing colored lights and different sounds through headphones. The theory is that artificially inducing an emotionally aroused state uncouples the traumatic memory from the person's emotional response. Anyway, when we put the headphones on Marty and turned up the volume, he totally lost it. He had a very violent reaction ..."

"Wait," Duggan said, "did you say Fisk freaked out when you made him wear headphones?"

"Yes," Palladino said. "We had to discontinue the therapy."

"What kinds of sounds do you play when you do EMDR therapy?"

"We use all kinds of sounds—loud tones, raucous music."

"You treat patients by playing loud music," Duggan said, "through headphones."

"Sometimes. Yes."

"What about words?"

"No, that's not my technique. But maybe some other psychologists do that. You'd have to ask them."

"You said a drug is helping Marty Fisk."

"Prozosin."

"But Prozosin only treats the symptoms, just the nightmares, right?"

"As far as I can tell, it's been helping. There's a cabin in the woods where Marty goes to get away ..."

"To fish?"

"To hunt demons," Palladino corrected. "Look, considering what these soldiers go through, I'm surprised more of them don't crack.

Marty's a strong guy. I helped him get a job in the athletic department at Gonzaga. I'm pretty sure he's going to get through this."

"This cabin where Fisk goes—do you know where it is?"

Palladino shook his head. "Did you ask Laura?"

Duggan exhaled. "Maybe I should ask her again."

Palladino's gaze hardened. "Maybe you should leave Marty alone."

"I can't do that."

"Listen, Agent Duggan, veteran suicide is an epidemic—twenty vets kill themselves every single day. A few, like Westlake, become a danger to society. But the vast majority of these guys find a way back from the edge, and eventually they adjust. They can take care of their families, hold down jobs, and watch sports on Sunday afternoon. With proper therapy, most of these broken soldiers can be repaired. The thing is, one way or another, we just keep making more of them."

Tom looked at himself in the mirror and used his hands to push the wrinkles out of his favorite T-shirt, black with a single white lightning bolt on the front. Tonight was his Skype date with Lucy, and he wanted to look good, at least from the neck down. He had run the options in his head a hundred times, but showing his face to her was out of the question. Too dangerous for both of them.

Tom went back to his workstation and found an e-mail from toke:

meta militia wants to meet u. log on to 4chan/mm/. click on green hair, passwd: silky. 9 p.m.

The first thing that got Tom's attention was that he was being summoned to a meeting on a 4chan IRC channel for an unspecified reason, which was unusual. The second thing was that there was no /mm/ section at 4chan.org, at least not officially. He had browsed a few backdoor IRCs, but this was different: a password-protected channel created specifically for a private chat between Swarm and Meta Militia, whatever that was. As Tom expected,

4chan.org/mm/ led to a 404 File Not Found message decorated with an anime image of a girl with green hair. He clicked on the hair and entered the password. Two people were waiting to chat, toke and mm629.

toke: hi swarm thx for coming
swarm2020: no prob what's up
toke: my friend mm629 has a gift for you
swarm3711: really? what's that?

Tom's screen refreshed, and a new user name replaced toke's.

mm629: hi swarm. I'm a fan of yr stuff, and the boys
    on 4chan say you're ok. I have something very
    special, something that could be very powerful in
    the right hands … in yr hands
swarm2979: really?
mm629: it's potentially very dangerous, too dangerous
    to be kept secret. Do u understand?
Swarm9331: nope
mm629: just look at it. no strings. if you like what
    you see, we can talk more. If not you destroy
    it. Deal?
Swarm8206: i know you're not heat because toke is a
    pal. I'll look if you want but no promises
mm629: no promises, no strings. we'll send an onion
    encryption to your server. the file will only
    download once. then the channel will self-erase.
swarm5082: gotcha
mm629: i hope we'll be talking again soon, swarm
swarm4646: what's meta militia?
mm629: self-explanatory. i'll wait till you open
    zeph.r

Swarm0716: zeph.r?
mm629: yr wasting time …

Tom watched as zeph.r began to download. The progress bar inched across the screen counting megabytes: 300 … 400 … 500 … It stopped at 629.

From the instant he opened the file, Tom knew that this was no ordinary piece of code. He had expected a malware virus of some sort, but this was completely different. Besides instructions for various controls, there was a variable frequency generator and transducers for audio outputs. The bulk of the software was diagnostic, similar to an MRI brain scanner, except that it seemed to be connected to a transmitter of some kind. He was intrigued.

Tom saved the file to his hard drive and flipped back to the IRC chat.

Swarm6593: where did you get this?
mm629: ha. not yr problem
Swarm2356: it is now
mm629: DOD
swarm8144: really?
mm629: the one and only
swarm4778: jesus. why is it called zeph.r
mm629: u can call it whatever you want. it's yours now
swarm5348: what's the point of giving me something like this?
mm629: zeph.r increases the susceptibility of the human brain to visual and audio suggestion. it can be broadcast through airwaves or embedded in an app. you already rule the smart mob scene … imagine the possibilities …
Swarm2671: do you realize what you're suggesting?
mm629: fuck yeah

```
swarm8801: I need time to think
mm629: understood. just don't think too much or you
    might change your mind
mm629 has logged off
```

Tom checked the time and opened a specially encrypted version of Skype. He had considered using one of the various VR dating apps, but he ruled them out as too public, glitchy, and hackable, not to mention the mood-killing clumsiness of donning an ocular headset. Skype was simple, familiar, and relatively secure, and Tom knew several people in long-distance relationships who swore by it. Adding a live visual dimension to his trysts with Lucy was a big step, with plenty of potential to misfire. Maybe taking it slow on their first Skype date was the wisest option.

Tom clicked on the camera icon and watched as the screen filled with Lucy's creamy skin, full red lips, and flowing hair. But it was that smile, so knowing, playful, and warm, that dissolved his resolve to keep a PG rating.

"Hi, stranger," Lucy said. She giggled. It was a friendly, inviting sound.

Tom raised his hand and waved. "Hi."

"Oh, thank you," Lucy said, clasping her hands in pretend prayer. "Thank you, dear God!"

"What?"

"At least now I know you're not some fat hairy stalker. Not to be so judgmental, but you have no idea how worried I was."

"Yeah, it was a possibility, I guess."

"More like a *probability.*"

"Well, thanks!"

"You're welcome. And even though it's a little fucked up that you still won't show me your face, I can see already, just from your arms and body, that you're, hmm, late twenties or early thirties and nice looking."

"Really? You can tell?"

"For real. And your voice … It's just how I hoped you'd sound—masculine yet sensitive."

"Are those mutually exclusive?"

"Too often," Lucy said. "How about me? Do I sound the way you expected?"

"Yeah, actually." Tom added, "I already knew what you looked like, remember? From the Fourth of July flash mob." He decided it was best to leave out the part about hacking into her laptop and eavesdropping on her phone conversations.

"Right, I remember." Lucy ran her hands over her breasts and hips. "So you've seen me naked already. And you're looking at my face. And what do I get? A torso shot from a men's T-shirt catalog. Does that sound fair to you?"

Tom swallowed.

"Wait," Lucy said. "I'll make it easier for you." She lifted her top and leaned into the camera lens. Her presence filled the high-def screen, almost to the point where he could smell her.

"Jesus," Tom said.

"You like what you see?"

"Sure, I mean, it's just that the way you looked at me right now … It was like that first time on the Fourth of July."

"So then let's have some fireworks. Your turn to lose the shirt, Mr. Don't-Worry-I-Won't-Say-It."

This was exactly what he had hoped for and exactly what he had feared. Tom peeled off his shirt. He knew that their Skype tease was a degrading sideshow, a compromise that was equal parts sacred consummation and college dorm cyber porn. He had gone along with it anyway, against his better judgment, yet there was no denying the insistent throb in his pants.

"Get closer," Lucy commanded. She stood up, and he watched as her hand slid down into her underwear. "Now you."

Tom unbuckled his belt and pulled down the zipper.

"Nice Calvins," Lucy said. "Keep going. Don't be shy. Show me what you've got."

Tom did.

"Well, well, " Lucy said. "I see someone was ready to come out and play!"

Luminescence, for all its limitations, had been their iridescent Garden of Eden, a protected oasis of pre-carnal innocence. Now they'd graduated to the realm of visual contact, sexual lubrication, and self-conscious shame. He could feel the pastel flowers fading and the iron gate clanging behind them; no more carefree idylls in softly glowing pastures, no more delusions of a normal life, whatever that was. Could that cold exile be the forbidden knowledge denied by God to mortals, the knowing that some lives were meant to be lived on their own terms, that sometimes normal wasn't good enough, that there was something sublime out there beyond the fringe of the pedestrian comforts his mother so ardently wished for him. And anyway, wasn't this blessed body delirium normal too? It was easy to imagine it was Lucy's hand on him, tugging him farther into the mossy meadows of Pan's forest, gripped by an elemental force dating back to the first time homo erectus took hold of his own erection while staring intently at the original Lucy lounging insouciantly on a branch in the next tree. She was saying something, but it was hard for Tom to hear over the huffing bio-hydraulics, no longer caring what this might cost him, the last vestiges of prudence and restraint swamped by roiling spasms of original sin, just as he had dreaded and rehearsed it in the mirror so many times. He always knew that once they crossed the line, there would be no turning back, no redemption or forgetting the tart tang of apple, the silky slither of serpent, the vertiginous, delicious fall from grace.

10

Laura Fisk took a lot longer to answer the door the second time. Even then, she left the safety chain on and shouted at him from inside. "I already told you—he's in the mountains fishing!"

"I know about the cabin," Duggan shouted back. "It's important that I find him. I have information about Donald Westlake, but I have to tell Marty myself."

An elderly woman tending her garden across the street lifted her head and regarded him like a deer calculating whether to freeze or bolt. Duggan heard the scrape of the chain and the door opened, this time wide enough for him to step inside. There were children's toys strewn on the living room floor and dishes piled in the sink but no sign of actual kids. Duggan ignored the mess as he took a seat on the sofa. She was beautiful in a disheveled, unkempt way. He could tell from the way she glared at him that she was in no mood for friendly chitchat.

"I really don't mean to bother you, Mrs. Fisk," Duggan said. "Just tell me how to find him. It could be a matter of national security."

"Hasn't Marty already done enough for this country," she said. It wasn't a question. "He's trying like hell to get his life back, but you people won't let him."

For the first time, Duggan detected a slight Western drawl.

"What people? Did someone else come to talk to him?"

Laura Fisk seemed perplexed. "I thought you said you were with the government."

"I am," Duggan said. "The Department of Homeland Security. My job is to make sure that what happened to Donald Westlake was an accident."

"And why should I help you do that?"

"Because I'm starting to feel pretty sure that it wasn't."

Laura Fisk pursed her lips and reached for the purse beside her chair. "Mind if I smoke?"

"It's your house."

She acknowledged his comment with a shrug. He watched her pull out a Marlboro 100 and light it. "Is Marty a suspect?"

"I think Marty tried to save his friend."

She took a long pull from the cigarette before speaking. "And who's gonna save Marty?"

"All I can tell you is that I'm the only person who's trying to find out who's responsible. I don't know who's behind it or what side they're on or where they're hiding, but I'm running out of leads. My boss doesn't even know I'm here. You and Marty are my last chance to find out what really happened in Afghanistan."

Laura Fisk closed her eyes and took another drag from the cigarette. When she exhaled, the smoke made intersecting whorls in the air between them.

"He's at Priest Lake, across the state line in Idaho. A friend of his has a cabin there. Take US 2 north for about two hours to Fifty-Seven, then follow East Lake Shore for about eight miles. You'll see a wooden sign for Breuer on a dirt road. Take it to the trailhead. You'll have to go on foot after that. It's about a fifteen-minute walk to the cabin."

She nodded to the door and turned away from him in the same motion.

"Thanks, Mrs. Fisk."

"Anytime."

She didn't get up to let him out.

The road to Priest Lake took Duggan deep into a postcard flashback of the Idaho lake region, past dockside cocktail dives with neon martini glasses and stucco-sided motels shaped like cigarette cartons. At one point, a speedboat full of laughing teenagers tried to race him along a roadside river. A girl in a yellow bikini waved as the bow sliced into the turn and pulled her away, leaving a scar of white foam on the cobalt surface. Eventually, the Jet Skis and resorts thinned out to an occasional fishing skiff or wind-boarder, then the road lifted from the beach into a thicket of hemlock and cedar and he was there. Duggan parked next to a wooden sign that read "Breuer's" and hiked up the slope, past patches of ferns and mushroom-studded stumps, across a trickling creek to a cliff-edged glen. The cabin faced a grove of ivory-barked aspens, but the deck out back had a sumptuous view of Priest Lake. He could understand why a man might come here alone to watch the water turn violet at sunset, the trees and solitude muffling the city racket and the silent screams of moving shadows on a remote-controlled camera feed.

"Can I help you?"

Duggan turned to the voice, which belonged to a muscular young man with cropped hair and a rash of blondish stubble on his jaw. It was easy to picture him kicking a soccer ball with Westlake and Wasson and the boys on the base. Fisk was half hidden by some bushes about ten yards back on the trail, meaning that he had watched Duggan for a while before deciding to reveal his perch. From the lowered tilt of his right hip and the way his hand hovered out of sight, Duggan guessed that his inquisitor was armed.

"Are you Martin Fisk?"

"Maybe."

"Peter Palladino told me you had a cabin out here. Your wife told me where it was."

"Is that a fact?"

"I need to talk to you about Donald Westlake."

"I had a feeling you weren't here to catch bass," Fisk said. "Besides, there's nothing you can tell me about Donny that I don't already know, Mr. ..."

"Jake Duggan, cyber-ops division of Homeland Security. Do you know who was sending those signals to Donald through his computer?"

Fisk's posture shifted to the other foot. "Agent Duggan, would you do me a favor and turn around, take out your ID, and hold your hands up where I can see them?" Duggan did, and a few seconds later, he felt himself being patted down. Fisk returned Duggan's credentials, holstered the gun in his jeans, and strode toward the cabin. "C'mon inside," Fisk said, motioning to his guest to follow. "I just made some coffee."

The cabin was obviously owned by a man of means—tastefully functional furniture in dark tones, a stuffed elk head, Bose stereo, the odor of burnt wood wafting from the wide granite fireplace, a stack of *Esquire* magazines on the floor, and a half-read copy of *Drunk Tank Pink* on the mantle. The book's subtitle was *And Other Unexpected Forces That Shape How We Think, Feel, and Behave.* Duggan took a seat on the Holstein cowhide sofa and waited for Fisk to fix their coffee.

"A pal of mine from college is doing pretty well on Wall Street," Fisk said as he poured. "He got this place to remind himself where he came from. Unfortunately, he's too busy making money to enjoy it. Kinda ironic, don't you think?"

Duggan gestured to the book on the mantle. "Do you believe people can be influenced without their being aware of it?"

Fisk followed Duggan's gaze to the mantle. "Hard to say. Is that what Palladino told you?"

"He told me that you came back from Afghanistan with nightmares and an aversion to loud music. He told me that you had to take down your own best friend."

Fisk swiveled back to face Duggan. He was smiling, but the tendons on his neck were rigid. "Palladino's a good man, but he's a bit of a head case."

"Is that supposed to be funny?"

"Yes."

Fisk raised a bottle of whiskey over the coffee cups. "Black is fine," Duggan told him.

"More for me," Fisk said. He poured a couple shots worth into his cup and brought the bottle with him. Fisk sat and kept his eyes on Duggan as he drank. "You know, I come here to get away from people like you."

"If it's any consolation, I didn't drive all the way out here to enjoy the view."

"So why did you?"

"I was sent to your base at Kandahar to make sure that there was no terrorist involvement in the events leading to Donald Westlake's death, particularly to certify that there was no evidence of a cyber breach by unauthorized individuals or foreign agents. I met the master sergeant, Quinn Davis, and talked to some of the guys in your unit. I did a diagnostic on Westlake's laptop, but it was already wiped. Davis told me you were honorably discharged, voluntarily."

Fisk's gaze narrowed, but he kept his composure. "Did they tell you what Donny and I were doing on the base?"

"You were training the Afghans to fly their own drones. The air force couldn't count on bringing Muslims to Nevada without attracting attention. So they flew you guys to Kandahar instead."

"Correct." Fisk took another gulp from his cup and topped it off again with whiskey. "But you didn't come here to talk about drones, did you?"

"If you ever repeat what I'm about to tell you, I'll deny it," Duggan said.

Fisk shrugged. "I have a pretty lousy memory these days."

"The Department of Defense wants me to certify that there's been no cyber intrusion from outside, which is probably the case," Duggan said. "I do think there was a breach, but it came from the inside. I think Donald Westlake was the victim of some kind of test, some kind of experimental research by the DOD. I think the military is responsible for what happened to your friend, but they're trying to deny their involvement and bury the facts. I think that's why you were discharged. I think that's why you're hiding out in the woods, waiting for someone to come along and try to shut you up."

It was only when Fisk exhaled that Duggan realized he'd been holding his breath. "I'm really glad I didn't shoot you," Fisk said.

"Me too."

Fisk's upper lip twitched as he drained his cup. "You know I gave back my medal."

"I heard about that."

"Donny was a good man. He deserved better."

"So do you. Palladino said you had an adverse reaction to the therapy that involved listening to loud sounds through headphones. The air force report said that Westlake was wearing headphones when the shooting took place."

"It was that fucking music," Fisk blurted. "That heavy metal shit. That's when it all started."

Duggan drank some coffee. "All what started?"

"He joined a group. They met on the base two or three times a week. He didn't talk about it, and I knew better than to ask. Then I noticed the change."

Duggan held his tongue as Fisk reached for the bottle again.

"His flying got a lot better at first. It was weird how almost overnight he was so much quicker and smoother on the controls. Lots of pilots take Adderall and other stuff, but this was different, a total game change. He was like a machine. He was so much better than me that I started to feel inadequate."

"Did you talk to him about it?"

"He wouldn't talk to me or anybody. All he wanted to do was fly drones and listen to that goddamned skinhead garbage. I mean, he even shaved his head to look like one. I followed him one night to a building on the far side of the base. No windows. Two guards posted outside the door. It creeped me out. Then ..."

"Then what?"

"The bad stuff started. The headaches, the nightmares. He started messing up on the job, overshooting targets. He said he wasn't getting enough sleep, but I knew that wasn't the problem. I warned him, goddamn it. I told him not to do it."

"Not to do what?"

Fisk was slumped down in his chair hugging himself, a crumpled, diminished version of the strapping, confident fellow Duggan had encountered in the woods.

"Like I said, he wouldn't tell me. All he said was that he got an offer to join a special program, something that would earn him time off his tour, but he couldn't talk about it. Not even to me."

"And during this time, when things got worse, he was still listening to heavy metal."

"All the fucking time." Fisk sat upright, but his arms were still wrapped around his torso. "It didn't make any sense. He was obsessed with it—hard-core head-banger crap. I mean, we're talking about a guy who's favorite band was *Dave Matthews*, for Christ's sake. We all teased the shit out of him, but it freaked us out."

"You and Wasson and the rest of the soccer crew?"

Fisk nodded. Then, more to himself than to Duggan, he said, "I knew it! I knew it! I knew it! Those lying motherfuckers! They made Donny their bitch, and then, when the shit hit the fan, I was the one who had to clean up their mess." Fisk was holding his head in his hands and breathing hard, and Duggan started wondering if his questions and the whiskey had nudged him too far.

Fisk looked up at Duggan. "Do you know what it feels like to shoot your best friend in the head?"

113

"No," Duggan said. "I don't."

"Well, Agent Duggan, let me tell you something. I don't know either."

Fisk saw Duggan's confusion and let it stew a few seconds before adding, "I pulled the trigger and splattered the shooter's brains halfway across the base, but that wasn't my best friend. Do you follow me, Mr. Cyber Cop?"

"Sorry, I don't."

"The man I killed wasn't him—*it wasn't Donny*. I saw his eyes when he left the barracks. And after he went ballistic, when I got close, I could hear that fucking metal music drilling through his brain. He knew I was standing behind him. I knew he could hear me yelling. I put the barrel of my gun against the back of his head, and he still wouldn't stop. So my conscience is clean. If anything, I was doing him a favor."

"How's that?"

Fisk's eyes were red but his gaze was defiant. "I'm saying that what I did wasn't murder."

"Why not?"

"Because the guy I loved like a brother was long gone. The Donny I knew was already dead."

The bees buzzed furiously, fanning out from the hive, circling and attacking the intruder. It was impressive how quickly the insects had mobilized to repel the threat, each individual instinctively assuming its role in the frantically humming organism. Cara knew that even as the warriors pelted her bee suit in protest, a battalion of soldiers was heading deep into the hive, some to secure the precious stores of honey, others creating a last-ditch line of defense for their queen. The fact that this particular bee colony was situated on the roof of the Fairmont Hotel in San Francisco didn't faze Cara or the bees.

"Shhhh," Cara hushed soothingly. "I'm not here to hurt you. I brought you here, remember?"

The hotel's managers had approached her years ago to advise them on a project to cultivate bees on the roof, partly to make sure that its elevated micro farm of herbs and vegetables would get properly pollinated and partly to help reverse the colony collapse disorder in the global bee population, which had plunged more than 90 percent since the 1980s. The hotel's beehive colony, up to two hundred thousand bees that produced eight hundred pounds of honey annually, had since been successfully replicated at hotels in other parts of California, Washington D.C., Toronto, and even China. Tending to the bee colony always lifted Cara's spirits, and for a few moments, she forgot all about the evolutionary biologists conference going on in the ballroom downstairs. She lifted out a honeycomb with gloved fingers, inspecting the concentrated nectar for color and viscosity.

"Dr. Park?" Eric, who had joined her on the roof, was standing back at a safe distance. "Sorry to interrupt, but you've got to get ready for the awards ceremony."

Cara looked at her watch. "Oh, damn. Thanks, Eric."

She followed him to the elevators and went to her room to change. A few minutes later, she was sitting with Eric and several hundred colleagues, all of them happily picking at goat cheese and arugula salad and sipping Napa wines. After some introductory comments, Cara's name was called and she obligingly rose to accept her Beagle citation for innovative research. As Eric had predicted, the PHAROH experiment in Africa yielded data that advanced the understanding of hive-mind intelligence and stirred wide interest in the global community of evolutionary biologists. The applause reached her ears, but she took no pleasure in the acclaim and kept her remarks to a more or less perfunctory thank you.

What her applauding colleagues didn't know, and never would, was that what she encountered in the Serengeti the morning after the PHAROH test had left her horrified and disgusted. The unspeakable trauma of what she saw that day in Africa followed her back to the US, where she spent weeks in a demoralized funk. Cara had initially resisted Eric's entreaties to write a paper about PHAROH and their field experiment in Tanzania. Eventually, though, Eric convinced her that it was unscientific to dismiss an entire area of inquiry over a single inconclusive experiment. Plus, the United Nations was expecting something for its money, even if the result of their research would probably never bear humanitarian fruit. Cara had rushed to make the deadline for the conference, the theme of which happened to be emergent patterns in biological organisms. If a locust swarm could learn to defend itself even in midair, Cara posited in her paper, then maybe it could also be trained to do things other than ravage crops and grasslands. If the biochemical and environmental triggers that caused emergent behavior in locusts, bees, termites, and other animals could be harnessed and channeled, Cara concluded, then why couldn't swarms be domesticated and trained like any other animal to deliver medicines or do other jobs that required large groups of small highly mobile messengers?

Writing the paper, along with doubling down on yoga on the weekends, fended off her nagging sense of failure, at least until she received a call from a man who identified himself as Barry Rodman at DARPA. He told Cara that he was a big fan of her work and that it was an honor just to be speaking to a scientist of her caliber. Then he asked if she would be interested in a grant to explore how bees and other swarming animals could be used to deliver lethal viruses, biological weapons, and even miniature explosives to enemy targets. She listened in disbelief to Rodman's pitch before clearing her throat to interrupt him. How, Cara wanted to know, did the military know about the contents of a scientific paper that hadn't even been published yet? Rodman declined to say, but he made it clear that a contract of this kind would be lucrative and generously funded. In fact, Cara was aware that bees and stinging insects had a history of being employed as weapons of war going back to the

Romans, who had catapulted beehives directly into the ranks of advancing enemy troops. But what the military's messenger was proposing was unlike any bio-weapon that had ever existed before. Rodman hinted that DARPA scientists were close to perfecting a way to train insects to follow instructions by interfering with their natural navigation systems. He added that PHAROH showed some very promising applications along the same lines. "What you're doing and what we're doing look like a natural fit," Rodman excitedly told her. "We think the combination could double the speed of development and deployment. We already have a small testing facility in the Bay Area, so there'd be no need for you to travel."

For Cara, the mere possibility that her research could be used to kill people instead of help them was so distressing that she had to force herself not to hang up. Instead, she apologetically explained that her teaching schedule and research workload had forced her to put PHAROH on indefinite hold. Besides, she added sincerely, "The damn thing doesn't even work."

"Before you say no," Rodman persisted, "think of all the things you could do with a budget and a lab twice as big as the one you have now." Cara politely but firmly told him she wasn't interested, well aware that her negative response would probably have a deleterious effect on her career in ways that she would never discover. As disturbing as the whole episode had been, it was something else that was bothering her, something she feared might somehow be related to the DARPA offer she had rejected.

When she got back to her table, Eric, who had already imbibed more than his fair share of small-batch organic brews, was waiting with a fastidiously dressed woman who looked familiar. "There she is!" Eric announced, holding out a chair for Cara. "This is Rosalyn Cooper from the CDC. Ms. Cooper wants to talk to us about a possible collaboration."

Cara shook the woman's hand. "Nice to meet you. I recognize you from the beehive tour I gave earlier today, before the luncheon."

"Yes," Cooper confirmed. "That was lovely and very interesting. I think it's wonderful that they serve the honey to the guests in the hotel."

Eric held up the bottle in his hand. "Case in point: Honey Saison Beer, brewed with sweetness from Fairmont's own rooftop buzzers!"

Cooper smiled at Eric. "Yes, dear, but that's not what I want to talk to you about." She turned her attention back to Cara. "I was fascinated by your suggestion that insect swarms could be cultivated and taught to perform specific tasks. As I'm sure you know, the bee population is suffering from a viral infection, one that moves very quickly from one infected hive to another. Well, I was thinking that what if the bees' ability to transfer viruses was adapted for something good? I mean, could bees be used to inoculate vulnerable populations in remote areas where it's physically or economically difficult to reach the target population?"

"Are you talking about training bees to use their stingers to inoculate humans?" Cara asked.

"No, of course not—I mean, eventually perhaps," Cooper answered. "But initially at least, the bee-delivered vaccines would be introduced to crops that they fertilize and maybe even injected by their stingers into livestock, which also become food for people. There are some tests going on in Africa using specially treated mosquitoes to inoculate people against malaria, for example. But mosquitoes don't swarm intelligently, and they certainly can't be trained to zero in on a specific population or geographical area."

"But maybe bees can!" Eric interjected. "And who knows, with any luck maybe we can pay back the little buzzers by curing the bee virus while we're at it."

"I have a budget for research along these lines," Cooper continued, "and I can't think of anybody who is doing more exciting work in this area than the two of you. Would you consider such a project with the CDC?"

Eric was already beaming. *Maybe this is how it starts,* Cara thought, *meeting the right person at the right time with money to push the envelope, willing to try something daring and new, something that might actually move the needle.* Maybe the science behind PHAROH could redeem itself by paving the way for bees to help people avoid diseases. Maybe the bees had brought her good luck; maybe this was karma payback for giving them a safe haven on the roof of one of San Francisco's most luxurious hotels.

"We are very interested, Ms. Cooper," Cara said. "I've also been thinking about what you said about bees transmitting viruses. Eric and I have been talking about developing a computer model that uses beehive migration patterns to make a predictive map of pathogenic viruses."

"What if viruses are also following emergent models?" Eric exclaimed. "What if they have a form of collective intelligence that hasn't even been identified yet?"

Cooper's eyes were twinkling with enthusiasm. "I can give you access to our virus-tracking databases, assuming you decide to work with us."

"Consider it done," Cara said. "Eric will set up a conference call to discuss details and next steps." The women shook hands again.

"A toast," Eric intoned, hoisting his beer. "To the future of viral medicine, and God bless our winged friends on the roof. May they flirt with flowers forever!"

Cara felt a surge of gratitude for her young assistant's dogged optimism. It was Eric's refusal to abandon PHAROH and his persistence in getting her to write the paper, which, after a dark detour with the DOD, turned out to be the doorway to what she was seeking: an unexpected and much-needed chance to redeem herself with positive, purposeful work.

"Yes, long live the bees!" Cara chimed in as she tipped her glass. But there was a tinge of sadness in her voice because, based on her inspection, she knew the Fairmont's hive colony was already dying.

11

In all his countless hours of stringing ones and zeros together, of weaving batches of electrical impulses into actionable commands, Tom had never encountered anything like zeph.r. The person or persons he met in the secret 4chan chat room might or might not actually exist, but the code itself was indisputably real. Mm629 said Tom would know what to do with zeph.r, but he wasn't even sure how it worked, let alone what it was supposed to do. Zeph.r wasn't just a piece of software; it was a whole suite of different algorithms bundled together and delivered into his hands.

Mm629 had implied that zeph.r could be fused into a multimedia signal, but for what purpose? In some ways it looked like a diagnostic tool from a medical lab, yet it was also designed to deliver an audio output. What did the acoustic manifestation of an electromagnetic wave generator sound like? Tom sat in his chair and bounced a rubber handball against the ceiling as he deliberated the pros and cons of finding out, but he had already made up his mind. It didn't take him long to transfer part of the code into an audio equalizer he was developing for Xander's upcoming gig in Vegas. Tom put on his headphones and looked at the clock: 3:04 p.m. He clicked PLAY and raised the input until he detected a faint hiss of static. Gradually, gingerly, he increased the volume. What at first seemed to be white noise, he realized, was actually a dense cluster of different sounds, like instruments in an orchestra tuning up. Then the sonic curtain pulled back to reveal the main event, two strands of oscillations moving in tandem. As they wobbled and throbbed,

Tom felt their binaural vibrations penetrating his entire body, two frequencies creating a third entity. There was a rising, writhing tower of tessellating textures, each one separate yet fused to the others and seething, like a flame igniting, and above it, behind it and around it, a bigger wave cresting into a sound that he had never heard before.

Tom opened his eyes and saw his mother's tear-streaked face staring down at him.

"Oh my God, Tom," Sonia said. "You scared me so much."

Tom sat up and looked around. The room was in a shambles, his collection of books, DVDs, and games strewn across the floor, framed posters and pictures tilted or off their hooks, chairs pushed over. There were scratches on his arms, and his T-shirt was ripped halfway down his chest.

"What happened?"

"I heard noises," Sonia told him. "I didn't want to bother you. I thought somebody was with you, and then I started to worry because I heard you talking, but it wasn't English. When I came in, you were like this. I thought you had an attack. I'm taking you to the doctor."

"No, I'm fine," Tom said, getting to his feet.

"*Mira* me," Sonia commanded. "Are you doing drugs?"

"No," Tom told her. Normally he would have laughed, but he was still getting his bearings. "Mom, really, don't worry. I'm okay."

Sonia peered at her son skeptically. "Just promise me you'll be careful, M'ijo."

"I promise, Mom," Tom said. "Just leave me alone and close the door."

As he was cleaning up the mess, he noticed a sticky dampness in his crotch. He put his hand down his pants and was horrified to feel a slick residue of semen.

"Jesus," Tom muttered. "What the fuck?"

After he showered and changed, Tom checked out his workstation. The headphones had been yanked out of the plug, but otherwise everything seemed fine. Tom righted his chair and sat down, trying to piece together what had just happened. The timer on his audio player had stopped at 3:13:52. The episode had lasted nearly ten minutes, but most of Tom's memory of it was a vague jumble of images and sensations. He remembered listening to the zeph.r signal and being drawn in by its fractal effect—the closer he listened, the more he heard. It was almost as if his own consciousness was being drawn into the signal, becoming part of it. He didn't recall removing the headphones, but at a certain point, he no longer needed them because zeph.r's augmented presence had spread to everything around him. Every object in the room had become incredibly visceral, as if the molecules in his metal desk, the plastic mouse in his hand, even the air he was breathing had suddenly taken on more heft—each material, texture, and shape contributing its own song to a magnificent chorus that he had joined just by hearing it.

Eventually, the sensations that had filled Tom's head and body evaporated, dissipating back into the program like a genie returning to its lamp. But he had seen something that was still seared in his memory. He took out a sheet of white paper and started to draw. Tom made six circles that represented a sequence of overlapping images. In the center of the first circle, he drew a cluster of dots, like a distant galaxy hundreds of light years away. In the second circle, the dots were larger, taking on spherical shapes. In the third circle, the dots had grown even larger, with the dots now appearing in their own cores, almost filling the first circle. By the fifth circle, the largest dot had nearly eclipsed the original, and the dots inside it were spawning the next generation of advancing spheres. When the diameters of the fifth and sixth circles aligned, a green aurora signaled their fusion and the beginning of the repetition of the cycle.

Tom put aside the drawings and reopened the zeph.r program folder, scouring the files for clues to what had just transpired. Working backward, he could almost trace the line of reasoning, several styles of programming converging in a core microwave frequency generator surrounded by audio and visual tools and controls and, in some cases, slightly modified versions of the same program.

Then it hit him. So obvious, it had been right under his nose all along: the format of the file was part of its instruction manual. It was a test, and he knew the Meta Militia was waiting to give him his score.

Tom opened the 4chan/mm/ channel and initiated the request for a chat with mm629. The response came almost instantly.

mm629: hi swarm—did u enjoy the ride?
Swarm1209: wtf is zeph.r? where did it come from? who are you?
mm629: lol. You took a little trip into the wormhole
Swarm672: I guess you could say that
mm629: then you already know who we are. the medium, in more ways than one, is the message
Swarm2636: zeph.r is unfinished, isn't it?
mm629: please explain.
Swarm3007: that's why you gave it to me. u want me to finish the code. u want me to help u make it fully operational
mm629: did you hear that?
swarm8729: hear what?
mm629: applause and champagne corks popping ;) our faith in your cognitive acumen was not misplaced
swarm7877: tell me who you are. i dont care what yr name is. how did you get this? are you the architect?
mm629: i didn't do it alone. i was one of many
swarm7511: was?
mm629: i'm with Meta now. we don't answer to anybody

swarm4018: if you trust me with the zeph.r software,
then the least you can do is tell me what it's for

For almost a minute, there was no response. Then mm629 resumed the thread.

mm629: we think the less u know, the better for
everybody
swarm6199: I deserve the truth

There was pause, shorter this time.

mm629: the people responsible for the initial
development of zeph.r were motivated by fear,
and fear begets death, and death must have
consequences
swarm8908: that's not an answer
mm629: all that matters is what u do next, swarm.
that's why we chose u to take zeph.r to the people.
use zeph.r to open their eyes, make them see
swarm7355: what makes you so sure i will?
mm629: because now you know zeph.r is too potent
for any single entity to own or control, because
you feel the change coming, because you are the
change coming, because there's no turning back,
not 4 u, not 4 anybody
swarm4835: u make it sound like a war
mm629: listen harder
mm629 has logged off

Tom was still staring at the screen when a familiar gait drew his attention to the window. Xander's vault over the sill was even jauntier than usual. He opened his hand to reveal a thumb drive.

"What's this for?"

"It's a copy of "Stardust," Xander explained. "It's the new single I want to break in Las Vegas. I want you to design the video graphics and the app. There's also a program in there for live visual effects that's pretty cool."

Tom started to plug the thumb drive into his computer.

"Do that later," Xander said, grabbing Tom's hoodie and tossing it on his lap. "We've got things to do."

"Where?"

"You'll see. Our carbon frame steeds await."

Xander looked at the drawing of Tom's zeph.r vision on the desk. "That's cool," he said. "Can you make an animation of that for 'Stardust'?"

"Yeah, sure."

"Awesome. It's perfect for the track. I'm using an Omnisphere."

"An Omni what?"

"It's a program that let's you play an instrument with the harmonic characteristics of any other. So you can play a guitar that sounds like a piano and drums that sound like a sax. It can inject voice effects too."

"That sounds sick, Xan."

"It is. But right now, brother, we gotta get moving."

It was a clear, breezy evening, perfect weather for an impromptu outing. The bikes were waiting for them outside, and Xander watched approvingly as Tom gaped at his and ran his hand over the high-tech frame.

"Holy shit, Zan."

"Pretty sweet, no? They're Nashbar Carbon 105s. More than a grand each, but who's counting. Are you ready to roll?"

"Hell yeah."

Xander steered them in the direction of downtown, a trajectory that usually led them to a new bar or band. The interlocking sizzle-click of their gears, with Xander thrumming a counter-tempo on the handlebars, was a reassuring soundtrack. Tom discarded his initial annoyance at being hustled away from zeph.r. Getting outside his head and into the fresh air on a bike that he'd only seen in magazines was exactly what he needed. Xander produced a flask of rye whiskey, which the pals passed back and forth as they rode. Xander slowed and pointed to a billboard across the street. "Look at that. What do you see?"

"An ad for bacon cheeseburgers?"

"Look closer—at the shine on that juicy tomato, the glistening slab of meat wedged between two perfect brown buns. What do you see now?"

"Fast food porno?"

"Exactly!" Xander effused like a professor praising a clever student. "Just think about it—a photo that stimulates physical lust for something with no substance or redeeming social value. That's the very definition of pornography. Yet it's perfectly legal—even for children! My God, have they no shame!" This was one of Xander's favorite personas: sardonic sociologist.

"That's pretty deep, Xan," Tom said. "I can't wait to hear your Freudian analysis of KFC."

"Oh, you just wait …" Xander's coyote howl echoed off the stucco buildings as he zoomed ahead. Catching up, Tom asked, "So are you going to tell me where we're going?"

"Sure, but first eat this." Xander gave Tom a hand-wrapped energy bar and took one for himself. Tom bit and chewed warily. The granola and chocolate were real enough but there was also a gritty, earthy ingredient that Tom didn't recognize.

"What's this?"

"Some food for thought," Xander answered. "Breakfast of champions."

They rode and chewed without talking for a while. "I miss this," Xander said. "We used to do it all the time, remember? Carefree compadres, going nowhere, everywhere."

"That was before you got famous and the bikes got expensive."

"And before you got a girlfriend. By the way, how is the eternally elusive Lucy in the Sky? Still hooking up for safe sex at the cyber Yotel?" Xander chuckled at his own joke. "Dude, I mean seriously, how can you even be sure that Lucy isn't a guy, not that I personally give a shit."

"How does she know I'm not a girl?"

"Ha—so true. What do you know about Critical Mass?"

"The bicycle flash mobs? Not much," Tom lied. "I think it started in San Francisco. Green cyclists, anti-car activists who use their bikes to create giant traffic jams."

"Not traffic jams," Xander corrected. *Collective social engagements.* They've got affiliates in hundreds of cities around the world."

"Cyclo-guerrillas international," Tom translated.

"*Exactamente.* The goal is to raise awareness for alternative energy sources and, of course, to have some fun along the way."

"Like Swarm?"

"Not exactly. Have you ever been to a mutant vehicles rally?"

"No," Tom said truthfully.

"Well, that, bro-migo, is about to change."

They had arrived at the plaza bordering the east side of the Texas State Capitol Building. Already hundreds of bikers were milling around the visitor's center and overflowing onto the sidewalks and parking lot. While bicycles dominated, there were also unicyclists, two-man go-karts covered in yellow fur, shopping carts rigged with blinking Christmas lights, almost anything and everything with wheels. Several people with portable boom boxes blasting various strains of EDM and a contingent of riders in nineteenth-century sporting attire added to the madcap atmosphere. Whenever a car tried to squeeze through the hubbub, a trio of stunt riders would rear up and twirl on their back tires to stop it, raising a chorus of whoops and cheers.

Xander surveyed the scene with impatience. "If we don't mobilize," he observed, "this thing will get busted before it even starts." He produced an air horn from his backpack and let out a couple of authoritative honks. "Yee-haw!" Xander shouted. "Let's ride, people!" Several bikes on the edge of the crowd sprang into motion, and the rest began to follow, a careening cavalcade spilling onto Congress Avenue and stopping traffic. The herd turned right, presumably with the goal of looping around Lavaca before charging into the tourist zone from the west.

"Shouldn't we turn left?" Tom asked. "Aren't you one of the leaders of this thing?"

Xander chuckled at the thought. "No, man," he said. "You can't publish a route map, because then the cops will know where to put the roadblocks. There's a general idea, which is to get to Sixth Street, but the exact path is decided by whoever's in front at any given time."

"So the people in front are in charge?"

"Nobody's in charge; everybody's in charge."

Tom found Xander's comment incredibly, inexplicably hilarious. As he laughed too long and too hard, he felt a sudden weight of atmospheric pressure on his skin and a rolling wave of nausea emanating from his core. He noted that the leaves in the trees were completely translucent and everything around them, even the air, seemed tactile and sentient. Of course: the magic energy bar.

"Oh boy," Tom said, leaning forward on his handlebars as the pavement under his tires seemed to bend with space-time.

"Yep," Xander said.

As Swarm, Tom had instigated dozens of flash mobs, but this one was different. Everywhere around him, his fellow mutaneers were smiling, talking, singing, laughing, seemingly clueless and unconcerned about the how and when of their ultimate destination. This amorphous collective had a beginning and an end but no front, middle, or back. It had an objective but no preordained path. As the group rolled along, hundreds of other alt-bikers joined, some of them waving flashlights and holding signs that read "Drink, don't drive" and "Gas fuels wars." Someone had brought along a high-def mobile projector, and Tom turned to see a life-size blue whale undulating across the building facades like a gargantuan mascot. The whale's eye peered at Tom, telling him, "Yes, go ahead. You're on the right track; don't look back." He experienced a sensation of being levitated and propelled forward by something much bigger and deeper than a mushroom-spiked parade of provocateurs. *So,* he thought, *this is what it's like to be part of the organism, inside the spontaneous heart of the happening.*

The neon signs were saturated and streaking as Tom pedaled, liberated and exhilarated, to drift along with the coursing congregation. Xander was just ahead, talking to a girl with pink and purple glow lights on her bike frame. He looked back to check on his pal. "Tommy, how are you doing back there?"

"I just had a great conversation with a whale."

Xander grinned and turned his attention back to his comely companion. Tom felt an inexplicable surge of euphoria, a sudden flashback of what he had felt earlier in the day when he tested the zeph.r signal. This was the part he had forgotten when he blacked out: how good it felt—inside and outside and all around him. No wonder he had ejaculated; it was an involuntary reflex to something that had nothing to do with sex or cheeseburgers. His body was responding to a stimulus somehow connected to the essential chemistry of the human condition, both macro and micro, to everything and everybody pouring down the streets, spinning in tandem around him, to *this*.

A familiar halo of luxuriant blond hair floated into Tom's view. It could only belong to one person in the entire world. And there she was, riding her bike just a few yards away. Lucy in the Sky. In the flesh. He even recognized the red sweater that she had worn to one of their Skype dates. Tom pedaled faster. How close could he get without revealing himself? Even after all these months, she still hadn't seen his face. But if he caught up and looked at her, would she know?

The bikers lurched left on Sixth Street and surged toward Austin's main drag, where bars, drunk revelers, and Friday night traffic would ensure maximum chaos and press coverage. Tom was just a few feet behind Lucy now. He was pulling up alongside, still debating whether to reach out to touch her hair and let her see him, when he saw the police barricades. The bike mob gave a collective shudder, splitting the main group and sending bikers spinning in all directions. Some of the riders sped up and charged directly into the police line, while others did everything they could to avoid it. Lucy was swept up by the panicking crowd and pushed away from his orbit. "Lucy!" Tom shouted. She turned but was already too far away to identify the caller—then she was gone.

The local TV stations had been tipped off and were already on the scene, setting up camera angles, blocking the sidewalks and adding to the confusion. Tom watched as an officer trotted into the first wave of bikes and tackled a rider like a linebacker, both of them hurtling to the ground in a bundle of fists and spinning wheels. On cue, dozens of bikers whipped out their phones and began to video the altercation, managing somehow to be participants and spectators simultaneously. Tom watched as the woman Xander had been talking to moved in closer to record the melee and started screaming, "Recording law enforcement officials in a public place is legal! You are the ones breaking the law!" Her shouts only enraged the officers further, and when they went after her, Xander sprinted to her defense. As Tom ran to back up his friend, he felt bulky arms gripping him from behind, dragging him back and pushing him into a police van. He tried to yell out, but the officer's chokehold was squeezing his esophagus. As the vehicle pulled away in the tear gas haze, Tom got a last glimpse of Xander holding his ground against at least three police officers, whirling like a dervish and gathering speed in the eye of the cycle-strewn storm.

Tom's mom bailed him out around midnight, but he had to wait until the next morning to visit Xander at the hospital. DJX had two cracked ribs, three sprained fingers, a black eye, and a busted lip. Bandages covered half his body, and his left arm was suspended in a splint, but considering the circumstances, as the doctor solemnly noted, he was a lucky man. True to form, Xander was in a sanguine mood.

Xander jiggled his arm sling in greeting. "Did you have fun last night?" he asked, lifting only the part of this mouth that wasn't bruised. Tom pulled up a plastic visitors' chair.

"Not as much as you."

"True that." Xander said. "Those bastards. It's all over Twitter. There's going to be an investigation."

"What about the bikes?"

Xander waved beneficently with his good hand. "No worries, bro. We'll get new ones, better ones. By the way, she looks really nice."

"You saw Lucy?"

"Yeah, I saw your virtual squeeze. I'm just glad she's not a figment of your imagination or some fat guy wearing his mom's underwear."

"Nah, that was the cop that clubbed me," Tom said. "You could have warned me about the chocolate-mushroom bar."

Xander jiggled his broken arm dismissively. "Where's the fun in that?" He motioned to Tom to come closer. "Go to the closet and get my apartment keys out of my jeans."

"You're still high, aren't you?"

"Shut up and listen to me," Xander said, suddenly serious. "I want you to go my place and get my hard drive and keep it safe until I'm out of here. Fabian says I'll be fine in time for ARK, but I want you to have the master of 'Stardust' so the cops can't confiscate it and you can make the visuals. Plus, you can start working on that app that embeds code into music. I left a Leap Motion controller for you, too."

"What's that?"

"Just take it, " Xander ordered. "I'm trusting you with my music, Tommy. Make it great; make it amazing."

"Don't worry, buddy. I will."

Tom did as Xander asked, fetching his friend's hard drive and placing it on his workstation along with the thumb drive with the visual effects software, the Leap Motion controller, and the laptop loaded with zeph.r. Tom took off his hoodie, locked the door, and cracked open an energy drink. For the next several hours, he tinkered with the various programs, stitching them together and weaving their commands into a kind of binaural audio-visual device. The Leap Motion was the coup de grâce. By sensing and tracking the movements of human hands and fingers, it allowed Tom to not only manipulate visual effects but also to create shapes and images in three dimensions without even touching a keypad or mouse. Tom smiled at the thought: ten fingers, ten digits, digital. Tom put on his headphones and cued a 3-D rendition of the "Stardust" video graphic to the Leap Motion software. Then he lifted his hands toward the screen, which instantly sprang to life, awaiting his next instruction. As his extremities flexed and danced in the air, the pixels on the screen responded to his orchestral gestures, spiraling, spinning, and revealing a dazzling realm of infinite immersive possibility, one that he had somehow dreamed but never seen, a vast panorama that now, for the first time and forever, he could summon and command with his virtual fingertips, warping reality with a twist of his wrist, stopping and starting time with upraised palms, weeping as he felt himself morphing and merging with the machines around him like a deity who was finally, tentatively at first but with increasing aplomb and assurance, grasping the source of his nascent power and flowering intention.

Part II

EMERGENCE

12

October ████████████
Duggan, Jake
National Cyber Security Division
Department of Homeland Security

FIELD REPORT #917-406
SUBJECT: Airman Donald Westlake, U.S. Air Force, Kandahar,
Afghanistan
TO: SIMON GUPTA, DIRECTOR OF H.S. CYBER-OPS
FROM: J. DUGGAN

Three weeks ago, I was entrusted with a mission coordinated
with the ███ and ███ to investigate the possibility of a security
breach at Kandahar Air Force Base in relation to the shooting
of allied Afghan soldiers and the subsequent death of Airman
Donald Westlake, a member of a ███████████████████████
███████████████ directed by the AF in conjunction ████████
███████ authorities. An inspection of the ██████████████████
at Kandahar base barracks showed no signs of ███████
███████████ or ██████████ by unauthorized personnel, but
there is reason to believe that such █████████, if it exists, was
██████████ prior to my arrival at the base. The ████████████
████████ by agents of the ██████████████████ led me to believe
that the real goal of the ███ was to █████████████████████
███████ facts or circumstances or activities, involving ███

135

and/or DOD agencies and/or external forces, that either caused or increased the likelihood of the death of Airman Westlake.

I have also come across anecdotal testimony related by Westlake's drone teammate, Martin Fisk since discharged and being treated for PTSD outside Fairchild AF Base in Spokane, WA, to the effect that Westlake did not suffer a combat-related, psychotic episode, as described in internal govt documents, but was in fact acting under the influence of internet-delivered messages, signals, or instructions that may have origins overseas, in the U.S. or both. Interviews and background checks suggest that the source of the signals could be undisclosed experiments by the DOD related to mind control, either defensive or offensive in design and nature and other viral or internet-bourne inducements. While I have found no direct evidence linking the CIA or DOD to specific experiments or covert programs that could have produced Pvt. Westlake's actions in Kandahar, research and backchannel interviews suggest that the possibility is real and cannot be responsibly ignored.

Given the unknown origin, capabilities and distribution methods of those signals, and the magnitude of the potential threat that they represent to American citizens, I strongly recommend the following course of action:

1. A formal request to the CIA and DOD for all documents and evidence related to the Westlake incident, including interviews with military personnel in Kandahar and in the U.S. who had direct or indirect contact with Westlake and members of his platoon.
2. A full accounting of all special ops, covert training and mind control

███████ involving ████████████████ or any other █████████████ applied via computer ████████████████, or that could be transmitted via the Internet, private online networks, or other █████ ███████.

3. A request to the NSA for any and all related data and materials that pertain to this case, including the ██████ ██ working on ███████ like the ones described above.

4. An immediate elevation of this case to the Director of the Department of Homeland Security to flag what seems to be ██████████████████████████████ ████████████████████████████ between the ████ and the ████ and ████.

5. If any of the assumptions and conclusions of this memo are true and accurate, it's possible that the ████████ ████████████████ of the ██████████████ have been ████████████████████████████████████ ████████████, which would require the immediate notification of the Director of ██████ and the Director of the ████████████████████████████

6. Permission for this agent to continue the investigation of the Westlake case and all related concerns and potential ███████████████████████████ with the sole intention of containing and neutralizing any possible ████████████████████████████ either now or in the foreseeable future, and to ensure that ████████████ is steadfastly avoided henceforth by ████████████████████ and taking immediate and appropriate organizational action.

13

Throngs of half-naked young people sporting mouse ears, Burger King crowns, DayGlo body paint, and oversized sunglasses waved at the limo as it approached the ARK festival. Xander and Tom waved back, marveling at the fantasyland of streaming banners, faux medieval towers, carnival rides, and waterslides ringed by a trio of giant stages that loomed like Mayan temples over the postpubescent playground. Platoons of festival workers were attending to the first wave of what would grow into a bronze carpet of fifty thousand bodies. Even with the sun sinking in the west, it was still scorching hot, and in the middle of the carnival several hundred revelers in surfer shorts and bikinis were doing a rain dance around a giant dripping mushroom made of hydraulic misting tubes brought in to blunt the heat.

"Jesus," Tom said. "Are you ready for this?"

"I've been ready forever," Xander answered.

In a couple of hours, Xander and Tom would join the sultans of spin as they whipped the faithful into fits of aerobic abandon. But for now all they could do was gape in awe at the sheer scale of the spectacle gearing up around them. ARK was the latest and biggest in the new breed of mega-EDM events. For years, the electronic dance movement had been building on the outlaw foundations of Detroit techno and Chicago house, amplifying and consolidating the countless permutations of trip-hop, dubstep, techno, and trance, elevating the DJ from a booth at the back of the room to the front stages of sold-out arenas and stadiums. With Tom's surreptitious help, Xander had caught the mega-rave wave just as it was cresting into a multibillion-dollar enterprise and EDM festivals were metastasizing into massive multidimensional attractions.

The opening acts were warming up the crowd as the limo pulled up to the backstage entrance, where staffers politely asked to see their passes before waving them into a compound of deluxe Bedouin-style tents. Balloons swayed lazily overhead, and a propeller plane used smoke to etch an invitation to a casino after-party, the puffy white letters slowly smudging to nonsense in its wake.

Tom and Xander were escorted to the VIP enclosure behind the main stage, where the other DJs and their entourages sipped cold tequila cocktails and acknowledged new arrivals with a glance and courtly nod. An elaborate buffet and open bar awaited, as did a bottle of vintage Dom Perignon with regrets from Fabian, whose note begged forgiveness for having to shepherd another client at the Sacred Music Festival in Fez, Morocco. When Xander popped the cork, several heads turned and Tom felt curious eyes on them. Then a fawning actress and her manager/boyfriend approached their table and asked if they could please have a pucker of bubbly. Xander made a graceful bow as he filled their glasses and the invisible membrane was breached effortlessly, seamlessly, as if they had always been on the inside track, as if their ascendance to the royalty of EDM had been preordained and blessed from the very beginning. Where Tom and Xander came from and how they had arrived at the technorati apex made no difference, not with the thrumming vibrations of half a million watts of audio equipment massaging them through the evening air and thousands of fans eagerly waiting for DJX, as Xander was now officially known, to assume his place on the illuminated platform and rattle the heavens with his sand-shuddering beats.

Xander's animated gestures and lopsided grin said it all—this was where he belonged, these were his kin, this gleaming chain of social silver was his element. Tom knew that someday, probably very soon, he would remember this moment as the precious pinnacle of something that was about to be overwhelmed by events even more irresistible than music or money or fame. Xander was absolutely right about their fates being tied, but Tom now saw that rising to the upper echelons of the EDM elite was just the beginning of a much steeper trajectory.

Even though he was young and fresh on the scene, or most likely because of it, DJX had been awarded a plum slot to spin, just when the sky behind the stage became an orange-violet aurora laced with iridescent chem-trails. A female show runner materialized and whispered into Xander's ear, signaling that it was nearly time for him to go on. Tom and Xander followed her onto a tarp-covered riser behind the stage, which overlooked a vast ocean of people already applauding and calling for their groove-wielding hero. Tom and Xander were shaking their heads and laughing even before the crowd let out a guttural roar of anticipation. "Let's make them remember this," Tom said, heading to his perch a hundred yards opposite the main DJ stage at the elevated A/V console that controlled a curved wall of fifty-foot-tall LED screens.

A thudding cadence announced the beginning of the set, and Xander stepped onto the turntable deck under a halo of bluish light.

"Hello, everybody! Are you ready to touch the sky?"

He raised his arms in greeting to the cheering throng, at once blessing and bowing to the sea of smiling faces. Then he donned his headphones and started turning dials and pushing buttons, adding layers of percussion until he had a samba-like foundation riding the insidious bass line. Thick waves of synthesizer slowly wobbled and then sped up to a rollicking strut that got the crowd kicking and bouncing. In the video control booth, Tom was echoing the aural textures with whirling shapes that dissolved and merged into each other like spin art. It occurred to him that neither he nor Xander played an actual instrument, yet here they were manipulating sounds and images in concert before a vast and appreciative audience, a foot-pounding pageant performed by an emphatic cast of thousands.

Xander looked at Tom from across the crowd and raised two fingers, meaning that there would be only two more songs before the world premiere of "Stardust." Tom reached into his pocket and retrieved the flash drive that he hoped would demonstrate the potential of the Meta Militia's contraband code on a live audience. In addition to recalibrating the zeph.r signal and synching it with microwave-enabled audio and visual suggestions, Tom had taken the extra precaution of separating his and Xander's earphone channels from the main feed to shield them from zeph.r's mind-warping effects.

Xander launched into a patch of fast-paced electro with a counter-pattern of peeling saxophone—or was it guitar? In response to the song, Tom brought the circular shapes on the LED screens into sharper focus, making them synch with the beats like single-cell creatures pulsing to the rhythms. Out in the audience, glow sticks drifted over the thicket of hands and arms like mitochondria.

Xander looked over and held up a single finger.

Tom pulled out the key drive and uploaded zeph.r, checking to make sure that his visual loop was queued up and ready to go. Xander was building tension with scratchy guitar riffs over tumbling synthetic drums and a corroded lower register. He took the tempo down to a lumbering crawl, and Tom followed suit, initiating the fractal egg animation and aiming a battery of industrial-strength lasers upward to intersect like the interior arches of a celestial cathedral. Xander raised his hand, and the symphonic overture of "Stardust" rose along with the lights, a single searing note that coalesced with the lasers overhead to create a portal to the Milky Way.

Tom turned a dial to stream zeph.r into the mix and scanned the crowd just as the light and music swooped back to Earth in a cascade of pulverizing thumps and the dancers reeled with mouths open, heads bobbing, bodies bending like rubber under the sonic pummeling. Xander was nodding and staring into a faraway place, pacing himself. Through the lens of the Orion software, zeph.r was a neon red rectangle with pulsing control nodes, blinking in time with the music, guiding him as he adjusted the blend and raised the amplification another notch.

The crowd was heaving in tandem to Xander's motions like minnows swimming in some unseen current, their heads bowing in perfect agreement. Almost *too perfect.* Just to be sure, Tom boosted zeph.r another notch, and that's when he saw it: an enormous murmuration shuddering through the audience, like the ripples emanating from a stone dropped into a pond, except that this pond was a mass of several thousand people suddenly lurching in unison, an impossible concurrence of limbs perfectly synchronized to the beat as the song's lyrics shuffled and blinked on the giant screens:

Move.
Be
the
beat.
Now be
Stardust
Again.

Tom looked over at Xander, who seemed perplexed by what he was seeing in the crowd. Their eyes met, and Tom shrugged, pretending not to know what was happening, pretending not to be thrilled by what he was seeing. Tom gazed out at ARK city—twenty thousand eyes glued to the screens, feet stamping, arms pumping, all of them responding to the same internal metronome, not separate anymore, not from the images inside or outside, not from the world around them or each other. The throng simultaneously heaved and screamed in approval, the conscious attention of a single beast consuming its audiovisual feast.

Be
Stars.
Move
with
Each other.

Xander arched his back and rotated on his heels, the same action that had momentarily mesmerized the police in Austin. He pounded the air with his fists, absorbing the approval of countless roaring mouths, basking in their feral screech. He turned his palms in a gesture of benediction to his tribe, and leaned forward over the controls, constructing a swirling melody around an amplified Middle Eastern tattoo. Xander had returned the crowd to solid ground, and now Tom took them deeper, immersing the dancers in a sulfurous haze of smoke and blood red light. The giant words flickered and flashed, a kaleidoscopic scrabble of letters and shapes coalescing into a call for action.

Move
Live
Love
Each other
Live
Love
Now

A thousand yards away, on the other side of the ARK festival grounds, Eric Wightman heard a thunderous racket from the main stage and cursed his friends. He had come to ARK at the last minute, convinced by his chums that seeing DJX would be the highlight of the summer. They had all agreed to arrive early for his set, but that was before his pals, most of them drunk or rolling on ecstasy by now, had insisted on waiting in line for the *fucking Ferris wheel,* like little kids distracted by the candy-colored ring of pretty lights. Don't worry—we've got plenty of time, they'd assured him. And then the wheel had lurched to a halt because someone had thrown up and had to be carried away to the medical tent, and now Eric was trapped in limbo, literally up in the air. Even from this distance at the top of the mechanical loop, he could tell that whatever was happening on the main stage was epic. The light show on the screen and the cluster of lasers rising over the crowd like a castle of white light were hypnotic, incredible. And the new song—so stirring and soulful, was triggering memories, things he hadn't thought about in years. The feeling he got from the music erased his anger but not his frustration. He wanted to be there with those people. He wanted to dance with them, all of them. "Shit!" was all Eric could say. "Shit, shit, shit!"

Tom felt the energy in the audience morphing again, moving inward from the edges. Then he peered into the teeming crowd and saw something inexplicable—people going at it like animals in heat, not just making out but having actual intercourse. Already stripped down to swimsuits and flip-flops, it didn't take long for the boys and girls to get naked and nasty with their neighbors, total strangers instantly available and irresistible. Meanwhile, in the middle of the humping horde, dozens of delirious dancers were passing out, their limp silhouettes carried on a cushion of hands to the edge of the crowd, where they were gently lowered to the ground. ARK security, alarmed by the licentious groping and growing pile of bodies, pushed into the heart of the crush to disperse the mob, but instead of making them docile, zeph.r accentuated their natural aggression. Anyone who resisted became the object of their wrath, until the lovers and the fighters were all trading blows in the expanding brawl.

This wasn't the plan, people going crazy, getting hurt. Tom disengaged the zeph.r signal, but it was too late. As the tangle of humanity churned into a violent mash-up, Tom's elation evaporated and Xander gave him the signal to pull the plug. The show was over. Tom cut off the sound, uncoupled his hard drive, and erased all traces of zeph.r before joining Xander in a mad scramble to get away from the chaos and back to the enclosed VIP area. They fought their way through the stampede, miraculously managing to locate their driver.

"Get us the hell out of here!" Xander ordered. As the limo pulled away from the exit, a caravan of Nevada State police cruisers barreled through the gates, followed by ambulances and fire trucks, all with lights flashing and sirens screeching.

"What the fuck happened back there?" Xander wanted to know. "Everybody went berserk."

Tom was busy making whiskey drinks at the other end of the limo. "It was fun at first, and then it got kinda weird."

"Ya think!?"

Twenty minutes later, Xander and Tom were back in their high-roller suite with wraparound views of the Las Vegas Strip. The ARK after-party and the nightlife lords and ladies of Las Vegas awaited them, but right now it was just the two of them, still trying to digest the magnitude and meaning of what had just transpired.

"Did you freaking see that!" Xander was pacing and typing into his phone. "I mean, the crowd went absolutely apeshit!"

"Yeah, I saw it," Tom replied. "Totally insane."

Down below, gamblers and gawkers streamed through gleaming mazes of carefully calculated temptation, most of them hoping in vain that they'd get a chance to do something that was supposed to stay in Vegas. During the ride from the airport to the hotel and during a short exploratory sprint on the jammed sidewalks, Tom was astonished by the sheer range of humanity pouring through the streets, an endless parade of pedestrians who had converged on this shameless Shangri-la to forget their woes and escape the inertia of the familiar, the comfortably safe and sound, where the chances of winning big were even lower than a streak on roulette.

But Tom and Xander had managed to beat the odds, both of them still in a state of suspended disbelief, trying to digest the magnitude of what had just happened. What difference did it make that Tom had engineered Xander's stardom from the shadows? None of it would have happened without their unique combination of ability, guts, and ambition. After all, Xander's talent and charisma were real, the ARK extravaganza was real, the lavish suite they were staying in was real. Zeph.r was real. The power of its signal had outstripped Tom's expectations, but he had also witnessed its limitations. He now understood why the Meta Militia had passed it on to him; the software was a ticking time bomb. In its present form, zeph.r was too unpredictable, too blatant, too random. But what if it could be tamed, focused, and controlled?

Xander poured some stiff drinks from the bar and motioned for Tom to follow him out to the terrace, which overlooked the famous fountains of the Bellagio. Tom's eyes followed the river of light flowing like lava past their hotel and down the Strip to the edge of town. Just a few minutes ago, they'd been running for their lives, and now they were on top of the world. Tom felt a shiver of vertigo, a tremor of understanding that by breaching the boundaries of what was possible, they were now teetering on the threshold of the unthinkable.

Arms resting on the railing, Xander gripped his glass with both hands and leaned in toward Tom. "It was 'Stardust,' man," he said. "That's when everybody went nuts, dancing like maniacs, tearing off their clothes. It was a goddamn free-for-all out there. It was like, like ..."

"Like *The Rite of Spring*?"

"Yeah, exactly!" Xander blurted. "You know what I think?"

Tom waited for Xander to tell him.

"I think we've got a monster hit on our hands." He held up his glass. "We did this together, Tommy. We're a team. I want you to come on tour with me as chief of technology and visuals. Full partners in crime. I keep the publishing rights but everything else we split down the middle, fifty-fifty."

Tom glanced at Xander to make sure he wasn't kidding. "Gee, Xan, thanks. I mean, when and if that happens ..."

"It already did." Xander grinned like a dealer pulling an ace from his sleeve. "ARK asked me to join the tour as one of the headliners. Ten cities in thirty days. All expenses paid. Fabian just texted me. He's working on the money part, but it's middle six figures minimum. Are you with me?"

Tom wasn't particularly fond of traveling, and he didn't need the money, but the chance to keep testing zeph.r in public was enticing. He had assumed that its signal could only affect people within a few hundred yards of the speakers, but there also seemed to be a halo effect of some kind passing from person to person across a much larger area. Doing more ARK festivals would give him ample time to fine-tune the software and probe its uncharted dimensions.

From their perch on the twenty-ninth floor, Tom watched the Bellagio's swaying strands of pressurized water flex and twine like a double helix of DNA preparing for cellular mitosis, the chemical chain that had programmed the destiny of every human cell since the dawn of the species, including the occasional mutation, a random glitch that reshuffled the genetic deck and opened the door to variation and, under the right conditions, biomorphic evolution. In fact, it occurred to Tom that the entire Vegas strip was an annotated history of human civilization, from the Bellagio's spurting gene pool to the Egyptian pyramid at Luxor, on through Caesar's imperial Rome, the canals of Venice, and even the Eiffel Tower and its saucy American sister, the Statue of Liberty, with her beguiling gaze and promise of unfettered democracy in the home of the brave and the land of ATMs that spat out crisply minted hundred-dollar bills.

"Hell yeah," Tom said, gripping Xander's shoulder. "I'm all in!" Then he opened his wallet and tossed a wad of twenties into the air, the buddies howling as they watched the money corkscrewing like confetti into the fountain's fanning tendrils.

14

Duggan stared at the document in his hands in utter amazement. Then he shoved the redacted report into the shredder and took a Maalox. He had never had an internal memo censored before, and he'd never heard of it happening to anyone else either. Gupta wouldn't return his calls or e-mails, which only intensified his anger and disappointment. Was the pressure on NCSD coming from inside or outside or both? He was going to find out even if it cost him his job. He had every intention of walking down the hall to Gupta's office for a showdown, but when he opened his door, JT was blocking the threshold, looking sympathetic and gently pushing him back inside. "Easy, easy, I know how you feel, but don't ever do anything while you're still mad," he told Duggan. "C'mon, buddy, you know better than that."

"They censored my report, JT"

"I know, but what makes you so sure it was Gupta?"

"Then who?"

"I've been getting some vibrations," JT told him. "Give me a chance to find out what's shaking. Meanwhile, keep your head down and don't do anything rash."

For the next couple of days, Duggan pretended to stay busy, tracking routine cases and pitching in on investigations when asked, wondering when the ax would fall.

Then the word came that Gupta had agreed to grant him an audience. Duggan braced himself for the worst and walked down the hall, past the cubicles and meeting rooms, to the corner office. Gupta was waiting, his desk scrupulously cleared of clutter.

"Jake, have a seat. I want to apologize."

"For what, sir?"

"Your memo, the edited version that was sent back to you, was a mistake. I'll take responsibility for that. You did good work, Jake. There are some patterns and issues you raised that merit our attention, especially the possibility of interagency manipulation. That's serious stuff. And I promise to look into it."

"But you want me to back off," Duggan said.

"I want you to wait."

"Wait for what, sir?"

Gupta grimaced. "Just give me some time, Jake. These are serious allegations that raise sensitive questions. We're on tricky terrain here. We've got to proceed carefully."

"And what about me? Am I expected to forget what I know?"

"I expect you to be patient. Take some vacation. We'll talk again when you get back. I promise."

"Is that all?" Duggan asked.

"Yes, Jake. That's all."

There was no sign of JT, so Duggan decided to call it a day and sweat out his frustration at the gym. The brisk walk cleared his head, and he was looking forward to a rigorous workout when he opened the combination lock and reached for his sneakers. The Post-it was stuck to the inside of his locker. It said that a ticket to see the Washington Capitals at the Verizon Center for that night's game was waiting for him at will call. Duggan peeled off the sticky square, which was the same lime green as the one that had been left for him on Westlake's laptop in Kandahar. He was pretty sure the Post-it would be free of fingerprints, as would his ticket. Duggan pulled on jeans and took a cab to the stadium, fully aware that whoever left the ticket probably had zero interest in hockey.

The arena was noisy and crowded, and his seat was good—third row of section 111, right behind the penalty box. Spectators were already lambasting their favorite players, and Duggan did his best to look involved in the brutal ballet. His understanding of hockey was limited to knowing that it was dominated by Canadians and brawny brawlers with incomplete sets of teeth.

The seats to Duggan's left were occupied by an older man and a boy who appeared to be his grandson. The seat to his right was empty, and it stayed that way until the end of the first period. The score was still zero to zero when the spot was claimed by a man casually dressed in jeans and a polo shirt, carrying a beer and a box of popcorn. Duggan regarded his companion askance. Middle-aged. Nondescript. Could be anybody. Especially since he was wearing a red-and-blue Capitals Warface hockey mask, just like the ones for sale in the fan merchandise store.

"Hey, buddy, did I miss much?" the stranger said to Duggan.

"Hockey mask. I have to remember that one."

"Team spirit is an undervalued virtue," the man said, his voice muffled by the mask and the noise of the game. "It's getting too risky to have a conversation like this online."

"Works for me, as long as you're not here to talk about hockey."

"I know about your memo," the man said, "and I know why you're being told to stand down. Interested?"

"Is hockey a contact sport?"

The puck was slapped toward their section before being intercepted at the last second, sending it ricocheting against the Plexiglas barrier, which afforded them an excellent view of the ensuing shove-fest. They waited for the commotion to settle.

"You were right about the DOD trying to cover something up, and you were also right about Westlake being in a covert program involving mind control."

Duggan nodded. "Tell me something I don't already know."

The man paused to sip his beer and clap for a visitors' goal. "What do you know about microwave experiments by the US government?"

"I know that that there was a horse race between us and the Soviets during the fifties and sixties," Duggan said. "I know that offensive uses of microwave beams were tested by the United States on its own personnel until the shit hit the fan in the seventies, when the whole shebang went underground. I'm guessing that whatever Westlake was exposed to is just the latest iteration of something that isn't supposed to exist."

The visitors charged and nearly scored again with a zinger right up the middle. "C'mon, you pathetic losers!" the man shouted. "Get it together!" He gulped his beer and belched. Without turning his head, he said, "It's kinda funny, don't you think?"

"What's funny?"

"Well, everybody's all upset about the government wanting a back door to your smartphone, and meanwhile it's busy building a back door to your brain."

"Keep your day job," Duggan said.

"Tough crowd tonight," the man said, clearing his throat. "The program is called zeph.r, and it was being tested to increase the learning curve and effectiveness of drone operators, or at least that was the idea. At some point along the way, as you have already deduced, the experiment went awry. Something about increasing the bandwidth, but it's all too technical for me. Anyway, after the massacre, as you know, the DOD did their best to build a cover story. But one of the scientists who worked on the project underwent a change of heart, you could say. His name is Kenneth Ulrich, and he went AWOL with a copy of the zeph.r code. DOD thinks we're holding him hostage to keep them off balance and take back some of their jurisdictional turf."

"Are you?"

They were interrupted by the older man getting up to take his grandson to the bathroom. When the kid saw the man's mask, he said, "Cool! Grandpa, can I get one, please?" The grandfather gave Duggan's companion a sour look.

Hockey Mask waited for them to leave before continuing. "The answer, unfortunately, is no," he admitted. "At first, we thought he might have been a mole for the Chinese or the Russians, but now we believe that he's still in the United States."

"Doing what?"

"That is exactly what we'd like to know. But there's reason to believe that he has turned against his previous employer."

"You think he's a domestic threat?"

"Westlake and Ulrich were close."

"How close?"

The man shrugged. "Who am I to judge? But Ulrich's former colleagues say that he blames the air force for Westlake's death and for publically lying about the actual causes, depicting a patriot as a nutcase. Ulrich thinks the military behaved less than honorably and should be held accountable."

"How does he intend to do that?"

For the first time, the man in the hockey mask turned to face Duggan. "We were hoping you could help us find out."

"Who's 'we'?"

The kid was back, wearing an identical fan hockey mask and carrying a souvenir stick. "I've got a mask and a stick, so I can beat you up," the boy said. The man playfully put up his dukes, and the kid pretended to bonk him on the head with his stick. Everybody chuckled and retook their seats.

Hockey Mask spoke again. "Let's just say that there are two different camps on whether your investigation is a constructive development. As your boss knows, some of those people might go to considerable trouble to keep you from digging any deeper."

"Well, at least I know you're not DOD," Duggan said. The man said nothing and sipped his beer. A player caromed into the Plexiglas with a loud thump, followed by a referee's whistle. "But you still haven't given me a reason to help you."

"Do the words Meta Militia ring a bell?"

Duggan shook his head.

"The term popped up in a few of the e-mails Ulrich received before he flew the coop. It could be significant, or maybe not."

"That's not much of a lead," Duggan said. "And how do I know it's not just another red herring?"

Duggan thought he heard a sigh from behind the hockey mask. "Look, I'm not going to ask you to trust me, but protecting the United States from a domestic cyber-attack is the one thing we all agree on. The fact is, if there's a rogue DOD scientist with a grudge running off his leash with a dangerous technology in his possession, we all want him stopped. And if he's in this country and using the Internet to transfer or transmit the zeph.r code, then the responsibility lands squarely on the NCSD's turf. Am I right?"

"I follow your logic."

"That's all anyone could reasonably ask," the man said. "I'm only here to tell you that there's more support for what you're doing than you might think. Thanks for your time. Now I think I'll go get myself another beer."

Duggan stayed for the rest of the game knowing that the man in the hockey mask wouldn't be coming back. In the last five minutes of the period, he watched men in padded uniforms rush the goalie box and pile on top of each other like seals. Then a Capitals player faked left and right before bouncing the puck off an opponent's stick to set up a teammate who slammed home the winning shot. The maneuver was proof that under certain circumstances, even an enemy can help you achieve your goal. Duggan decided that maybe hockey wasn't such a dumb sport after all.

Cara Park was at her desk having her usual working lunch of quinoa, roasted soy, and lemongrass tea when her office phone rang. It was Rosalyn Cooper from the CDC, calling to ask if she knew anything about the strange outbreak of mass hysteria and fainting reported at a recent techno rave in Las Vegas.

"I hate to sound old-fashioned, Rosalyn, but I don't know anything about techno or raves."

"I'm sure you don't, Cara, and I'm sorry to call you out of the blue like this, but you're the only person I know who might be able to help me," Cooper insisted. "Local hospitals are required to issue reports of injuries that affect more than a few people, and normally this kind of thing would be of more interest to the DEA than the CDC. But this case is different. What got my attention is that the victims' symptoms are nothing like the usual alcohol or ecstasy overdoses. I mean, some of them match—the euphoria and sexual permissiveness. But it's not just the symptoms that have me worried."

Cara put her lunch aside and reached for a pen and scratch pad. "Go ahead. I'm listening."

"At this particular event, at least five thousand people experienced similar symptoms at pretty much the same place and time—simultaneous dementia, plus blackouts and memory loss, and the effects lasted, in some cases, for several days. Strange, don't you think?"

"Yes," Cara agreed. "And it sounds like you've ruled out controlled substances."

"I'm double-checking with the DEA, but it doesn't match the profile of any drug I've ever heard of. And how could so many people ingest it at the same time? Unless it was in a vapor or gas form."

Cara's eyebrows arched as she scribbled on the pad. "Or an airborne pathogen of some kind?"

"That's the concern."

While Cooper was talking, Cara started a search for reports on the ARK "Rave Zombie Riot," as one journalist had dubbed it. "There's definitely something strange about it," Cara said. "But what kind of virus could induce symptoms like that across such a large group so fast?"

"Well," Cooper replied, "that's why I'm calling. There was something about the descriptions of the people that made me think of you. I just sent you some links. Take a look and tell me what you think."

Cara said she would and then hung up.

She found plenty of news reports, most of them with sensational headlines like "Techno Beat Bacchanalia" and "Randy Rampage at ARK." But none of them could explain the phenomenon of thousands of ravers apparently convulsing in unison, although one state senator proclaimed it "proof that our permissive society is poisoning its youth and sowing the seeds of its own destruction." Even the police were flummoxed. The only article containing any useful information was by a reporter from the Las Vegas *Sun*, who had interviewed Monica Blair, an ER nurse at Desert Springs Medical Center. Blair had treated dozens of those who arrived at the hospital in various stages of disorientation or physical distress. "It was spooky," she recounted, "I've seen plenty of kids on ecstasy, but this was something else. The symptoms were more like brain damage or high fever, conscious but unresponsive, lots of moaning, blinking, and twitching. But within twenty-four hours, most of them seemed fine, so we let them go home. There's either a new drug out there or some kind of weird flu. Either way, it's bad news."

"Knock, knock," Eric said. Cara beckoned him inside, but her eyes stayed on the screen. "I've got the visuals of the bee colony migration patterns," he said, spreading a sheaf of maps across her desk. "There's some pretty interesting stuff here. The migration isn't linear. Look!" He pointed to a web of lines emanating from different hubs.

Cara stared at the printouts. "They're asymmetrical."

"Right? I noticed that too," Eric said. "But, no, I mean, look at these vectors. It's incredible. The scout bees are communicating with each other miles away from the hives. See?" Eric used his finger to trace a pair of hubs with several intersecting spokes. "There's no way to explain this from a biochemical standpoint."

"Terrestrial magnetic navigation?"

"But then how do the scouts know about each other? There's no way these convergence patterns can be random. There's something else telling them where to go. But what and why?"

"I don't know, Eric. But this is good work."

"Thanks. I'll rerun the data to make sure, but I'm guessing Rosalyn will be interested in whatever's going on here."

"I'm sure you're right," Cara agreed. "I just spoke to her, actually."

"Really? What about?"

"She thinks that there might be some kind of viral outbreak in Nevada. Apparently, a bunch of kids went berserk at a rave in Las Vegas last weekend."

"You mean ARK?"

"Yes, have you heard about it?"

"I was there."

"You were at the zombie rave riot?"

"What?" Eric was flabbergasted. "Wow, Dr. Park. Honestly, it was just a music festival."

"Why didn't you say something?"

"Say something about what?" Eric's face reddened. "I saw some police and ambulances at the end of the night, not a big deal. I mean, the authorities are always trying to close these things down. And I wasn't high on ecstasy, if that's what you're getting at."

Cara shook her head. "Forgive me, Eric. That's not what I meant. Naturally, what you do on your own time is none of my business. I'm just trying to understand what happened. The reports from the hospital are really weird—something about collective brain damage, mass psychosis. Did you or your friends see anything like that?"

"Actually, we were stuck on the Ferris wheel," Eric said glumly. "By the time we got down, it was all pretty much over."

Cara couldn't decide if she should be sympathetic or relieved. "Rosalyn is worried that we might be seeing the start of some kind of pandemic. Apparently thousands of people were infected at exactly the same time."

"Whoa, *infected*? By what? Mushrooms and ecstasy can make people freak out but thousands of people at the same time? No way."

"Rosalyn thinks it might be a new virus."

"Jeez," Eric said. "A *rave germ?* The buzz online is that it was the best EDM festival ever—great music and light show, everybody grooving together, letting loose. I mean, that's why people go to these things."

"What about the ..." Cara caught herself, realizing that a question about rampant sex at the ARK festival was inappropriate for a slew of reasons. "Never mind. Rosalyn is doing an analysis of the medical reports. Maybe we'll find a pattern."

"Sounds good," Eric said. He paused at the door. "Listen, I'm heading downtown to meet some friends for pizza. You're more than welcome to join us."

"I've still got work to do. But thanks for the invite."

"No prob," Eric said. "I'll update the hive migration data in the morning. Do you need me for anything else?"

"No, I'm going to stay and finish up. Good night, Eric."

"Just text me if you change your mind."

"I will. Thank you."

When Eric was gone, Cara clicked on the links that Cooper had sent. The first video showed scads of smiling kids playing Frisbee and cavorting under the blazing sun. The second video was taken after dark. Cara was astonished by the scale and intensity of what she saw: tens of thousands of people jammed together, dancing in lockstep and waving their arms in tandem, absorbed and transported by the mutual surrender to sensory overload. And the music. She'd heard techno before, but this was different—industrial beats and flashing lights but also layers of something else, a guttural drone, like Tibetan monks chanting. Could it be coming from the crowd? In the midst of it all, numerous couples were writhing and twining like salacious serpents, seemingly oblivious to their surroundings. Letting loose, as Eric would say.

Watching the video made Cara feel like an over-the-hill voyeur. The mating rituals of the young had apparently changed since her own college days, when the drug of choice was marijuana, a substance known for its ability to magnify the social distance between inebriated individuals. What she was looking at was the opposite of alienation; it was social communion of a degree to which she had no reference, except maybe the congregational bees and ants that she considered her extended family. Not that she looked down on pot or other countercultural pastimes. Carter, a musician, sculptor, and her last real love, had been a connoisseur of THC, with a whole shelf of hydroponic buds in jars meticulously labeled with fanciful names like Purple Horizon and Big Bang. The lovers would take long walks in Golden Gate Park, stumbling onto a saxophonist playing Coltrane in the arboreal maze, planning backpacking trips to Bali and Patagonia, reading each other's horoscopes and auras. As a kind of den mother to Carter and his beat poet pals, she would help them sew blinking lights on their outfits and make sure he was stocked up on psilocybin brownies and avocado veggie wraps for their annual pilgrimage to Burning Man.

The libertarian bond they shared seemed natural and honest to Cara, and their countercultural community flourished until a trip to the Yucatan to celebrate a galactic alignment at the pyramids of Chichen Itza. As drummers and fire dancers paid homage to the Mayan God Kukulkan, they watched the winter solstice coincide with the moment that Earth, Jupiter, and the sun made a straight line to the center of the Milky Way, a cosmological event that wouldn't occur again for thousands of years. It was there, at a place and time that many believed marked the return of the rain god, that Carter kneeled and presented her with a silver ring forged by a local shaman. "In La'

Kesh," he said to her as conch shells bellowed the beginning of a new Age of Aquarius. "It's Mayan for 'You are another me, and I am another you.' I want to be reborn with you and have kids together so our love and blood will mix and last forever."

Cara tried to give him the answer he expected, but the words wouldn't come, and she watched helplessly as the light in his eyes drained away. It was not the old world but their relationship that ended that day. Being centered, Cara realized, was not the same thing as being grounded, or ready to be buried in diapers and nannies and non-toxic toys, or becoming another's significant other without understanding one's own inner self. The idea of putting her career on indefinite hold and settling down, even temporarily, to take on the responsibility of raising a family with an income-averse free spirit triggered a sudden attack of claustrophobia. Before long, Cara had moved back into her own apartment, and their agreement to take a breather elongated into a permanent separation.

Since then, she had limited her relationships to no-strings affairs that left her free to concentrate on her work while steadfastly shunning online dating sites. She was repelled by the notion of putting herself on display, of tagging her photos, and/or listing her interests and hobbies and favorite authors for all the world to devour. The modern compulsion to publicly expose every detail of your life struck Cara as indecent, a kind of digital exhibitionism. Willfully uploading personal pictures, experiences, and thoughts for free, Cara felt, cheapened the intrinsic value of one's existence, like seeing your mother's wedding ring in a pawn shop window.

Cara replayed the ARK video. When did summer music festivals become uninhibited orgies of hyper-sensory connection? So many people packed into a single place, rubbing up against each other, breathing the same air. It wouldn't take much for a virus to replicate exponentially through such a dense population, spreading quickly to other cities, states, and continents. Cara switched off her computer, locked the doors, and headed for the BART station, feeling hopelessly unhip and wondering for the first time if it was her destiny to live the rest of her life studying creatures that would never know the excruciating freedom of being alone.

Duggan didn't wait for an invitation from Gupta before storming into his office the next morning, but the person behind his boss's desk was a stranger, a woman immaculately coiffed and clearly in charge. Duggan recognized the other person in the room as Jordan Sharpe. JT was there too, barely concealing an I-told-you-so smirk.

"Hello, Jake," the woman said. "I'm Jessica Koepp. I'll be your primary supervisor until further notice."

Koepp extended her hand, and Duggan took it. It was a firm, confident shake.

"Where's Gupta?"

"Mr. Gupta has been reassigned," Koepp said without elaboration. "I believe you've already met Agent Sharpe from NSA. And of course Agent Nutley."

"JT and I go back to cyber boot camp."

"Yes, I know," Koepp said. She was dressed in a tailored gray suit and shiny black pumps. The pearls around her neck were discreetly expensive. She motioned to Sharpe to close the door.

"Jake, let me start by apologizing for the misunderstanding between you and your former supervisor. Sometimes things happen that require action outside the normal channels. This is one of those times."

"So now we're flying under the radar."

Koepp smiled kindly. "For now, yes. As you already know, the integrity of two or possibly three agencies has probably been compromised. And until this all gets sorted out, it's best to be conservative about who else is privy to the details of our investigation."

"You mean the Westlake case?"

"Yes," Koepp confirmed. "A research scientist at DOD who was working with Airman Westlake has gone missing with some sensitive technology."

"His name is Kenneth Ulrich," Duggan interrupted. "A DOD researcher who was working with an experimental software called zeph.r."

JT shot Duggan a look that said *touché*.

Koepp and Sharpe exchanged a glance.

"That's correct," Sharpe said. "We know that Ulrich is off the reservation but still have no idea if he acted solo, or whether he's remained in touch with any confederates at DOD. The zeph.r project was funded and operated outside federal guidelines, which makes it a black box with powerful sponsors inside the DOD, sponsors who would probably like this whole problem to quietly go away."

"What you mean is that we're basically in a sack race with the DOD to find Ulrich, and until he's brought in and debriefed, it's going to be hard to tell the good guys from the bad guys."

Koepp nodded appreciatively. "Gupta did say you were a man who doesn't mince words."

"I've already been contacted by an anonymous source who knew about Ulrich and zeph.r," Duggan said. He watched Koepp for a reaction, but she remained impassive. "So I'm guessing none of this is going to stay secret for very long."

"Which only adds another layer of urgency to your assignment," Koepp agreed. "Operation Zeph.r was designed to embed messages and behavioral direction in human brains to boost concentration and efficiency. Apparently, one of the experiments included embedding a subcutaneous receiver chip into the test subject's head ..."

"To boost the signal's bandwidth. And Donald Westlake was the lucky GI who got to test DOD's new toy."

"Yes. The chip increased the intensity of messages, which, in theory at least, could be transmitted via visual and aural signals hidden in music, pictures, and other sensory stimuli."

"Who's running the program now?"

"No one," Sharpe said. "Officially, anyway. Zeph.r was dismantled by DOD a year ago after early tests showed that the effects of the software were too erratic and unpredictable to be useful as a military weapon enhancement."

"But somebody didn't get the memo."

"Or maybe that person wrote it," Koepp said. "For all we know, Ulrich might not be the only entity with a disruptive interest in zeph.r."

"You mean China, Russia, the North Koreans," Duggan said.

"Or somebody closer," Sharpe said. "You would know better than us who might be willing to aid and abet a computer scientist determined to expose secret government mind control research."

"It's a pretty long list," Duggan said, "not even counting international interests. Can you get me a summary of attempted hacks into DOD research facilities during the past year?"

Sharpe nodded.

"One more thing, Jake," Koepp said. "You've developed a reputation as something of a loose cannon, an operative who doesn't respect interagency protocol. There have been complaints from certain quarters, a concern that you knowingly overstep organizational bounds."

Here it comes, Duggan thought.

"You want me to stop," he said.

"No, I want you to keep it up. Just make sure the three of us know what you're doing so we can watch your back."

JT spoke for the first time. "Jake, we're confident that NCSD will soon be given the authority and resources to address this threat at the proper level," he said. "Meanwhile, you're stuck with us."

Duggan paused to consider his options. Koepp didn't seem like the type to take the helm of a sinking ship, but if NCSD took the fall in an interagency power struggle, his head would be first on the chopping block. On the other hand, JT's survival skills were matchless and his comment was as close to an endorsement as he would ever get. Duggan looked at Sharpe.

"Can you get me a universal term search on the NSA global database?"

"I'll do it," JT volunteered. "I can get somebody to discreetly run a wordcluster analysis for Ulrich, Kandahar, DARPA,mind control, and all the usual hacktivist groups. Anything else?"

"Get me everything you can find on the Meta Militia."

"What's that?"

"Every revolutionary needs followers to help him fight for the cause," Duggan said. "And I think Ulrich might have found his army."

15

It was probably a coincidence that Fabian, looking like a Bible-thumping evangelist in his spotless white suit, seemed to be channeling an unseen power as he commanded Xander and Tom to close their eyes and hold out their hands. "Can you *feel* it?" he said solemnly, drumming the palms of their hands with his fingertips. "Pennies from heaven."

Xander pretended to pluck invisible coins from the air and stuff them in his pocket. "Can we open our eyes now?" he asked.

"Baby, you can do anything the hell you want," Fabian gushed. "To paraphrase my friend Jay-Z, you're not a businessman; you're a *business*, man!"

Tom smiled, and not just because he enjoyed watching Xander, after barely scraping by on so little for so long, fulfill his artistic aspirations. The morning after the mob meltdown in Las Vegas, the ARK promoters announced the addition of DJX as a featured headliner of the tour, and within twenty-four hours, Xander and Tom were on a plane to a sold-out event in Detroit. Over the following weeks, they had played Seattle, Vancouver, Los Angeles, Miami, and several other towns before landing in Chicago, where they were resting up and doing some recording work before the upcoming ARK festival finale in New York. Fabian had joined them in the Windy City with news that "Stardust" was topping the EDM charts in the United States, Europe, and Japan. Offers were pouring in for media interviews, TV appearances and book deals. Fabian had arranged a press conference and reception at their Lakeshore hotel to promote the launch of an entire line of DJ equipment under the brand MuseX.

"The media mongrels await," Fabian said. "I hope you guys are ready to get blingy, because the lucre is coming, lots of it."

As it happened, the rise of DJX was about to become a jackpot for Swarm too. The dark nets that Xander and his pals used to procure their drugs, entire black markets that lurked in the ether and the untraceable crypto-currencies that financed them, had given Tom an idea. What if Swarm created his own peer-to-peer currency, a chain of digital credits that were dispersed and collected off the grid, passed surreptitiously from person to person, hard drive to hard drive, a virtual fortune that could be used to buy real influence and things? He had even minted a name for this new kind of crowd-sourced cash: Nuero$.

"Tommy," Xander said, reaching for his jacket, "c'mon. Let's do it."

"Nah, you go ahead," Tom said. "DJX is the star. I'm just the dark matter around it that nobody sees."

Xander grunted. "Yeah, the invisible force that holds everything together."

"You guys are nuts," Fabian blurted, grabbing Xander's arm and steering him toward the elevators.

"Just don't forget to meet me at the studio," Xander called as he headed out the door. "Seven o'clock. I texted you the address."

Tom picked up the *Chicago Tribune* lying on the coffee table. A headline on the front page asked, "Is Mad Raver's Disease the new AIDS?" The article explained that the mysterious illness detected in Las Vegas was spreading even faster than the CDC's most dire projections. Outbreaks of the Rave Plague, as the media dubbed it, were surfacing throughout the country, mobilizing a backlash from groups that regarded the epidemic as a symptom of unchecked social decadence. Laws banning EDM festivals were being introduced in several states, and a senator from Texas was calling for a shutdown of all outdoor music events until the source of the affliction was identified and contained. EDM fans and their allies had pushed back, invoking the First Amendment and free market principles to defend raver's rights. The FBI, meanwhile, was quietly gathering intelligence on the organizers, promoters, and patrons of the house music scene.

It didn't help that Ravers' disease seemed to have no identifiable cause or cure, or that random patches of people who had never even been to an ARK event were showing less severe but similar symptoms of euphoria, dementia, and nymphomania. Conspiracy theories bloomed in the blogosphere. Certain members of the clergy preached that the epidemic was an act of God, a curse on a sinful civilization that signaled the end of days. Others accused the North Koreans and Iranians of biological terrorism or blamed global warming. Parents stopped letting their teenage kids go out at night, and some small towns and cities had enacted weekend curfews. Those most risk-averse had started wearing gauze masks in public, adding to the freakish atmosphere of encroaching emergency. But woven into the clamor and concern, like a loose thread being gently pulled, was the unspoken dread that the malaise creeping across the land was not just a loose thread in the social fabric but the start of a permanent unraveling.

Just to play it safe, Tom had restricted zeph.r's signal at ARK events to short, controlled bursts, which still allowed him to isolate and catalog a wide range of effects. He learned that some people were more susceptible to zeph.r than others and that the receptivity of the crowd was enhanced proportionately by incorporating spoken and written language into the audiovisual mix. Tom was on the verge of giving zeph.r a peer-to-peer capability, an open source dimension that would act as a psycho-acoustic echo chamber, amplifying individual brain waves across each other like synapses firing on a magnified grid. Not even the Meta Militia could have envisioned such a thing: a zeph.r super-wave without limits, self-generating ad infinitum, a flash mob with a mind of its own. Tom had also started adding a new zeph.r code into the "Stardust" app, a sleeper signal of sorts that could be enhanced and activated remotely.

As Tom's ability to tweak the moods and actions of Swarm's followers and recruit new ones from Xander's expanding fan base grew, so did his appreciation for the transformative implications of his elaborate pranks. In Chicago, a crowd of twenty thousand inexplicably organized into a two-mile-long conga line and danced to city hall as a protest against the anti-rave crackdown. A week later, Xander made his video debut in an unauthorized Web documentary called *Music Messiah: Revolution From the Dance Floor to the Streets.* Tom had even bigger plans for New York. It was the last stop on the tour, and he couldn't resist marking the occasion with a final zeph.r-charged flourish of coordinated flash mob disruptions. Tom had started to translate the ideas welling up inside him into a communiqué of what was happening and what could come next, a manifesto and roadmap for terra incognita.

Prolonged exposure to zeph.r was affecting Tom personally too. Swarm's talent for mobilizing large numbers of people and zeph.r's ability to mold human consciousness were starting to seem interconnected and interdependent, like two magnetic poles of the same phenomenon. As he probed zeph.r's endless pathways and neural vistas with Leap Motion commands, Tom felt his fingers both controlling and being absorbed by the molecules in the air, blurring the distinction between action and thought and alerting him to the possibility that he was on the brink of a major discovery, a quantum shift that would change everything, including himself.

When Tom arrived at the studio, Xander was in the control room, listening as a singer named Maxine dubbed her vocals for a new DJX single in the soundproof recording booth. The track oozed from the speakers, an electro-soul hybrid with clear commercial potential. Xander pulled off his headphones and took a puff from his latest toy, an e-joint that vaporized the THC in marijuana without actually burning it. He saw Tom and held up the smokeless device.

"We've come a long way, baby!"

Xander laughed at his own joke, looking like an updated James Dean in his Levis and white T-shirt, hair cropped close on the sides and untethered on top.

"Sorry I'm late."

Xander pointed the vape at Tom. "You want some?"

"No, thanks. I gave it up for Lent."

"Ha, Fabian's little sermon really got to you!" Xander took another drag. "Hey, guess who I ran into at the press conference today?"

"Your tantric yoga instructor?"

"Nope."

"I give up."

"The Federal Frigging Bureau of Investigation!"

Tom pressed the mute button on the studio monitor. "Wow, Xan," he said casually. "Your fan base is really expanding. What did they want?"

"They wanted to know if I had noticed anything ..." Xander stifled a giggle, "...*unusual.*"

"I see your point," Tom said. "Two Tex-ass greenhorns from Nowhereville sticking to their guns and in no time at all shooting to the pinnacle of the EDM industry, hundreds of thousands of kids losing their minds and going berserk at their ARK shows, the CDC talking about air dusting outdoor raves with anti-bacterial gas ..." Tom paused. "Nothing unusual here, Officer."

"But actually!" Xander stomped his designer boots on the ground.

"Xan, it's not *that* funny. What did the FBI want?"

"They wanted to know if I had been approached by terrorists or subversives, or if any of the other DJs are working for the Iranians, or if I thought the Taliban or Isis are into trip-hop or techno house ... Ridiculous shit like that. A total waste of taxpayer money, if you ask me."

"And what did you tell him?"

Maxine was waving to them from the recording booth. Xander clicked on the intercom. "What's up, Maxie?"

"Hi, Tom." She blew him a kiss. "Did you guys like the last take?"

"Beautiful, baby." Xander slowly clapped his hands together. "We loved it, didn't we, Tom?"

"Yeah, really nice."

"I think we've got what we need, baby," Xander told her. Maxine did a little celebration dance and started packing up her stuff.

Tom turned the monitor off again. "So what did you say to them?"

"Dude, chill," Xander scolded. "It was just one guy, Agent Lance Chen." Xander produced Chen's card and handed it to Tom. "It was a clueless fishing expedition. Obviously. Don't get all spooky on me." Maxine was on her way to the control room. "I hear you, though. Things are getting a little weird out there. Humpty Dumpty in da house."

"All fall down," Tom said.

"That's where we're headed."

"What?"

"I meant we're going to the Varvatos party—*downtown*. That's where it's at tonight."

Maxine entered the control room and looped her arms around Xander's neck. "You guys, you sexy sonic sorcerers, your fabulous beats make me feel like …" Maxine made a sound that started as a squeal and ended in a suggestive purr.

"Gosh," Xander said. "Our beats are *that* arousing?"

"Even better," Maxine said, running her finger along Xander's jaw. "C'mon, Tom. Come with us. You know you want to."

"I do, and I would," Tom said sincerely. "But I've got a date."

"It's a *cyber* date," Xander whispered sotto voce in Maxine's ear. "Very off the grid."

"Oh, safe sex," Maxine said, her hand inching down Xander's shirt. "Without touching. How fucking romantic."

"You'd be surprised," Tom said.

Xander stood up and gave Tom a friendly fist bump. "C'mon, Maxi. Let's give Tommy some privacy."

When they were gone, Tom connected to their secure mobile network and fired up his laptop. Lucy was already logged in, waiting for him with a glass of wine in her hand and a feathered mask on her face. She knew he was traveling, but he never told her what city he was in or why he was there.

"Are you going to a costume party?" Tom asked.

"Yeah," Lucy said with a slight slur. "It's always Halloween when I'm with you. In fact, it's a fucking ball, a masquerade ball."

Tom sighed. A few weeks after they started Skyping, Tom installed a program that distorted his features just enough to conceal his identity. The semblance of normalcy had mollified her—at least for a while.

"Baby, I'll do anything you want," he said.

Lucy took off her mask and glared into the camera. "Yeah? In that case, why don't you go fuck yourself? I'm tired of jerking off a ghost." Lucy raised a glass of red wine toward the camera and took a slurp. "I figured if I got my own mask, then I could get a girlfriend to fill in for me once in a while, just to keep things interesting. Not that you'd notice."

"That's not fair."

"I'll tell you what's not fair," she said. "Having a relationship with a guy I've never met or touched, a guy who must be ashamed of himself or me or both. A guy who says he's hiding his face to protect me but won't tell me from what, a guy who says he loves me but treats me like a fucking cyber hooker. I could make a thousand dollars a night doing this shit."

"Lucy, c'mon."

"You don't think I can get it?"

"Oh, you're hot enough," Tom said, taking the bait. "Going all the way, having cybersex, that was *your* idea, remember?"

"You call this going all the way? Fuck you, Swarm, or whoever the hell you are. I'm sorry, but I can't do this anymore. I can't take it. It has to stop."

Lucy's demeanor transitioned from angry to sad, and Tom realized that she was on the verge of breaking it off with him. "Wait, wait, listen to me," he said. "I'm sorry, but I told you already that what I'm doing is against the law. You mean too much to me. I can't have you mixed up in this."

"I'm already mixed up in this. At first, I was intrigued. You were so different and mysterious and, yes, sexy. The novelty of it all was kind of exciting, but not anymore. Not like this. And I finally realized that nothing is ever going to change, least of all you."

"Oh, baby, my lovely Lucy in the Sky." Tom grabbed the side of the screen and leaned in. "I've already changed. I'm changing so fast, in so many ways. I wish I could show you. I know it's hard to deal with, but I need you more than ever. You can't leave me all alone, not yet, not now."

Lucy watched the live feed of a man with no face professing his love to her. "How the hell do I know you're not already in jail?" she asked. "I'm sorry, but you are no Prince Hamlet, nor even an attendant lord. I thought you were the fool, but now I understand— the fool, you see, is me."

Tom had one last card to play. He braced himself for the consequences of what he was about to say. "All right, you win. Listen to me."

"I'm done, my dear. I've had it with your pretty speeches ..."

"You know that secret project I've told you about, the reason we can't meet, the thing that speeds up evolution?"

"Please spare me more Darwinist bullshit. I'm not your fucking chimpanzee."

"No," Tom said. "It's real. If I show you what it is, if I let you try it, if I prove to you it's not bullshit, will you give me a break?"

Lucy stared at the screen and drained her glass. "I'll tell you when I get back from the bathroom," she said.

Tom pulled a key drive out of his computer bag and uploaded the most recent version of zeph.r, and sent Lucy a copy that would self-erase after one use.

When Lucy returned, Tom asked her to lock the door of her room, download the app, and put on her headphones. "This better be good," she said.

"Just keep the headphones on, no matter what happens," he instructed. "It'll sound like static at first, or a high-pitched whine, but just keep listening."

Tom booted the zeph.r code and used the control panel to create a link to the app on Lucy's computer. Then he donned a pair of headphones himself. During the tour, he had done some research on microwave mind-control experiments. It turned out that the Russians had published data on the frequencies that they knew affected people's moods and thoughts, but what they didn't have was the ability to embed language and thought into the signal itself, and vice versa. By distilling the code through the Omnisphere software and modulating it with pro tools, Tom could actually play the human brain like an instrument, an instrument with an infinite scale of tones and modulations mimicking music and speech, an instrument capable of fusing with other instruments, other minds, until it was like a chamber orchestra tuning up or, in this case, an intimate binary fugue, a duet between a guy and his girl.

Lucy's expression was impassive at first, and then her eyelids began to flutter. As Tom worked the controls, both guiding and following, he began to sense what she was hearing, feel what she was thinking. He approached the porous surface of her awareness, the trembling anticipation of surrender, two signals coming together, transmitting and receiving, sharing energy like strings vibrating in perfect pitch, communicating without talking, embracing without touching.

As Lucy listened, the room around her dissolved, replaced by a weightless void dotted with shimmering dots that expanded into pulsing concentric circles, yawning elastic portals pulling her closer, drawing her in. "I don't ... I can't," she stammered. "My God. Oh my God."

Tears streamed down Lucy's cheeks as she experienced herself as a child bouncing on her father's lap, the thrill of her first ride on a carousel, centrifugal bosons of self-stretching the colors, spindles and hubs, across memories and fantasies, round and round, into the nested Chinese boxes of birth and death and genetic roulette and the sublime chorus of her own being and everything echoing around it and through it, an atonal aria that twined and chimed with the life force that had bought her to this moment. And there was something else, something far beyond sound or physical sensation, coming closer, until she felt herself in the presence of another essence, and she understood who he was and what he was doing, why he couldn't reveal himself, why he wouldn't say good-bye and why he had to go, and in a way that could never be painted or photographed or rendered into an actual image or shape, she finally saw his face.

16

Governor's Island, it turned out, was the perfect setting for a cyber insurrection. A 172-acre patch of wooded land located only eight hundred yards from the southern tip of Manhattan, it had served as an early trading post for Dutch settlers, a US Army base in both world wars, and as a defensive hub for the Continental Army during the War of Independence. Now, more than 250 years later, Swarm would raise a battle cry of a different kind, storming Manhattan by way of mobile phones and water taxis provided to shuttle ARK ticketholders back to the city. The three-day assault would employ all of Tom's skills as a flash mob general and require the mobilization of recruits from across the northeast corridor. He was prepared to deploy every weapon in Swarm's arsenal, from the newest iteration of zeph.r to the national network of flash mobbers he had been building for months, teaching them how to strike out of nowhere without warning and then retreat back into the population, an updated rendition of the same guerrilla tactics used by George Washington to draw the Red Coats into a fight.

Tom stood on the northern edge of the island, at the confluence of the East and Hudson rivers, trying to picture what it must have been like to look toward Manhattan and spy a massive armada of British battleships arriving to quash the rebellion. Did the insurgents feel their hearts sink at the display of so much raw military force? Or did they take comfort in the knowledge that once people had a taste of freedom, they would fight to keep it and risk everything to win? What Tom knew for sure was that the patriots who took up arms in the war of independence were mostly in their twenties and thirties and even teens, with a fondness for ale and drinking songs, the same music that was ringing in their ears as they fought and died for a new order, just as EDM evoked rebellion and transformation in the age of Swarm. Because revolutions are always waged by the young, and the music that inspires and rouses them to action is by definition the soundtrack of inexorable change.

"Pretty dope perspective of Madhattan," Xander said, visibly pleased with his own pun. He was standing next to Tom, admiring the sight of Wall Street skyscrapers jutting abruptly from the busy harbor. "Looks almost close enough to swim."

"I wouldn't try it," Tom said. "Too many sharks."

"In the water *and* on the land," Xander said. "Whaddaya say we get this sound check done, commandeer us a sailing vessel, and go have ourselves some fun in that sleepless concrete island over yonder?"

"Aye-aye, Captain."

Xander and his coterie were already up and out when Tom regained consciousness the next morning. He shuffled though the snapshots in his head of nightclubs in Brooklyn and Manhattan, naked women dangling from the rafters and raunchy vaudeville improvs playing tongue in cheek to people who were impossible to shock. It was nice to have the suite all to himself, the dawn patrol debris of empty bottles and dirty dishes notwithstanding. He dialed housekeeping to clear away the mess and called Xander, who tried to get Tom to join him for brunch in Chelsea with Bjork and Alt-J.

"You gotta come down here, man," Xander pleaded. "I just got invited to spin inside a glacier in Iceland! But right now we're going to an after-party in a water tower."

"They took the water out first, I hope."

Xander snorted. "Preferably, right? Just throw on your clothes and grab a taxi. I need a water tower wingman."

"Sorry, bud, cannot do. I've got some errands to take care of. I'll meet you backstage at six."

Tom ordered a continental breakfast in the lobby, which looked strangely sanitized in the daylight, like a negative image of the same place and people he had seen just a few hours ago, everybody still a little high but pretending to look civilized after a shower and four aspirin. He decided to take a stroll around the hotel, memorizing the street signs to make sure he'd find his way back. New Yorkers, he noticed, had a knack for flickering eye contact and staying equidistant from vehicles, buildings, and each other, as if they had a built-in GPS, which of course they did. It was the unconscious behaviors of self-conscious Gothamites that made them interesting, Tom decided.

After making sure that the augmented reality signposts for the flash mobbers were all in place, Tom went back to the hotel and spent the rest of the afternoon working on Swarm's missive to the masses. He didn't need to imagine what Swarm would say, for the thoughts and actions of his virtual alter ego were increasingly his own. Since his mind-melding Skype session with Lucy, Tom had started reading books about history and science and philosophy to help him understand and better articulate the unfamiliar dimension of his feelings. His electromagnetic union with Lucy had convinced him that humanity was squandering its evolutionary potential. If people could come together the way he had with Lucy, there would be no suffering, no famine, and no war because the destructive division between oneself and other human beings would no longer be possible. The manifesto that Tom was scribing was just another variable, another tool in the service of Swarm's mission, which was itself a work in progress, revealing itself incrementally with each modification of zeph.r software, each public transmission of the signal, each word that was uttered by and in the name of Swarm. It was time for the emergent rebellion to be heard and seen and felt. Once unleashed, could the genie be put back in the bottle? Or was zeph.r strong enough to replicate endlessly and trigger the next step in human evolution?

A private launch was waiting for Tom at the South Street Seaport pickup point, and even over the noise of outboard engines, he could hear an elephantine electro thump as the boat approached the private dock behind the main stage. Xander greeted Tom with a thumb and forearm clinch that he'd learned from his new friends and led him to the greenroom tent. Tom was even more eager than usual to check the A/V deck since this was his first attempt to use ARK as a springboard for a multi-pronged event in a major city. He had embedded a custom set of visual commands directing the ravers to rush the ferries to Manhattan at the end of the set and join their flash mob brethren at Grand Central Station.

Xander tapped Tom's shoulder and nodded toward the stage. When Xander reached the top of the stairs, the crowd went ballistic and a corona of photons seemed to emanate from his dark silhouette, like a solar eclipse in the shape of a man. There was a second, lesser roar as Tom took his place at the A/V station, and he made a mental note to stay completely out of sight during their gigs from now on. Fame was the last thing Tom wanted or needed, not with feds sniffing around and their impending realization that the apparently harmless pranks going on right under their noses were in fact field rehearsals by a posse of neo-insurgents.

Maybe it was the salt air, or the proximity to one of the world's most sybaritic cities, and most probably, at least in part, because it was the final stop in the ARK tour, but there was an extra jolt of energy in the air. The other DJs, the crew and the producers, everyone could feel it, and the grin plastered on everybody's face reflected the mood of relief and mutual congratulation. Even with the Vegas mishap and the growing ranks of anti-EDM picketers at every stop, the ARK festival tour had been a huge critical and financial success and a clear victory for anyone who liked music loud and unmuzzled. But what Tom and the rest of the ARK team did not know, what they wouldn't discover until it was far too late, was that at that very moment an armed flotilla from Long Island was landing on Governor's Island, preparing an ambush designed to teach the plague-infested techno geeks a lesson they would never forget. The intruders, their features obscured by face paint and ski masks and carrying wooden clubs and chains, vaulted the fence easily, overwhelming the few security guards in their path and breaking into a trot as they zeroed in on their target.

As the finale of their set approached, Xander started the countdown to "Stardust," and Tom was ready with a specially tailored message:

Do what you want.
Think what you want.
Be what you want.

Go to the city.
Keep on dancing.
Take the boats.
Take the city.

The dancers responded slowly at first, like a huge ship changing course but then turning and spilling toward the exits with gathering momentum, still moving in tandem to the beat but with a freshly charted destination. Some held their phones up, using the Swarm AR app to navigate their path to the boats and their destinations on Manhattan island.

Go to the city.
Take the boats.
Take them now
to the city,
together,
now.

The dark wedge sliced into the exiting crowd like a V-shaped raft of ducks swimming against the current, forcing their way toward the stage, pummeling anyone and everyone who got in their way. At first Tom mistook it for a fight, but the blob of black was grinding through the crowd with a clear objective. In another minute or two, they would reach the DJs, and then what? Tom hastily typed a new message into his A/V program and uploaded it. Most of the people had already surged out to the docks to board ferries and water taxis back to the city, but several hundred dancers were still in the music's grip, their eyes on the screens as they heeded Tom's new call to action.

> *Stop the men in masks*
> *Turn them back.*
> *Stop them*
> *Now.*

What happened next was inexplicable and unforgettable to anyone who witnessed it, a random collection of individuals suddenly acting with a single objective, a hundred fists raised like a hammer against those who would do them harm. The wall of hands and arms created a barrier in front of the advancing attackers and then encircled them. The intruders froze in their tracks, lashing out blindly, trying in vain to find the leaders of the countercharge. The pulverizing beat grew louder as the thugs lowered their weapons in disbelief, predators turned into prey. Then the rearing surge of humanity closed in and took them apart.

Dear brothers and sisters:

We are living proof of the transformative energy of human consciousness and the distributed genius of the crowd. As our numbers and power have grown, so has our understanding of what is possible, of why instant collective action matters. In the course of evading the authorities and helping those in need, by being ruthless provocateurs of fun and whimsy, by exploring the boundaries and possibilities of technology and common cause, we have bonded and evolved together.

Now it is time for us to change and grow again.

Listen: Do you hear that sound in the clubs and on the streets? Have you noticed that the mindless dance has lost its frivolity and taken a quantum leap? The same bold rhythms that make us smile and pump our fists are the marching drums of a militia on the move. Strength in numbers is an invisible wind, a zeph.r blowing across the land from the west, the bringer of spring and rebirth after a long, cold winter.

But before we can grasp our destiny, we must understand our history—not last year, or last century, not even to the earliest traces of man. I mean the memory buried inside, embedded in our DNA, like the gills that briefly appear on the human fetus in the womb, submerged, dormant, waiting. Look around you, my brothers and sisters—the old order is dying. But something else is being born. The networks and technology we need are already here, the hive mind is wired and globally aware. Who will control and deploy the means of our morphogenetic rebirth? Who will own the future? Better us than them. Better now than never.

We are approaching the end of the third Gilded Age.

The power of money, what money means and what it can do, all of this will be washed away by the surge of the collective, which moves at the speed of thought yet does not actually move at all, like a tsunami. We think of a tidal wave as something that travels between continents with the speed of a jet plane, crossing the ocean until it smashes against the coastline. But in fact, for most of its journey, a tsunami is simply energy being transferred from one water molecule to the next. The water itself doesn't actually move. Only at the very end of the tsunami's journey, when the shallows compress its hydraulic fury against the shore, does the wave reveal itself, rearing up in a cold-blooded curl, crushing and carrying away everything that stands before it. The new community will not be compromised by the cloud; it will not be collected and sifted by servers. It will be viral in the truest, deepest sense—person-to-person, peer to peer, phone to phone, mind to mind.

Swarm + crypto currency = Nuero$

At this moment, we are more than a million strong and multiplying every minute. Now imagine if each of us contributes one hundred dollars anonymously to the cause. That would instantly become one hundred million dollars. But if that money is collected and reissued to millions more as Nuero$, what we will have actually accomplished is the monetization of the hive mind, crowd-funding as a global financial event, immediately spawning a new crypto currency worth billions.

The enemies of distributed democracy will say that we are demented radicals, that our goals are beyond the fringe. But what threatens them most is the mobilization of the mainstream, the awakening of the masses—not just immigrants who came here looking for a better life or native-born Americans no longer welcome in their own country, but all of us together. Do you feel the cameras watching? Can you trace the moment when your phone became a leash and turned you into a moving target? We have become refugees in our own cities, the walking dead in the war against the everyman. What the pundits call politics is the pathetic clamor of mongrels fighting over scraps. Even our masters have lost their bite.

Come, my brothers and sisters, join me in the crystal waters. The wave is approaching. Some will float, and some will sink. It's high time we took them all for a swim.

Duggan looked up from his computer screen at JT, who was waiting for his reaction.

"Where did this come from? And what the hell is Swarm?"

JT shifted uncomfortably in his chair. "Well, actually, Jake, the answer is not that simple. As you requested, we ran a relational term search across all platforms, the entire NSA database, and this blog post had the highest keyword correlations from the list you gave us: militia, EDM, zeph.r, sometimes with a slightly different spelling but still statistically valid. We did a search for the Swarm's IP number, and it turned up over two hundred thousand individual addresses, none of them viable. Or I should say all of them viable since the message from the Swarm went viral."

"How is that possible?"

"We think they're using some new kind of cloaking software to disseminate their propaganda," JT explained, his tone straddling alarm and admiration. "The message is erased from the hard drive as soon as it's opened, but not before spitting it out to the next round of recipients from the receiver's own e-mail address book."

"Like a spam bot?" Duggan asked.

"Yes, but much smarter. It looks like Swarm has tapped into a phone-to-phone network that uses Bluetooth to transmit messages completely off the telecom grid. The only reason we have a copy of the transmission is because we got lucky when someone on our side took a screenshot with his camera before it self-erased."

Duggan could barely contain himself. "This Swarm manifesto— you're saying more than a quarter million people have already read it and passed it on God knows how many times, and that despite having the resources of the entire government at our disposal, we can't track it or identify the source of the damn thing?"

JT bit his lip. "All we know so far is that the message was initialized through a distributed worm-bot designed to self-publish and replicate at a particular time."

"When was that?"

"It went live the same day as the ARK festival incidents in New York."

"No kidding."

"Yeah, it's probably not a coincidence. And there's something else you should see."

JT handed Duggan a sheet of paper with words inside overlapping circles of varying sizes. "It's a word cloud. The bigger the circle, the more times the word came up in e-mails, blogs, text messages, social media posts, telephone calls, whatever. As you can see, Swarm, zeph.r and Meta Militia have a high degree of coincidence with EDM, rave plague, ARK and DJX."

"DJX?"

"That's the stage name of an electronic music star who toured with the ARK festival."

"Which was ground zero for the shit show in New York. And this revolutionary postcard hit the Net the same day."

"Correct."

"So you think this DJX is associated with the Swarm?"

"Possibly. His real name is Xander Smith. He's a self-taught musician born and raised in Austin. An FBI field agent interviewed him in Chicago a couple weeks ago. But the agent says there's no way this kid is the author of the Swarm manifesto."

"So that leaves us with Kenneth Ulrich."

"Looks that way."

"Is he the brains behind the Swarm?"

"Swarm is a metaphor," JT corrected, "an amorphous crowd-sourced symbol to rally the faithful. But the Meta Militia, as far as we can tell, is an actual organization. We've been able to intercept some of the group's internal communications, but they're encrypted, naturally."

"Can't we break the code?"

"Most likely, but it takes time. Meanwhile, if we sift through Ulrich's e-mails and monitor the grid, we might be able to correlate if and when he first made contact with the militia and whether or not he's with them now."

"So what are we waiting for?"

"Right," JT said, rising to leave. "I'll keep you posted."

Duggan rested his elbows on his desk and rubbed the bridge of his nose. Nothing about this case made sense: a deadly clash between pro- and anti-EDM groups on Governor's Island that may or may not have been orchestrated by a rogue DOD scientist, who may or may not have joined forces with a hacktivist group that called itself the Meta Militia. To top it off, the ARK incident corresponded with a series of flash mobs that were described by some observers as having been carried out with almost military precision, coinciding with a call for a cyber uprising by a dark-net movement called the Swarm.

Duggan reopened the file of media reports that JT had given him. The flash mobs began the same night as the rave and had continued into the following day, each one larger than the previous one and following its predecessor by close to exactly six hours. In the first, two hundred people in business suits converged on Grand Central Station and froze mid-stride like mannequins for more than five minutes before dispersing. In the second, four hundred musicians dressed in marching band uniforms showed up at Lincoln Center and replayed "The Battle Hymn of the Republic." At the third, six hundred people in clown costumes gathered on the streets around the New York Stock Exchange and performed zany circus routines for several minutes, before leaving trails of banana peels in all directions. All told, the rave and flash mobs resulted in nine deaths—six had been beaten to death by angry dancers on Governor's Island, the other three drowned during the ferry crossing back to New York, and dozens more had been injured at the concert or during one of the flash mobs.

Duggan browsed on to a story that explained why there were so few arrests, considering the scale of the disruptions. According to a spokesperson for the NYPD, the flash mobbers had been so organized that police didn't have time to react or even to realize that what they were witnessing wasn't some sort of promotional event for a movie, Broadway show, or the circus. "It looked to me like they rehearsed their routine a hundred times at least—I'd pay to see it again," one officer had quipped. "The strange thing was that afterward most of them said they couldn't remember why or how they got there. But you know—that's kids nowadays."

Another clip quoted an evolutionary biologist at UC Berkeley named Cara Park who had been in New York as part of a CDC task force on the Rave Plague. Park had examined ravers and flash mobbers admitted to New York hospitals and suspected a connection between the two. "What got my attention about the flash mobs," Park told the reporter, "is not just that they happened the same day as the EDM festival but that some people admitted to being present at both. They all showed some of the same symptoms of a kind of group psychosis that we've been seeing at some EDM events, namely synchronized action, post-activity depression, memory loss, and unaccountability for their actions. It was almost as if something or somebody, at least temporarily, had taken over their minds."

Duggan opened his browser and found the phone number of the UC Berkeley biology department and asked for Dr. Cara Park. When she answered, he introduced himself as an agent of the cybersecurity division of the Department of Homeland Security.

"I'm sorry, Mr. ..."

"Duggan."

"I'm very sorry, Mr. Duggan, but I already told your associate that I wasn't interested in military funding for my research."

"You didn't tell me, Dr. Park. I'm not with the DOD."

"Well, maybe not you specifically. But it was somebody else from the government. Don't you all work together?"

"Ideally, yes," Duggan said. "But that's not why I'm calling. I read your interview about the flash mobs and ravers sharing certain symptoms of mind control, as if they'd been brainwashed."

"No, not brainwashed," Cara said. "What I meant was that they seemed to share a kind of collective amnesia that may or may not be related to a virus or to some other unknown pathogen. Until we can isolate and identify the cause of the syndrome, we have no chance of finding a cure. Honestly, certain alarmists to the contrary, we're not even sure what we're dealing with here. Forgive me for getting a bit technical, but MRIs of some of the injured demonstrators showed brain alteration but no damage per se, at least not in any overtly or permanently disabling way. It's the most extraordinary thing."

"It sounds like you've started developing some theories about it."

"No, actually, we've hit a dead end, or a cul-de-sac," Park said. "I'm just a research scientist advising the CDC. I'm not a neurologist or a virologist, and I shouldn't even be speculating because it's outside my area of expertise."

"But you are a doctor, aren't you, Ms. Park?"

"I have a PhD, if that's what you mean."

"In evolutionary biology," Duggan said.

"Well, yes, that's right," Cara said, succumbing to flattery in spite of herself. "So in any case, I'm very sorry I couldn't be of more help, but I need to get back to my work."

In some part of him that was still latent and unformulated, Duggan began to like this woman. He liked the way she put sentences together and the timbre of her voice. He liked how she was smart and to the point and made sense and was confident but stopped short of arrogance. He even liked the way she was trying, politely yet firmly, to get rid of him.

"Dr. Park," Duggan said, "I'm calling because I have reason to suspect that these flash mobs we're talking about, and the illness or virus that's causing the symptoms, could be a threat to national security. There are potentially many lives at stake. It seems to me that especially because you're not a medical doctor, you might be able to help me understand what's going on here, who's behind it, and how we might be able to stop it."

"No offense, Mr. Duggan," Cara responded stiffly, "but these young people you're talking about aren't criminals, and while I certainly appreciate that you have a job to do, I really can't be a part of some government crackdown or any investigation that infringes on a person's privacy or civil rights."

Duggan paused, deciding to try a different tack.

"Excuse me, Dr. Park, but I think we got off on the wrong foot here. First, I have absolutely no intention of cracking down on people who like techno music or infringing on anybody's rights. I called you because I'm trying to find a particular person, a scientist who is in possession of government property that could be dangerous, very dangerous, to the public. These ravers—it's the techno fans themselves who are possibly in danger. My impression is that your work with the CDC has the same goal—to protect innocent people from harm. Am I right about that?"

Cara hadn't expected this—an undercover government agent talking about the welfare of ordinary citizens. He seemed nice enough, but she feared that if she cooperated with this man, sooner or later, one way or another, she would end up regretting it.

"Mr. Duggan, I appreciate what you're trying to do, and I'm happy to assist the government whenever it's using its resources for the common good. But for you to understand what my work is about and how it may or may not be useful for your investigation, you would have to come to San Francisco and see the lab and get an educated grasp of my research, and then maybe we could have a coherent discussion about the flash mob syndrome, and any possible connection between it and this person or persons you're looking for."

"I agree," Duggan said. "You tell me when you're free, and I'll be there."

Cara looked at her phone in disbelief. "That's very accommodating of you," she answered, "but I don't think that's going to be possible." Her tone was apologetic, but what she was actually thinking was, *Back off, you pushy bastard.* "You see, I'm leaving in a couple of days for a conference in Asia, and unfortunately I won't be back in the Bay Area for quite some time ..."

"In that case," Duggan interrupted, "I look forward to seeing you at your office at two in the afternoon tomorrow."

"Excuse me? Mr. Duggan, I don't think you ..."

But Duggan had already hung up.

17

The taxi took Duggan north from downtown San Francisco through the Embarcadero and across the Bay Bridge to the Telegraph Avenue entrance of the UC Berkeley campus. Though it was his first visit to the city, he barely noticed the quaint cable cars clinging to surreally sloped streets, the paint by numbers Victorian facades, the way the fog barreled across the bay and collided in slow motion against the Oakland hills. His thoughts were continually reverting to the Meta Militia's potential to hatch thousands of Donald Westlakes, all of them running amok and pointing their guns in the wrong direction.

Duggan paid the fare and wended his way past squads of backpack-toting students, across a small grove of redwoods, until he reached the biological sciences building. The door to Cara Park's office was open, but instead of seeing the intriguing woman he had spoken with on the phone, Duggan found himself facing a young man who introduced himself as Eric. Duggan noticed Eric regarding him with a bemused head-cocked expression.

"Something the matter?"

"You don't look like Big Brother."

"You don't look like Cara Park."

Eric made a noise indicating amusement. "Fair enough," he said. "I'm Dr. Park's research assistant. She's waiting for you up at the lab. We figured it would save time if I drove you up the hill. It can get a little tricky, especially when there's fog."

"It doesn't seem very foggy now."

Eric craned his neck at the sky. "That's something only a first-time visitor would say. The Bay Area is a giant collection of microclimates. The weather can sneak up on you."

"Is that why everybody here wears fleece hoodies and Gortex?"

"Yeah, I guess," Eric said. "But mostly people tend to lie around on the grass with their shirts off."

"Because it gets so warm?"

"Because it's standard behavior."

Duggan followed Eric to a faculty parking lot, where he unlocked a blue Prius. As he navigated the windy road toward the Lawrence Livermore Laboratory, Eric said, "Dr. Park told me you're with cyber intelligence."

"Yeah, Homeland Security," Duggan confirmed. "Cyber Security Division."

"Gee, that sounds pretty serious. Do you arrest guys who share music files without paying ... or people who hack PlayStations?"

Duggan decided to let the gibe slide. "I'm here to talk to Dr. Park about some software that was stolen from the Department of Defense."

"You got hacked?"

"I guess you could say that."

"What's that got to do with EDM?"

"You mean electronic dance music?"

Eric glanced at Duggan and nodded slowly. "Yeah," he said. "Cara said you were chasing some kind of techno terrorist."

Duggan crossed his arms and looked out the window. The panorama of bronze hills and eucalyptus trees overlooking schools of sailboats skittering against San Francisco's mist-shrouded skyline was breathtaking. Farther west, the crimson tiara of the Golden Gate framed the Pacific and announced the edge of the continent.

"So, Eric, what kind of work do you do at the lab?"

"Different things, but mostly software development and statistical bio-modeling. I run the numbers on the colonies, population counts, hive migration patterns—bees, ants, termites, grasshoppers, slime molds, all kinds of adorable critters."

"What's that got to do with the Center for Disease Control?"

"We're helping the CDC look for correlations between hive migration patterns and epidemics, like, for instance, signs of distributed intelligence in human pathogens, applying predictive models from one thing to the other."

"You mean correlations between bees and viruses?"

"Sure, and basically the different ways that certain populations organize and interact as single entities, or anything else with a distributed brain that can teach itself new tricks."

"The hive mind," Duggan said.

"Yeah, exactly."

A gauzy mist had begun to creep across the road, smudging out the vista. Eric eased the car into a parking space on the edge of a group of bunker-like structures. "I warned you about the crazy weather up here," he said. "Wait till you meet the people."

In the thickening fog, the buildings looked as if they could withstand a nuclear blast, which was probably the case. Eric led the way inside and down a long corridor with concrete walls and fluorescent lighting, halting in front of a pair of steel doors. He entered an access code and rested his hand on the scanner. The red LED light turned green, and the doors swung open.

"Welcome to the Berkeley bug motel." Eric grandly waved his arm over several dozen crate-size Plexiglas-fronted containers stacked in the middle of the room and against the walls, each one home to a particular species. "Just please don't feed the residents." He halted in front of the first box. When Duggan realized what he was looking at, he reflexively took a step backward. "Don't worry; they don't get out," Eric said, adding, "very often."

Duggan watched as thousands of ants, oblivious to their human spectators, clambered over each other, marching through winding tunnels with tireless determination, an endless stream of insects hauling morsels of food and mulch dozens of times their body weight, soldiers and civilians all going about their business. He noticed that some of the ants were carting lifeless bodies through the tunnels.

"I didn't know ants were cannibals."

"They're not" Eric said. "But they carry their own dead. That tunnel leads to the graveyard."

"The colony has a graveyard?" Duggan asked.

"Yup," said Eric. "It's in a chamber farthest away from where they store their food."

"Really? How many ants are in a colony?"

"In this one about one hundred thousand," Eric said. "But a super colony discovered in Hokkaido, Japan, had more than three hundred million. Each ant brain has about two hundred and fifty thousand brain cells. A human brain has about a hundred billion cells. So collectively a super colony could have ..."

"More brain cells than a human being," Duggan concluded. "So then why isn't an ant colony as smart as a man?"

"That depends." The voice belonged to a stunningly attractive woman in a lab coat.

"On the colony or the man?" Duggan asked.

"On how you define *smart.*"

She was tall and slender, with flawless caramel skin and long black hair pulled up in a businesslike bun. "Hello, I'm Cara Park," she said, extending her hand. Duggan gladly took it.

"Your associate has been showing me your little zoo."

"So I see," Cara said coolly. "They might look small to us, Mr. Duggan, even inconsequential. But as a species, ants have been doing pretty well, wouldn't you say?"

"Only a man with half a colony in his head would disagree," Duggan replied. Cara's almond eyes rested on him for a few seconds. "I'll take over from here, Eric. Thanks."

Eric bowed slightly. "I'll be in my office if you guys need me."

"Let me show you the lab." Cara led Duggan through the spotless high-tech facility, where half a dozen or so researchers were huddled around high-resolution LCDs. "Observing our insect friends is the key to what we do, of course, but biology is increasingly about analytics too."

"You're doing some fascinating work here," Duggan said. "I can see why you said I couldn't understand without coming to see the lab for myself."

She scanned his face for sarcasm. "I hope the trip doesn't turn out to be a waste of your time, Agent Duggan."

"Not much chance of that." Cara didn't ask him what he meant.

"Are all these people your students?"

"No, only Eric and two others. We share the facilities and divide the costs between various department budgets." Cara circled back and walked him down the avenue of insects. More ants, bees, grasshoppers, and he was loathe to guess what else, with less than a quarter-inch of plastic keeping them in their own separate worlds. "We have more than five million insects in the lab," Cara told him, "but there are many millions more in those computers over there."

"A synthetic model of insect colonies and hive behaviors," he guessed.

"Yes, that's right," she said.

Duggan could feel the perspiration gathering in his armpits. He couldn't remember the last time an admiring look from a woman had had such a physical effect on him, but it was time to get to the point. "When you said that the ravers and flash mobbers in New York both showed signs of mind control, did you mean that it seemed as if someone was telling them what to do, or did you mean that they were under the influence of something that made them more susceptible to suggestions?"

"I honestly can't say," she answered. "Possibly both. At this point, we still don't have enough data to make even an educated guess."

"What about the reports of people losing control of their sexual impulses? I mean, I know young people are normally kind of promiscuous, but the news articles and blogs I read made it sound like some of these events turned into full-blown orgies."

He could sense her reevaluating him, trying to read his intentions. It occurred to Duggan that ideation was an aphrodisiac, and this tentative probing of each other's mental acuity, the back-and-forth volley of hypothesis and validation, was a form of cerebral foreplay. There was something about the way Cara tilted her head ever so slightly that told him she felt it too. Some of the student researchers, two females in particular, were discreetly glancing at Duggan and whispering to each other. Was their subtextual flirting that obvious?

Cara motioned to him. "Let's go talk in my office."

She shut the door and took her seat behind her desk. The only non-office-type furnishing, aside from a couple of colorful designer lamps, was a painting of the open sea, a blue-green haze of waves and sky with no discernable horizon. There was a comfortable-looking sofa on the other side of the room, but Duggan chose a steel straight-backed chair closer to the desk. He did his best to ignore the way her maroon skirt peeked out from under the white lab coat when she shifted to face him.

"My point is that I can't I can't isolate a single cause from all the variables," Cara was saying. "I flew to New York because of the reports that the ravers were acting as a collective entity, and the CDC wanted to know if a virus could somehow be passed from insects to people. But what got my attention was that the symptom profiles of the people at the rave and the flash mobs were almost exactly the same. How could any pathogen spread so fast? My contact at the CDC promised me a summary of the lab analyses from the New York hospitals. Any correlations, or lack of them, will tell us a lot about whether we're on the right track or following a dead end."

"Please make sure you let me know when you get the data," Duggan said. "It could be important." He pointed to some large sheets of paper lying on a worktable against the wall. "Is that a map of Rave Plague outbreaks?"

"Actually, they're image maps of beehive migration patterns," Cara said, moving them over to her desk. Duggan rose and leaned over her shoulder to look. He could smell her perfume—refined, slightly citrus. Cara pointed to the lines radiating from the main hubs, which followed their own trajectory like storm bands around the eye of a moving hurricane. "These lines show the trajectories of the scouts from various hives getting ready to move. The hives are also in motion but still manage to stay at an optimal distance from each other."

"It's funny," Duggan mused, "because the maps we made of social media networks around traveling rave festivals look just like that."

Cara's eyes grew wide. She picked up her phone. "Eric, do you have the CDC's map of known Raver's Disease incidents? Yes, the national map. And while you're at it, bring that list of EDM festivals. Yes. Thanks." She turned her attention back to Duggan. "What made you think about that?"

"Well, your assistant told me that you were looking into parallels between insect migrations and viral pandemics, so I just assumed ..."

"We compared the known outbreaks to viral infection patterns," Cara explained. "But there didn't seem to be a match, which is why I don't think we're looking at a contagious viral event. But it never occured to me to cross-check the outbreaks against beehive scout trajectories. Look, they show a different kind of navigational intelligence. It's not biochemical; it's more ..."

"Electromagnetic?"

"Yes."

They were interrupted by a knock on the door. Cara let Eric in and asked him to put red dots on cities where there had been a major EDM event and superimpose those dots onto the map of Rave Plague outbreaks. She took a ruler and started connecting the outlying virus dots to the red EDM festival dots, starting with the closest ones and moving outward. The pattern revealed itself quickly—a hub-and-spoke configuration that moved on a linear axis. She placed the EDM-virus map on her desk next to the schematic of the beehive-scout patterns.

"Look at that," Eric said." The EDM raves are the hubs that connect the viral spokes...."

"Which is why the infections didn't match a classic viral-contagion pattern," Cara interjected.

"I'll bet the remaining dots form secondary hubs," Duggan said, "and that they follow the same pattern as the main signal."

Eric looked up from the maps, for the first time reading the body language between Duggan and Cara. "What signal?" he asked.

"Have you ever heard of something called the Swarm?"

"Not something," Eric corrected. "Someone." He told Duggan about Swarm's unrivaled reputation as a maestro of flash mobs and the militant blogs that had started appearing on the Internet. "He used to be a prankster," Eric said. "His flash mobs used to be mainly about having fun. But about a year ago, something changed. He's been getting more dogmatic lately. I mean, who knows, it might not even be the same person anymore."

"You said you didn't think Rave Plague was caused by a pathogenic virus," Duggan said. "And it's certainly not being caused by some flash mobber's blog. But what if it's being transmitted wirelessly by some sort of viral software? It would make a similar pattern, wouldn't it? It would look just like the scout bees looking for a new place to start a hive, and the random spokes would be following the communication pattern of individuals using social networks."

"Wow," Eric said. "I've never thought of a viral infection profile like that before, but it could be possible..."

"What could be possible?" Cara asked.

"What if Swarm's viral message is spreading through live streams sent out by the ravers themselves?"

Cara's eyes opened wide. "You mean, the same way that the bee scouts use electromagnetic signals to instantly trade information about their flight paths."

"Exactly!" Eric could barely contain himself. "Anyone watching a live feed of a Swarm EDM event on their phones would be exposed to the same frequencies as the people at the actual rave. Maybe less potent than the source, but still...The dancers' own social networks become the pathway for the Swarm's brainrave to spread!"

"Do social media platforms kept a record of who's watching somebody's else's live video stream?"

"Well," Eric answered, "they sure as hell track everything else. No offense, but good luck getting them to share it with the government."

"Let's let Agent Duggan worry about that," Cara advised.

"Eric, I definitely think you're onto something," Duggan allowed. "But for now, let's stick with the data we have. When you analyze the pathway of an actual pandemic, is it possible to run the sequence in reverse?"

"To locate and isolate the origination point of the outbreak," Cara said, completing his thought. "Eric, how soon do you think you could do it?"

"I don't know—a day or two," Eric said. "If you guys are right, then the reverse simulation should lead us right to the point of origin, assuming it came from one place. I'll set up the database script before I leave tonight. If we're lucky, I could have a synthetic model by the day after tomorrow. It all depends on how fast we can populate the program to get a rich enough data set. Some of the guys in my class owe me a favor." He looked at Duggan. "Can you give me keywords for a meta search across media platforms? How far back do you want to go?"

"Two years?"

"Shouldn't be a problem."

Cara glanced at Eric approvingly. "That's great, Eric," she said. "Let me know when you have something to show us."

"I thought you had to catch a plane to Asia tomorrow," Duggan said.

Cara and Eric traded a look. "I'll cancel it," Cara said. "This is more important."

"Thank you, Dr. Park," Duggan said. He handed her his card. "It's been a pleasure. Call me on my cell when you get the data."

Cara looked at his card. "Jake Duggan." She turned to Eric. "You go get started on the model and I'll call Agent Duggan a car."

Cara picked up her smartphone. "Are you going to the airport?"

"No, I'm heading back to the city."

"Oh, I assumed you'd go back to Washington," she said casually as she typed in the request.

"I booked a room at the Fairmont, just in case something like this happened."

Cara looked up from her phone. "Pretty sure of yourself, aren't you, Agent Duggan?" He would have taken umbrage if not for her slightly teasing smile.

"Actually, I was pretty sure about *you*," he said.

The office phone rang, and Cara picked it up.

"Hello? Rosalyn, how are you? Yes, listen, there's something I need to ..."

Cara fidgeted with a paper clip as she listened. "I see, I see. Thanks for letting me know. Bye."

"Bad news?" Duggan asked.

"That was my contact at the CDC," she said. "The director is giving a press conference in the morning."

"So what does that mean?"

"We'll find out soon enough," Cara said.

One of the researchers signaled to Cara. ""Your ride's here, Agent Duggan. I'll definitely be in touch."

On his way out of the lab, Duggan paused in front of a windowed bin containing an entire bee colony. The proximity of the buzzing creatures reminded him of growing up in Illinois. During the humid

Midwestern summers, his family would picnic with friends in the park and his mother would put out glass jugs of sugared water to catch the bees and wasps zooming over their plates. He would sit with his juice and PB&J sandwich, transfixed and terrorized by the drama of insects losing traction and falling into the gleaming death traps, an unwitting witness to the excruciating struggle that followed, antennae bent, legs akimbo, stingers thrusting fecklessly, slowly drowning in his mother's lethal nectar. Even now, he couldn't keep from imagining what would've happened if the bugs managed to escape and take revenge on their executioners.

On the way back to town, Duggan dialed JT. "Swarm is a person," Duggan told him. "A flash mobber."

"Makes sense," JT said. "So is Swarm Ulrich or the DJ?"

"Not clear yet. I'm waiting for some data at UC Berkeley that could help us find out, so I'll be working out of San Francisco for the next few days. Meanwhile, it would help if we could get the data any live video feeds made by Swarm's flash mobbers."

"You mean from people's phones?" JT asked.

"We think it might be how the Rave Plague is being transmitted to people beyond the EDM events."

"You realize that what you're asking would practically take an act of Congress," JT said incredulously. "I wouldn't even know where to start."

"Let's start with the victims," Duggan said tersely. "Maybe we can get some of them to willingly share their live video history."

There was a long pause before JT said, "I'll see what I can do, but don't get your hopes up."

"Slim chance of that."

JT guffawed. "Hang in there, pal. We're still trying to get a fix on Ulrich's location, working a possible angle through his sister in Norway. I'll keep you posted."

Duggan was about to hang up when he became aware of the clicking noise on the line. "Hello?" he said. The clicks continued for a few more seconds and then stopped.

After checking in at the Fairmont, Duggan unpacked and went to a nearby gym for a workout and a swim. It relaxed him to plow through another medium, the water enveloping him like a second atmosphere, the repetitive motion of major limbs, the automatic breathing. Swimming was a form of meditation for him, a way to wipe away the clutter. His thoughts drifted back to Cara Park. She was brilliant, insightful, and irresistible, a potentially disastrous combination if he crossed the line. He'd slept with sources before, but she was becoming indispensable, which raised the stakes on whatever did or didn't happen. Either way, it was tricky—one wrong move and he'd be back to negative one, chasing ghosts in the fog with no one to catch him if he lost his way.

The CDC's announcement was all over the media the next morning. Duggan immediately called Cara at the lab. "Did you hear? The director just declared Rave Plague a national health emergency."

"Yeah, I know," she said. "If our theory is right, this will only make things worse."

Duggan asked her to lunch, and she accepted. She told him to meet her at a Mediterranean café on Shattuck Avenue, a couple of blocks from campus. The restaurant was funky and vaguely vegetarian, with an abundance of potted vines and leafy plants flourishing in the front window. Cara arrived slightly late and a bit flustered. Her hair was loose and shiny. He ordered hummus and the lamb burger with fries and a beer. She asked for a kale Caesar salad and an organic iced tea with lemon.

"You seem a little upset about the CDC announcement," Duggan said.

"Oh, no, I mean it's great if you're a fan of martial law."

"How do you figure?"

"Invoking the All Hazards Preparedness Act is tantamount to declaring a state of war," Cara explained. "If the local and state authorities agree, there's almost no limit on government intrusion. Mandatory testing and inoculation by oral tablets, injection or aerial spraying, forced quarantine—you name it—all just became legal. Due process is out the window."

Duggan dipped a pita chip in his hummus. "You make the cure sound worse than the disease."

"Oh, yes, you're right," Cara said tightly. "Let's look on the bright side. It's probably just a cyber psychopath running around with brain-conditioning software from the Department of Defense. At least it's not infectious!"

Duggan was taken aback by her outburst. "Let's not get too optimistic here," he said.

"Believe me, I hope I'm overreacting" Cara said. "Although calling the outbreaks Rave Plague on national television is probably enough to send people running into the streets with cans of Raid and shotguns."

Duggan took his time chewing. "How's the contamination modeling going?"

"Eric's pretty sure he'll have something by tomorrow. I just hope it's not too late."

"It's not too late," Duggan said. "The software that's probably causing Rave Plague is every bit as dangerous as any biological pathogen, which is why I'm enormously grateful for your help."

Cara's demeanor softened. "What does your girlfriend think about your staying on the West Coast for a whole week?"

"What made you think I had a girlfriend?"

"I don't know. You're handsome, confident, and probably carrying a gun. I figured there was no way you could be single."

Duggan laughed. "Well, I'm not that stable, and the only guns I use are in video games. What about you? I'm guessing you aren't armed and dangerous."

"Hmm, humorous and diplomatic," Cara observed, sipping her tea. "I like that in an unstable single guy. If I were the kind of person who discussed things like that with somebody I just met and hardly knew, I mean."

Duggan smiled. "I'd expect nothing less," he said. "But just for the sake of argument, if you, for whatever reason, decided to discuss your personal life, what would you say to that person?"

"Fair enough," Cara said, pushing her hair from her face, "I suppose I would say that about three years ago, I was engaged to a wonderful guy who was looking for a cosmic soul mate, and for a while, I was that for him, and I liked it. But I was always wondering when he'd grow up, and the day that he asked me to be his wife, I ran for the hills. When he called my bluff, it turned out that—surprise!— I was the one who couldn't commit."

"Sounds like maybe he didn't know you very well after all," Duggan observed.

Cara took a bite of her salad without taking her eyes off him. "And what about you, Agent Duggan? What would you say if you were having a conversation with a woman you barely knew and she told you that she was allergic to serious relationships?"

Duggan finished his beer before answering. "I'd say she didn't strike me at all as a commitment-phobe."

"Oh, really? Based on what?"

"Well, I'm no expert, but as far as I can tell, this hypothetical woman is obviously conscientious, kind, and brilliant. Those all seem like essential and excellent partner traits to me."

Cara rolled her eyes. "You're not from the West Coast, are you, Agent Duggan?"

"No, I'm not," Duggan answered. "And I think you should call me Jake."

"Then you have to call me Cara."

"Happy to oblige, Ms. Cara."

"So, Jake, where is this mythical paradise where they make unstable single straight men who are also perceptive, amusing, and gallant?

"Chicago," he said. "But I'm probably the only one in San Francisco."

Cara seemed to mull that over for a bit, and then she waved to the waitress to bring the check. "One is all she would need."

18

Xander wandered over to Tom's bookcase and started reading the titles aloud: "*The Fantastic Inventions of Nikola Tesla, The Origin of Species, Beyond Good and Evil, Dynamical Systems and Chaos Theory, Optiks, Cryptocurrency ...*" He ran his finger slowly across the spines of the volumes. "I know about you and Swarm, Tommy," he announced. "I gotta admit you really had me fooled."

"Huh?" Tom kept fiddling with the visual-generator program on his computer, but his heart was pounding.

"You sly dog. I'm looking at your private little library—Nietzsche, Darwin, Jung, Hofstadter, Kauffman. I mean, c'mon, it's pretty obvious."

Tom did his best to remain nonchalant. "What's obvious?"

"That you've been reading Swarm's blog, man! Evolutionary catharsis, the next paradigm of humanity—that's his whole thesis! The only thing I don't get is that I've been telling you about him for ages but you were never interested. So what changed your mind?"

Tom tried to look chagrined. "I don't know. The mutant vehicles rally, all those people flowing together like a river ... I just finally got curious, I guess. You were right—Swarm's ideas are pretty provocative, all the stuff about an evolution of the collective mind. Do you think he's right?"

"Well, let's just say that I don't think he's wrong," Xander answered. "If light and matter are just bundled states of energy, different forms of some universal force that we're all made of, then who's to say that human thought isn't just another kind of wavelength on the spectrum? Sometimes when I'm spinning, I can see the music travel through the dancers, like a physical thing, and I stop seeing individual people. I don't even see a crowd. It's more like a presence, a huge shapeless animal that moves and breathes."

"A movement with a million eyes and hands, a mind with a thousand brains," Tom said.

"Yeah." Xander was squinting at his friend. "You know, it's kinda weird how much you sound like Swarm right now."

Tom laughed. "Wow, that's quite a compliment, I think."

Xander's expression was unchanged. "I'm not kidding, Tom. There's something going on out there, and I'm not sure it's a good thing. That night in New York, I saw a guy pulled to pieces right in front of me. People died, and all those flash mobs happening the same night in Manhattan … They say that this Rave Plague they keep talking about is connected to the music, the whole techno dance scene. What if they're right? What if there's something out there, drilling into people's heads? What if someone is trying to sabotage the EDM movement by releasing chemicals or viruses? The haters, you've seen them, they'll do anything to kill our groove."

Tom and Xander had only texted a couple of times since getting back from New York. After the altercation on Governor's Island, Xander was unusually subdued. He had texted Tom that he wanted to talk, and Tom had guessed immediately that something was amiss. "Xan, Xan, lighten up," Tom said. "You can't believe everything you see on the news. They make shit up just to fan the flames."

Xander was undeterred. "I saw it with my own eyes, Tom. They tore the arms off his body. I saw the looks on their faces, the way they walked. It scared me. Those people were tuned into some kind of negative frequency."

"I know. It was pretty weird."

"Plus Homeland Security gave me a buzz."

"They *called* you?"

"Yeah."

"Not the FBI guy?"

"No, somebody named Duggan, Agent Jake Duggan. He asked me about some hacker group called the Meta Militia, and Swarm, too."

"He asked you about Swarm?"

"He wanted to know if I knew him or if I'd ever been contacted by him."

"What did you say?"

"I said that everybody knows Swarm and nobody knows Swarm. He's the grand guru of flash mobs."

"True enough."

"Tom, I came to tell you that I've decided to lay off live performances for a while. With Homeland Security sniffing around and the paranoid vibe that's taking over the whole EDM scene, I need a break. What if we're responsible somehow, even indirectly? What if Swarm was on Governor's Island? How in hell would we even know? And this freaking techno flu. The government just declared a national health emergency, in case you haven't heard."

"It's all bullshit, Xan," Tom said. "Propaganda from the fearmongers."

"Maybe, but it's just not worth it anymore. Not to me. Not if there's even a possibility that somebody's using us to hurt people and sabotage EDM. Anyway, the ARK tour is done and we've got plenty of money. So who cares if we take a time-out? Just until things settle down."

"If we give up, then the bad guys won."

"Look, I'm just talking about the live stuff. We can keep recording. I've got a ton of new song ideas. We'll write the next 'Stardust.' Then we'll see. I told Fabian, and he's cool about it. He says I'm ready to go more mainstream."

"So you're just going to drop everything and hang out in Austin, trade in your Maserati for a platinum pedicab?"

"LOL," Xander said. He started drumming on the bookshelf. "There's a girl in Barcelona. I met her on the tour, and she invited me to visit. I've always wanted to see Spain. I think I'm gonna take her up on it."

Tom could tell that Xander's mind was made up. He also knew that getting off the grid for a while was the smart thing to do. Homeland Security was only one or two steps away from connecting him and Xander to Swarm. Better to play it safe, lay low for a while, and plan the next move without the feds snipping at their heels.

Tom held up his arms in a sign of surrender. "You're right, Xan. It's a good time for a break. You'll see, in a couple of months, nobody will remember the Rave Plague. Go see your girl; have some tapas. The last few months have been nuts. Maybe I'll take a vacation myself."

Xander brightened. "Yeah, man, that's what I'm saying. Come join me in Europe. We'll do a road trip to Morocco or, even better, Berlin. The Germans will never shut down techno, it's in their DNA. We'll have some techno kicks and sauerkraut!"

Tom had heard the stories about Berlin, the legendary mecca of EDM, where people from all over the world convened to rave for days at a time without stopping to eat or sleep. It would be easy to disappear in the ether of the afterhours, careening through the clubs, flying under the radar.

"Sounds like a plan, Xan."

Xander gave Tom bumped fists. "I'm glad we powwowed."

"Me too," Tom said.

A chat request popped up on Tom's screen, which Xander took as his cue to leave. "Give me a few days and then get ready to buy a ticket to Germany," he said. "Auf Wiedersehen!"

"Ciao."

LucyintheSky: why won't you answer my Skype requests?

Swarm1171: you know why

LucyintheSky: tom, what happened that night was beautiful. i never
    felt so close to anybody. so alive—ever. i can't explain it, but in

my dreams I can hear your thoughts sometimes. what you're planning to do is insane

Swarm2791: really?

LucyintheSky: once u start this, how do u know u can stop it?

Swarm8696: who says i'll want to stop it

LucyintheSky: you don't know the full effects. nobody can

Swarm9075: that's exactly why it has to happen

LucyintheSky: just let me see u, touch u. one time.

Swarm1113: I told you. it's too risky, now more than ever

LucyintheSky: not fair! ☹

Swarm2022: I'm sorry, Lucy. I'm going away for a while. maybe after I get back

Lucyinthesky: if you don't meet with me i'll go to the police

Swarm 0716: stop talking crazy

LucyintheSky: you're breaking my heart!

Swarm0327: ;(

LucyintheSky: i love u

Swarm3309: i luv u 2

LucyintheSky: then please, please, please

Swarm4649: we have lingered in the chambers of the sea. don't blame me. Forget me. i don't exist.

Swarm4649 is offline

Duggan was having dinner in his room when Cara called. He had spent the past twenty-four hours reading over the background materials JT sent him, including a set of decoded messages between members of the Meta Militia. Most of it was rambling neo-anarchist nonsense, but one post had stopped him cold. It claimed that the militia had recently taken possession of a "top secret weapon." The message included the warning that the weapon was "being tested and readied for use against its own makers" and that the militia would not rest "until the sovereignty of the human mind was acknowledged and protected under international law as a universal and inalienable right that can never be suspended, amended, retracted, or denied." The post ended with the boast that "the Swarm is raging around you, if you just know where and how to hear and feel it."

Duggan still wasn't sure if Swarm was an individual, a splinter cell, or a false idol devised to inflame and distract, but the danger he represented was definitely real. If Swarm had zeph.r, then Swarm knew Ulrich, or was Ulrich, and one or both of them were members of the Meta Militia. What he still didn't understand was how the militia planned to use the zeph.r code to punish the DOD. Or had the covert operation already begun? Duggan had a queasy feeling that the Rave Plague was just the opening salvo of a much broader offensive.

Duggan's mobile lit up and rang like an old analog phone. It was Cara, and she sounded stressed.

"Jake, I need to see you right away."

"Are you okay?"

"Yes, I'm fine," she said. "It's the hospital report summary. I don't think we should discuss it on the phone."

Duggan hesitated, feeling the heat on his face even before he uttered his response: "Why don't you come to the hotel? I'll meet you at the bar."

Thirty minutes later, Duggan watched Cara stride into the Fairmont looking effortlessly swanky and carrying a leather portfolio. This time he allowed himself to consider the implications of the black cashmere sweater, designer jeans, and coyly lavish diamond stud earrings.

"I need a drink," Cara announced, sliding into seat next to him. "I'll have a Booker's Bluegrass, neat, please."

"Two," Duggan told the bartender, who looked at Cara and said, "Nice to see you again, Dr. Park."

"Nice to see you too, James." Before Duggan could say anything, she explained, "I work here sometimes. We helped the hotel establish bee hives on the roof."

"It's none of my business," he replied. "Your roof project sounds cool, but there's nothing more impressive than a woman with good taste in bourbon."

"Is that so? A friend of mine likes to say, 'Reality is an illusion created by a lack of alcohol.'"

Duggan grinned. "You have good taste in friends too." When their drinks arrived, he raised his glass. "To bees and bourbon." They drank.

Cara bit her lip before lowering her voice. "What I came to tell you is directly related to your case, which is why I didn't want to talk about it over the phone. Just trying to be careful."

Duggan thought about the strange clicks on his phone. "I appreciate it," he said.

"Rosalyn Cooper just sent me some data."

"The woman from the CDC?"

"Yes, I think I told you she had agreed to send me the lab summaries from the people who were hospitalized after the flash mobs in New York. The CDC is operating under the assumption that the Rave Plague is being caused by some kind of infectious agent, a virus or bacteria. But when I saw the lab summaries today, there was something else, something I've seen before, except not in people."

"I'm listening."

"The flash mob patients in New York showed signs of dehydration, traces of various party drugs, alcohol, and psychological trauma, but they also showed extremely high levels of serotonin."

Duggan took another gulp of Booker's. "Wait a minute—you think the Rave Plague is a reaction to serotonin?"

"No. Well, yes, to a certain extent, but it's potentially much worse than that. As you know, one of my areas of expertise is locust swarms. Locusts, most of the time, are ordinary grasshoppers. But under certain conditions, principally a lack of food combined with overcrowding, the grasshoppers' serotonin levels skyrocket and they enter what entomologists call a gregarious phase, which is marked by aggression, increased strength and sexual activity, and an impulse to gather and move in huge numbers. The grasshoppers transform physiologically into locusts. They literally get bigger, stronger, and meaner, but also they become capable of acting as a single entity."

"The locust swarm becomes a hive mind."

Cara nodded.

"And you think serotonin is triggering locust behavior in the ravers?"

"Possibly—it would explain a lot."

Duggan was feeling lightheaded, and not just from the Booker's. "Okay, so let me ask you this: if humans enter this gregarious phase, could they be controlled, directed to do things against their will?"

"I think so—or the things they already want to do get amplified, impossible to resist."

"And could the same state of hyper suggestibility be caused by aural stimulus or an electromagnetic pulse?"

"You're talking about the flash mobs, the hacker who writes the blogs?"

"Yeah," Duggan said. "I'm talking about Swarm."

"Let me show you something." Cara unzipped the portfolio and pulled out several color printouts of the human brain. When Duggan saw them he drained his glass and raised two fingers to the bartender for another round.

Cara laid the images out on the bar and leaned close to Duggan. When their hands touched, she didn't move hers away. "Some of the hospitals did MRIs of ravers who had lost consciousness. See this?" Cara pointed to a chart of left- and right-brain functions. "The right brain is generally considered the nexus for creative and emotional expression, nonlinguistic sounds, and music. The MRI scans showed that the patients' right hemispheres were lit up like Christmas trees."

"You think the signal was still transmitting to them?"

"The signal—or something else," Cara said. "What worries me is that if whatever is causing this locust effect in people keeps spreading, or if the rave crowd gets big enough, there may be a threshold point at which it triggers a locust-like transformation. It could create a human swarm with similar properties as actual locusts."

They savored the bourbon in silence for a minute. Then Duggan turned and took Cara's hand. "You are absolutely incredible," he said. "I'll warn my bosses at NCSD, but you've got to tell the CDC that there's no virus."

"Jake, I can't do that. I have no scientific basis for it. The locust effect is just a hypothesis, pure conjecture. You don't even have proof that Swarm actually exists. I could be totally wrong—and so could you. Besides, it's already too late."

"It's not too late to prepare for the worst," Duggan said.

"Fine. But first you've got to find who's doing this, Jake. Maybe Eric's model will help."

"I'm counting on it." Duggan pulled back and gazed at Cara. "You know, you'd make a great federal agent."

"Oh, really? Even though I don't like guns?"

"Believe me, all you'd have to do is show the bad guys those brain charts and they'll surrender immediately."

Cara laughed. It was an honest, inviting sound.

"Wow," Duggan said suddenly, "I can't believe what's happening!"

"What is it?"

He pulled her close and whispered into her ear. "I think I feel my serotonin rising." This time they laughed together.

He could feel the warmth of her leg against his. Their hands found each other, fingers gently probing, skin cells sending signals to their brains. He kissed her and nuzzled her neck.

Duggan moaned. "This is such a bad idea," he said.

Cara reached for her glass and took a slow, thoughtful sip.

"A terrible idea," she agreed. "Plus you're unstable and ..."

Duggan kissed her again and waved for the check.

"From Chicago," he said.

19

Duggan's head ached as he surveyed the familiar flotsam of a one-night stand: half-empty whiskey tumblers, furniture festooned with discarded clothing, a faint whiff of perfume on the pillows. But Duggan knew there was nothing trivial about what had just happened, and not merely because Cara Park was a crucial source and collaborator on the most important case of his career. In the midst of their carnal calisthenics, the tumbling tangle of bodies and limbs, skin to skin, he could feel himself being pulled into her glowing orbit like an asteroid basking in the sun's invitation to stick around and unfurl its inner comet. The eye-watering catharsis of self-discovery was not an emotion Duggan usually associated with torrid sex, but when he attempted to articulate his feelings, she had placed her finger on his lips as if to seal the words inside him, keeping them safe from unnecessary exposure or scrutiny, available only on a need-to-know basis, along with the rest of their clandestine affair.

After showering and ordering a large pot of black coffee, Duggan's first instinct was to send a message to Koepp, but he needed Eric's map before he could call for backup. Instead he called Cara, who was out for the morning with teaching obligations, her administrative assistant informed him, but Eric would be happy to meet with him at the lab at eleven. Duggan confirmed the appointment and turned on the TV while he dressed. The CDC pronouncement had ignited a firestorm of paranoia and public outrage. At least fifteen states were considering laws that would indefinitely outlaw public gatherings of more than a hundred people for any reason, and pressure was mounting on the federal government to take a stand. Drugstores and pharmacies were experiencing a run on Cipro, an antibiotic known to be effective against anthrax, and schools were suspending assemblies and playtimes. Never mind that the CDC had yet to identify a single virus or bacteria responsible for Rave Plague syndrome or confirm that the outbreak was in any way contagious.

Erik was waiting outside the building when Duggan's car pulled up. "Cara's sorry she can't be here—it's her day to teach—but she told me to tell you to meet her at five forty-five pm in front of the campanile," he said. "Do you know it?"

"The big clock tower on campus."

"Yep, that's the one," Eric affirmed. "Anyway, Cara told me about your, um, conversation last night. I mean, about how the Rave Plague might be a manifestation of the same serotonin surge as locust swarms. And she told me that you think that what happened in New York was possibly caused by some kind of electromagnetic pulse. Pretty amazing stuff."

Duggan shook his head. "But it's not enough," he said. "Cara said the locust connection was still just a theory, without hard evidence. I don't even have a solid link between Swarm and the Rave Plague outbreaks."

Eric raised his finger and smiled. "I think you're going to like the results of the Rave Plague geo timeline I just finished," he said. "But first I want to show you something."

Eric led Duggan down a hallway and ushered him into a storage room stuffed with discarded electronic gear. He pointed to a dishwasher-sized heap of sheet metal, transistors and wires held together with duct tape and bungee cords.

"This," Eric announced with a sardonic impresario's flourish, "is PHAROH."

"Pharoh?"

"It's an acronym for Poly-Harmonic Audio-Redactive Omnidirectional Hardware," Eric said. "It's designed to interrupt the neurons that trigger serotonin production in locust swarms. We field-tested it in East Africa last year on actual locusts. PHAROH's signal succeeded in canceling out the emergent cohesion of the locust swarm, it even killed a few, but the electromagnetic field was only a few hundred yards wide...."

"So PHAROH was a failure."

Eric frowned. "That's what Cara would say. But the test confirmed an emergent link between the locusts that had never been scientifically measured, which was pretty big news at a recent conference, and, most important, it actually did neutralize and disable the locusts that were flying in a proximity bubble around the plane."

"So what went wrong?"

Eric pointed to another clump of metal next to PHAROH. "See that battery pack? Batteries like that are expensive and really heavy."

"So if it had more power, you think PHAROH would have worked."

Eric shrugged. "More power, more money, more time ..."

"You're suggesting PHAROH could be used to disrupt an electromagnetic signal at an EDM rave?"

"I'm not suggesting *anything*, Agent Duggan," Eric said, using a conspiratorial tone. "In fact, for the record, I never even showed you this. But I'm sure that if anyone can keep a secret, it's you." Eric closed the storage room door and led Duggan back to the lab, where he halted in front a jumbo-sized LCD screen and opened a folder marked "Swarm."

"This first image is, of course, a map of the USA," he said. "The orange dots show the location of every outbreak of Raver's Plague recorded by the CDC, which means that the hospitals had to suspect a cluster or something else out of the ordinary to report it to the feds, which takes us back only about six months. The smallest dots represent outbreaks of five people or fewer; the biggest ones are outbreaks of five hundred or more."

Eric opened a second US map with a series of green dots on it and superimposed that over the first one. "Now this one shows every stop of the ARK EDM festival, all twenty dates nationwide."

Eric was waiting for Duggan's reaction. "You see it, don't you?"

"The Rave Plague outbreaks don't match up with the ARK festival."

"Not until Las Vegas."

"So we're back to square one."

"Not necessarily. It just means that there was some kind of game change in Vegas, no pun intended."

"You think Las Vegas is the source of the Swarm signal?"

"I was thinking the same thing, but then I remembered that Cara said the New York ARK show—and you can see it's by far the biggest orange dot—and the Manhattan flash mobs seemed to overlap, both in symptoms and participants. So I called a buddy of mine who is a fanatical flash mobber. He had an IM trail of every Swarm flash mob for the past 18 months. I charted Swarm's flash mob events with yellow dots, which made it possible for me to do *this*."

Eric called up a third map with yellow dots and layered it over the other two patterns. "Beginning in Vegas, Rave Plague outbreaks and flash mobs correspond in every US city, except for one in Texas, where Swarm's flash mobs preceded the Vegas correlation by almost a year." The yellow dots were so thick that they almost blotted out the name.

"Damn," Duggan said. "Swarm started flash mobbing in Austin!"

"Bingo! And it looks like he joined, or started shadowing, the ARK festival in Vegas. So all you have to do is find out which DJ from Austin joined the ARK tour in Vegas ..."

"And I'll find Swarm," Duggan said.

The Berkeley bio-emergence engineer and the Homeland Security agent high-fived, causing several heads to turn.

"Will you e-mail me a copy of those maps?"

"Sure thing, Agent Duggan. Just give me a few minutes to compress the files ..."

But Duggan was already typing into his phone, heading toward the exit.

An hour later, as Duggan was logging in to the NCSD secure conference line with his boss and JT, a file popped up in his secure in-box. It was a government photo of Kenneth Ulrich. He was younger than Duggan expected, with cropped blond hair, steel-rimmed spectacles, chiseled features, and a meticulously trimmed beard. He walked JT and Koepp through Eric's map and waited for their reaction.

"This is very interesting, Jake," Koepp said. "But we were hoping you were going to tell us that you'd found Ulrich and had him in custody."

"Not yet," Duggan said. "I think I know where he is. I think I know what he's been doing. If I can find him, then I'll know what he's planning to do next."

Even over the video screen, Koepp was visibly disappointed. "Do you think you could be a little more specific, about Ulrich's location, I mean?"

Duggan realized it was going to be a harder sell than he expected.

"I get that you suspect Ulrich has been using the stolen DOD software to cause the Raver's Plague," JT said, trying to sound supportive. "Meanwhile, the Austin-based DJ who was questioned by the FBI, Xander Smith, has left the country with no forwarding address. But you don't think he's Swarm, because you think Swarm is still in Austin. Is that right?"

"It's mainly circumstantial at this point, but yes," Duggan admitted. "I think I know a way to smoke Swarm out, but I can't do it alone."

"Is the Meta Militia based in Austin too?" Koepp asked.

"Impossible to say since it communicates via slave PCs and encrypted IRC channels on 4chan/b/," Duggan said. "The militia base, if there is one, could be anywhere. I've been working with an evolutionary biologist at UC Berkeley. One of her people made those maps I just showed you. But we need to move on this guy before he changes tactics or disappears again."

"Ulrich, you mean."

"No, a flash mob blogger named Swarm, who's working with Ulrich and who's probably also connected to the militia and several other cyber-anarchist groups."

"Let me make sure I'm following you," Koepp said. "You think an attack is imminent, but you have no material proof except for some threatening blogs by the Meta Militia and someone who calls himself Swarm and who may or may not be Ulrich, or associated with Ulrich, but you have a biology-based theory that he's hiding out somewhere in Austin, Texas?"

Duggan fought to tamp down his impatience. He knew the case was still half-baked, but his gut told him that every hour of delay increased the chance that Swarm would slip away. He was also annoyed that JT seemed to be playing devil's advocate by taking Koepp's side against him. He took a long breath, choosing his next words carefully.

"When I came back from Afghanistan and said the DOD was hiding something about the Westlake shooting, nobody believed it," Duggan said. "My report was blacked out and put in my boss's bottom drawer. But my hunch turned out to be right, didn't it?"

"Sure, Jake," Koepp allowed, "You were absolutely vindicated. But Kenneth Ulrich is an actual person, and the zeph.r signal really exists. This Swarm character is pretty nebulous. There's just not enough tangible evidence. You're asking us to ignore the CDC, sound the alarm to the director, and put all our credibility on the line for a hunch."

"If you're wrong, it won't be just your neck on the chopping block, Jake," JT added.

There was a lull, and Duggan sensed he was about to get shut down. He knew the prudent course was to submit to reason and err on the side of caution, live to fight another day, but he couldn't bring himself to do it.

"Let me put it this way," he said. "As officers of the National Cyber Security Division, I think you would have to agree with me that Stuxnet, Olympic Games, and Conficker are real; the blackouts in New York, India, and Rio were real; the cyber-attacks on Google, Sony and Apple were real; and WikiLeaks and Anonymous are real; and the unprovoked massacre of allied Afghan troops by a US drone pilot named Donald Westlake really did happen."

"Of course," Koepp said.

"Then you should know that what seems like impossible crackpot science fiction one day can all too suddenly become a hard cold reality the next. In fact, it's almost guaranteed. You just haven't accepted it yet because there isn't enough tangible evidence."

"Jake, Jake," JT protested, "nobody is saying—"

"Let me finish," Duggan growled. "I'm telling you on the record that Swarm and the Meta Militia is real, and if the zeph.r software that Ulrich stole from DOD is deployed, we'll all be facing something a hundred times worse than any of those other incidents. And all I'm asking of you, as two fellow agency officials entrusted with protecting the nation from precisely this kind of threat, is to help me do everything in my power to stop it from happening *before* it happens." Duggan paused. "This conversation is being recorded, right? I just want to be sure."

Duggan's colleagues looked at each other. Their flattened faces stared back through the screen and he could almost see the audio tape replaying in their heads.

"All right, Jake," Koepp said. "Tell us what you need."

The UC Berkeley campanile was the same building identified on Duggan's campus map as Sather Tower. He could see why Cara liked it, a gray-stone spire that lorded over a grove of gnarly sycamores with a kind of monolithic grandeur, a good place to take a break from class, read a few pages of poetry, or wait for a surreptitious tryst. He spotted Cara heading toward him on the sloping path. In her skinny jeans and leather jacket, her head bent over a smartphone screen, she could easily be mistaken for a graduate student hurrying to meet her thesis adviser. She was almost on top of him when she looked up.

"Oh, you're already here."

"I'm very punctual," he said.

"That's good," Cara said, "because the concert starts in ten minutes and we've got some climbing to do." She took his hand and led him toward the base of the tower, pausing to fish in her purse for a key to the door that opened toward a small interior lobby with an elevator. "C'mon in—don't be shy," she said.

"Did you say a concert?"

"Never mind," Cara faux scolded. The elevator doors shut, and the car began a slow climb to the observation deck. "Now pay attention because there may be a quiz. Please keep your hands to yourself, Mr. Duggan. There's no groping the teacher during class. After dinner is another story."

"Yes, professor."

"Where was I? The campanile you are presently inside of is the third largest bell and clock tower in the world. It's three hundred and seventeen feet tall and was built in 1914 and designed to resemble the famous clock tower in Venice. Have you ever been to Venice?"

"Not yet."

"That will cost you half a grade, but you can make it up by taking me there someday." The elevator doors parted, and Cara pointed the way up a steel-stepped staircase.

"There are sixty-one bells in the tower, the largest of which weighs ten thousand, five hundred pounds. Do you know why there are sixty-one bells, Mr. Duggan?"

"No idea," he said.

"It's because the top of this campanile is home to a full-scale carillon."

They had reached a wooden landing and entered a chamber filled with church bells of every conceivable size. Duggan felt himself transported to a time when bells weren't just for marking hours and announcing the next class period but also a means to alert populations to impending danger and amplify moments of profound significance. Something moved in the rafters, and he braced himself for a Quasimodo apparition.

"Hi, Agent Duggan. Glad you could make it!" Eric waved to him from the raised platform. "I'm starting in about sixty seconds. I hope you like Philip Glass."

"You should see your face, Jake," Cara said, reveling in his astonishment. "A carillon is a concert instrument made of bells that can be played with a keyboard."

"What's Eric doing here?

"Eric is a fellow at CNMAT, the Center for New Music and Audio Technologies. CNMAT includes the carillon in its curriculum and allows qualified students to perform concerts in the campanile several times a week. And tonight is Eric's turn."

The bells began to peel, a plangent, minimalist chord cycle. Two higher notes mitigated the melancholy and anchored it to a haunting, repeating progression. Duggan felt the mammoth chimes reverberating through his body, saturating his senses. During the stirring recital, he noticed some words engraved onto the biggest bell, a tone poem in every possible way.

The music stopped, and Eric emerged from the belfry to greet them. "What did you think?"

Cara and Duggan broke into heartfelt applause. "It was one of the most incredible things I've ever experienced," Duggan said. "I didn't know much about Philip Glass, but I just became a fan." "Well done, maestro. Bravo!"

Eric took a bashful bow. "So glad you liked it. The piece is adapted for carillon from his solo piano works—'Metamorphosis One.' It's a reference to the novel by Franz Kafka."

"Which is about a man who turns into a cockroach," Duggan pointed out.

"Indeed it is," Eric said.

"Eric has a fine ear for music and bio-irony," Cara observed proudly.

"Now, I understand why bells are put in churches to summon the faithful," Duggan said. "And the music they make is fantastic, but what's their connection to advanced technology?"

"A number of things, actually," Eric said. "We're working with the Music Genome Project. It's what powers that app on your phone that finds the name of a song you like that's playing in a bar or a restaurant. Anyway, we're working with them to identify the numinous elements of music, the common denominator in religious hymns, African slave spirituals, Handel's *Messiah*. You know, the sound of inspiration and rapture."

"The voice of God," Duggan intoned.

"Yes, exactly!"

"Kind of like the poem inscribed on that bell over there." Duggan pointed and enunciated the words:

> *We ring, we chime, we toll.*
> *Lend ye the silent part.*
> *Some answer in the heart;*
> *Some echo in the soul.*

Eric clasped his hands over his head. "Whoa, that's freaking awesome. I can't believe I never noticed it!" He retrieved his phone and took a photo of the inscription. "Anyway, the other project with CNMAT is about hooking up the bells to the Internet. See those magnets up there?" He pointed to several oblong contraptions mounted next to the bell clappers with motorized hammers and dangling wires. "Eventually they'll be connected to a wireless remote control digital player. A church in Siberia already uses the same software to perform for masses and holidays. The priest loves it."

"And the congregation too, I'm sure," Duggan said. "So once it's wired up and operational, a pianist in Russia could do a guest gig on this carillon without ever having to get on a plane and actually be here. You could hook these bells up to another keyboard, a laptop, anything."

"Yeah, pretty much," Eric agreed.

"How about a DJ deck?"

"Ha!" Eric crumpled over, pointing to Duggan. "Dr. Park, this guy! This guy is *too much!*" Eric righted himself and took a breath. "Sorry, it's been a long day," he said, composing himself. He gathered his things and bounded for the stairs. "I gotta run. Thanks for coming, and enjoy your dinner. I hear the place is dope!"

Duggan turned to Cara. "That was an amazing surprise. Thank you."

"You're very welcome."

He leaned in to kiss her, then caught himself.

Eric's voice echoed up from the stairwell. "No worries. I already know, and I definitely approve. My lips are sealed—unlike yours."

Duggan took her to dinner at one of the Bay Area's new gastronomic hot spots. Bearded waiters in crisp striped shirts and wool waistcoats hovered vigilantly. Duggan and Cara sat at a dimly lit table for two and ordered a Santa Barbara Zinfandel and postmodern tapas made from organic ingredients grown at local farms. Duggan's rising euphoria was tempered by his corresponding vulnerability. He felt like an emotional hemophiliac. One little scratch and he might bleed to death.

"Gee, a smart, beautiful woman, good food, *and* church bells—I must be in heaven," he said.

"Or at a wedding," Cara quipped. "You haven't even tasted the duck yet."

"Listen to me." Duggan reached across the table and intertwined his fingers with hers. "You are an incredible woman. I'm ecstatic about this, about us. But I must confess that I have a terrible track record with relationships. The last thing in the world I ..."

Cara held up her hand. "Wait. Before you go any further, I have my own confession to make. I am a total relationship-*phobe*. I mean, not partially but totally. Especially when I feel like this, the knowledge that there could be real emotion and connection, it's like a self-destruct button. I start analyzing and second-guessing every move, yours and mine. I start thinking it's all just chemicals and synapses firing, biology taking its course. Hormones, the genetic imperative, commanding us to have sex, to *think* we care."

"Wow." Duggan retracted his hand and leaned back in his chair. "I'm just wondering who's going to fight for this relationship, because it's certainly not one of us."

Cara shrugged. "Beats me. And I'm not into threesomes."

"Me neither," Duggan said, "for the most part."

"Then I guess we're screwed," Cara said.

"Yep," Duggan agreed. "So can I sleep at your place tonight?"

"Absolutely."

They stared into each other's eyes, and he refilled their glasses. Somehow they'd managed to sidestep the usual booby traps. Despite their personal baggage, so far it was a clean slate, a good start. The food, the wine, and the vibe all conspired to convince Duggan that this was the real deal. He put down his glass and waited for her attention. "There's something else we need to discuss," he said.

"Shoot."

"I saw Eric's maps, and I showed them to my bosses at the agency."

"How did that go?"

"They're giving me the federal and local authority to make an arrest. Now all I have to do is produce a suspect."

"Jake, I get it. You need to find Swarm. And you will."

Duggan took a long sip, steeling himself. "Cara, I have no right to ask you this, but I'm getting desperate."

"I already said I'd sleep with you."

Duggan smiled wanly. "I want you to go on TV and talk about your theory, just the way you explained it to me at the bar the other night. I'm asking you to make a public appeal to Swarm as a scientist, to tell him that what he's doing has potentially disastrous effects that he doesn't understand, that he can't control."

"That's all true," Cara said as she ate.

"And I want you to say that you're willing to meet with him. I want you to pique his interest, make him come to you."

Cara stopped chewing and slowly wiped her mouth. "You want me to go on TV and ask for a date with a cyber-terrorist?"

Duggan nodded. "That's exactly what I want."

"And you're not even a little worried about my safety?"

"Of course, I am. That's why when he contacts you, you're going to insist that the meeting happens in a public place. You can let him choose the venue, but it has to be out in the open. That way I can protect you."

"And you can catch your mystery man, your elusive Swarm."

"That's the idea."

She seemed stunned, appalled. He reached for her hand, but she pulled it away.

"What makes you think this sociopath you're after will even talk to me?"

"Cara, he's a techno-anarchist, not a serial killer. This person is extremely intelligent, a former Defense Department scientist who defected for personal reasons. Trust me—he'll want to hear your theory. There'll be a small army of agents and police on the scene. You know I'd never do anything to put you in danger."

"The Rave Plague signal is military software?" Cara shook her head. "Jesus Christ, Duggan. And you guys wonder why the government gets a bad rap."

"Cara, this guy is a public menace. Innocent people have already died, and if I can't stop him, this is only the beginning. Because of you and Eric, we're on the right track to get him. Nobody has your skills, and you've helped me get this far. Do this and you'll have done your country a great service and saved many lives, including mine."

"Okay, hold it right there," Cara said. She picked up her glass and drained it. "I liked it better when you were asking me for a sleepover."

"I still am," he said.

Tom was blasting Joy Division's "Love Will Tear Us Apart" as he hurriedly packed and reviewed his mental checklist. The song always cheered him up, which was arguably counterintuitive for an English band that had taken its name from the prostitution wing of a Nazi concentration camp. In a couple of days, he would be joining Xander in Berlin, but first he had some loose ends to wrap up, one of which was attending a meeting with an evolutionary biologist named Cara Park, who had appeared on local TV to appeal for an audience with Swarm.

"You don't know me," she said to the camera in a video clip that had gone viral on YouTube, "but if you really care about your followers, then you have to hear me out. There are dangers in what you're doing, consequences and repercussions you can't possibly anticipate. Please contact me before it's too late, for your own sake as well as the millions who have heard and heeded your message." The talk show host tried to get her to say more, but she insisted that only she could deliver the details of her warning to Swarm—in person.

Park's message had both intrigued and disturbed Tom. He obviously had a weakness for beautiful women who spoke directly to him through a camera lens. But what, if anything, did she actually know about zeph.r? Was it a fishing expedition or a trap? He was going to

225

find out, but he would take proper precautions. It didn't ultimately make any difference, because the Tom Ayana who lived in Austin was part of a life that he was leaving behind, like a snake sloughing off its old skin in order to keep growing. He would miss his mother, but in most ways that mattered, he'd checked out a long time ago.

Tom took it as a positive sign that Austin's annual South by Southwest Interactive conference happened to be in full swing. The city was packed with techies and social media mavens who had come to mingle and swap business cards during the nonstop barrage of meetings, product demos, and sponsored parties overflowing with free food, drink, and branded industry swag. The hordes of hackers, software engineers, and mid-level media managers were his kind of people, the kind that checked their mobile devices every ten seconds to get details about the next presentation or event they absolutely couldn't miss, the kind who knew that the only thing cooler than being in the know about a paradigm-shifting innovation was having co-written the business plan.

It wasn't hard to find Cara Park's e-mail and send her an encrypted message to meet him at a place where he controlled the environment and everything that happened in it. The zeph.r code was safe in the cloud, but now that Park knew Swarm was in Austin, the feds wouldn't be far behind. Tom decided that Xander had picked an opportune moment to take a vacation and that Berlin was a perfect place to get high and lie low, moving by night through the underground club circuit, an internationalist hyper-creative community that would embrace them, absorb them, and conceal them for as long as they needed or wanted. He didn't even have to learn German.

Cara called Duggan the minute she received Swarm's text.

"Read it to me exactly as he wrote it," he told her.

"All it says is this: 'Dear Professor Park, I saw you on television talking about Swarm. You seem unusually informed and intelligent for an academic. I'd be happy to hear your theories about human evolution. Meet me Thursday for the SXSW Gaming Expo at the Palmer Center. Find the Luminescence multi-player contest and log in under your own name. Wait for me in the grove of aspens behind the castle at exactly three in the afternoon. I'll join you there as Mr. Aws.'"

"That's all?"

"Yes," Cara confirmed. "What's Luminescence?"

"It's a virtual reality game."

"He wants me to meet him in a game?"

"It's a fantasy world where people appear as avatars who can communicate with each other by typing or talking into voice-recognition software."

"Like a chat room."

"Yeah, but more visually elaborate," Duggan explained. "You know, as in speech bubbles. You need to answer him."

"What should I say?"

"Just say you'll be there."

"Anything else?"

"After you answer, don't touch your computer," he instructed. "I'm sending some men over now to do a trace on the text. I'm sure he's covered his tracks, but just in case he made a mistake. My associates are heading to you now with a copy of the game and headgear. They give you a crash course on Luminescence today so you can navigate the game and find the virtual meeting place tomorrow. They'll bring your credentials for the conference too."

"You're not coming?"

"I've got to make sure we've got a proper reception waiting for Mr. Aws. I'll be there to meet you at the Austin airport at noon."

"Jake, how can you be sure that Mr. Aws is Swarm?"

"Typical hacker humor," Duggan noted.

"What do you mean?"

"Mr. Aws is Swarm spelled backward."

Tom had cleared his room of incriminating material and was ready to go by the time he sat down at the kitchen table for a farewell lunch with his mother. She was humming a Mexican folk tune as she served him his favorite home-cooked meal—huevos rancheros with beans and rice and plenty of chile verde sauce. She put the plate in front of him, with a cold glass of limeade to wash it down. It gave her pleasure to watch her son eat. It was the only time she had his full attention. "Why are you going to Shanghai?" she asked him. "You don't even speak Chinese."

Tom laughed and wiped his mouth with a hand-embroidered napkin. "It's for business, Mom," he lied. "Besides, everybody in the world speaks English, even the Chinese. I've got to do something downtown, and then I'm heading straight to the airport to catch my plane."

Sonia frowned. "How can you go so far away without taking any luggage?"

"My bags are already at the airport." He got up from the table and wrapped his arms around her. "Don't worry. I'll call you from Shanghai in a week so you'll know I'm okay." He put a wad of thousand-dollar bills in her apron pocket. "Here's some money, Mom. All the bills are paid for the next six months, and your bank account will be refilled automatically."

Sonia pulled out the cash and tried to give it back. "It's too much, M'ijo. What am I supposed to do with all this?"

"Buy yourself something nice," Tom said, slinging his backpack over his shoulder. "Or give it to the church."

"I'll ask the Virgin to watch over you and keep you safe," Sonia said. "I told Chevo the same thing when he left."

Tom felt a familiar pang, but all he said was, "I love you, Mom. You know that, don't you?"

"You're just like your father," Sonia said matter-of-factly, "always moving between the light and the darkness, living in two worlds." She took his hands in hers and squeezed them. "He says he's proud of you for helping your *tía*. He says not to be afraid of this thing you're doing in the electric world, that place the computers take you. He says to trust the meaning of your name."

Tom was absolutely dumbfounded. For all these years, ever since he was a child, Sonia had never spoken so frankly about his father. He was a shadow, a cipher that only festered in his imagination, a yawning abyss banished and buried by anger and grief. And now here she was, suddenly chatting about Chevo like it was no big deal.

"Mom," Tom said. "How do you know Dad wants me to trust my name?"

"Because he told me," Sonia said. "He talks to me all the time."

Tom walked out the front door and down the steps to the car waiting to take him to the Palmer Center. Better to let the authorities think that Swarm was still in Austin, or if they somehow managed to track him back to Tom and his mother, she would point them to Shanghai. Besides, the megabucks grand slam version of Luminescence to which he'd invited Dr. Park was restricted to players who registered for the Austin expo. Millions would be watching online and betting on the outcome, but you had to be present to compete. SXSW Interactive was Tom's home turf in his hometown, and he couldn't imagine a more fitting setting to take a final bow before disappearing in a puff of pixelated smoke.

Tom took a last glance at the house where he'd grown up and saw his mother standing on the front porch. The potted prickly pears clustered around her feet reminded him of the painting of the *Virgen de Guadalupe* that she kept in her bedroom. Had Sonia stood amid the cactus thorns to watch his father on the day he left to catch the plane to Alaska? Tom knew she didn't wave good-bye to his dad, because she had never accepted his departure. She never lost hope that he somehow avoided or survived the crash, or if he did fall from the sky, that the Virgin would find his spirit wandering the icy slopes and guide him home. For all of Tom's life, even with the years piling up and grinding her down, Sonia never stopped taking care of herself, keeping the house ready, cooking Chevayo's favorite foods, cleaning up, and sitting by the window until long after dusk.

She didn't wave to Tom either.

It was hard to imagine anything trickier than apprehending a nameless and faceless suspect in a crowded, cavernous space that was equal parts trade show, amusement park, and video game arcade. In the hour that he'd been at the expo to prep for the takedown, Duggan had been engulfed by fake fumes from ersatz volcanoes, accosted by a loquacious robot, and nearly run over by a pack of remote-controlled racing cars. Applause and laughter mixed with Wagnerian music, floor-shaking thuds, and amplified explosions as roving gangs of conference attendees clogged the aisles and collided with queues of fans waiting to take their picture with costumed actors from the latest superhero hit.

"How are South by Southwest techies like beauty queen contestants?" Duggan overheard someone say. "One, they want to make the world a better place. Two, they want to be Googled but won't let you touch. Three, they get free drinks everywhere they go."

Duggan had taken every conceivable precaution to ensure that Swarm was captured and removed as a threat to the nation's peace and cyber security. Fifteen plainclothes NCSD agents, two of them posing as gamers, were strategically placed around the interior of the expo. At least as many Austin police officers were stationed outside

230

the exits on the unlikely chance that Swarm somehow managed to get that far.

Cara had taken her homework seriously, adjusting the virtual reality headgear and playing Luminescence with her federal tutors until the wee hours before packing to catch her flight from San Francisco to Austin, practicing diligently to make sure she didn't get lost, captured, or killed on her way to her tête-à-tête with Mr.Aws at the castle. To her own surprise, once she acclimated to projecting herself into a digitized doppelganger in a dreamlike 3-D environment, she found the fantasy kingdom and its strange denizens oddly captivating. She liked the way the players' thoughts appeared in speech bubbles above their heads and how shape-shifting between avatar personas was an accepted form of self-expression. The scientist in her wanted to know, for instance, why the trolls clustered together and shared a cranky, pugilistic disposition. Were irascible people drawn to trolls because they reflected their actual temperament or did being a troll mold one's personality the way Halloween costumes tailored the dispositions of those who wore them? Not to mention the unicorns. But as the minutes until her meeting with Mr. Aws ticked away, she found her thoughts shifting to the even stranger reality of agreeing to meet with a suspected real-life cyber terrorist in a make-believe world to discuss an untested theory that might or might not prove to be Swarm's undoing. And the whole thing was happening in the congested sensorium of a technology conference crawling with undercover federal agents, one of whom was her secret lover. *My God,* Cara told herself. *You have fallen into the rabbit hole and are about to have an audience with the Mad Hatter. How will you ever find your way out?*

The meeting with Swarm was still forty minutes away, and Duggan's stomach was churning. He took an antacid and adjusted his wireless mike for the fourth time. Cara had already taken her place with the other early arrivals at one of the video game consoles clustered under an array of oversize HD LCD screens that would soon come alive with the sights and sounds of 250 fanatical contestants engaged in an accelerated cash prize round of Luminescence. He decided to take a stroll around the expo's perimeter and check on his agents.

As he walked past a row of demo laptops, he noticed the LED camera lights blink on as he passed. Duggan stopped and so did the cameras. He stared back at the unblinking apertures, refusing to accept the possibility that he was being tracked and watched. *Relax, it's just a computer display gag.* He pushed the more disturbing possibility out of his mind and circled back to the Luminescence arena, where many of the player consoles were already occupied, mostly by men in buzz cuts, baseball hats, and hoodies, all of them waiting to don their headgear and storm the virtual kingdom and collect their share of the half a million dollars' worth of enchanted gold coins strategically sprinkled across the realm.

Duggan alerted the agents on his closed communication network. "Keep your eyes out for the man in the picture," he instructed. "To join the game, he has to be sitting at one of the player consoles." He had circulated the DOD staff photo of Ulrich to his agents, but most of the men in the room were wearing VR goggles and sporting varying degrees of facial hair. "Stay frosty and keep in mind that he might have shaved or changed his appearance."

There was a trumpet fanfare and an ebullient roar as the LCD screens lit up to announce the official start of Luminescence. The players activated their virtual devices, and within seconds creatures of every description were storming through the gates, fanning out in every direction. The clang of crossed swords mixed with howls of pain as the players in the vanguard were cut down by a squad of black knight bots on horseback. A growing clot of SXSW spectators gathered to watch the crusading contestants on the giant monitors and cheer them on, but Duggan kept his eyes on the screen that projected Cara's activities. He knew Swarm was somewhere in the room, but they wouldn't know for sure until he revealed himself by making contact. Cara had picked a yellow-and-black bumblebee as her avatar, and he spotted it soaring above the mayhem in a steady course toward the castle. It circled and drifted down into the grass and pretended to browse some flowers as NCSD agents incarnated as white knights loitered nearby. Within moments, a hooded figure in a long monk's robe glided into view.

"Let the monk pass," Duggan instructed the agents. "Duel with each other so he doesn't get suspicious." The knights did as instructed, and the monk advanced. The bee turned to face the intruder, and the monk bowed in courtly greeting. The speech bubble created by the word translation software in the player's headset microphone appeared, and Duggan knew the game was on.

Dr. Park, I presume.

Mr. Aws. Nice to meet you.

The pleasure is mine. I like your bee. I hope it doesn't sting.

The bee danced in a circle and fluttered its wings.

No, of course not. I came to warn you. The signal you are using raises the serotonin levels in the brains of your subjects. I've seen this before in locust swarms. The serotonin induces morphosis.

The monk came closer and bowed.

Interesting. Tell me more.

The bee transformed into a green grasshopper.

All locusts begin as grasshoppers. Starvation and crowding triggers the serotonin secretion, and they begin to change, both neurologically and physically. They become stronger and more aggressive, sexually and otherwise. They also begin to exhibit emergent behavior, a unified consciousness that's driven by primal urges and appetites.

The mild-mannered grasshopper began to change. It got darker and bigger and started to buzz angrily. Then it reverted back into a harmless bumblebee.

Very impressive, but your demonstration just proves my whole point: as Stuart Kauffman argued, self-organization and complexity are already built into our DNA, and now we have our finger on the biological trigger.

I'm sorry. I'm not sure I follow. What trigger?

Darwin was only half-right; he couldn't have anticipated the impact of technology on our capacity to initiate change in our own environment. You see, all we need to do is create the correct conditions for an accelerated form of human emergence.

My God, Duggan thought, *it's him.* He recognized the syntax from the Swarm blog, the same intelligence and chilling confidence, the erudite rant of a terrorist with bio-global ambitions. Duggan was proud of Cara. She had quickly earned Swarm's respect and had gotten him to open up to her. He wanted her to understand what he was doing and why, one scientist to another, they were sparring on neutral terrain before retreating to their respective corners.

It's too dangerous, Mr. Aws. We've seen the brain damage and violence that comes with uncontrolled emergence. The locusts become ravenous, marauding predators, cannibals. We don't know the immediate implications or longer-term consequences for our own species, especially if the mutated humans are allowed to reach critical mass. What if you can't control what you've started? Are you ready to take that risk?

The monk chortled dismissively.

Human beings routinely slaughter each other by the millions. They assassinate, torture, and mutilate, often in the name of their supposedly benevolent gods. They create systems and hierarchies that crush the weak and the poor. They stuff their faces while others starve. They build weapons of mass destruction to protect arbitrary borders and obliterate their rivals. Children are given guns or are sold into prostitution. Innocent people are jailed and tortured for their skin color or social class or religious beliefs. Others blow themselves up for the same reasons. And you're worried that I might encourage bad behavior?

The white knights stopped fighting and were beginning to creep closer.

Tell your knights to back off, Dr. Park, or I'll make them go away.

What knights?

The monk raised his hand, and twin bolts of lightning struck at the hapless swordsmen. They changed color and flickered, and then they were gone.

"What the hell happened?" Duggan demanded into his mike. Nobody knew. "He's right under our noses at one of those consoles. I need a visual ID—now!"

"Sir," an agent responded, "everybody looks the same with those headsets on."

"Then get closer to the players and see if you can hear him talking to Dr. Park through his microphone."

Mr. Aws, maybe what you say is true, but shouldn't people be allowed to choose? Who gave you the power to decide how and when they evolve?

That's rich, Doctor! Who gave me the power? Why, it was you—the white-coated sorcerers of the governing class! It was scientists like yourself who devised the means to supercharge human minds the better to fight your wars without errors or moral reservations. And how long would it be before someone decided the same technology could be used to shape the thoughts of ordinary people, turning them into unquestioning slaves, for their own good, of course. Just look at history and ask yourself if I'm wrong.

So fine, then let democracy run its course. Let the people decide for themselves.

No, that's my point—the choice was made by our government when it declared war on the free will of its own soldiers, when it failed to recognize and respect the sovereignty of the human mind. The only remedy, the perfect justice for this crime, is to unleash the hive on its would-be masters.

Swarm, it's me, your Lucy in the Sky. I'm sorry to interrupt, but I've got to see you before you leave.

Cara wasn't sure how long the pretty princess avatar had been watching them. She had luxuriant blond curls cascading around her shoulders and was regally attired in a white dress and a crown of floating diamonds. Mr. Aws turned and faced her, but there were no thunderbolts.

Lucy, what are you doing here? This isn't a good time. Go home. I can't talk now.

Can't you feel how connected we are? Ever since that night, I see you in my dreams, even when I'm awake.

Please don't make me hurt you.

"Sir, I think we have an audiovisual." Two agents zeroed in on a player in the middle of the tenth row. The man seemed agitated, as if fending off something—or someone.

"Get ready," Duggan said. "I want you to keep your distance, but cut off his exits. I want a takedown plan with double backups. What the hell is that princess doing there? Who the fuck is Lucy?"

What about your own freedom, Mr. Aws? You know they'll try to stop you. What good can you do in prison? Is it worth it?

Yes, you have a point, Dr. Park. In fact, I should probably take my leave before those agents lurking in the aisles make their move. It's been a pleasure.

Mr. Aws, don't go yet. I can help you.

Swarm, I'm sorry about what I said last time. I'm not mad anymore. I understand what you're doing. You are a prophet, and I see that now. I just want to talk. I'll wait for you in the lobby. I'm wearing white, just like my avatar. I love you.

But the monk was already raising his arms, summoning a breeze that became a howling wind that swept across all the player's screens and battered the battlefields and forests and alien habitats of Luminescence. The hurricane became deafening as it grew in size and ferocity, lifting up trees and buildings, knights and dragons, trolls and unicorns, draining the lakes and sucking the blue sky itself into a voracious funnel that wrenched the entire kingdom loose from its circuits and wiped it off the LCD screens, erasing every trace of Luminescence, leaving nothing but a gaping void of dead black frames.

Pulling the plug on a virtual world in the middle of a half a million dollar competition at a packed expo had a number of instantaneous effects, not the least of which was hundreds of apoplectic gamers jumping to their feet and screaming at the organizers and producers, who were scrambling around with flashlights, desperately trying to figure out what had gone wrong. The outcries of shock and dismay attracted another crush of gawkers who rushed over to see what the ruckus was about, fueling the mayhem.

"Don't let him get away!" Duggan ordered into his mike, but it was already too late. Did Swarm also set off the fire alarm that triggered a stampede for the exits? Duggan didn't have time to speculate. "Outside! Tell the Austin PD to grab him on the plaza! Do you still have a visual?"

"Yes, sir. We're in pursuit. Except—"

"Keep on his tail. I'll be out in a minute."

Duggan fought his way across the clogged rows of game consoles to reach Cara, who was shaken but otherwise unscathed. "I'm fine," she said. "Go on. You have to catch him!"

Outside on the jammed sidewalks, the exiting crowd had been joined by more than a hundred amateur clowns. Big ones, small ones, scary ones, and funny ones, all of them juggling, tumbling, and mugging for the pedestrians, who stopped to laugh and gape. It was as if Luminescence itself had spilled from the servers and emptied onto the streets, spreading its madcap spell over people and things, a fun zone of players being played by the game. On every intersection surrounding the Palmer Center, convoys of mutant vehicle bicyclers and teenage student drivers inexplicably converged and collided helter-skelter into each other, snarling traffic, oblivious to angry shouts and honks from stalled commuters. Before the agents and police could apprehend him, Swarm melted into the mayhem, just another geek in the teeming techie mash-up.

"Which way?" Duggan demanded. The agents pointed to a hooded man who had broken from the pack a couple of blocks away, hurrying up the avenue, his head down as he typed into his phone. The agents' vehicles were trapped in the student driver gridlock, so Duggan and his men continued their pursuit on foot, dodging clowns and cars, gradually gaining ground. They were closing in when a flurry of pedicabs materialized around their target, moving in formation with uncanny precision. Duggan watched helplessly as their quarry jumped into the lead cab and disappeared with the foot-powered fleet down a side street.

"Goddamn it!" Duggan shouted, winded and seething.

Cara was waiting for him back at the Palmer Center. The look on his face told her what had happened. "I'm so sorry, Jake," she said. "But maybe it's not over yet." Cara turned to the young woman standing beside her. "Agent Duggan, there's someone I'd like you to meet. This is Susan Oliver. She says she's Swarm's girlfriend."

Part III

EVOLUTION

21

The dust devil did a manic mambo on the blacktop and moved across the road to molest a gaggle of camera-toting tourists before unspooling. Watching from the car, Tom considered the cruel genesis of the wrinkled arroyos and stratified spires protruding from the desert floor like exclamation marks. He knew the scenic overlooks along Arizona's Route 179 did a good business catering to visitors intent on capturing digital recollections of the red rock vistas. But out beyond Sedona's commercial encampment of psychics and shops full of vortex maps and Jackalope postcards, he also glimpsed the sculpted remains of a geological last stand against entropy, a graveyard of mineral-rich mountains stripped to their bones and left in the sun to bake in their own pretty ashes.

Xander insisted on sending a driver to pick Tom up in Phoenix and bring him to the hideaway he was leasing from an A-list actor shooting a movie in Asia about Genghis Khan. "You'll never find it on your own," Xander boasted, "not even with a GPS."

Arizona was quite a departure from their month-long hiatus in Berlin, where they had immersed themselves in the local EDM demimonde, staying with DJ friends in the louche former East Berlin area of Friedrichschain. Their lair was stumbling distance from refitted power stations and factories where insomniacs roamed murky chambers outfitted with heavy shades to blot out the dawn and keep them undulating to the beat, alone and together, grinding their hips inside the rhythm machine, taking refuge from their worries and obligations, napping for short intervals in the crannies and nooks around and between the monolithic speaker banks, oblivious to everything except the steady thrum of electrons spinning and sparking in the artificial night.

During their fourth week in Germany, Xander announced that he was looping back to Barcelona for a few days and then flying home to rekindle his muse and work on some new music. Tom stayed behind in Berlin, content to continue sampling the post-Soviet charms of Bitte, developing a taste for Bavarian beer and bratwurst and monitoring the EDM scene through industry colleagues and the 4chan b-tards, who were busy helping Anonymous take down a gang of Russian ransomware pirates. Since absconding to Germany, Tom had continued his campaign of electronic samizdat, and Swarm had begun to surface in the cultural mainstream, sometimes in reference to a shadowy cyber insurgent who had amassed an underground army of followers, sometimes as a catchphrase to describe a dawning realization that the true danger posed to society did not come from any single person or group but from the metastasizing grip of the Internet itself, reigniting the debate over the nature and limits of personal responsibility and social freedom, except that this time the argument was being monitored and measured in an echo chamber of blogs, texts, and tweets.

Was Swarm a person or a movement or something much more elemental, something hidden in plain view, like air, and just as ubiquitous? That day at the expo in Austin, conjuring flash mobs to flummox the feds, Tom had never felt more liberated and empowered. It was almost as if he had stepped out of Luminescence and into the physical world with a corresponding power to summon an unstoppable wind. By commanding the minds and actions of others in real time, his synapses had begun to fire in concert with a larger nerve center, a brain that was no longer his alone or limited by the physical and neurological limitations of his own body. How else to explain Lucy's uncannily timed appearance at SXSW than the possibility that, under certain circumstances at least, zeph.r's effects were not completely temporary. The intensity of their fusion had opened a door that could never be completely closed, no matter how much he tried to shake off his emotions or forget her desperate pleas as he pulled the plug, not just on their relationship but the entire virtual world that had once contained it.

Sitting in a café built of bricks recycled from the Berlin Wall, Tom pondered his predicament. He had created Swarm to protect himself, but the twined tango with his shadow self had become symbiotic. He was no longer merely speaking through Swarm; he was relying on Swarm to give him a voice that was echoing through the cyber-verse to a degree that even Tom found astonishing. But how could he lead the insurrection as a furtive fugitive in European exile? The cutting-edge video installations of W33.tv, Room Division, and other Berlin innovators were tempting platforms for a widespread zeph.r transmission. But the anti-rave backlash trying to shut down EDM culture in America, or the new *Kulturekampf*, as the Berliners called it, had also started to surface in Europe. Tom couldn't risk attracting attention to himself, certainly not at a time when the search for Swarm was becoming an international cause célèbre. By hopscotching across dark nets in cyberspace, Tom could communicate with anyone anywhere without leaving a digital footprint or deliver the mesmerizing graphics from "Stardust" along with his blogs and the zeph.r code in a downloadable app. He had even updated Swarm's avatar so that a single pixel was added to his image with the arrival of each new viewer, rendering his visual appearance as a pulsating aggregation of microdots, the hive mind in a faceless humanoid form. Newspapers and websites around the world started publishing screenshots and video clips of Swarm's stochastic silhouette, and one night, on his way home from the clubs, Tom passed a young German sporting a Swarm T-shirt. Tom wondered what the journalists and fans would say if they knew that every version of Swarm's protean portrait, by virtue of becoming minutely modified by the very act of being seen, was intrinsically unique.

Despite his close call with the authorities in Austin, Tom was undeterred from his quest to use zeph.r as a bridge between the ineffable energy of collective thought and the quantum holy grail of particle physics, a tool that could pierce the membrane between omnipresent but unseen forces and reveal a unified supersymmetry of pure, transformational awareness. He knew that the laws of evolution were on his side and that it was only a matter of time before he found a way to gather the cranial critical mass that Dr. Park had warned against. But where and how? Maybe there was a clue to his next move in the way Swarm's call to action was ricocheting around the planet, across borders and languages, gaining traction by the nanosecond. Tom had been scouring the Web for the latest manifestations of his alter ego, tracing the semiotic Braille of hyperlinked meme pathways, when he got the text from Xander inviting him to Sedona.

"We're almost there," the driver announced as they approached the end of a box canyon. Just when Tom was sure they could go no farther, the car took a sharp right and started climbing an escarpment on a dirt road that eventually dead-ended at a speaker box welded to a rusty red gate. The driver pushed the call button, and Tom heard Xander say, "Open sesame!" The motorized gates swung aside. They drove another ten minutes before Tom saw the house, a protruding blade of glass and steel stabbed into the mesa overlooking the north exposure of Cathedral Rock.

The front door was ajar, and Tom entered the sleek, cool interior, following a muffled thrum through the bamboo-floored rooms until he found Xander ensconced in the center of a makeshift studio, bobbing to the beat with a pair of headphones covering his ears, surrounded by a panoply of glowing consoles, LED screens, and keyboards, all connected to a tangle of wires strewn across the floor like linguini. Tom spotted an analog Moog Sub Phatty synthesizer and a vintage theremin in its original wooden console with what looked like a stubby car radio antenna poking up.

Seeing Tom, Xander removed the headphones and opened his arms wide. "Ditat Deus!"

"Amen, brother."

Xander dropped his arms. "Dude, it's the Arizona state motto. It's Latin for 'God enriches.'"

"Music to my ears." Their hands clenched in greeting.

"You have no idea." He pointed to the theremin. "Ever seen one of those?"

"Yeah, in books anyway," Tom replied. "It's the first instrument designed to be played without being touched. You could use it in our next gig."

"Whatever," Xander said. "I missed you, man. I have to say, I wasn't sure you'd actually come. Still too much heat in Austin to go home?"

"It's why you're here in middle of nowhere, isn't it?"

"Maybe I just needed a change of scenery."

Tom pointed to a silver metal box about the size of a toaster oven stashed in the corner. The front-panel display had old-fashioned knobs and dials and a gleaming cathode-ray tube. "What's that little gizmo?"

"Oh, that's a Rife square wave generator," Xander said. "It was built in the nineteen thirties by a scientist named Royal Rife. He believed that by exposing the brain to specific microwave frequencies, you could change people's moods, improve their health, and even cure cancer. Our host—whose name I'm forbidden to utter by a legally binding NDA Agreement..." Xander leaned forward and silently mouthed the actor's name. "He said I could use it, so I thought it might be interesting to see if the Rife beam box could be synched with the Omnisphere, you know, to intensify the audiovisual effects."

"That would be sick," Tom said,

Xander flipped the switch, and the Rife sprang to life. The dials flexed behind the indicator panels, and the cathode throbbed with a purplish glow. Even from across the room, Tom could detect a faint oscillating whine, a sound that was unexpectedly, excitingly familiar.

"Wow, that's pretty intense," Tom said, covering his ears with his hands. "Are you sure it's safe?"

"Well, my landlord uses it all the time, and he looks pretty healthy." Xander clicked off the Rife. "I thought this would be a good place for us to get some work done. No interruptions, just like the old days, you know?" He got up and gripped Tom's shoulder. "C'mon, let's have a drink. In the freezer is some ice wine I brought back from Berlin. There's some killer sativa too."

Xander retrieved a pair of tumblers and a tall, thin bottle filled with a clear liquid from the mesquite and granite bar and led the way out to the terrace. "This stuff will blow your mind, and if it doesn't, the spice in the pipe definitely will," Xander said as he uncorked the bottle and filled their glasses. "It's made from late harvest grapes that freeze in the first frost. The pulp separates from the skin, releasing concentrated flavors and, some say, the grape's true spirit."

Tom lifted his glass. "To icy spirits and warm climates!"

"To hot women and cool mixes!"

The ice wine was dense, sweet, and bracing. Tom gazed into the gaping canyon and marveled anew at the g-force of their social acceleration. In less than two years, Xander had progressed from drug-dealing DJ wannabe to discerning oenophile and friend of unnamable movie stars who kept vintage microwave-beam generators in their bathroom. "This kind of reminds me of Vegas," Tom said, "only better."

Xander's smile melted. "Nope, it's nothing like Vegas or New York." He lit the pipe, took a hit, and passed it to Tom. "This house is built on a vortex, you know, a geo-dimensional power spot. Do you feel it?"

"I do," Tom said, holding his breath. "I most certainly do." He exhaled and took another exquisite sip. "So, Xan, the ice wine and this cool-ass crib definitely don't suck. But what are you really doing here, besides ignoring the headlines and playing with Rife beam in the bathroom?"

Xander's gaze hardened. "I told you, I came here to work. I'm writing stuff for the next record and working on music for a film. Fabian thinks it's a good move for my artistic cred. He says sound tracks are the next big thing."

"No kidding. What movie?"

"Hang on." Xander dashed into the house and came back with a Velo-bound typed manuscript.

Tom read the title aloud: *"Ocean's 9/11."* He flipped through the pages. "It's a joke, right?"

"Yeah, definitely," Xander agreed. "It's a rom-com about a terrorist attack on Vegas."

"Didn't that kinda already happen, during ARK?"

"But *actually*!" Xander took another drag and put it on the table. "I'm glad you brought it up. You know, I've been reading J. Krishnamurti, the Indian philosopher. He says we all want to be famous because we think it will give us freedom, except that the moment we aspire to be famous, we are no longer free."

"Is that why you stopped touring, because you felt trapped by your fame?"

"No, I already told you. I stopped doing live gigs because the vibe went sour and people were getting hurt. In Spain, some people were saying that EDM DJs are techno terrorists."

"That's bullshit."

"Agreed, but still. In the Spanish press, they called me a murderer, Tom. A *matador*." There was an ache in Xander's voice that Tom had never heard before.

"Look, I hear what you're saying. I feel it too, a change in the barometer, a shift of gravity. But I can't back away or hide from it. We can't stop being who we are."

"Who are we, Tom?" It was more of an accusation than a question. "I've been thinking that maybe things happen for a reason.

Maybe there's a lesson, a message of some kind, in all the strange shit going down."

"Who's message?"

"I don't know. But I thought if I turned down the volume for a while, I might be able to hear it." Xander deferred to the yawning silence before continuing. "I went on a little excursion the other day, up to the Hopi reservation. It was pretty interesting. Maybe we can take a ride tomorrow and I'll show you around."

"What's at the Hopi reservation?"

"Injuns!" Xander made a savage face emitting tribal hoots and Tom had to laugh. "There's a guy who's friends with my actor pal," he continued, "He took me to a ceremony, you know, with a shaman, near a place called Prophecy Rock. It's kind of a big deal to get invited, but this guy's pretty plugged in with the locals. Anyway, it made an impression. I see things differently now."

Tom considered the impassive walls of sandstone across the valley, tiny fissures burrowing into the rock for thousands of years, then one day the whole cliff collapses. "I feel the same way, buddy."

"So then you'll come to the reservation with me?"

"That's not what I meant," Tom said. "But, yeah, sure. Why not?"

"Awesome!" Xander jumped to his feet in celebration. "Wait, I wanna show you something." He went into the house again and came out with a book-sized tablet. He tapped the screen, and sheets of water began to spill along the patio roof, glistening panels of liquid enclosing them on three sides. The temperature dropped immediately, and the acoustics shifted. Cathedral Rock was still visible, deconstructed and blurred into a flickering watercolor.

"You're kidding me," Tom said. Even in his enlightened state, Tom noted, Xander hadn't tired of cool toys.

"It's called hydro-architecture, walls made of moving water." Xander stood up and pushed his finger through the translucent plane. "Tom, let's try something. If you go out and get on the other side, I'll get my camera and take your picture through the water." Tom went outside on the terrace and slowly pushed his hands and face through the liquid curtain.

"Wow," Xander said, snapping away. "The colors are fucking incredible. You look like you're passing through the portal to another dimension. It's kinda scary."

"Yeah," Tom said. "It is."

Fluorescent lighting was cruel to most people, but Susan Oliver looked poised and lovely as she patiently waited in the interrogation room at Austin police headquarters. Her blonde curls and long white dress clashed with the drab surroundings, making her seem like a creature from another world, which, Duggan considered, was more or less true given the circumstances. There was nothing remotely exotic about the man in the blue suit sitting next to her, who reflexively glowered at Duggan as he entered the room and took his seat.

"Hello, Susan. It's nice to see you again. I want to you thank you for taking the time to come in today."

"Hi," she said sweetly. "Nice to see you, too, Agent Duggan. I think you've already met my lawyer, Mr. Reyman."

"Yes, I have," Duggan affirmed. "I'm sure he's informed you that you are not a suspect and that I just want to ask you a few questions."

"On the condition that I can ask you some questions too," she replied.

"I can't promise that I'll answer them, Susan, but you're certainly welcome to ask."

"You can call me Lucy. I mean, it actually makes more sense, you know?"

"Whatever you prefer, Lucy. Is that why you're wearing the same dress you had on at the gaming expo?"

"I guess."

"And maybe you could help me understand why you changed your mind about coming to talk with me?"

"Agent Duggan," Reyman interrupted, "may I remind you that my client is here of her own volition and doesn't have to answer any of your questions if she doesn't wish to."

"It's okay, Mr. Reyman," Lucy said with a rebuking tone. "Agent Duggan, I'm here against my attorney's advice. But it's only fair that you know I didn't come here to help you. I came to help Swarm, you know, Mr. Aws. It took me a while to figure that out, so here I am."

"What do you mean by help Swarm?"

Lucy shifted in her seat and tugged on a lock of buttery gold hair. "Well, like I told Professor Park, the main thing is I don't want him to get hurt. I was there at the expo, and I know he's in a lot of trouble ..." Lucy put her hand up to her mouth, her eyes glistening with concern for her phantom lover, a person she knew only as a faceless body and an avatar called Swarm. "If I help you catch him, will you promise me he won't get hurt?"

"You know I can't do that, Lucy."

"Then can you at least promise me that I can have a couple of minutes alone with him before you take him away?"

"A couple of minutes, yes," Duggan said. "Alone, no."

Lucy wiped her eyes and pushed her hair back behind her ears. "I figured that was the best I'd get."

"You really care about him, don't you?"

"Do you know what it feels like to love somebody, to touch each other's souls across space and time, and yet you can't ever be with that person? Physically, I mean."

Duggan tried to look empathetic.

"So tell me, Lucy, what did you touch in Swarm's soul?"

"Agent Duggan," Reyman objected, "we had an agreement that you would respect certain boundaries about Ms. Oliver's relationship with Mr., ah, Swarm. This man played with my client's heart, and he owes her an apology and an explanation."

Hearing a lawyer refer to a suspected cyber terrorist as if he were some kind of deadbeat boyfriend was almost too much for Duggan. He looked at the ceiling and took a breath before resuming.

"Lucy, in your online dates, did Swarm ever talk about his plans, about where he was going next, what he was planning to do, anything like that?"

She nodded and sat up straight in her chair. "Right before he left for China, before that last time I saw him in Luminescence, he said that he was close to reaching the critical mass for bio-emergence. I mean, he didn't actually say it. I just knew. He was looking for a big event, lots of people, a party or a concert. And he was working on a device to make the mutation process go faster and mobile."

"What did he mean by making mutation mobile?"

Lucy shook her head. "I don't know," she said. "I really have no idea. But if you take me to where he is and let me talk to him, I'll do my best to find out."

"But you've never seen his face, so how can you even be sure it's him?"

"I know what he looks like inside. I'd see it in his eyes. Trust me, I would know."

"And you're willing to travel if necessary?"

"Sure, whatever it takes."

Reyman held up his hands. "That's absolutely out of the question, Agent Duggan. How could you possibly ..."

Lucy gave her lawyer a fierce look of reproach that froze him midsentence.

"I'll go wherever you want, Mr. Duggan," Lucy said. "I can feel him changing. Don't ask me how, but I can. I know he misses me, and he feels bad about hurting me. He's afraid of me because I'm the only thing that could hold him back from the next level."

"The next level?"

"Morphosis, the next evolutionary step in our species."

"But how could you hold him back?"

"Because I'm the only one who knows his other self. You know, the part that's still human."

The looping threads of oscillating notes and beats were still echoing in Tom's ears as the murmur of men's voices reached him from the other end of the house. Tom and Xander had spent the remainder of the previous night in the studio, listening to DJX's latest tracks and experimenting with ways to integrate various electrical patterns and riffs with the Theremin and Ominsphere, blasting weird ululations at decibels that literally raised the hair on their arms. After Xander had turned in for the night, Tom carefully unlatched the Rife generator and used headphones to secretly sample its mesmerizing modulations. The device itself was quaintly primitive, but the four-hundred-page instruction manual stored in the machine's carrying case, with its meticulously indexed menu of mind-altering frequencies and recipes on how to manage and mix them, was a gold mine. Tom now had all the components he needed for a full-scale deployment of zeph.r. He could hardly wait for a chance to fine-tune zeph.r's turbo-charged capability to fuse words and music into electromagnetic commands.

Tom pulled on shorts and a shirt, poured himself some coffee, and padded barefoot out to the terrace. Xander was basking in the late morning light in a white caftan, having toast and coconut water with a man in faded jeans and expensive-looking cowboy boots. The visitor's plaid Western-style shirt was partially unbuttoned, a navy bandana knotted around his neck. His longish hair was streaked with silver and his aviator Ray-Bans reflected the mesas and buttes of the Verde Valley with polarized precision.

"Ah, good, you're up," Xander said as Tom emerged from the house blinking. "Tom, meet Travis B. Marlow. Travis, this is my best friend and creative partner, Tom Ayana."

"Nice to meet you," Marlow said with the slightest tinge of a Western drawl. He raised his lip at Tom but didn't offer his hand. "Tom Ayana," Marlow intoned. "Interesting."

"What's interesting?"

"It's just that in Sanskrit, *ayana* means ..."

"I know what it means," Tom said.

"Travis is going to be our guide to the Hopi nation," Xander offered. "He says we're very lucky to be allowed to join the ceremony tonight. It's a gathering of the tribal elders, Indian shamans. Outsiders usually aren't allowed."

"It's only because I told them you were friends of Ryan's," Marlow said. "They love his movies."

"The Hopis watch movies?" Tom asked.

"Yes, they do," Marlow said, staring at Tom with a look that said, *Dear Lord, spare me from these clueless city slickers.* "The Hopi are old souls, but they're not Luddites," he said sternly. "They have DVD-R and satellite Wi-Fi and MacBook Pros. Some of them even went to college."

Tom shrugged. "I'm not from around here."

"No kidding. So where *are* you from, son?"

"Austin."

"Well, that explains a lot," Marlow said with a chuckle. "You guys killed all your Indians a long time ago. I'm surprised you even know what they look like, except for what you've seen in the movies, of course."

A gust of wind blew Xander's napkin off the terrace, and they watched it flutter into the canyon like a startled dove. "I've gotta say, I expected more from someone whose name means 'voyager, the one who follows the path.'"

"The path to what?" Xander asked.

Marlow tilted his head toward Tom. "Only your buddy can answer that question."

Xander was nonplussed. "Tommy, you never told me."

"It's just a name," Tom said.

"The ceremony tonight is in the Hopi village of Old Oraibi, not far from a petroglyph called Prophecy Rock," Marlow continued. "I thought we'd swing by there first, get you guys oriented."

"What's a petroglyph?" Xander asked.

"It's a series of drawings etched into the rock," Marlow answered. "Think you guys could be ready to go in an hour? A jacket, sunglasses, and hiking shoes are all you'll need. The Hopi and the desert will provide the rest."

During the ride to Prophecy Rock, Marlow became more relaxed, pointing out various landmarks and talking about his upbringing as the son of a fighter jet test pilot at Warren Air Force base, near Laramie, Wyoming. The technicians on the base had taken young Travis under their wing, teaching him basic computer programming and introducing him to a network of linked computers that was being developed by the military to provide fail-safe communication in case of a nuclear attack. It was called ARPANET, short for advanced research project agency network, and it was designed to avoid sabotage or destruction by allowing messages to seek their own path from point A to point B across the global computer grid. Long before the Defense Department decided to open up ARPANET for commercial use by the public, Marlow was smitten by the notion of a digitized Internet that increased in power exponentially with each computer that joined it. To Marlow, the untracked borders of the World Wide Web were the final frontier, an untamed territory with limitless vistas to be mapped and explored.

"It didn't take me long to figure out that computers, once they were linked together in sufficient numbers, behaved more like organisms than machines," Marlow explained. "This turned out to be an idea that people would pay me to talk about. Before I got out,

I worked as a consultant for Gates and Jobs and just about every technology company you ever heard of—and quite a few you never did … or will."

"So why did you stop?" Xander asked.

Marlow chuckled grimly. "Well, in the beginning, cyberspace was the most interesting place in human history. The World Wide Web was untamed territory, and everybody in it had unlimited freedom. You could be anybody, do anything, and the only speed limit was your imagination—terra incognita, the final frontier. For a while, it operated as a kind of boundless, victimless Manifest Destiny. But then the settlers moved in and staked out their little plots of html, and their little plots of mind, and they furnished their cyber suburbs with all the familiar baggage. And soon enough, the cyber bordellos opened up, followed by the neon storefronts and banner ads for five cents a click, and everybody was back to the same old tricks. Like Joni said, "They paved paradise and put up a parking lot.""

"What about AI?" Xander asked, "You know, uploading our brains into the cloud, the singularity?"

For a few seconds, the only sound was the engine and the thrum of wheels on packed earth. "Maybe," Marlow allowed, "but computers won't be as smart as people until they're capable of building humans who are smarter and faster than they are."

"Wouldn't that make them God?" Xander asked.

"Or the opposite."

They drove for a while through forests of wind-carved hoodoos and flat-topped mesas lording over flat playas of silicon. The stark landscape was interrupted now and again by fleeting views of unadorned ranches and adobe huts. This was a vision of the West minus steam engines, strutting cowboys, or whiskey-soaked saloons. *No Lone Rangers and Tontos, no Pale Riders*, Tom mused. There was nothing Hollywood-esque about this reservation, and Tom wondered if the Hopi watched Westerns when they logged on to Netflix on long, lonely nights.

"What if you could find another place like the early Web," Tom asked, "a place that was still full of open space and possibility? What if the Internet wasn't the final frontier? What if there was another human dimension still waiting to be explored?"

Marlow peered at Tom though the rearview mirror as if to get a better look at him. "Why in the hell," he said with a sly grin, "do you think I'm here? You see, this is the original sharing economy. And when city people are renting out their toasters and washing machines because they lost their job to a new algorithm, the eternal lessons learned in places like this will come in real handy."

The SUV arrived at the foot of a craggy butte. They got out of the car, and Marlow led the way beyond a jumble of boulders toward a series of red-walled bluffs. They passed a cypress pine so tortured by the wind that it had coiled completely around its neighbor. "An arboreal love story or fratricide?" Marlow muttered. "Take your pick."

He halted in front of a large stone slab inscribed with a series of interlocking drawings. At the lower left corner, a stick figure held a vertical line that forked into two secondary vectors flowing to the right. The top path was adorned by three human figures before turning into a jagged staircase that seemed to lead nowhere. The lower path was decorated with cornstalks. Three circles intersected with the lower path, and a second vertical line connected the two horizontal paths on the right.

"The Hopi believe that the world of men has been destroyed three times," Marlow began. "We are currently in the Fourth World, which the Hopi believe is about to end."

Marlow pointed to the human figure on the bottom line. "The great spirit presides over a thousand-year timeline and the two choices facing mankind. The top line is the path of materialism and technology. The zigzags at the end show that this path becomes unstable and ends in destruction. The other path is the path of life, which is the path of spirituality and coexistence. The Hopi believe that we still have a choice. We can take the path of greed and materialism, which will trigger the great purification and the end of our existence. Or we can reconnect with nature and pursue the path of the Great Awakening and emerge into the Fifth World."

"How will we know when the Fifth World arrives?" Xander asked.

"According to the prophecy, the end of the Fourth World will be signaled when the Blue Star Kachina removes his mask during the ceremonial dance and reveals himself to the children. The unmasking of the Blue Star Kachina and the appearance of a blue star will signal the beginning of a time of great turmoil and transformation. The survivors will enter a new era of spiritual rebirth and global consciousness."

Marlow glanced at the shadows elongating on the rocks. "The ceremony of elders will be starting soon. We should go."

The old Oraibi village was a cluster of crumbling brick houses and newer shacks perched on the edge of the first three mesas that overlooked the Hopilands, a twenty-five-hundred-square-mile tribal homeland with its own government and time zone. Off in the distance, a dome of thunderheads dragged a dark veil of rain behind it. A delegation of children and dogs greeted the SUV and followed it to a compound of one-story structures on the ridge. A few minutes later, one of the villagers approached the driver's window and spoke to Marlow in a language that Tom didn't recognize. The man had a weathered face and was wearing jeans and a battered brown leather jacket.

The man left, and Marlow shifted in his seat to face them. "They want us to wait."

"Wait for what?" Xander asked.

Marlow reached under his seat and extracted a bottle of tequila. "I'm not sure," he said, taking a swig and passing it along. "But we could be here for a while, so we might as well make ourselves comfortable." From time to time, a villager would pass near the SUV and shoot a furtive glance in their direction. The bottle was half gone when the man came back and spoke to Marlow again. After a few minutes of conversation, they solemnly shook hands, and Marlow started the engine.

"So what's happening?" Xander asked.

"Nothing, not anymore," Marlow replied. "The tribal council has canceled the public ceremony."

"Why?"

"We've still got some tequila, don't we?"

"Sure do." Xander handed him the bottle, and they watched as he drank and drove with one hand on the wheel. It was getting dark when Marlow finally broke the silence.

"The tribal elders are spooked," he said. "One of them saw the Blue Star Kachina dance in his dreams last night. They didn't let us stay because they thought we were part of the elder's dream."

"*We* were in the elder's dream?" Xander repeated. "How cool is that?"

Marlow shook his head. "It's not cool," he said. "In the elder's dream, the Blue Kachina removed his mask during the tribal dance and the dancing stopped; the children cried because it was the sign of the reckoning, the end of the Fourth Sun and the beginning of the great purification."

Marlow took another swig of tequila before continuing. "The elders decided to mark the vision with prayers and stories so the people would understand what has happened and to explain the visit of the brothers."

"What brothers?"

"The Blue Kachina signals that the world we know is dying. It's a sign that a war is coming. Columns of smoke will rise from the cities; mind will fight matter. The prophecy also says that in the final days, the Hopi will witness the return of two brothers, one from the East and one from the West. The brothers' arrival will herald the return of the blue star. One brother will live, and one will die. That's when the Fifth World will emerge."

Marlow waved the bottle in their direction. "I think they were talking about the two of you. The elders think you are the two brothers from the prophesy."

Xander craned his neck to look at Tom in the backseat. "That's crazy shit, man. They don't know anything about us. Besides, we're not even brothers."

"Not brothers of the womb, maybe," Marlow countered, "but what about brothers of the mind and spirit, the drum and song? Which one of you is from the East?"

"We're both from the West," Tom replied.

Xander seemed rattled. "I was born in Maryland," he confessed abruptly. "My folks moved to Austin when I was two. Tom, I never told you because there was no point. I mean, I'm ninety-nine percent Texan."

Tom turned his attention back to Marlow. "Which one dies?"

Marlow chuckled and rocked in his seat, though he didn't seem the least bit drunk. "Even if I knew," Marlow said, his face a featureless black mask in the car, "why would I tell you?"

Nobody spoke during the rest of the ride home.

They were almost at the house when Marlow's mood suddenly brightened. "Guys, I'm sorry if I freaked you out with those Indian fables," he said. "The Hopi can get a little intense sometimes. The elders are storytellers. They speak to their people in metaphors. I wouldn't take it personally."

"So you don't think the world's actually going to end?" Xander asked.

"Hell if I know!"

"But that stuff about the two brothers and the elders knowing I wasn't from Texas. How do you explain that?"

"I can't," Marlow said flatly, "because I'm not Hopi."

"But you subscribe to their philosophy."

Marlow waited for the red gate to open and drove through it before picking up the thread. "Some would say that the only real difference between guys and the opposite sex is dicks and broad shoulders, but I'm among those of us who harbor a suspicion that there's a reason men exist beyond fucking and lifting heavy objects," he said. "Maybe, just maybe, part of our job is to carry the burden of discerning cycles of destruction and rebirth and accepting responsibility for them. If that's what you mean by philosophy, then I guess you can count me in."

Marlow kept the engine running as they got out. "Look, believe whatever you want," he said. "I personally am going to go home and spend some time with my wife and kids. *Cuidense.*"

Marlow's last words kept Tom from sleeping that night. At the first inkling of dawn, he grabbed a flashlight and his jacket and hiked up the trail behind the house until he reached the rim of the canyon. He watched the sun rise through a cataract of milky periwinkle and magenta. Then he descended back to the house and searched for paper and something to write with. The light on the rocks was already fierce when Xander found him hunched over the dining table, working intently on a series of drawings and diagrams.

Xander grabbed a beer from the refrigerator and was halfway through it before curiosity got the best of him. "Okay, I give up."

"It's a polyhedron, in this case a three-sided pyramid made from four equilateral triangles that all meet at their vertices. The tetrahedron is one of the five Platonic solids, which are believed to have mystical healing powers and the ability to resonate and interact with other Platonic shapes across the universe. As it turns out, these shapes are repeated at the molecular level, and some believe that they can channel and amplify human brain waves."

"Okay, thanks for the science lesson, Mr. Wizard, but is there any particular reason why you got up at dawn to draw three-sided pyramids?"

"What Marlow talked about last night, taking responsibility for our actions, I think I know a way for us to do that. Look, if you stack the pyramids at their vertices and revolve them at their central axes, they form an *X*."

"So?"

"The *X* is a point of conversion, a crossroads, an hourglass of transformation that can be seen from three perspectives at the same time, especially if we light it up from the inside."

"Why would we light it up? And what's that thing that looks like a spaceship in the middle of the *X*s?"

"That's the DJ booth."

Xander turned away and dumped the beer can into the recycling bin. "You're kidding, right?"

"No."

"Tom, I already told you, I'm done with live gigs!"

"Hang on, Xan. Just hear me out."

"I'm not listening."

"You were in the car last night. You heard about the Hopi belief that one world is ending and a new one is being born, about the two brothers who help create a new consciousness."

"C'mon, Tommy, get a grip. It's a religious *fable*."

"How did the Hopi elder know you were from the East, something that not even I knew?"

"It doesn't matter how," Xander said, reaching into the fridge for another beer.

"You're quitting what you love because you're afraid of being blamed," Tom said. "That just makes it look like you ran off to your desert bunker to escape your own guilt."

"So what do you want me to do, Tom? Spin my greatest hits and save the world?"

Xander stalked out to the terrace, and Tom followed him. "Let's do a concert, Xan, one last show, a free concert, a benefit for the victims of Governor's Island, a demonstration against division and hate. Do it for them, do it for yourself, do it for us."

"A free concert *and* a benefit," Xander said mockingly. "That doesn't even make sense."

"We'll use crowd funding," Tom persisted. "If we don't raise a million dollars for charity and at least two million more for the concert itself, then everybody walks away, no harm done. But if the money comes, then everybody who's there is a co-owner. It won't be a commercial venture. We won't make a penny of profit, if that makes you feel better."

"Tom, this is all very noble, but raves have been outlawed in twenty-five states. You'll never Get a permit for a gig that size."

"Then we'll do it in one of the other states, like New York or Pennsylvania. There are some pastures outside of Philadelphia where we could fit thirty thousand, maybe more. We'll donate another million to the state so they'll let us do it. We'll even hire our own security to make sure nothing bad happens."

Xander looked dubious, but his resistance was waning. "You crazy motherfucker—you're actually serious, aren't you?"

"The *X* will be illuminated from the inside, with the speakers embedded in the extremities," Tom said. "We'll drop virtual walls of water, a giant replica of your hydro-architecture, from the edges of the stage and shoot bolts of electricity and fireworks from the top. It'll be cutting-edge sound and lighting effects. We'll get the guys from Berlin to help us build the *X*."

"*X*, as in X-pensive," Xander deadpanned.

"*X*, as in X-istence," Tom countered. "Dancing in the moment—forever."

"X-isting together"—Xander hoisted his beer—"one last time!"

"Xan, that's what we'll call it: X-ist—and DJX marks the spot!"

"Hang on, Tommy. I need you to hear me." Xander laid his hands on Tom's shoulders and stared into his eyes. "I'm willing to give it a shot, but if we don't raise four million dollars within twenty-eight days, then X-ist is off and we never talk about it again. Agreed?"

"You have my word, brother."

Xander ran his hand over the drawings, and Tom knew he was imagining the real thing, a mighty translucent totem of communal celebration, the greatest EDM sight-and-sound system ever built, surrounded by thousands of cavorting collaborators. Xander's finger loitered on the fifty-foot X with its revolving DJ control module.

"We should make it bigger," he said.

23

Dear citizens of the emergent nation,

I am here to tell you what you already know, what you feel in your bones and fear in your heart. You see it coming yet are blind to what it means. You don't want to hear it, but still you listen. You know what I'm about to say, don't you?

The answer is already there: on the tip of your tongue, on the edge of your seat, in the pit of your stomach, in the stagnant air around you. Don't worry; we will get to the question.

Our country, our world, is ailing. We take our pulse in the daily news, but the symptoms are clear and our temperature keeps rising. Hope dangles from a thread, unraveling over a spreading pool of dread. During commercial breaks from *Dancing with the Stars*, we watch the smoke rising from our cities, we hear the distant thunder creeping closer, and we open another cold one. We worship the rich and famous, our gleaming media gods. We grope for money and sex, but the fun has gone out of both. There are no blessings that can cover the cost. Even Dionysius has failed us.

Across this frayed and fractured republic, we hear the same watered-down wisdom: We should have seen it coming. We have only ourselves to blame. It's true that we have merrily planted the seeds of our own destruction, but self-laceration and rock-hard abs will not bring physical or spiritual redemption.

The revolution will not be YouTubed. The revolution will not be Googled. The revolution with not be Facebooked. The revolution will happen in mind space and real space, a militia of morphing minions seeing with a billion eyes. Thinking with a billion brains. Moving on a billion feet. Stepping together into the new now. Our now. Right now.

This is not the first time the axis mundi has reshuffled the deck, my friends. Four worlds have already come and gone, their footprints buried in shifting dunes of dust. The plague we fear has been raging in our souls for decades, but the purification has other plans for us. This time, the children will not cry when the Blue Star Kachina removes his mask in the plaza. This time, we will save ourselves by saving each other. This time, we will lift the ark before the rains come. This time, we are the flood.

Cara was thrashing and moaning, her arms lifted as if fending off an invisible demon.

Duggan shook her gently. "Baby, wake up. You're having a nightmare."

"What?"

"You were having a nightmare," Duggan whispered. "It's okay. I'm here. Go back to sleep."

The clock on the nightstand read 4:47 a.m., barely more than an hour until his video conference call with NCSD. He stayed in bed until Cara's breathing became deep and steady, wondering if it was merely selfish or an act of treason to be grateful for the crisis that had brought them together. He got up and closed the bedroom door, showered, dressed, and brewed a pot of coffee. Then he took a seat in the kitchen, fired up his laptop, and entered the key code for the secure communication link.

While he waited for his colleagues to come online, he sipped bitter breakfast blend and reread Swarm's latest communiqué, captured in fragments and pieced back together by the NSA computers as it rippled and caromed across the planet. The message had only confirmed what Duggan already suspected: Swarm was preparing to strike, and the window to stop him was closing fast. Swarm's incendiary manifesto was resonating far beyond its natural EDM and computer geek constituency, attracting the attention of bloggers, pundits, and talk show personalities from across the political spectrum. The gist of Swarm's appeal seemed to be in his zeal not to replace or repair the status quo but rather to transcend it altogether. His manifesto was equal parts revolution and evolution, an inflammatory bio-determinism that spoke to anyone with a hankering for seismic change.

Swarm's cathartic call to arms was spreading and metastasizing, online and in real space, faster than the authorities could track or understand it. In churches and statehouses, Swarm was denounced as a cyber-Satan who posed an existential threat to everything good and a scourge that had to be stamped out before it went too far. Isolated scuffles between pro-Swarm citizens and local law enforcement were becoming routine in the South and the mid-West, but Duggan knew the looming danger was much more insidious. The agency's language filters had detected an uptick in Internet traffic linked to Swarm's missives from every county in the nation, evidence that his incendiary cryptolect was seeping into the mainstream, becoming routinely cited, paraphrased, and excerpted in hundreds of thousands of blogs and websites.

The pop version of Swarm's dystopian doctrine was seductively simple: people would come together or they would perish in underground bunkers and luxury yachts, in skyscrapers and mountain cabins, in mansions and trailer parks, gated communities and sweltering slums. Homo sapiens would either ensure each other's survival or they would drag each other into the widening crevasse between "us" and "them" and be swallowed. And since human history showed that our species had a stubborn tendency to fall back on bad habits, evolution was the only solution. And Swarm, with his ascendant celebrity and gospel of hyper-communal redemption, was the movement's medium and messenger, catalyst-in-chief, and interactive messiah.

Duggan nervously drummed his fingers on the table. Could a camera-shy hacktivist with a knack for apocalyptic sermonizing actually instigate a morphogenetic uprising? Concern over the nature and dimension of the threat had elevated Duggan's investigation to a national security priority. Thanks to Koepp's persistence and JT's administrative aplomb, they were now the joint heads of a special interagency task force created with the specific goal of containing and eliminating the Swarm-Meta Militia threat. The president himself was following the team's progress via daily updates from his chief counterterrorism adviser, with copies going to the FBI, the CIA, the NSA, and the Department of Defense Cyber Command.

Duggan looked at the clock: 5:59 a.m. His laptop chimed and blinked into a conference room at NCSD.

"Good morning, Jake."

Koepp, JT, and the faces of about a dozen men arrayed around a large oval table stared back at him. He recognized Jordan Sharpe and the director of Homeland Security, but the rest were unfamiliar. "Gentlemen, I won't waste time on introductions," Koepp began. "You know what this group represents and why we're all here."

Since the presidential endorsement of the NCSD's mandate to locate and neutralize Swarm, Koepp's disposition had taken on a terse efficiency that underscored the gravity of the situation. She turned to the men at the table. "I'd like Agent Duggan to begin by giving us an update and his interpretation of the latest Swarm communication, and then we can fill him in on the latest developments on our end. Jake, maybe you could start with the woman who claims to be his lover."

"Well, for starters, I wouldn't describe her as his lover, exactly," Duggan said. "They had a relationship online with an erotic dimension. They've never met physically, and he never revealed his face to her, but she claims that she would be able to identify him if she saw him."

"And you find this credible?" one of the men asked.

"Yes, I do, and I'll tell you why. For one thing, her descriptions of their chats and the time periods in which she said he was traveling match perfectly with the ARK raves in Las Vegas and New York, where we know Swarm was present. Also, she describes an incident during which the suspect subjected her to an audio signal of some kind that she says allowed their minds to merge. I think it's pretty safe to say that she was subjected to a modified form of the zeph.r software."

"But it didn't make her sick or crazy," the man from the CIA said.

"No, as far as we can tell," Duggan clarified. "But I can tell you Ms. Oliver is cooperating voluntarily and shares our desire to find him. One thing I'd like to make clear is that the so-called Rave Plague, early reports from the CDC notwithstanding, is neither a virus nor a disease in any conventional sense. The real culprit is a device that transmits electromagnetic signals into the brains of its victims, controlling their thoughts and actions via applications and smartphones—and in some cases at electronic music festivals."

"So you're telling us that we're up against an army of dancing zombies?" somebody asked. Duggan waited for the chuckles to subside.

"What I'm telling you is that Kenneth Ulrich, or whoever it is that's behind Swarm, has been experimenting with different frequency variations of the original code. It seems that lower doses of zeph.r, like the earliest ones at the raves and the one that Ms. Oliver experienced, can induce euphoria and a profound sense of well-being and connectedness. The symptoms you're referring to are generally triggered by higher doses of the zeph.r signal, where the synapses of individuals become joined in a kind of feedback loop. Sometimes the victims who are exposed to zeph.r can get ill, but I wouldn't call them crazy. They can be very alert and organized. That said, the stronger the signal, the more likely you are to see various degrees of aggression, dementia, and violence."

"What happens if somebody aims a high-strength zeph.r beam at a large crowd?"

"That," Duggan said, "is something I hope we never find out."

"So, Jake," Sharpe interjected, "as you've reported, the data trail around this big rave in Philadelphia next month, the X-ist party, fits the patterns of the rave riots in Las Vegas and New York. Do you think Swarm is behind it?"

"I'm not sure if Swarm is behind it per se, but I'm pretty sure he'll see it as an opportunity for another field experiment, a human petri dish to test zeph.r's power. This is looking to be one of the biggest raves in recent history, which is why Swarm will find it irresistible."

"The place where the children dance in the square." Heads turned to JT, the new co-leader of the expanded zeph.r task force. "Some of the references in Swarm's most recent blog pertain to the Hopi myths of apocalypse. The appearance of the Blue Kachina, when this Hopi deity removes his mask to the children— meaning the general population—it signals the beginning of the end of the world."

"You're saying the 'children dancing in the square' is a coded reference to attendees of the X-ist rave?" Koepp inquired.

"There's no way to be absolutely sure," Duggan said, "but it could be code or a euphemism for a major attack."

The eruption of urgent commentary that followed was interrupted by a scowling man from the FBI. "I'm sorry, but that doesn't sound at all like Ulrich to me," he scoffed. "Scientists don't dabble in Native American witchcraft, not even criminal ones. And they don't go to techno raves."

"I'm sorry," Duggan asked. "You are?"

"Patterson, executive assistant director for FBI Criminal Cyber Response."

"Excuse me, Assistant Director, but what makes you so sure Ulrich won't be at X-ist?"

"Well, lots of reasons," Patterson replied, "but the main one is that thanks to cell phone data filters and GPS triangulation, we've tracked Ulrich to a warehouse in Worcester, Massachusetts. A squad of agents from Critical Incident Response is preparing to strike in a few hours."

Duggan dialed through surprise, indignation, and outrage before settling on diplomatic restraint. "That's certainly good news," he said. "But as the lead field agent in this case, I'd like to know why I wasn't alerted."

"I'm alerting you now, Agent Duggan. I'm sorry, but there just wasn't time ..."

"There was time," Duggan said firmly, "and if I just heard you correctly, there still is."

JT spoke up. "Jake, I'll meet you in Boston and we can take a chopper to Worcester together."

Duggan looked at Koepp, who nodded her assent.

"Of course, you're welcome to observe, Agent Duggan," Patterson allowed. "It's only fitting for you to be there when we take down our prime suspect."

"Except that if Ulrich is in Worcester," Koepp asked, "then who is the man Agent Duggan almost captured in Austin?"

"That's a good question," Duggan said, doing his best to stare through the camera at Patterson. "Logic suggests that Ulrich and Swarm are not the same person but actually collaborators, and most likely comrades in the Meta Militia. So Ulrich is no longer our only prime suspect."

There was another burst of conversation, and the representative from the State Department joined the fray. "Duggan, you said Swarm needs a big crowd to set off his zeph.r brain beam, right? So all we have to do is shut down the concert in Pennsylvania and he'll be dead in the water. By then, with any luck, we'll have Ulrich in custody too. Problem solved."

There was a murmur of relief and self-congratulation around the table.

"Excuse me, gentlemen," Duggan said as loud as he could without waking Cara. "Hear me out, please."

Their attention turned back to his screen. "I'm sorry, but shutting down X-ist is not a course of action I'd recommend," he chided. "For starters, it won't stop Swarm from continuing to release the zeph.r virus in isolated batches via the Internet and who knows how and where else. The effect is diluted when distributed on social media or a peer-to-peer live streaming basis, but it's not insignificant. It's possible that the outbreaks of civil insurrection we're seeing across the country might be at least partially caused by ongoing low-voltage wireless transmission. Second, we're pretty certain that regardless of whether or not we capture Ulrich, Swarm won't be able to resist showing up in Pennsylvania. We narrowly missed getting him in Austin, and as you know, his influence and the danger he represents is increasing every minute. If he goes off the grid again, we might not get another chance to make an arrest. But if we plan this right and use Swarm's ex-girlfriend as bait to smoke him out, I think we can corner and capture him in Philadelphia. Which is why we encouraged local officials in Pennsylvania to approve the application for the X-IST event."

A gray-haired man in a military uniform leaned toward his microphone. "Lieutenant General Bruno Mansfield, field commander of the US Fifth Army. Mr. Duggan, what exactly do you mean by 'lose control'?"

"I can't say exactly, sir, but Swarm already has more than a million followers in this country alone. If he finds a way to broadcast zeph.r at full power outside of a tightly defined geographical area, if he can 'light the fuse,' as he puts it, and fully activate the mind-control weapon in his possession, we could be facing a situation of mass hysteria and civil disobedience."

"Is there a way to contain or deflect this mind control beam you're talking about?" Mansfield asked.

"You would know better than me, General. But a cyber confrontation on the scale of what Swarm seems to be planning would make every existing contingency plan instantly and permanently obsolete." Duggan paused to let his words sink in.

"And now, if you ladies and gentlemen will excuse me, I've got a stakeout to catch."

It took Tom two hours to design the X-ist festival app and another day to lay out and launch the crowd-funding proposal page. Within a week, two hundred thousand people had pledged fifty dollars each to become "partners" in a "transformative X-perience of music, light and collective energy" on a five-hundred-acre parcel of farmland twenty miles from the City of Brotherly Love. Two million dollars of the proceeds had already been earmarked for the X-istence Foundation, the nonprofit entity set up to assist and compensate casualties of the New York ARK riots and fund research into the still unidentified aliment associated with EDM raves. In exchange for their support, "X-isters" would receive admission and a camping pass, as well as an interactive LED bracelet that would serve as their digital ticket and allow an interactive relationship with the audio-visual elements of the X-ist sensorium.

"You realize that without playing a single note, you've already changed the economics of all music festivals forever!" Fabian's designer topcoat flowed behind him as he excitedly paced around Xander's Arizona pad. "Eight million dollars in twenty days! It's incredible!"

"But can we build it in time?" Xander asked. "If we can't do it this summer, while it's still warm, I won't do it at all."

Tom spoke up from his seat on the sofa. "Not to mention that the money disappears in ten days if we don't accept it."

Fabian stopped pacing and rubbed his goateed chin. "It's doable, but we're going to need every penny from the fund to make it happen. I'll need to double everybody's salary."

"Well, at least you won't have to pay me, because I'm doing it for free," Xander quipped.

Fabian looked close to tears. "My dear boy, you just became the most famous DJ that ever lived. I'm not worried about your salary. After this, you can write your own ticket."

"So you'll do it?"

"Absofuckinlutely! But I need you both on the East Coast ASAP. There's a shitload of work to do, logistics galore, and I'm sure not launching this monster by myself."

"Don't worry, I've already rented a town house in Brooklyn with an a/v studio in the basement," Xander told him. "It'll be our command center."

"X-Central," Tom said.

"That's perfect for getting social media buzz," Fabian enthused. "Maybe you can host a dinner for the biggest donors. We all can move to a hotel in Philly right before the show."

"Tom's in charge of the audiovisuals," Xander continued. "I'll work on recruiting the talent. Armin, Joel, Alex and Nicolas already told me they'll do it for nothing if we cover their expenses." He jumped up from the sofa, eyes gleaming, arms extended winglike. "Each of the five guest DJs will get to do a forty-minute set, with me as the closer. I'll get the Chinese dude who plays the mouth harp and the gourd flute, a single light shining down on him, segueing into thunder and rain, jungle sounds of the primordial ooze. Then I'll add some Omnisphere and take them through the origins of the galaxy and human civilization, past and future, inner space and outer space. Plus, some real instruments: guitars, Mellotron, a theremin, and some singers."

Tom was nodding and smiling. "You're the man, Xan."

"I'm sure it'll be outrageously dope!" Fabian said. "I'll take care of finances and construction and media—you guys conjure the magic." He hovered over the 3-D model that Tom had 3D-printed on the dining room table. The tower of intersecting *X* s rose up from the clutter of empty wine bottles and scratch pads. "Tom, can you please explain this to me again?"

Tom pointed to the circular platform in the center of the model. "The module here at the fulcrum is the three-hundred-and-sixty-degree revolving DJ deck. The arms of each *X* are translucent Plexiglas, seventy feet tall, lit from the inside by high-intensity LEDs that change color. The lights and the music, everything will synchronize with the participants' radio-controlled wristbands, which also vibrate and change colors in sync with what's happening onstage. Water walls will flow from the edges of the towers, and pointed rods of St. Elmo's fire will burn at the top. We're telling everybody to wear white so that their clothes pick up the colors on their wrists and in the show."

"I flunked science in high school," Fabian said, "so tell me, what the fuck is St. Elmo's fire?"

"It's a field of luminous blue-tinged plasma created by an electrical discharge from an object pointed into the atmosphere," Tom said. "It's named after St. Elmo, the patron saint of sailors, because it would appear on the tips of ships' masts during electrical storms. We'll turn off the St. Elmo's when the acrobats go up to the roof to rappel off the edges into the crowd, which happens when we shoot off fireworks at the climax of Xander's set."

Xander was behind them with his hands on his hips. "Pretty cool, eh?"

"Beyond belief," Fabian uttered.

"Believe it," Xander said.

"How soon can you guys be in New York?"

"We have tickets to fly in two days," Xander told him. "I'll text you when we land."

After Fabian had left, Tom and Xander did shots of Patron blanco and took a walk along the ridge behind the house. Xander staked out a spot on a level boulder and Tom stood beside him to savor the luxury of so much uncompromised space.

"How did you do it, Tom?"

"How did I do what?"

"How did you get the money so fast?"

"It was a snap," Tom said lightly. "I just harnessed the power of the cloud."

Xander's features looked inflamed in the wasting daylight. "Don't bullshit me, Tommy. Nobody has raised so much money so fast since the early days of crowd sourcing."

"It's not bullshit, Xan. Every cent of the money is from real people. Go ahead and do an audit if you want, and you'll see that the funds are completely legit. I think you're underestimating your marquee value."

"Sorry, pal, but I'm not buying it."

"Okay," Tom relented. "What I just told you is true, but I left something out. You know I used to work in cyber security. My job was to keep hackers out of my clients' business, to protect them from scammers and bandwidth bandits."

"Yeah, I already knew that."

"Well, then it shouldn't surprise you that I got to know a lot of people on both sides of the firewall. Most of them hack for kicks. Sometimes they go after the real bad guys when no one else will or can. The point is, the Internet is riddled with dark nets, organizations of people who trade and share information, and sometimes they join forces to help each other out, or to do something that they agree is important."

"Like Anonymous."

"Yeah, but there are hundreds of groups like them, all different but connected, all over the Internet, all over the world. Each individual in the group might have links to hundreds or thousands of other people, other computers. Networks of networks. They know how to manipulate the levers of social media in ways that nobody else can see, invisible hands pulling the strings."

"You sound like Swarm right now. Did you talk to him too?"

Tom had the sudden sensation that the laconic buttes and hoodoos around them, the million-year-old survivors of a time before

276

time, were leaning closer to hear his next words. "Look, Xan, honestly, there's no way I can answer that question, because Swarm is not an individual. Swarm is an idea. Like you said, he's everybody and nobody. He's a collective of collectives, the ghost in the machine."

Xander turned away and spat into the dirt, and Tom could feel the whole planet tilting slowly away from the sun. "Whatever, man. Anyway, you admit you did that—you got your cyber buddies to pull the strings for X-ist."

"Yeah, but they did it because they believe in what we're doing Xan, just like the thousands of the regular people who contributed their PayPal dollars and credit card numbers. They're coming to Pennsylvania because they believe in X-ist, in what it represents, and because they believe in you. The music, the vibe, the EDM community, and everything around it matters to them, just like it matters to us."

"Really? What part of this actually matters to you, Tom, because I honestly can't tell anymore."

Tom was engulfed by a wave of sadness, like a warm spring welling up from a subterranean chamber. The stress of the past few months, the running and hiding and truth twisting, was taking its toll. "I'm sorry, Xan," he said, swallowing hard. "I'm sorry I lied to you. It's just that this concert is really important. It's the culmination of everything we've done. Brothers in everything, always, including this."

They both watched as the sun melted into an orange pool of lava. Xander draped his arm on Tom's shoulders. "Hey, no worries, man. It's not the end of the world." He paused before adding, "Not yet anyway."

"Ha," Tom said.

The desert around them seemed to exhale in the encroaching evening. Xander zipped up his jacket and turned back to the house. "C'mon," he said. "Let's go back and fire up the grill. Just make sure you keep your word. This is the last live gig, brother. When the Blue Kachina dances, we're done."

25

The helicopter whirred and hovered over an empty parking lot near the Amtrak station on Worcester's south side. As they drifted down to their makeshift landing pad, JT pointed to an intersection a couple of blocks away, where SWAT trucks and Massachusetts PD cruisers had encircled a three-story brick building with an American flag draped across the boarded-up entrance.

"Here, you'll need these," JT shouted over the din, handing Duggan a set of laminated police credentials. Once they got clear of the chopper, they flashed the passes to get past the armed policemen manning the perimeter barricades. They were less than a hundred yards from the building when the first shots rang out. Duggan and JT reflexively ducked behind a dumpster as a tear gas canister tore through a window on the second floor. Machine-gun fire peppered the pavement and a half dozen FBI and local police officers returned fire.

"Good timing," JT said good-naturedly. "Remind me to travel with you more often."

A man with a bullhorn warned the occupants that they had five minutes to surrender before the use of lethal force, and Duggan braced himself for the next fusillade. JT raised his head to get a peek at the building. "I have a bad feeling these guys aren't going to surrender."

Duggan watched a young man in a brown suit talking to a cluster of SWAT commandos like a football coach on game night. The group dispersed, and a moment later he heard shouts and lifted his head to see a pair of armored agents run up to the entrance and release a satchel before scurrying back.

"Fire in the hole!" somebody cried. The explosion was strong enough to knock down the door and blow out most of the remaining windows, which were obscured by billowing smoke. There was another volley of tear gas projectiles, followed by a squad of commandos who rushed the building. The gun reports, isolated at first, escalated to a ricocheting crescendo, like popcorn on a hot stove, before becoming more intermittent. There was a lull and then a single final bang.

"Goddammit," Duggan said.

"I'm sorry, Jake. I tried to get them to wait, but you know how it is with the FBI."

"I sure do."

They waited for the all-clear signal and then got up and walked over to the man in the brown suit, who was on his phone requesting medical support for the dead and wounded. When he saw them, he raised his finger for them to wait. They did.

"Vid Rico, FBI Critical Incident Response team," he said, extending his hand. "I heard you guys were coming."

Duggan shook Rico's hand. "You were supposed to wait until we got here."

Before letting go, Rico answered, "Couldn't do it. We could hear them destroying evidence inside."

The men simultaneously released their grips. "I'm sure you were just following orders," Duggan said acidly. "Can we go inside before your men destroy the evidence you were so worried about?"

"Sure thing. I'll walk you in myself." Rico called out for gas masks and handed a couple to Duggan and JT

They entered the building just as the ER vans arrived on the scene. The first floor was a smoldering obstacle course of overturned desks, smashed computers, and corpses. Piles of paper were still burning in one corner. A Celtics basketball jersey nailed to a blood-splattered wall had been crudely customized with the words "Meta Militia."

They climbed stairs to the second floor, which had served as a makeshift dormitory, and judging from the pile of bodies draped across the bunks, that was where the surviving defenders had made their last stand. There was a thick trail of blood leading up to the third floor.

"Get behind me," Rico ordered.

They followed the red smear up the stairs and though a warren of small offices, all of them empty except for one. Kenneth Ulrich was hunched over his desk with a gun in his hand and an expanding puddle of blood under his chair.

"Is that the guy you were looking for?" Rico asked.

"Yeah," Duggan confirmed. He looked back at the stairs, retracing the final frantic moments of Ulrich's life. "Why would someone who was mortally wounded drag himself all the way to the third floor just to get to his desk?"

JT shrugged. "Workaholic?"

"His computer's still on," Rico noticed. "And it looks like he just sent somebody a file."

Duggan leaned in to look at the computer screen. "It must have been a pretty important message." He looked at JT. "Can you get me a copy of that file ASAP? And I want to know where it went."

"I'm on it," JT said. He pointed to a snapshot tacked to the wall next to the desk: two young men leaning toward the camera in a double selfie, smiling. "That's Ulrich, right? But who's the other guy?"

Duggan took out his phone to take pictures of the Post-its arranged in a neat grid around the photo, all of them lime green. "That's Donald Westlake," he said.

The rented Esplanade descended into a bucolic valley bordered by a two-lane paved road on the north and a meandering tree-lined creek to the south. In the center of the valley, on a two-hundred-acre grassy plain, teams of construction workers were putting the finishing touches on a towering *X* polyhedron buttressed by lighting rigs and hi-res LED screens. Arriving at the cluster of temporary tents serving as the X-ist festival's onsite headquarters, Tom, Xander, and Fabian emerged from the SUV and marveled at the full size realization of their crowd-funded vision.

"Holy shit," Xander exclaimed, leaning back to take in the scene. "It's unbelievable what people can do when they put their minds together."

"So true," Tom said.

"It's a goddamn miracle is what it is!" Fabian proclaimed. "Eighty-five feet tall, plus twenty feet for the base and another sixty-five for the trapeze platform and Elmo's fire rods!" Fabian surveyed the buffet and beverages laid out for lunch and fished out a Diet Coke. "One hundred and seventy feet—three feet taller than U2's three-hundred-and-sixty-degree claw stage. We're going to make it into the Guinness Book of frigging World Records!"

Fabian's phone emitted the sound of money being shoveled over the bass line from Pink Floyd's *Dark Side of the Moon*. He raised his hand before answering. "Speaking of which," he said. "Yeah, escort the media from the press tent to the front of the base platform, and we'll do the video Q&As in the DJ module. See you in five."

"We don't need any publicity," Xander said peevishly. "X-ist was completely sold out three weeks ago."

"If even half of the people who bought tickets actually show up next week, this place will be mobbed," Fabian agreed. "Don't worry. I've got two helicopters booked to fly you and the other VIPs back and forth from Philly. And I got you guys this ..." Fabian reached into a small case he'd been carrying and pulled out a handgun that Tom recognized as a Walter PPK—compact, beautiful, and capable of stopping anything on two feet.

"Whoa!" Xander exclaimed, recoiling from the weapon. "I'm not touching that thing!"

"You don't have to," Fabian said. "It'll be taped to the underside of the master mixing board in the DJ module. Just a little insurance." He looked at Xander and Tom. "You guys are the only ones who'll even know that it's there. Anyway, that's enough housekeeping. Here's what's important: The DJs, the contributors, the fans, the foundation, the workers who broke their asses at double wage to get this done in time, they all deserve to be recognized and celebrated. I've kept the interviews to a minimum, like you asked, so please let's show a little enthusiasm here."

"Tommy, come with me," Xander said. "This is your design more than anybody's. I'm not even sure I understand this augmented reality thing you've cooked up."

Tom raised his arms in a gesture of deflection. "Sorry, bro; it's your mug that they want," he said. "All you need to say about augmented reality is that we'll have special 3-D visual effects that people can view with their smartphones in real time. The radio wristbands will automatically upload the software to their phones to create an unprecedented collective experience."

Fabian looked up from his texting. "He's the smart one, isn't he?"

"Nah, we're equally smart," Xander corrected. "I'm just better-looking."

"Okay, whatever. *Motherboard* is waiting." Fabian hustled his star client in the direction of the giant X. "Tom, I told them one hour max, plus a photo shoot. There're plenty of food and drink."

"Take your time," he told them. "I've got some stuff to do for the augmented reality script."

Tom took out a tablet and started scanning the perimeter of the area. Then he videotaped the lighting towers and the main stage. His phone was chirping more than usual. The 4chan/b/ boards were going crazy over an FBI assault on a Meta Militia safe house in Massachusetts. The media was reporting that all the militia members had been killed on the scene, but according to the 4chan posts at least a few had escaped. The news only reinforced Tom's resolve to initiate X-ist before the authorities clamped down.

When he got back to the SUV, a husky man with a red beard wearing a Led Zeppelin T-shirt with red suspenders was sitting in a folding chair drinking a can of Rolling Rock.

"Hi, I'm Jed," he said, extending his paw.

"Tom."

Jed nodded toward the soaring structure. "You gonna get on top of that thing?"

"Ah, yeah, eventually."

"At night?"

"Definitely."

"I can't imagine what that's like, looking out at thousands of people, controlling their bodies."

"Excuse me?"

"With the music and lights, I mean. You make them dance, right? The hot girls. And then you take them to your trailers backstage and ... you know."

"Yeah, that's what we do," Tom said.

"Awesome!"

Tom unfolded a Pennsylvania state map and pointed to a circle he had inked onto the heart of Amish farm country. "We're here, right?" He rotated toward the river. "And that's south." Then he pulled the tourist pamphlet from his back pocket and spread it out on a plywood worktable.

"Gee," Jed said, "I didn't take you for the sort of guy who was into Amish hayrides and Hershey's candy factories."

"I'm just getting my orientation. I like to know what's around me. How long would it take to get to Washington, DC, from here? On foot, I mean."

"Hmm, let's see. A hundred and twenty miles at about five miles an hour. Thirty hours, maybe." Jed grinned. "That's with no stopping for sleeping or eating, of course. But you don't seem like the extreme hiking type either."

A low rumble echoed through the valley, and Jed craned his neck toward the source. He pointed over the trees to where black anvil clouds were massing. "Looks like some big thunder is brewing. Summer squalls can come out of nowhere this time of year."

"No doubt."

"Don't worry," Jed said. "We'll put some rods at the top of the tower to catch any stray bolts. The electron discharges can be pretty darn spectacular."

There was another ominous rumble, but Tom ignored it. "I'm bringing my own lightning," he said.

Duggan had made a reservation at the same restaurant that was the setting for their first real date. Nursing a sparkling water as he sat at the bar to wait for Cara, he fidgeted with his cocktail napkin and suppressed the urge to check his phone. He wasn't the type to be nervous before meeting his girlfriend for dinner, but the stakes were unusually high tonight. Duggan looked up and watched her saunter in, entranced all over again by her angular allure. But first there was a bit of business to address.

"Are you going to tell me where you've been the last couple days?" Cara asked once they'd been seated. "Your phone was turned off the whole time."

"It's better for both of us if I don't tell you."

"Of course," Cara said. "Why do I even bother?"

The waiter appeared with the top-notch cabernet Duggan had preselected, and Cara raised her eyebrows as it was poured. "We'll, aren't you the clever one," she said approvingly. "Looks like someone is expecting to get lucky tonight."

"You bet I am," Duggan said, tipping the rim of his glass against hers.

They savored the wine for a few seconds before Duggan spoke again. "I don't mean to be obnoxious, baby, but the truth is that where I was and what I was doing is irrelevant. What matters right now is that I'm finally getting the support I need, which means I have to go back to headquarters and put together a task force for X-ist."

"Exist?"

"It's an EDM festival that's happening about thirty miles west of Philadelphia. It could be our last chance to catch Swarm. We think he's preparing to use a new, stronger version of the zeph.r beam, one with a mobile capability."

"The girlfriend in Austin didn't lead you to him?"

"No, not yet, but she still might. She says she'll know him if she sees him, and I'll make sure he sees her. When he takes the bait, I'll be waiting."

"But, Jake," Cara protested, "if the zeph.r signal is strong enough, there could be an enzootic spillover effect."

"Please translate."

"There's a whole field of cross-species spillover effects leading to viral contamination," Cara explained. "You know, diseases that people get from exposure to animals, like bubonic plague from fleas, avian flu from birds ..."

"Or human swarming from locusts," Duggan said.

"No, this is different, although there are some significant parallels. In an emergent scenario at least, the people exposed to zeph.r aren't catching swarm behavior from locusts. They are assuming the symptoms of swarming from morphogenesis within their own species."

It was the opening Duggan had been waiting for. "Cara, didn't you do some experiments in Africa to control locust swarms?"

"The experiments were a failure," she said tightly.

"That's not what I heard." He had never seen her so upset. Duggan waited while Cara took a sip of wine and regained her composure.

"You spoke to Eric, didn't you?"

"Don't be mad. It's not his fault. If I locate Swarm, maybe I can at least use the PHAROH beam on him before he releases zeph.r."

"Absolutely not," she protested. "Did Eric also tell you PHAROH killed some of the locusts? We have no idea what it might do to people. I don't care how dangerous Swarm is—I'm not going to be an accessory to murder. But I will go with you to Pennsylvania, if you want me to. Eric can watch the lab and maybe I can help you figure something out once we're there."

The waiter arrived with their food, and they disengaged like boxers returning to their corners. The food was delicious, but Duggan was too stressed to enjoy it. He chewed slowly and wiped his mouth before resuming the bout.

"Actually, I was thinking of inviting Eric," he said. "He's been to some of the raves; he knows the EDM scene. Plus, he can help me protect my men from zeph.r."

"That's ..." Cara's voice faltered. "That's very nice of you."

"I'm not being nice, just practical. I need his expertise on the task force team. It makes sense. Just like it makes sense to use PHAROH as a backup at X-ist."

Cara's expression curdled. "Jake, I already told you, I won't allow it."

"I thought you became a scientist to help people," Duggan persisted. "You just explained to me how dangerous zeph.r is. What could happen if Swarm uses it on a crowd that size? Aren't you being a little selfish?"

Cara's face reddened. Duggan knew that if he pushed too hard, it could spoil the whole evening, but he had to try.

"Listen, I get it," he said. "You have to protect your reputation in case something goes wrong. Nobody has to know where PHAROH came from except for the three of us. I'll make sure of it."

"Jake, you don't know what you're talking about," she said sharply. "The man from the Defense Department wanted to use my research on insects to create swarms of bees and *flying clones*, a cloud of killing machines acting as a single organism. I think they've been doing experiments in the Bay Area. The bees at the Fairmont have something wrong with them. I found evidence of unexplained supersedure—that's when the hive kills its own queen. The other night in my dream, I saw ..."

Duggan watched helplessly as Cara's throat constricted, her eyes welling up with the blind panic of a recurring nightmare. He watched as she replayed the horrific memory of returning to the scene of the experiment in Africa, only to encounter legions of locusts, twitching and clicking and oozing green fluid as they convulsed and expired, shattered by PHAROH's disruptive death ray.

In her dream the locusts metamorphosed again, this time into millions of drones the size of dragonflies, with squadrons of insects of all kinds becoming smarter and faster, grasping their advantage, taking to the air by the trillions, blackening the skies and rallying their quiescent comrades, conquering their only competition on the planet by drilling into the fighting machines and uniforms of their former masters, gnawing through wires and clogging triggers, passing on the tricks they had learned in their cages at the DOD, micro-mercenaries recruited and armed with poisons and miniature bombs, and rogue mobs of vengeful warrior bees dancing to point the way and spread the word that the time had come to wage holy insect war and rid the planet of its human infestation once and for all.

"Cara, Cara!" Duggan reached out to touch her hand, but she flinched and pulled away. "I'm sorry. I didn't mean to ..."

"Of course you did," she snapped, using her napkin to blot away the tears. "I'm such a fool. I thought it could be different this time. I thought *you* could be different this time."

"Cara, what are you talking about?"

"I'm talking about why it can never work between us."

Duggan stared into his glass until he was sure she wasn't joking.

"Look, I'm sorry about leaving town so abruptly again, but you of all people know how important this is. I'd stay if I could."

"Right now, that's the last thing I want you to do," she said coldly.

"Hey, don't be like this. I was looking forward to a ..."

But Cara was still seething. "Whatever we've been doing the past few months, whatever this is, it isn't love, or even commitment. Our whole relationship is a checklist of complementary attributes that satisfy our work schedules and physical needs."

It was Duggan's turn to take umbrage. "Really? That's all I am to you? A 'checklist of attributes'?"

"Within the first ten minutes of us meeting," Cara continued, "I had subconsciously capitulated to the relationship. Hormones were rushing into my brain, affecting my perception of you. What I didn't actually know about you was filled in by the *idea* of you. That's what everybody does. I was seeing what I wanted to see ..."

"Wait a minute," Duggan interrupted. "I want to make sure I've got this right. You're telling me that we're too compatible to stay together, that my feelings—and yours too—are just a biological convenience. I'm sorry, but if that's what you learned in college, I think you should ask for your money back." He took a bite of his food, which was flavorless. "If you want to break up, then so be it, but please spare me the bio-psycho bullshit."

"I don't blame you for being angry," Cara said. "I know this must all seem bizarre and academic. But over the past few weeks, I've felt myself becoming dependent on you, feeling incomplete when you're not around. It's been a depletion of my independence. I don't recognize myself."

Duggan groaned and rubbed his face. Her last comment was like a final piece of the jigsaw falling into place. "Oh boy," he said. "I didn't see it coming, but now I get it. You're threatened by your feelings for me because it means a loss of control. Your seamless hermetic shell has been breached, and now your only defense, your brilliant solution, is to back away, to run for cover and call it quits."

"That's too simple, Jake."

"Excuse me, but it actually *is* that simple. You're safer when you're alone." Duggan paused, almost choking on the words. "But what about me?"

"You'll be okay," Cara stammered. "You're a sexy guy with a sexy job. You'll forget me, and eventually I'll forget you. That's how it happens, right? You told me yourself that that is how it always ends. And then you move on to your next conquest."

Duggan murmured an expletive, a curse on women and on himself. "I only told you that because I felt that this time was different. I still do. Or at least I did." Women wanted guys to bare their feelings, to confess their deepest doubts and desires. Alcohol and sex loosened men's tongues, but sooner or later, one way or another, the same words uttered in postcoital bliss came back to haunt them.

Duggan pushed his plate away. Dinner was over. He wordlessly paid the check and went to get the car. When Cara got inside, Duggan was gripping the steering wheel so hard his palms ached. "I'll tell Wightman he can't come to DC," he said, "if that makes you happy."

"Don't be stupid, Jake. You need him there. Like you said, it makes sense."

"Nothing makes sense right now."

Duggan didn't speak again until they were pulling up to Cara's apartment. "The bottom line is that I can't imagine my life without you," he told her. "And if that's just my enzymes and hormones talking, I really don't give a fuck, because they're the only ones I've got. Take it or leave it—it's what I am. What you perceive is what you get. After this thing in Philadelphia is over, I'll be back. And if you still think we should split, I promise I'll get out of your life and never bother you again."

Duggan stopped the car, but Cara wasn't done surprising him. Without turning her head, she asked, "Want to come up and tuck me in?"

"Is this breakup sex or makeup sex?"

Cara put her hand on Duggan's lips to silence him and then got out. He sat behind the wheel for a minute, thinking of all the good reasons he had to keep driving. Then he killed the engine, locked the car, and followed her up the steps.

26

···

JT was waiting in Duggan's office when they arrived from the airport. He handed a temporary credential to Eric, who accepted it with a ceremonial bow, and briefed them on the meeting that was scheduled to begin in a few minutes.

"Be careful what you wish for," JT told Duggan. "All the agencies that matter will be in attendance, and you know what happens when you put a lot of big dogs in the same room."

"Mutual ass sniffing?"

Eric blinked and sniggered like a schoolboy.

"Not if we stick to the game plan," JT said. "Koepp and I have your back, and so does the director, but our time flying under the radar is over."

Duggan nodded. "I get it. This is prime time and everyone's watching."

"One more thing, Jake." JT handed Duggan a manila envelope. "It'll take a while to shift through the hard drive on Ulrich's computer, but here's the message he sent right before he died, plus the transcripts of the Post-it's on the wall in his office and some text from the memo utility on his smartphone."

"Thanks." Duggan nodded and put the envelope into his desk drawer.

JT focused on Eric. "I've heard a lot about you," he said. "Think you can help us catch this cyber creep before he does any more damage?"

"I don't know if I can help you catch him," Eric said, interlocking his fingers over this head. "But I think I can give you and your men some protection from any zeph.r beams bouncing around at the concert."

JT turned his hand into a gun and pointed it at Eric. "I like this kid," he said. "Let's go. We can't be late to the rodeo."

Duggan led the way down the corridors that he normally found so dull and stifling. But Eric seemed wonderstruck when they passed a framed portrait of the Homeland Security director. "Will he be at the meeting?"

"The director usually attends by video feed," JT informed him, "but he'll be able to see you."

Eric had been like a puppy on the ride to NCSD headquarters, staring out the window at the Beltway commuters, practically pissing himself with anticipation. The youthful alacrity of Duggan's new sidekick made him realize how blasé he'd become about working as a federal cyber agent. It was a kick to see it all again from Eric's dewy perspective. It must all seem to him like something out of an action-adventure video game, Duggan thought, except that the bad guy in this case was real and the fuse for his microwave bio-bomb was probably under construction on a farm somewhere outside of Philadelphia.

They entered the packed conference room and took their seats. Koepp nodded and called the meeting to order. Sharpe and Mansfield were there, as well as a dozen or so operatives from various federal agencies. "Thank you all for coming," Koepp began. "As you all know, the apprehension of the suspect known as Swarm has been elevated to a national security priority. Agent Duggan, who is our lead field operator on the case, will give us an update in a minute. But first I'd like us to start with some important news from Deputy FBI Director Joseph Osheyack. The floor is yours, sir." A man in a pin-striped suit cleared his throat and leaned toward the microphone. "Ladies and gentlemen, I'm very pleased to tell you that one of our prime targets,

Kenneth Ulrich, was taken down three days ago at a warehouse near Worcester, Massachusetts."

"Were you able to question him?" somebody asked.

"The suspect is deceased," Duggan interjected.

"There was gunfire as we approached the building," Osheyack continued, "and FBI agents responded appropriately. Ulrich was already dead from a gunshot wound when we entered the premises. In addition, nine of his co-conspirators were killed."

"They're not talking either," Duggan muttered, feeling Koepp's eyes on him.

"I'm sorry about the collateral damage, but I think we have to look at this as a net gain," Osheyack asserted. "Ulrich was a traitor and a dangerous criminal who has now been neutralized. We've confiscated some equipment and software that's consistent with the zeph.r software design, proving his complicity." He glanced up at the video feed from the director's office. "I really don't understand why Agent Duggan would have a problem with that."

"The problem," Duggan said sternly, "is that we don't know anything more about Swarm's plan, and everyone in the building who could have told us something is dead. If Swarm feels threatened, it'll only make him more dangerous and harder to catch."

"Which is why," the director of Homeland Security chimed in from the screen, "we're giving Agent Duggan the full support of our agencies, including the FBI and NSA and DOD."

"Mr. Director," General Mansfield added, "Ditto that from the Fifth Army of the US Northern Command."

Duggan's gaze shifted to Eric, who was holding his hand up like a college student waiting for the professor to call on him. Koepp peered across the table. "Yes?"

"I was just wondering ..."

"Could you identify yourself to the task force, please?"

"Oh, sure. Sorry. Eric Wightman, from the biomorphics department at Lawrence Livermore Laboratory at the University of

California, Berkeley, ma'am." He glanced at Duggan, who gave him the nod to proceed with caution. "I was wondering if there might be a way to use the government's computing resources to design a predictive model of locust swarm behavior projected onto a crowd of, say, twenty thousand people. If we can identify the threshold of emergence, maybe your agency can work with local officials to restrict the numbers of attendees and prevent zeph.r from reaching critical mass..."

"Mr. Wightman," Mansfield broke in. "As an expert in this field, do you really think that this de-centralized uprising is even containable?" Mansfield groped for the words. "I mean, what do you call a subversive movement that anyone can join anywhere at anytime for any reason, just by downloading an application?"

There was a lull as faces turned to hear Wightman's answer.

"Open-sourced terrorism?"

A kind of psychic shiver rippled through the room. Then a man with a trendy buzz cut cleared his throat. "Michael Bragin from the NSA, sir. We concur with Mr. Wightman's suggestion, and we'd be happy to work with him on building a predictive computer model."

Koepp nodded. "Thank you, Mr. Wightman and Agent Bragin. Jake, will you make the introductions and so forth?"

"Happy to do it."

After adjourning the meeting, Koepp called Duggan and Mansfield into her office and shut the door behind them.

"Jake, I think you've met General Mansfield."

"Only remotely till now, but yes, of course."

"We're only a few days away from D-day," Koepp said. "Besides the fifty armed agents you requested, you'll have jurisdiction over the local county and state police; that's another eighty or so men. I've also asked the joint chiefs to have the Northern Command on alert. As a precautionary measure, General Mansfield is moving a fully equipped force of six hundred men from the US Fifth Army in Houston to a concealed position a few miles away from the festival grounds."

"And I've got a direct line to the joint chiefs and the president himself, if we need it," Mansfield added.

"Excuse me, but did you just say the Army Northern Command is being deployed in Pennsylvania?"

"That's correct," Mansfield said. "Duggan, you've made a very convincing case that due to his customization of the zeph.r software, Swarm might already have the capability to control the minds of his followers."

"I said that he might, but ..."

"And if that's the case, then by extension, those people have for all intents and purposes become enemy combatants who are subject to the same policies and actions that apply to all foreign terrorists."

"And the president is okay with this?"

"The White House is in accord with the calibrated use of extreme force against terrorist threats on US soil. The way we see it, US citizens who do not have full control of their minds and therefore can no longer be responsible for their own actions are ipso facto no longer protected by citizens' rights and privileges provided by the US Constitution. The governor of Pennsylvania agrees, which is why he has authorized the deployment of federal troops in his state, plus a few other surprises, like MEDUSA."

Duggan and Koepp waited for Mansfield to elaborate.

"It's an acronym for Mob Excess Deterrent Using Silent Audio. Whatever's going on in those ravers' heads, MEDUSA's sonic beam will stop them cold."

"And what if it doesn't stop them cold?" Duggan asked.

"Then we'll resort to more conventional weapons."

"As in the US Army using lethal weapons against American citizens?"

"Correct."

Duggan was incredulous. "So you're saying that from a legal standpoint, anyone who comes under Swarm's influence is by definition an enemy of the state and therefore fair game for US troops?"

"If we get to a point where that distinction has to be made, then the answer is yes."

JT and Eric were huddled in deep conversation when Duggan got back to his office. "Sorry to interrupt guys," he said. "You did well in there, Eric. But we need that predictive model. X-ist is just a few days away."

"Did well?" JT gushed. "Hell, he was magnificent! I'll bet you that before this is over, the NSA offers him a job."

"I thought you said you liked him," Duggan said mirthlessly.

JT was studying his friend with concern. "Jake, exactly what happened back there?"

Duggan waved off the question. "I'll tell you later." He looked at Wightman. "Eric, I want you to spend some time with the NSA and DOD tech guys. Find out what else they got at the warehouse in Massachusetts. Help them if you can, but mainly keep your ears open. JT, please take Eric over to NSA and introduce him to Bragin's team, and while you're at it, find out anything you can about a sonic crowd control cannon called MEDUSA. Meet me back here at six and we'll all go for a good steak in Georgetown."

Duggan shut his door and tried to shake off the anxiety from his conversation with Mansfield—too many variables on a potential collision course. Then he opened the envelope that contained Ulrich's files from the Meta Militia raid. Inside was a printout of the text on the Post-its and a USB thumb drive with the contents of Ulrich's last e-mail. He scanned the Post-it transcripts, which were in a jargon that made no sense to him, and downloaded the contents of the thumb drive—a single high-definition video, some photos, and a text file from Ulrich's phone memo app. The photos showed Donald Westlake in a bare-walled room sitting shirtless in a chair under a bright light. A plastic mesh dotted with brain wave sensors was wrapped snugly around Westlake's shaved head. Wires dangled down the side of his face toward a metal box with dials and switches and a strip of masking tape with a single word in black Sharpie letters: ZEPH.R. One of the photos was a close-up of a fresh scar about one inch long right behind his left ear.

Look for what isn't there.

The text file was an unaddressed draft of a memo to Ulrich's superiors. The document was clotted with technical jargon, but the gist of it was clear: Ulrich was asking his bosses for permission to discontinue the zeph.r tests. After several weeks of promising results, the high bandwidth treatments and a subsequent increase in the intensity of brain activity and performance was becoming counterproductive. Ulrich was worried that the zeph.r treatments were beginning to cause permanent degenerative damage to Westlake's brain. The memo closed with Ulrich stating that if his request was denied, he would have no choice but to tender his resignation, effective immediately. The memo was dated six weeks before Westlake opened fire on allied Afghan troops in Kandahar.

Lastly, Duggan played the video and watched as his screen became an eyewitness documentary of the last two minutes of Donald Westlake's life. The clip, which seemed to have been taken by a GoPro camera attached to an airman's helmet, began with the jerky movement of soldiers roused from their barracks by sudden gunfire, half-dressed and stumbling over each other as they scrambled for their weapons and rushed outside, expecting to confront the enemy and instead finding one of their own robotically gunning down Afghan allies. The camera must have been on Martin Fisk's helmet, because Duggan could hear him yelling over the clamor at his buddy, begging him to stop, over and over, before shooting him dead. The last few seconds of the video showed Westlake turning to face the camera and, in a flash of recognition and agonizing self-awareness, grabbing Fisk's rifle, holding the muzzle to his forehead, and waiting for his drone sensor and best friend to pull the trigger. The final seconds showed Westlake, his eyes bottomless black holes, silently mouthing the words *Do it, Marty. Help me do it,* before the rifle round sent pieces of his skull corkscrewing away from the back of his head.

Duggan vomited into his wastepaper basket and stayed in a crouch for a few minutes, waiting for the nausea to pass. Then he wiped his mouth, picked up the phone and dialed Peter Palladino in Spokane. The psychologist took the call right away. "I thought I might be hearing from you," he said somberly.

"Really? Why's that?"

"I figured you must have heard," Palladino said.

"Heard what?"

"I'm sorry to tell you this, but Marty Fisk is in the hospital. He took an overdose of tranquilizers and alcohol a couple days ago. It looks like he'll pull through, but it was a close call."

Duggan thought about the feisty and fit veteran he'd encountered at Priest Lake and how determined he seemed to stay alive. "Doctor, I know he was your patient, but the man I met didn't seem the least bit suicidal."

"Look, Agent Duggan, off the record, I agree with you. But as I explained before, these cases are very complicated. There's no way to predict, no way to be sure. Sometimes the healing doesn't go deep enough."

"Did he leave a note?"

"Yes, to his wife, Laura. It basically said how much he loved her and how sorry he was that this was the only way he could protect her."

"Protect her from what?"

"I really don't know," Palladino said. "He won't talk to me."

"Do you have Laura Fisk's home number?"

"She said something about going to stay with relatives for a while. But you're welcome to try."

Duggan hung up and called the number Palladino gave him. On the second ring, a man with a familiar voice answered the phone.

"Wasson?"

"Hello, Agent Duggan. How's your soccer game?"

"What are you doing at Marty's house?"

"They discharged me a week after you left—spineless motherfuckers. Maybe we weren't as covert as we thought. Should've known they were watching us the whole time."

Duggan could tell from the slight slur in Wasson's voice that he'd been drinking.

"You didn't answer my question," Duggan said.

"Laura's kinda messed up over Marty. We're all messed up, aren't we? Every fucking one of us. I came to help Laura with the kids, but nobody's home." There was a pause. "We should have helped Donny—bunch of dick-less cowards. We all saw the scar on Donny's neck, but we just looked the other way."

"Don't be so hard on yourself, Mitch."

"Agent Duggan, did you send Marty the video?"

"What video?"

"The video of Marty shooting Donny. That's why Marty tried to kill himself. I figured you already knew that."

"No, I didn't. The video came from Marty's helmet camera, didn't it?"

"Yeah. But those pictures of Donny all wired up and the memo ... That wasn't Marty."

"Who else knew about the video?"

There was another short pause. "After the shooting, a lot of people came and went. They confiscated everybody's stuff—cameras, laptops, you name it."

"And the video of the shootings was still in Marty's camera?"

"I guess."

"Was one of the guys who came and went named Kenneth Ulrich?"

"I don't know. Who's that?"

"Good-looking guy with steel-rimmed glasses and a blondish beard."

"Maybe. It's not something I would have noticed."

"Was it something Donny Westlake would have noticed?"

"I don't know. I suppose. It's none of my business. But I'll tell you this: whoever sent that video wanted everybody from the base to see it."

"Why do you say that?"

"Because they sent a copy to me too."

"Dr. Palladino told me that Marty's suicide note said he was doing it to protect Laura. Do you know why Marty would say that?"

"Maybe he was feeling like a liability."

"One more question: Did you leave the lime-green Post-it message for me on Donny's computer?"

"Yes."

"So you lied to me."

"No."

"How's that?"

"That night at the base, you asked me if I put the Post-it on Donny's computer, and I said I didn't, which was true. I wrote the words, but the Post-it was already there."

27

··

They came dressed in white from small towns and big cities, from the sunstruck suburbs of Phoenix and Miami and the hipster meccas of Williamsburg and Portland, from the well-heeled beaches of the Carolinas and the multicultural precincts of Atlanta and LA, from the redwood forest and the gulf stream waters, in cars and boats and planes and trucks and buses, from England and Brazil and Bali and Japan and Mexico and Denmark, and a hundred backyard backwaters where techno wasn't even in the vocabulary. They came alone and in couples and groups, friends and lovers, brothers and sisters, fathers and sons, saviors and sinners, orphans and outliers, drawn toward the intertwined Xs they could see from miles away, sensing that the translucent beacon soaring above it all was there for a reason beyond LED dazzle and dangling circus swingers. They wore the clear plastic bracelets on their wrists as badges of honor, physical proof that they had answered the call and paid tribute to the tribe, raising their arms for the automated scanners in an inadvertent salute to their fellow dancers and dreamers, whose numbers were increasing each second, until the burgeoning throng looked back to see who was behind them and returned raised fists to the fresh arrivals in a sign of solidarity and welcome and a roar of mutual recognition rose up from both sides of the turnstiles, a spontaneous anthem to the aggregation of familiar strangers before anything had even happened yet, except that something already had and everybody felt it and knew it.

Up in the DJ module, Xander and Tom heard the shouts and marveled at the parade of fans pouring past the jeering anti-rave hecklers and patrolling police vans. Fifty feet above the ground, with a view in every direction, the circular enclosure seemed to Xander like a starship hovering over a planet of upturned faces.

"God bless America," Xander effused. He turned to X-ist's first guest DJ. "Are you ready to take the helm?"

"Aye aye, Commander X!" The electronic luminaries and their comely crews feted each other with animated fist pounds and tequila shots. Somebody turned up the trip-hop on the capsule's monitors until the room was shaking on its hinges and all aboard were swept up in a pristine moment of unbridled levitation.

Tom tugged on Xander's shirt and pointed to the staircase. "Let's go higher. I want to show you something." On their way out, Tom hit a button and the peal of cathedral bells, pumped through a half-million-watt sound system, reverberated through the valley.

Duggan, who was checking e-mails at the NCSD command post set up under a row of weeping willows, flinched from the momentous clanging. It was like the Berkeley carillon magnified a hundred times. "What the hell?" He surveyed the crowd as several dozen agents milled around in white T-shirts and jeans, checking their guns and touching base with undercover spotters positioned around the grounds. Susan Oliver was there too, perched demurely on a plastic folding chair under the trees in her best Lucy in the Sky dress.

Eric handed Duggan a pair of earbuds connected to a wire running to a small plastic pack. "Put them on when the music starts," he instructed, "and they'll cancel out any microwave beams. I already passed them out to your men."

"Thanks." Duggan stowed the wave-deflector kit in his pocket. "What's so amusing?"

"Nothing. It's just that I never thought I'd see a bunch of Homeland Security agents dressed in white and rocking glow sticks and EDM backstage passes."

"Me neither," Duggan said. "Any sign of Swarm or zeph.r?"

"No, just the usual cell phone noise." Eric pensively tapped the screen of his mini-tablet. "I heard on Twitter that the US Army just joined the party."

"Yeah, they're bivouacked just a few miles away."

"Did you know the army was authorized to deploy MEDUSA? It stands for Mob Excess Deterrent Using Silent Audio."

"Believe me, I made it clear to General Mansfield that those things are only to be used as a last resort ..."

"That's not what I'm getting at. Remember when I told you about PHAROH and how the main problem in our field test was a lack of amplification? Well, it occurred to me that if PHAROH could be connected to MEDUSA, the signal might be strong enough to disrupt zeph.r."

"That's an interesting idea, but it's too late. Besides, Cara nixed that option, remember?"

Eric shrugged. "I'm just saying."

"What about the emergence computer model at NSA? Did you ever get a number?"

"Thirty thousand, theoretically. But there wasn't time to test the model for errors. Plus, the correspondence between density thresholds for grasshoppers and humans is still pretty inexact, to say the least."

Duggan barked into his wireless. "What's the count at the door? I need you to close the gates when it reaches twenty-five thousand." Duggan listened briefly before answering. "Because that's the limit— that's why. If the organizers push back, tell them they can take it up with the sheriff or the mayor or, if they prefer, they can talk to the commander of the Eastern National Guard." Another pause. "Yes, I'm serious."

Duggan turned back to Eric. "I want you to stay here with Susan Oliver. If you pick up a signal, text me immediately and I'll meet you both at the VIP entrance to the main stage."

"Roger that," Eric chirped.

A ticktock tattoo began to tap from the speakers, the sonic countdown to blast off. On cue, the crowd erupted as synthetic fanfares underlined the DJ's digitally distorted voice:

Are you
ready?
Are you
here?
Are you
ready
to
X-ist?

Duggan flinched again as his wristband lit up and started blinking in neon yellow.

Eric seemed mesmerized by his own flashing bracelet.

"You like this shit, don't you?"

Eric nodded. "What about you, Agent Duggan? You can feel the beat, right? I'll bet you've got some moves."

Duggan looked at Eric to make sure he wasn't joshing. "I can dance to anything if I've had enough to drink. But I'm more of a blues and classic rock kind of guy."

"That's cool too."

"Yeah, it is. Just keep your ears on the radio and your eyes on that screen. I'll be checking in every fifteen minutes." Duggan went over to where Susan Oliver was sitting. "Susan, I must say you're dressed appropriately."

"I asked you to call me Lucy, Agent Duggan."

"Sorry, Lucy. Are you still okay with what we're planning to do?"

"He's here. I can feel his energy."

"That's good, Lucy. Stay here with Deputy Agent Wightman. When we've confirmed that Swarm is on the premises, Eric will escort you to the VIP stage entrance and we'll take you up to the lower platform so your boyfriend can see you, okay?"

Lucy nodded, but her eyes were fixed on the rotating bauble in the sky.

"Damn, how tall is this thing?"

Xander was following Tom up the metal stairs encased in the upper arms of the polyhedron.

"Almost two hundred feet to the top, remember?"

"I mean the *X* part. You're not getting me up on that freaking Eiffel antenna."

"Don't worry," Tom said, "we're almost there."

They emerged through a trapdoor to the roof just as the clouds ignited in orange and violet streaks over the trees. The St. Elmo's tower rose another sixty-five feet above them, and four retractable cranes with trapeze bars attached to the cables were folded against its base. To the east, it was possible to discern the early evening lights of Philadelphia.

"Holy shit," Xander said, firing up a joint. "You can see the whole damned state from here." He pointed to the steel spire's pinnacle. "That's where you'll make your blue lightning, right? And those cranes are for the trapeze artists to fly over the crowd during my set."

"Yeah, but that's not what I want to show you."

Tom led him to a ten-by ten-foot cube made of wire mesh. "It's a Faraday cage." He opened the door, motioning for Xander to follow.

"I get it," Xander said. "This is where you incarcerate the guilty ones, right?"

"Actually, it's the opposite," Tom countered. "The first one of these was built by Michael Faraday back in the 1830s to shield people from electromagnetic radiation. I had it put in to protect the workers in case of lightning storms or if something went wrong with the St. Elmo's fire, but I brought you here so you know where to go if things get too crazy tonight."

"How crazy is 'too crazy'?"

Tom handed Xander a pair of binoculars. "See all those anti-rave demonstrators and cops?"

"Yeah, dude, that's why we hired our own private security."

"Now follow that road over there, about three miles to the south. What do you see?"

"Trucks, people."

"That's the US Army, Xan. The haters at the gates with their signs and insults are trying to pick a fight. They know the authorities are just looking for an excuse to come in and shut us down. The DJ booth is shielded, too, but if things get hairy, I want you to get the gun and meet me here, okay?"

Xander put down the binoculars. "If things get hairy," he repeated. "Why do you need a Faraday cage? There aren't any thunderstorms in the weather report."

"It's just a precaution, you know, for surveillance or stray microwave beams."

Xander's eyes narrowed on Tom. "Are you talking about the government or Swarm? You think he's here, don't you?"

"Swarm isn't a person or even a program, Xan. You said it yourself. Government troops are here because there's a war brewing, and X-ist just became ground zero."

Xander threw the joint down and stubbed it out with his shoe. "You knew this could be dangerous, and you still talked me into doing it."

"Because it's the right thing to do, Xan. Because it's time to take a stand while we still can. Look at that crowd—they're not here just for a good time. They showed up in spite of everything, because they want to belong to something. What Swarm is talking about—this fight for who controls the way we think, what we think, where and when we think—is just the beginning."

Xander shook his head slowly. "That's what the cage is really for, isn't it, Tom? You've bought into all this paranoid propaganda about mind wars, transmitters and cameras under every rock, mini-drones behind every cloud. You even have your own doomsday box on the fifty-yard line. Christ, it's just too rich, man. The cops don't have to put you in a cage; you're already doing it to yourself!"

"And what about Sedona," Tom shot back, "your little star-fucker fortress? Turning your back on the fans who follow you and need you, refusing to take sides—that's your cage, Xan."

"At least my cage has a view."

Tom put his palm on Xander's back and led him to the roof's edge. He reached over and raised Xander's arm to the crowd, and thousands below instantly responded with a deafening cheer of jubilation. "So does mine."

As the rave progressed, Duggan's wristband had changed along with each DJ set, from yellow to green to red. In minutes, DJX, the headliner and final act, would take the stage. What was next, purple? With a hologramic appearance by Prince? Still no sign of Swarm. Could someone have tipped him off? Then again, there was also the possibility that Wightman's crowd threshold theory was actually working.

Duggan spoke into his wireless. "Door status?"

"We closed it down at just under twenty-four thousand," the agent reported. "But I've got to tell you, sir, there are a lot of pissed-off people outside the gates, not to mention the anti-techno agitators. So far we've been able to keep them apart and hold everybody back."

"Good. Let me know if anything changes." Duggan's next call was to Wightman. "Eric, it looks like your crowd limit idea is working—either that or Swarm is saving his ammo for DJX."

"Or Swarm *is* DJX."

"We already checked into that. Xander Smith was in Spain when Swarm was meeting with Cara in Austin. If Swarm is here, Lucy is still our best bet to lure him out. How's she doing?"

"Lucy's fine," Eric said, "but she keeps saying she can 'feel him.' Kinda creeps me out. I'm picking up some trace zeph.r radiation from people's phones, but nothing more than you'd find at the local mall these days. Plus, the wristbands are making a lot of signal noise. I think X is planning something special for the grand finale."

"Just keep your eyes peeled and keep your phone on in case I need you."

"Will do. Ten-four."

Duggan's wristband and the *X* tower blazed alive in electric blue, and X-ist erupted in a paroxysm of screams and exultation. A bone-rattling tone, like the blast of an ocean liner's horn, announced the festival's namesake and main attraction. Swathed in a form-fitting white astronaut's jumpsuit, DJX emerged onto the elevated module and bowed to the cheering crowd as fireworks exploded and glassy sheets of water cascaded into a hidden moat. From his nook at the core of the DJ module, Tom oversaw the audiovisual effects, including a new set of hands-free controls he designed with the Rife manual to shape and modulate mood and intensity by transmitting signals to the X-ist bracelets.

Just as Xander had envisioned, the show began with the rubbery twang of an Asian Jaw harp, harmonically tweaked and boosted until it dissolved into a jagged waltz of shuffling beats, Native American chants, and thunderstorm effects. A churning polyrhythm began a steady ascent to the drop, where it wobbled and veered into a swaggering stomp, a goliath's footsteps shuddering deep into the planet's core. For the ensuing hour, Xander conducted an aural tour of the galaxy, buzzing past planets and spewing quasars, whizzing around moons and meteors, pausing to strum the rings of Saturn and evoke the scattered jostle of asteroid belts before resuming his astral trajectory toward the flaring heart of the solar system.

DJX stoked the crowd with flanged progressions and shredded chords, prodding the revelers into harder and faster gyrations, until the lights blacked out and the entire valley was illuminated by a pulsing ocean of blinking blue bracelets, each wrist oscillating with its own spiraling constellation. Then, as the aerialists descended from the cranes like spastic butterflies and St. Elmo's fire unfurled blue tendrils into the cloudless sky, Tom used flickering lasers to paint the air with the fractal prelude to "Stardust." This was the moment he had been preparing and waiting for. This was the prophecy that the Hopi elders had feared, and this was why Tom had spent endless hours rearranging ones and zeros into a program that could integrate the biotech matrix of music and nature and thought and spawn the next iteration of the species. "Let the Blue Kachina dance," he said.

"Oh, shit, it's happening!" The radio wave detector on Wightman's screen was jittering in the red zone. He texted Duggan:

Zeph.r signal is off the hook! Use your earbuds!

In the seconds before Duggan could find the signal deflector and activate it, he felt an electric tingle along with the startling sensation that he knew exactly what everyone around him was thinking and feeling—or could have if he completed the biochemical circuit by inviting their minds into his. His heart was beating so loud and fast … or was it the music?

He texted Eric: Bring Lucy to the VIP entrance next to the stage and I'll meet you there.

Duggan pressed ahead through the stew of sweating bodies, trying not to acknowledge the unavoidable contact of warm limbs and skin, the welcoming smiles and gently exploring hands, the alarming allure of liquid light and laughter and animal heat that was happening all around him and threatening to kindle the same flame inside.

The dancers moved as one, their attention focused only on each other and on the sublimely synchronized pulse. Tom could feel the texture of their radiance as he surfed the sloping trough of a giant signal wave, his entire body flexing and bending with it, until the frequencies were joined and enhanced by a galvanizing presence that had reached out across the Internet and rallied the faithful to this pivotal time and place.

Brothers and sisters,
the time has come,
this time,
our time.

Enemies surround us;
fear follows us;
evolution awaits us.

Open your eyes.
Can you see it?
Move your bodies.
Can you feel it?
Seize the moment.
Be the moment

The ravers faced the *X* and hoisted their phones in universal acceptance. Duggan realized that they weren't just hearing Swarm; they were also *seeing* him through the app streaming from their wristbands into any bluetoothed device. Swarm was revealing himself through the augmented 3-D mosaic of their handheld screens, like a spectral apparition conjured from a parallel dimension. As Duggan continued threading his way toward the stage, he had the unnerving awareness of being watched. He paused to look around, and his blood froze. Every person in his vicinity was staring at him with the same detached watchfulness, the way a video feed relays images without filtering or evaluation. Their eyes followed him as he moved, but the dancers made no effort to stop him.

The music lurched into a staccato military march, and woven into the cresting waves of synth, Duggan thought he could discern strings of words, incomplete sentences, uttered at different volumes and speeds, looping and overlapping as the crowd responded with increasing vigor to Swarm's avid exhortations.

Wake up.
Own your mind.
Be the future.
Save the nation.
Do it now.

Duggan could see Eric and Lucy standing on the lower platform about forty yards away. A young man emerged from the tower and approached Lucy, who turned and stepped toward him. They hesitated and embraced.

"Attention, all agents!" Duggan blurted into his radio. "Suspect sighted on lower tower platform! Approach with extreme caution!"

A man is talking to Lucy, Eric texted. What should I do?

Nothing. Just don't let them out of your sight.

Duggan's radio crackled. "Agent Duggan, we've got a situation at the gates!"

His worst-case scenario was materializing. Mobilized by Swarm's incantations and the optimized zeph.r signal, the thousands who had been stranded outside were overrunning the police lines and pouring through the turnstiles, pushed forward by those behind them, pressurizing the crowd. If this kept up, they would exceed Eric's density threshold in minutes. Duggan texted Eric, who was hanging back near Lucy and her soft-spoken suitor.

The people we kept outside broke through the police barricade. I don't think we can stop them

I know. I can see it from here. I've got more bad news. The zeph.r code has been modified. It's different, more potent than I expected. The bracelets are automatically binding the new arrivals to the group

What happens if the crowd reaches critical mass?

They'll begin to move to avoid being trampled by those rushing in behind them. If the morphogenesis is allowed to continue, the hive will begin to act as a single entity, one that will do anything it can to feed and survive

How will Swarm control it?

Distributed systems have no brain or central command. Once the hive mind takes over, Swarm can't control it. Nobody can.

As soon as Tom saw Lucy, he knew that this would be the first and last time they would ever meet. There was a man hovering nearby, unarmed and obviously harmless. Tom approached Lucy and gingerly caressed her hands and arms, inhaling the scent of her hair, kissing her neck.

"I'm sorry, baby," he said. "I've been a lousy boyfriend."

She turned to look at him, already smiling. "Don't apologize," Lucy said, pulling him closer. "I know you love me. I felt your presence all day. They thought I was crazy, but I'm not."

"You're not crazy, but it's not safe here."

Lucy looked over Tom's shoulder at Eric. "Darling, I've got to tell you something. There's a man named Duggan from Homeland Security. He's using me to get to you."

"I know." Tom brushed back her hair and kissed her. "Don't worry. He can't hurt me."

"I only went along with his plan because I had to see you, even if it was just once. Forgive me, my love."

"It's not your fault." Tom disengaged. "I'm so sorry, sweet Lucy, but I can't stay."

"No, it's not fair," she protested. "You can't leave me again! I don't even know your fucking name."

"It's Tom."

He touched her hand and felt something far beyond regret, a glimpse of something that was never meant to be, an alternate reality of home-cooked dinners and children laughing in the backyard, perfectly imagined and forever out of reach.

"I know, I know," she said between sobs. "Tom, don't go."

"Tom's already gone, baby. He left a long time ago."

Duggan watched Swarm disappear into the base of the *X* and cursed. "Suspect has reentered the tower!" he hollered into his handset. "I'm going after him." But before he could take another step, he was surrounded by a group of about twenty men, their vacant expressions replaced with a malevolent glare. Duggan remembered reading about the riots on Governor's Island. He wondered if he was about to find out firsthand what had happened to the intruders who made the mistake of taking on the hive. The first group of agents never had a chance. Before they could reach for their guns, Swarm's disciples overwhelmed them, breaking their bones and necks with unblinking efficiency, yanking out their tongues and gouging their eyes with their fingers and thumbs. Duggan drew his gun and shot the two attackers closest to him as a second squad of agents joined the fray. In the broadening tussle, Duggan managed to claw his way to the platform, glad for once that the music was loud enough to drown out all but the most piercing screams.

Xander was waiting for Tom in the Faraday cage. "Is this what you meant by 'hairy'?"

"More or less."

"Who's manning the decks?"

"Nobody. The program's on automatic."

Xander chuckled wearily. "I know it's you, Tom. It was you all along, wasn't it? You're Swarm."

Tom sat down across from his friend, who was squatting with his back against the wire mesh.

"What makes you think that?"

Xander took a swig of the champagne bottle he was holding. "I don't know—the way you've been talking lately, your crowd-sourcing trick. But it really wasn't until I saw you working the crowd tonight, the way you mirrored everyone's movements. I saw the mind meld." Xander pointed the bottle accusingly. "You lied to me, Tommy. All this time you've been making me your fool. I thought we were bros."

Tom dipped his head in penitence, relieved that the charade was over. "I'm sorry, Xan. I wanted to tell you, but I couldn't because I didn't understand it myself."

Xander passed the bottle to Tom, who accepted it and took a gulp.

"Cheers," Xander said.

"It started with the flash mobs, just for fun," Tom continued. "Then I used the Internet to help you get gigs, to make you an EDM star."

"You made *me* a star?" Xander leaned back and rolled his eyes. "That's rich, you bastard."

"Really? I thought maybe you'd thank me."

"Yeah, sure." Xander grabbed back the bottle. "Thank you for manipulating my career behind my back. Thank you for turning my

314

biggest concert into a battleground. Thank you for turning my fans into a bunch of dancing dunces!"

"That's not what's happening."

"Tom, do you realize you're a goddamn sociopath? You're wanted by the FBI, for Christ's sake. Cybercriminal Numero Uno!" Xander took another swallow. "That fucking brain wave machine. I saw the way you were drooling at the Rife. Did you write the code yourself? Or was it Swarm? Is he controlling your brain too?"

"Swarm isn't doing anything, Xan. Zeph.r is just a conduit for a transmutation that was already happening, that was always there."

"Blah, blah, blah," Xander sneered. "I've read your blog. What you're doing is wrong. If I had any sense, I'd lock you in this cage and call the cops."

"You don't need to—the feds are already here. They'll be up on a roof any minute."

"So when you're him, or it, whatever the fuck—when you're Swarm, can you read people's minds?"

"It's not like that," Tom said. "You dissolve and something bigger absorbs you."

"Row, row, row your boat," Xander slurred. "Life is but a dream."

"Yeah, and then you wake up dead—end of story," Tom said. "But what if you could be part of something beyond mortality? Something that never dies, something that's barely being born?"

"You make it sound plausible, Tommy, but it's not."

"You can't even see what I'm talking about unless you get inside of it. You can't see it from the outside, only the residue of where it's been."

Xander was silent for a moment. "Like the Higgs frigging boson."

Tom looked up at the St. Elmo's fire, its blue bolts spitting at the stars. "Yeah, a five-sigma event, protons colliding at the speed of light, a fusing of particles, a release of energy."

"Until there's nothing," Xander said. "Less than nothing."

"Until there's nothing we know and everything we don't know."

"And what happens after that? We all fall into a black hole? A bubble of dark matter swallows the fucking universe? What have you done, Tommy?"

"I did what I had to do."

"You selfish motherfucker."

"When gravity bends the light, when Swarm pulls us all to the next level, I won't matter anymore. I won't even exist."

"Ha," Xander said, but his eyes were glistening. "I can't go with you, Tommy. Not this time. I won't follow you into the black hole."

"I know," Tom said. After all that had happened and all that they had done, they had finally arrived at the fork in the road. "Kinda funny how things turn out. Who would have guessed? Not even us."

"Tommy, people could get hurt."

"People are already getting hurt, Xan. They're dying in their heads, and they don't even know it. When the change comes, you'll feel it and you'll see it. The future is inside us."

Xander averted his gaze. "I've heard the song, Tom," he said almost mournfully. "But you've been chugging too much of your own kool-aid, my friend."

"It's not about me or Swarm, Xan. It's about evolution, peeling away the layers, exposing the core."

"Yeah, until you get to iron. Then *ka-boom!*"

As Eric had warned and Duggan had feared, the zeph.r-fueled fusion of densely packed individuals had ignited a biomorphic ecosystem that followed its own rules. The dancers had begun to swirl and churn, their bodies merging into a pattern for seconds before disengaging and recombining in solidarity, wristbands blinking on flailing limbs, still moving to the music as they mobilized to eliminate the threat. Gunshots and screams of pain mixed with grunts and howls of pleasure as Swarm's legions became the twitching skin of something still groping for its true shape and purpose.

His clothes bloody and ripped, Duggan reached the stage along with a few agents who also managed to survive the mayhem. The music shifted gears again, and Duggan turned and blanched as the emergent organism raised its blazing blue bracelets and chanted the words projected on the enormous screens.

Own your mind.
March to Washington.
Tell the president.
Do it together.
Do it now.
Do it.
Do it.
Do it.
Now.

A hush fell across the valley, followed by a rising chorus of guttural yelps. Something new was happening. A concussive groan like a glacier cracking, cleaving, and sliding away. Then, like lava slowly flowing down a mountain, or a fledgling species taking its first steps, the swarm began to move. The police who hadn't been injured or killed in the turnstile stampede stood by helplessly as the cacophonous mass surged around the tower and began to stream south.

"He went inside," Eric told Duggan.

"I know. Two of you stay here to guard the door. The rest come with me." Duggan entered the tower and led the push against the torrent of terrified VIPs trying to escape down the narrow stairwell. Finding the DJ module empty, they paused to reload their guns and continued climbing.

Tom and Xander listened to the commotion coming from below. "You hear that, Tom? It sounds like the kids are getting a little, um, agitated. I guess the Blue Star Kachina took off his mask. Looks like we *are* the brothers in the elders' dream."

317

Tom nodded and stood up. "I need you to do me one last favor, Xan. I need you to lower me down over the side with the trapeze crane."

Xander tilted his head and rubbed the stubble on his chin. Yeah, well, you know what? You can just go fuck yourself, brother."

"I thought you might feel that way," Tom said, pulling the Walther PPK from his pocket and pointing it at his friend.

"Ha," Xander said. "I figured it might be you who took it, but I didn't think I'd be the target."

"You've got about ten seconds before I pull the trigger," Tom warned.

"I'm not going to be able to talk you out of this, am I?"

"Let's go—there isn't much time."

Xander got up, and Tom followed. "You'll always be my brother, Tommy."

"I know."

They reached the tip of the *X*, and the vertigo was almost overwhelming. Tom grabbed the harness as Xander took the controls. "Keep making music, Xan," Tom said. "I didn't invent your talent. The music was all you."

The door to the roof flew open. Duggan, with Eric and Lucy right behind him, was the first one to step out and see them. "Stop!" he shouted, raising his gun. "Homeland Security—stay where you are!"

"Don't shoot!" Xander yelled as he stepped forward, blocking Duggan's line of fire.

"Get out of the way!" Duggan warned. But Xander stood his ground. The bullet entered his right shoulder and exited just inches from Tom's head. Xander slumped against the base of the crane, his hand over his wound as he gazed up at St. Elmo's angry aura. "Hurts like a motherfucker," he said.

"I'm sorry, Xan," Tom said. He dropped the gun, raised his hands, and started backing away from his pursuers. "By the way, you're not the brother who dies. It's me."

"He's going to jump!" Lucy screamed.

"Good-bye, sweet mermaid," Tom said to Lucy as he teetered on the ledge. "'Till human voices wake us, and we drown.'"

Time slowed to a crawl as the scrambling actors in the rooftop drama simultaneously played out different outcomes in their heads. In a bizarre span of seconds in which everyone present saw Tom walking backwards, entropy's arrow seemed to hesitate, as if resetting the cosmic clock of what had already transpired, re-spooling what the double helix of chance and biological imperative had put into motion long before anyone involved knew their part in the unfolding events, or even if they had ever really had a choice except to follow through on an instinctual and molecular level that briefly but eternally tied them to the marauding mass of minds doing the same thing below.

Before Duggan could aim and fire again, Tom extended his arms, closed his eyes, and let himself fall backward into eighty-five feet of empty space. Duggan and Eric reached the edge of the roof just in time to see a hundred wrist-banded arms rise up to catch their precious cargo. They watched in disbelief as Swarm was carried away by the human tsunami surging toward the capital.

Duggan checked Xander's pulse and called to the other agents, "Somebody get EMS!" He put his hand on Eric's shoulder. "Listen to me. You've got to warn the president."

"But, Jake, I don't *know* the president."

"Call Agent Nutley. Tell him Swarm is headed to Washington and I'm in pursuit. I'll stay in contact as long as my battery holds up."

Duggan climbed into the harness and handed Eric the controls. "Lower me down," he ordered.

"What if it doesn't reach all the way?"

"Then I'll jump."

Eric looked down at the boisterous torrent of bodies marching south into the night. "Are you sure?" he asked.

"No, but do it anyway."

No arms reached up to soften Duggan's landing as Eric released him into the murmuring procession of biomorphic crusaders. Instead, at the last moment, the stampeding sea parted to make a space just large enough for him to reach the ground and get his footing before closing around him and continuing its forward rush. It took Duggan a few minutes to adjust to the unflagging pace and the familiar sensation that even without direct eye contact from his marauding companions, he was being observed. Duggan looked at his phone to confirm that they were heading south, straight to where Lieutenant General Mansfield would be waiting with part of the US Fifth Army. But before he could dial, fingers clenched his phone and snatched it away. Clearly, instant communication was out of bounds for the colony's newest addition. Now there would be no way to know if Mansfield had received orders to confront the marchers—or what might happen if he did.

The mob surged in a linear orientation across fields and highways, stopping traffic, trampling fences, and fording streams, all the while producing what seemed at first to be an inane yammering of repeated phrases and random outbursts but on closer listening turned out to be a patois of words and half sentences from Swarm's sermon blended with a polyglot blather of fast-food jingles and housing prices, the weather in Paris and TV newscasts spliced into sputters of letters and numbers. It was an open communications channel, a crowd-generated communiqué of unlimited bandwidth, a language beyond language that vaguely reminded Duggan of the jangling machine-to-machine screech of early computer dial-up connections.

Some of the marchers held up phones that showed blue arrows pointing the way, augmented-reality signposts planted by Swarm to guide his legions to their target in Washington. About forty minutes into the march, the din intensified and the emergent entity began to reorganize itself, with adult males moving to the front and sides and women and youths shifting to the middle and rear. Without even trying, Duggan found himself in the front ranks with the larger men, giving him his first glimpse of what had instigated the reconfiguration. On a ridge up ahead, a five-hundred-man unit of Northcom's Consequence Management Response Force was blocking the way to the capitol. Floodlights illuminated the grass and trees for at least a hundred yards around, telegraphing the warning that anyone who challenged the troops would be fair game for the array of MEDUSA microwave cannons. Remembering Mansfield's warning about the disposability of domestic cyberterrorists, Duggan started to move toward the back of the mob, away from the phalanx of troops in full riot gear. A web of hands clutched his shoulders and kept him where he was.

"This is an illegal demonstration," a bullhorn speaker announced. "Disperse immediately! You have one minute to comply."

Instead of heeding the army's order, the mob's male vanguard lunged forward in a V formation, gathering speed and numbers as they charged the government line. Tear gas shells ripped into the trees and sprouted like white mushrooms on the damp earth. Then Duggan heard a sickening hum and crackle as the MEDUSA cannons were activated. He crumpled in pain as the beam swept over him, a searing, deafening pressure in his head. As the rebels closest to the MEDUSA machines writhed on the ground with blood running from their ears, the men behind them immediately replenished their ranks while others carried the wounded away. A volley of rubber bullets and live machine-gun fire took out another row of attackers. But the rebels, moving with the organized vehemence of enraged insects, kept coming until the dumbstruck soldiers were overwhelmed and manually dismembered by their unarmed adversaries, some of whom stopped to pick up the fallen troops' guns and weapons while the others forged ahead. The rebels would have won the skirmish if it hadn't been for the tanks. Incendiary concussion shells blinded and scattered the attackers, who were forced to relent and rejoin the main group as it retreated to the west. Duggan noticed that the arrows on the ravers' phones had changed, like a GPS recalculating a new route to its destination. It now showed a circumventing path through Amish country, to Lancaster and across the Susquehanna River to York, before turning south again toward the District of Columbia.

The rebel battalion, still carrying the wounded and dead on its shoulders, continued its eastward trek. It wasn't long before there was another commotion ahead, and Duggan guessed that the Northcom force had circled around the marchers and set up a second blockade. Without discussion or apparent directive, the mob splintered into small pods of five to ten people, fanning out into the countryside to avoid the government troops, traversing a moonlit landscape of thatched-roof farms with pastures of grazing cows and rolled bales of sweet-smelling hay, scattering across grassy meadows bordered by wooden grain silos and pens of snuffling pigs and supercilious llamas. Duggan's group, four other men and one women, took a northwestern loop that would require a fast pace if they expected to rejoin the others at the river crossing south of Lancaster.

"Did you come to X-ist alone?" The woman spoke in a covert tone as they trekked down a dirt road leading to a covered bridge. Duggan wondered if the girl, a brunette in her late twenties with short hair and an athletic build, was breaking the rules by talking to him. Her sneakers were laced with pink glow sticks.

"Yes," Duggan lied. "How about you?"

"I came with my brother, but he got hurt in the fighting. Another group is carrying him to Washington." They entered the covered bridge, which smelled of gasoline and horse manure. "My name's Janice, by the way."

"Jake."

"Nice to meet you, Jake. What are your plans for the emergent reality?"

"Ah, I'm not sure," he said. "You mean the rave, right?"

"No," Janice said, lowering her voice. "X-ist is just the beginning."

"The beginning of what?"

The other men were walking in lockstep nearby, one of them making electric drum noises with his mouth. Duggan didn't have to try to run away to know they would stop him.

"Own your mind," Janice said, repeating it like a mantra. "March on Washington, own your mind, own your mind, own your mind. Do it now."

"Excuse me?"

"Good question," Janice said, picking up their conversation as if nothing unusual had happened. "There are so many possibilities, a world without borders or boundaries or war. Where do you start?"

"I guess you start right here."

"Exactly!" Janice whispered excitedly, her bracelet blinking. "*This* is where it starts. Not being alone or afraid anymore, not hating nature or each other, not constantly feeding the hunger for unnecessary things. That's the true definition of personal emancipation. The true self is not the individual ego; it's the sum of everything inside us and around us."

Duggan wondered what Cara would say about this conversation. Was Janice just parroting what she'd heard or was her bracelet transmitting the words into her head?

"Do you know why we're going to the White House?" Duggan asked.

"Oh, is that where we're going?"

The other men halted in their tracks and made a signal to stop. Duggan listened, but all he could hear were crickets and the muted snuffles of sleeping livestock. Then the outline of a man emerged from the murk. He was holding a rifle and waiting for them to get closer. Their flashing wristbands, Duggan realized, made them sitting ducks. "You people are on my damn land," the man growled. "Do you know what we do with trespassers around here?"

Before he could answer his own question, the biggest male in Duggan's group sprinted forward, the other men following close behind. The first bullet wounded the leader, but the other two reached the man in the shadows before he could reload. Duggan heard the wet smack of fists on skin and bones breaking, then a strangled scream. There was a short lull, followed by a splash in the creek below.

The two remaining rebels tended to the wounded marcher and motioned to Duggan and Janice. "Keep moving," they said. "March to Washington. Do it now."

They walked without talking again for several hours. Once a while, one or two of the men would dash into a house or a barn and come back with food and water. Duggan didn't dare ask what they did to get it. After a while, he could tell they were getting close to Lancaster. Gradually, like a condensed history of the industrial revolution, the pastoral surroundings and wooden structures gave way to gated stucco houses and electric lights, live animals became canned meats, dirt roads fed into the network of paved highways and billboards. Looming ahead were ads promoting the "Susquehanna Ale Trail" and a giant poster for a sight-and-sound spectacle called "Noah," which featured a forty-foot replica of the biblical ark floating in a man-made lake.

Human shapes began to materialize around them in the gloom, an influx of volunteers of all types and ages singing patriotic songs and carrying American flags as they joined the surge to the capital. The marchers converged in Lancaster's historic downtown, where TV crews broadcasting from the scene added to the carnival atmosphere. Hoots and applause echoed off the brick buildings as the swollen ranks of the rebel army greeted each other and fresh recruits passed out water, beer, and peanut butter and jelly sandwiches. Duggan watched in amazement as an expanding throng of newcomers from all directions joined the rebels in white. And as Tom paused to absorb the scale and implication of the impromptu people's pageant, he glimpsed something he had not seen in a very long time, maybe not ever: a self-regulating congress of Americans of every age, shape and social stripe, nodding and moving together, extremities linked and voices chiming in unanimous agreement.

A pickup truck loaded with apples crawled through the teeming streets with a trio of young men lobbing fruit from the back and shouting "Compliments of the Meta Militia!" A poster on the tailgate showed a picture that Duggan recognized—it was an image of Westlake wearing his microwave crown of thorns. The caption underneath: "Who killed Donald Westlake?"

Duggan caught two apples and handed one to Janice.

"Thanks," she said. "Is this Washington?"

"No, it's a city called Lancaster."

"Sorry, I'm from Kansas."

"We have to cross the river to a town called York. Then it's another hundred miles or so to Washington."

"Oh, jeez," Janice said. "I'm sure glad I wore sneakers."

"Listen," Duggan said politely. "It's been really nice meeting you, but I've got to get out of here. Will you help me?"

Janice frowned. "We're not supposed to let you leave."

"Who told you that?"

"Nobody. I just know."

"Janice, I like you," Duggan said, "and I can tell you're a good person. But if I don't get to Washington soon, a lot of innocent people could get hurt, and by that I'm talking about the people around us right now too."

"I believe you, Jake, but that's the whole point," Janice said. "We're not afraid anymore. It's the artificial isolation of individuality that makes us feel vulnerable and scared."

Duggan didn't need to turn around to know his two guardians weren't far behind. Would they abandon their limping comrade to chase him? His best opportunity to escape was before daybreak, which was just a few hours away. But he also had no doubt that if he tipped off Janice to his plan, she'd turn against him.

"Janice, what does 'own your mind' mean? How can you own it when you don't even control it?"

Her body stiffened, and when she turned, her eyes drilled into him.

"You're not paying attention, Agent Duggan," she chided in a low register.

A quiver of apprehension ran up Duggan's spine. "How did you know my name?"

"You're wondering if you are talking to a girl from Kansas or the man who jumped off the roof before you could shoot him," Janice said. Her bracelet was blinking again. "The truest answer is neither and both."

"Why are you doing this? Why are you leading these people to Washington?"

"Nobody is *leading* anything," Janice said sternly. "I'm nobody and everybody. I'm nothing and everything."

"So then why even bother to advance evolution? Shouldn't people be allowed to choose for themselves?"

"That's the whole point," Janice said. "It's time for us to embrace the obvious."

"So why are you leading your army to Washington?"

"Agent Duggan, I told you that I'm not *leading* anybody. The meta mind doesn't need an instruction manual. The path to our evolution is already inside us and all around us. Only those who oppose freedom of mind will be left behind."

"Like Donald Westlake?"

Janice made a face that didn't look natural on a pretty young woman. "He was a victim of your techno-industrial war machine."

"Is that your phrase? Or something you got from Kenneth Ulrich?"

"Ulrich's Militia and the Swarm are on a parallel course for the moment, but we don't share the same motive or ultimate destination."

"So then why declare a war on the government?

"Only free minds can fully flower. The government needs to understand and reflect that. There is no need for a material struggle. We only do what is necessary for our self-defense. It's you and your kind who turn weapons on the innocent and incite violence."

"So then why haven't you killed me yet?"

"Because it's important for you to see this, to understand what's actually happening. Our species is on the brink of an evolutionary leap, and you are on the wrong side of genetic history. But there's hope for you yet, Agent Duggan, because if the seed of transformation wasn't already taking root in your consciousness, you wouldn't be able to hear me."

Duggan took a breath and slowly exhaled. "Okay, so if I'm already part of you, can I at least borrow your phone?"

Janice gave Duggan a chastising look and wagged her finger. "That's the dumbest thing you've said all night."

As the rebels approached the Wrights Ferry Bridge, there were shouts and howls of dismay. The Northcom task force, reloaded and itching for a fight, was hunkered down on the other side of the river, waiting. Without hesitation, the mob altered course and spilled over the embankment toward the water. One by one, the biggest males took positions along the riverbank and locked arms until they had formed the first span of a human bridge. As the befuddled troops watched from above, succeeding waves of men climbed over the others and extended the chain until it reached the opposite bank. The rebels began pouring across the Susquehanna while a platoon of warrior males regrouped to confront the outflanked reserve. All at once, the main group poured down the bank toward the human bridges, pulling Duggan and his escorts along with it.

In the commotion of splashing limbs, detonating fragmentation bombs, and sputtering machine-gun fire, Duggan managed to discreetly separate from his captors and drift away. He waited until he was halfway across the living viaduct to dive downriver, staying submerged as long as possible to avoid detection. He surfaced gasping for air, exhausted and worried that at any second Janice and her goons would find him and drag him down to the bottom. He grabbed onto a floating chunk of wood and hand-paddled downstream, trying to conserve energy, waiting for the clamor of the battle of Susquehanna to subside behind him. After a while there was only darkness and the clammy grip of the current.

Duggan turned onto his back and allowed himself to be swallowed by the murk, imagining he had drowned, held down by Swarm's soldiers until his lungs filled and he sank like a stone. Was that how it felt to lose one's individuality, he wondered, and become one with the uber mind? Duggan didn't fear death, but during the past few days, as his sense of reality was upended by murderous cyber-terrorists and rampaging techno-rebels at war with the US army, he had begun to feel a gathering sense of dread, a disheartening unease that Swarm's goal of social catharsis had already been achieved. The deeper damage of Swarm's movement didn't come from the actions of his mesmerized followers, it was how his rants about the next phase of humanity had found tinder in the lives and minds of ordinary people, Americans who had reached a point of such faithless exasperation that they were willing to rip away the tattered façade of civilization just to find out what was behind it. The chill that Duggan felt wasn't just physical, it was also the creeping conviction that no matter what happened when the Xist-istas reached Washington, the country he knew and loved had jumped its rails in ways that that nobody had even begun to fathom.

Duggan drifted near a deserted boat dock, and he used the last of his strength to swim to it and haul himself out, dripping and covered in weeds and river slime, like a primordial ancestor taking its first tentative steps on dry land. Duggan staggered toward the deserted service road and tried to get his bearings. Hitchhiking was a lost cause in his current state, so he walked for what seemed like miles before he found a shuttered mini-mart with a working pay phone. His first call was to Cara.

"My God, when no one could reach you, I started thinking the worst."

"You have no idea how beautiful it is to hear your voice."

"Jake, are you drunk?"

Duggan managed a weary chuckle. "Just tired. Where are you?"

"I'm in Washington, with Eric. He's been working with the army to set up an amplification device for PHAROH."

"But I thought you said ..."

"Forget what I said. When Eric told me what happened at the festival and that you were in danger, I had no choice. Agent Nutley authorized a transport to pick me up and bring PHAROH to Washington."

"Jesus," Duggan said. "I don't know what to say."

"Where are you?"

"I'm not sure. A mini-mart somewhere in western Pennsylvania."

"In Lancaster? It's all over the news. They're saying it's the beginning of some kind of civil war."

"Just tell Nutley to GPS this phone and send a helicopter."

While he waited for the pickup, Duggan pondered his conversation with Swarm. The leader of a leaderless army that carried its own dead and built bridges with their bodies like ants, marching on Washington to do what? It didn't make any sense. If Swarm's goal was to fan the evolutionary flames of the entire species, why would he bother to start a war he couldn't win?

The pay phone rang. It was JT.

Hey, I'm glad you're okay," he said.

"Me too. It's a war zone up river."

"Are you sitting down?"

"No, but tell me."

"Kenneth Ulrich is alive."

"That's impossible. I saw his body at the Meta Militia shootout. So did you."

"Yeah, I know, but we just got the report from forensics. They checked Ulrich's dental records and fingerprints against the body we found in his office, and all the other ones too. None of them are a match. The FBI found a tunnel in the basement of the Militia's hideout. That must be how he got out."

Duggan cursed. "I want you to put out an APB on Ulrich immediately. Go wide—national, state, and local. We can't have another loose cannon running around with a copy of zeph.r on his thumb drive.

"So is Ulrich with Swarm?"

"I don't think so," Duggan said. "Right now I need you to send a security team to Washington to make sure that the president is fully protected from microwave intrusions of any kind."

"It's already happening," JT said. "A team from the NSA is on its way to the White House as we speak. I'll be there too."

"Good idea," Duggan said. "Make sure they all have protective earl plugs." He pressed the handset against his forehead and closed his eyes. "Fucking FBI."

"I know," JT said. "Don't worry, Jake. We'll get Ulrich." There was a pause before Nutley spoke again. "I've got more news you're not gonna like."

"Go ahead, make my day."

"That video of Westlake getting banged in the head by his best friend in Afghanistan?"

"What about it?"

"It's gone viral."

30

....

Eric watched intently as PHAROH was unloaded from a C-130 Hercules military transport and moved to a secure building on the base, where it was carefully unpacked and placed next to a vehicle that looked like a tank equipped with a microwave broadcast dish instead of a gun turret.

"MEDUSA, meet PHAROH," he said.

Never in a million years did Eric imagine himself trying to help the US Army modify a weapon designed to bake the brains of rioters and enemy troops. But here he was, surrounded by men in crisp fatigues, struggling to translate Defense Department jargon into a plan to build a supercharged mobile version of his resurrected anti-locust device. Working backward from the dish, Eric managed to isolate the amplification module that used brute electromagnetic force to disrupt the brain's cognitive functions. He turned to the lieutenant assigned to assist him and asked for the schematic. Eric perused the documents until he found a transducer that would accept audio inputs. He was about to lower himself into the MEDUSA's metal hatch when he heard someone call his name.

The voices were from Cara and Duggan, who had been granted clearance to visit the army's advanced weapons facility.

"You look right at home with all this hardware," Duggan observed.

"Not so much," Eric said. He held out his hand. "Good to see you, Agent Duggan. I was worried you might not get out of Pennsylvania alive."

"Me too," Duggan said. A couple of hours of sleep and a shower and shave at the hotel had restored him to a functional member of the twenty-first century. Cara had listened in utter amazement as he recounted the details of his nocturnal adventures among the Amish and Swarm's growing legions. "Cara filled me in on how you and she managed to get the army to approve airlifting your PHAROH device to Washington. I didn't know the CDC had so much clout."

"Doctors scare the hell out of people, even generals," Eric said.

"How's the US Army been treating you?"

"They've been quite hospitable," Eric said. "They even let me see their drone lab. You wouldn't believe what those things can do."

"How about the MEDUSA-PHAROH hybrid project?" Duggan asked.

Eric crossed his arms and looked over at the jumble of tools, open boxes, and electronic components surrounding the two machines. "It's a challenge for sure, kind of like getting two different species to mate, but I'm optimistic, sir."

"Optimistic isn't going to cut it," Duggan said. "Swarm's army moves fast, and it doesn't stop for naps. It'll be here by morning at the latest. I've seen what these people can do, and it isn't pretty. PHAROH might be our only shot to stop them from overrunning the White House."

Eric's levity vanished. "I'll get it done, Agent Duggan, but I can't guarantee that it'll work. These devices might look like cousins, but they run on completely different operating systems. But if I can hack into MEDUSA's amplification node, I think I can get them to shriek the devil's language."

Cara noticed Duggan's consternation and pointed to the boxy device on the floor. "PHAROH uses Selfridge's Pandemonium model to 'disrupt the demons.'"

"Pandemonium is Latin for 'many demons,' Eric added. "In emergent theory and artificial intelligence research, the 'demons' are simple programs that respond to each other, or 'shriek,' in a distributed bottom-up hierarchy that mimics not just human learning but also reproductive DNA and Darwin's theory of natural selection, among other things, including, of course, swarming locusts." Eric paused, a smile creeping across his face. "I guess you could say that PHAROH confuses MEDUSA by turning pandemonium into Babel."

"Let's hope it does because the Army is prepared to use lethal force to stop Swarm's rebellion," Duggan warned. "There's something going on out there besides zeph.r, something that might be even harder to contain."

"Are you talking about this?" Eric pecked at his phone and showed Duggan a photo of Donald Westlake wearing brain sensors and a link to the video that came from Ulrich's computer.

Duggan nodded grimly. "What about the danger of hurting bystanders if PHAROH-MEDUSA is deployed?"

"It depends what you mean by 'hurting,'" Eric answered. "My understanding is that MEDUSA isn't lethal at lower levels, but the version of zeph.r at X-ist was like nothing I've seen before." Eric held up a handful of zeph.r beam deflector headsets and gave them one each. "I brought these along, for me and anyone who needs them, just in case. Seriously, the PHAROH is just backup for a worst-case scenario, right?"

"That's what I'm hoping, Eric. I'll be with Cara at the NorthCom field command outpost."

"Roger that."

Duggan and Cara left, and Eric returned to his task, feeling like a freshman pulling an all-nighter before the big exam. The best he could do in the time left was patch PHAROH's processor into MEDUSA's output circuits. He unscrewed the cover to the access panel and began mapping a strategy to link the machines without overloading the system. His biggest worry was that the unprecedented combination of zeph.r, MEDUSA, and PHAROH could create an uncontrollable feedback loop. The other possibility was that the whole thing could simply overheat and blow up.

Eric's tech assistant was patiently waiting for further instructions. "We're going to need more wires," he said.

The black sedan approached the Pennsylvania Avenue entrance of the White House in the pre-dawn gloom and was immediately waved through when the guards recognized the man wearing battle fatigues in the backseat. General Mansfield saluted as he passed the checkpoint, steeling himself for a long, difficult day. He had spent most of the night on the phone with the joint chiefs, trying to find the midpoint between two crucial objectives. On the one hand, protecting the White House and the president was his top priority, but there was also the downside of unleashing excessive force against a civilian population in a climate of social instability. He had decided that political considerations were secondary to the safety of his commander in chief—and to hell with anyone who argued otherwise. Let the bureaucrats worry about public perceptions and Sunday morning quarterbacking from the media. He had more important things to do.

Mansfield got out of the car and stepped briskly toward the NorthCom control tower that had been set up near the West Wing. From there he could overlook the entire White House defensive barrier, a fortress of barbed wire, small artillery, ultrasound weapons, and five thousand battle-ready troops. On an elevated catwalk above the ramparts, snipers huddled behind sandbags with high-powered rifles at their sides. All wars had casualties, Mansfield reasoned, and anyone who attacked the White House was by definition an enemy of the state. Still, the ideal outcome, and what the general was essentially betting on, was that the mere sight of such formidable defenses would stop the mob in its tracks and deflect an attack without a single shot being fired.

Mansfield saluted the soldiers at the gate and climbed the steps to the command post where his deputy, Colonel Andrew Swain, was waiting for him.

"Good morning, General."

"Status?"

"Troops are ready and in position, sir, as is plan B," Swain said. "The first group of rebels is approaching the outskirts of the city."

Mansfield's brow furrowed. "Two hours ago you told me there was no way they'd be here before noon."

"Yes, sir, that was the original estimate for the main group coming from Pennsylvania."

"There's another group?"

"Affirmative," Swain said. "Helicopter and UAV surveillance spotted large numbers of demonstrators streaming in from the entire mid-Atlantic sector, sir. The front end of that force will be here in about ninety minutes, with the rest arriving not much later."

Mansfield grabbed Swain's binoculars and scanned the horizon. "Are these people civilians? And how many are we talking about?"

"Well, sir, we have to assume that anyone coming to the White House at this hour is aligned with the cyber terrorists. We're trying to get a count now."

"I want an update every five minutes. Make sure the media stay in their designated area behind the Washington Monument. And get me a line to the White House chief of staff. I told him to evacuate the president, but the damned fool refuses. What's he going to do, ask the cyber zombies to vote for him?"

"I don't know, sir."

Mansfield turned to the northwest, showing an elevated degree of concern. "Is Agent Duggan here yet?"

"He just arrived, sir."

"My God," Cara said as she and Duggan approached the White House defense perimeter. "It looks like they're expecting a siege."

"It just might be," Duggan said. He pulled out his phone and dialed JT. "Did you get a double selfie with POTUS yet?"

"Maybe later," JT responded. "He's a little busy right now arguing with his chief of staff, who wants him to transfer to the fail-safe bunker."

"Thinking about his legacy, I guess. What about the football?"

"It's secure with the vice president."

"And the NSA anti-microwave squad?"

"They're setting up their equipment in the West Wing."

"Okay, keep in touch."

"You too."

Duggan and Cara reached the command post and shook hands with General Mansfield. "Thank you for authorizing transportation for PHAROH, sir," Duggan said. "We've done our best to integrate it with a MEDUSA mobile unit. They'll be setting it up any minute now."

"Don't thank me, Duggan. Agent Nutley explained to me that DHS and the CDC have been involved in research along these lines for some time now. The approval for the airlift came from Homeland Security with the President's blessing." When he saw Duggan's expression, Mansfield chuckled. "You didn't know? Looks like somebody's been keeping you out of the loop." He turned to Cara. "Dr. Park, do you really think this contraption of yours will work?"

"Honestly, General, I hope we don't find out."

Mansfield peered across the metal catwalk elevated above the perimeter, where Eric was making final adjustments to the PHAROH-MEDUSA array overlooking the White House South Lawn. "Agent Duggan, those brain-rave demonstrators took out a hundred of my best men in Pennsylvania. The MEDUSA beam didn't stop them there, and frankly I'm skeptical that it'll do much good here either. But I can tell you right now that I'm not taking any chances with POTUS on the premises. Am I clear?"

"Very clear, sir."

"I understand that you spent some time among the rebels as their captive."

"Yes, sir. I managed to escape by swimming to safety during the Susquehanna River crossing."

"Impressive. My officers say that the rebels displayed superhuman powers. Do you know what they were referring to?"

"I wouldn't say superhuman, sir. It's more like post-human. The rebels are extremely organized and fearless. It would be a mistake to underestimate them."

Mansfield's mouth tightened. "That doesn't sound like a bunch of drugged-up cyber punks to me. Do you think they could be motivated by a religious or political ideology?"

"Sir, most of the people who walked here from the X-ist concert are under the influence of an experimental weapon based on stolen DOD technology. We think the enhanced MEDUSA cannons might neutralize or at the very least disorient them, but the weapon might also kill them."

"Duggan, I won't bullshit you," Mansfield said. "The only way you're going to get a chance to try out your microwave gizmo is if the demonstrators get inside the defensive perimeter, which I assure you is not going to happen. But you're welcome to stick around and keep the device powered up and ready go, just in case I give the order."

Swain handed Cara and Duggan flak jackets and put his hand up to his earpiece. "General, both rebel groups will be here in about thirty minutes, one from the northeast, the other from the southeast. I think you'll be able get a visual after sunrise."

"There are *two* groups?" Duggan asked. "Where did the other one come from?"

"We're not sure," Swain told him, "but at this rate, we could be looking at another fifty thousand or so demonstrators."

"Jesus." Duggan felt his belly tightening.

"Relax, Agent Duggan." Mansfield had his binoculars trained on the multitude approaching from the southeast. In the dawn's misty light, they seemed to extend all the way to the horizon. "They're carrying American flags," Mansfield said with evident satisfaction.

"Those people are patriots. It's pretty obvious they came to help us defend the White House."

"Fifteen minutes away, sir."

They all watched as the two groups came together like converging tributaries, mixing and swirling as they consolidated into a gathering mass in the National Mall, surrounded by a second circle of reporters with cameras and GoPro-toting tourists making videos of something so mesmerizing and strange that it left them wordlessly gaping in amazement.

Cara pulled her Kevlar vest tighter as she watched. "I don't like the look of this."

"Me neither."

"It's almost like they're trying to recompress to achieve more physical density."

"Which is the last thing we want," Duggan said.

"Okay," Mansfield said. "They see us and they've come to their senses, assuming they have any. This is all just a show for the six o'clock news."

Duggan watched as the crowd clotted and heaved, drawing the protestors from the fringes into the pulsing core and then pushing them out again, like cells dividing and realigning. There was a brief lull, followed by a roar of grunts and shouts from the mobilizing mob. Duggan cringed as the magnified mass flexed and bristled and began advancing toward the White House. There was also something else, a low, almost subsonic rumble, like the vibration of tectonic plates churning deep under the planet's crust.

Mansfield's smile curdled. "What the hell?"

"Sir, our latest estimate is a combined total of at least a hundred thousand," Swain reported, "and people are still coming out of the woodwork."

"Why are the terrorists dressed in white?" Mansfield groused. "It looks like a godforsaken holy war."

"Jake," Cara said. "Maybe we should get out of here."

"It's too late for that, Dr. Park," Mansfield said. "You're safer up here with us. The army invented crowd control. Just stay out of the way and let us do our job." He looked at Swain, who barked orders into his radio. Loudspeakers stationed along the perimeter warned the demonstrators to desist and disperse immediately or face lethal consequences, but the mob kept advancing.

Mansfield looked mystified. "Why won't they stop, dammit? Don't they know they're committing suicide?"

Swain looked at his commander. "At your signal, sir."

"They were warned," Mansfield said ruefully. "Fire at will."

The first tear gas canisters exploded along the front line of the throng while they were still crossing the National Mall. Each time, the crowd adroitly dilated into a circle around the point of impact, escaping the brunt of the blast. Those who stumbled and fell were carried away as others stepped up to take their place, closing ranks and increasing their speed as a veil of smoke wafted across the Washington Monument. A barrage of concussion bombs kicked up a shower of divots and felled hundreds more. But instead of dispersing, the males in the vanguard broke into an accelerated trot. They raised their arms in a signal of solidarity and unleashed a thunderous howl, the birth cry of a colossus taking its first exultant breath.

"Mother of Christ!" Mansfield muttered.

Storming the first line of defense, the rebels threw themselves across the bramble of barbed wire, layer upon layer, making a clear passage for the hundreds behind them who rose against the rampart by climbing over each others' shoulders, linking arms into human ladders so that those behind could continue the ascent. The army snipers, trained to eliminate high-value targets, scoped the unarmed rebellion fruitlessly for a kill. Only slightly more effective were the high-speed mini-guns mowing down the attackers, their screams mixing with the terrified shouts of soldiers watching their comrades being annihilated as their own captured weapons were turned against them. The insurgents fought as a single entity, hurling themselves on grenades, flipping jeeps, and overrunning machine-gun nests, using the growing pile of bodies as a ramp until they penetrated the defensive barrier and poured onto the South Lawn of the White House.

Duggan looked across the elevated catwalk to where Eric was crouching next to the MEDUSA-PHAROH control panel. Evidently, the mob only attacked those who threatened it with weapons or blocked its way. Huddled next to a Humvee-like vehicle festooned with radio dishes, Eric looked about as dangerous as a cable-TV repairman. Duggan pulled out his phone and texted him:

Jduggan: You okay over there?
EEric: Yeah, I think so.
Jduggan: Just stay put for now.
EEric: Don't worry!

The sea of white boiled and curled like a wave before cresting over the perimeter and swamping the terrified defenders. Mansfield was maniacally gesturing and barking orders into his wireless. Duggan had to grab his flak jacket to make him listen. "General, the swarm only attacks anyone who threatens it or stands in its way. Tell your men to stand down or they're all going to die!"

"Cease-fire!" Mansfield ordered his remaining troops. "I repeat: all units put down your weapons!"

The fighting abated, and the crowd turned its attention to the White House. There were no cheers of victory, just a muted jabbering of random words and noises in a dozen different languages. The murmuring blather that Duggan heard during the march from X-ist was percolating again. Every now and then, the word *president* would surface from the jumble of nattering yelps. Duggan listened to the polyglot chorus of fractured phrases and singsong chatter and remembered what Eric had said about the pandemonium model and how Selfridge's demons shouted their votes to each other to reach a collective decision. The swarm's escalating mumbles and shrieks, Duggan suddenly understood, weren't the sound of a triumphant army preparing to pounce; they were the emergent prattle of a giant brain sorting out its thoughts.

Inside the White House, in a suite of rooms in the West Wing complex that were sometimes offered to the staffs of visiting dignitaries, several members of the NSA's microwave security team were checking their audio deflecting equipment and methodically preparing their weapons. The guns had been given to them for self-defense, but even with the battle raging outside, the audio experts weren't worried about their own safety. Their official task was to monitor and reenforce the White House's microwave deterrent system, which was installed during the Cold War during the 1950s, after the American embassy in Moscow was famously "fried" by KGB beams designed to eavesdrop and pry and, some maintained, manipulate the moods and behaviors of the US ambassador and his staff. As a result, the White House defense had been bolstered with microwave-proof materials in the windows and walls as well as sensors and software to detect and repel any beams directed at the building.

The microwave intrusion alarms had been ringing off the hook since the first Swarm rebels stormed the White House perimeter, but not until now did the NSA cyber team receive permission to proceed with a thorough inspection of the president's offices and living quarters. The White House staff charged with escorting the NSA team to the Oval Office didn't blink when the technicians asked for directions to the emergency audio control system, nor did they think twice when the NSA team donned customized headphones and readied their weapons. The heavy metal rock blasting from the technicians' headphones would have definitely aroused suspicions in anyone close enough to listen, but by then the White House escorts weren't hearing a thing.

31

As the rebel mob on the South Lawn seethed and its vocal ruminations grew louder, Mansfield became agitated. "I think they're getting ready to attack again," he told Duggan. "You've got to try the PHAROH beam."

"General, stop and think about what you're doing," Duggan protested. "You can't use that weapon against unarmed Americans."

"Those rioters gave up their rights when they attacked the White House," Mansfield said. "End of conversation."

Duggan looked back toward the National Mall, which was packed with people as far as he could see. "General, you told me yourself that authority only extends to Swarm and people who are under his neural control. Only a fraction of these people came from the rave. What about the majority who came to protest peacefully?"

Mansfield shook his head. "I've already lost too many men. Besides, how can you even tell them apart?"

"Swarm's accomplices are dressed in white and wearing radio wristbands," Duggan said. "That's how he controls them!" Mansfield bit his lip. "General, see all those phones and cameras in the crowd? They are all capable of broadcasting live video streams. The images of PHAROH unleashed on unarmed civilians could help bring in fresh recruits. If there's a massacre, you'll want to be able to say you tried every contingency before resorting to extreme measures."

Mansfield crumpled his coffee cup and threw it to the ground. "What the fuck do you know about what I'll want?" he growled. "I'm not going to give Swarm's followers the chance to regroup and attack, not if there's even a small chance I can end this now. Colonel Swain, activate Hail Mary."

Duggan expected to see the soldiers raise their weapons again, but they seemed to be waiting for something. Then he heard it, a faint whirring, getting louder and closer. Cara saw them first, like a formation of geese approaching over the White House.

"Jake, what are they ...?"

The drones circled and hovered over the South Lawn, their shadows rippling like crosshairs over the rebels, who, sensing the danger, began to twirl and buzz like warrior bees preparing to protect the hive.

"Get down!" Duggan shouted to Cara, pulling her away from the exposed catwalk before he typed into his phone.

Jduggan: Eric, how long will it take to fire PHAROH?
EEric: About 30 seconds
Jduggan: Make it 15

Eric saluted from across the perimeter and moved to the PHAROH's control panel. "Put this on." Duggan handed Cara a microwave deflector headset and took one for himself.

"Jake," Cara whispered, "What are you doing?"

"I'm tired of cleaning up other people's messes," he said.

A rumbling buzz filled the battlefield as PHAROH cleared its throat and unleashed its sonic fury. At first, nothing happened. Then the rebels and soldiers nearest to PHAROH's swiveling dish began to contort and buckle, and Duggan could see the beam's effects rippling across the battleground in an undulating wave. Overhead, the drones suddenly wobbled and dropped to the grass like dead birds. For a while, there was nothing but PHAROH's unmerciful howl, an invisible hand clearing the airwaves of everything but its own pulverizing frequency. Duggan motioned to Eric to cut the power, and as if drained from the effort of breaking up the fight, PHAROH emitted a final high-pitched aria and shut down.

There was a new text from Eric: a thumbs up emoji followed by a smiley face and the words: *We need to talk. I'll come to you.*

Mansfield's radio crackled. "Get those things back in the air," he shouted. "Well then, fix it, goddammit!" He gave Duggan a venomous stare. "If you had anything to do with this, so help me, I'll have you arrested!"

"Excuse me, General," Swain stammered, "something's happening."

The crowd had begun to speak, a jumbled mishmash of repeated phrases and words that slowly started to coalesce and make sense. It was like listening to a child learn the words to a hymn, a fractured poem of broken promises that resonated far beyond the aggregation of souls on the White House South Lawn and the thousands more spilling across the capitol and beyond. "We ... the States of ... United people," thousands of voices proclaimed, "do this tranquility blessings ... insure a Constitution ... and secure ourselves America ... tranquility do ordain ... perfect general welfare ... establish the justice ... in form to order ... more common liberty ..."

Duggan was struck by the revealed gravity of scrambled words being uttered, not in the context of history but spoken with the sting of battle still fresh and the dead and wounded still present. Was it possible that Donald Westlake, an unknown airman from Spokane, Washington, had come to represent a set of principles and convictions worth fighting and dying for, worth marching on the capitol itself, to be endorsed and memorialized by a bio-emergent incantation of the people?

Jake, it's really important.

Before Duggan could respond to Eric's message, his phone rang.

"We've got a problem here," JT announced in a voice that bordered on panic. "There's been some kind of breach." Duggan could hear shouting and muffled gunfire in the background.

"The president?"

"The president and his family are safe in the control bunker, and the rest of us are barricaded in the Oval Office. Three White House staffers are down in the West Wing, and the NSA microwave team is missing."

"What do you mean by missing?"

"We can't find them, and they're not responding to texts or calls."

"What about the White House guards?"

"Jake, it's total bedlam in here!" JT shouted. "There's heavy metal music on the PA system, and everybody's gone crazy. We can turn the speakers off in here, but it's blasting through the whole building. The guards outside are fighting and shooting each other—it's a shit show."

"Stay where you are. And whatever happens, keep the president away from any kind of music or noise. Same for you."

Eric, still flushed and winded from his sprint to the command post, was waiting to talk.

"Do you have any more of those microwave deflectors?" Duggan asked him.

"Yeah, about half a dozen. They're right here in my backpack. Why?"

"I think somebody's broadcasting zeph.r inside the White House. We've got to help JT."

"My God. That's what I've been trying to tell you!" Eric unlocked his phone and opened the APB with Kenneth Ulrich's picture on it. "This guy, the one in the terrorist alert, I think I saw him going into the White House a couple hours ago. He looks different from the picture—no glasses and buzz cut—but I'm pretty sure it was him."

"Was he with the NSA microwave security team?"

"Yeah, I think so."

"Gimme a sec."

Duggan took Cara's hands. "I need you to stay here and keep me posted on what's happening outside. Stay close to the general and keep your phone handy."

"What about me?" Eric asked.

"Get out the deflectors. I need to have a chat with the general."

Duggan ignored Mansfield's hostile sneer as he approached. "General, the White House is under attack. I think it's Ulrich. One of my men from Homeland Security is inside with the president now. They're okay for the moment, but shots have been fired and they don't have much time."

The general shook his head and cursed. "I believe you, Duggan," Mansfield said, "but let the Secret Service and the White House guard do its duty. I don't have orders to enter the White House, and you don't either."

"Sir, according to my man inside, the White House guard has been compromised by electromagnetic beams. I'm asking you for a handful of your men to help me get to source of the signal before it's too late."

"The White House is already protected from microwave attacks, Duggan. Plus, all the doors are auto-secured during a red alert."

"Sir, the White House is fortified against microwave attacks from the outside, not the *inside*. I know this man, I know what he's trying to do, and I've got six deflector headsets for anyone you can spare to go in there and help me stop him." Seeing Mansfield hesitate, Duggan added, "Isn't protecting the president your core directive?"

"General," Swain interrupted, "what about the Executive Office Building?"

Mansfield looked out across the lawn to the White House as if trying to imagine what was happening inside. He turned to Swain. "Captain, take five men from your unit and accompany Agent Duggen to the Oval office to defend the president until backup troops arrive. And keep your radio on."

Duggan was a few steps away when Mansfield called him back. "Agent Duggan, do you have a firearm?"

"No, Sir."

Mansfield took out his gun and handed it to him. "Make it count," he said.

Eric handed deflectors to Swain and his men. "I'll stay with Cara," he said. "Don't get shot."

Duggan followed Swain and his squad away from the White House command post to the Seventeenth Street entrance to the Eisenhower Executive Office Building, where an armed officer led them through the lobby and into the basement. The officer unlocked a heavy steel door that opened into to a long concrete corridor. "Follow me," he said. Duggan had heard about the honeycomb of subterranean passages under the White House, but he never thought he'd be inside one carrying a loaded gun. The officer halted in from of a large blue door and pressed the code to unlock it. "Follow this passage to the stairs," he said. "You'll come out next to the kitchen pantry. Go up one level and the Oval Office will be to your right."

"Put on your headphones," Duggan told the men.

Swain nodded, and the group followed the officer's directions. Even before they emerged onto a carpeted hallway redecorated with blood-splattered wallpaper and splintered antiques, Duggan could hear the crunching bass and drums of heavy metal blasting from the White House sound system. They'd only taken a few steps when a deranged White House employee lunged at them with a knife. Swain dispatched the attacker with a single shot and kept the group moving until they reached a large varnished wooden door.

Duggan took out his phone and texted JT.

"Good to see you, Jake," JT said as he let them in and locked the door behind them.

"Likewise."

There were about a dozen men in the Oval Office, some of them wounded, all of them in various states of shock and disorientation. The air reeked of sweat, smoke, and gunpowder, and it was impossible to ignore the muffled din of heavy metal rock seeping through the door. Framed paintings of presidents lined the walls, but Duggan was looking for one in particular.

"Don't worry," JT said, reading Duggan's thoughts. "POTUS is secure in a microwave-proof underground safe room. He's been monitoring everything inside and outside on video monitors."

"What about in here?"

JT grinned. "Ever since Nixon, there's no taping or recording of any kind allowed in the Oval Office, which includes any kind of audio speaker system. The steel-reinforced doors have held the terrorists back so far. But I can't say the same for the rest of the building."

Duggan looked at Swain. "How long before the cavalry gets here?"

"Twenty minutes max."

Duggan looked at his watch. "Tell the troops to stand down."

Swain and JT looked at him blankly. "Eric thinks he saw Ulrich heading to the White House with the NSA security team," he explained. "The last thing we need is a battalion of armed soldiers coming in here and going bonkers."

"Sorry," Swain said. "I can't stop troops once we're inside. For all they know, the terrorists could be holding guns to our heads."

"Fair enough," Duggan said. "But then we've only got a few minutes to find Ulrich and deactivate zeph.r before all holy hell breaks loose."

"Son of a bitch!" JT's face contorted as he connected the dots. "That's exactly what Ulrich wants, isn't it? He's setting a zeph.r booby trap for the reinforcements!"

"Can you get me directions from here to the PA system control room?"

"Give me a sec." JT whipped out his phone and dialed the NCSD hotline, scribbling notes on the president's notepad as he listened. "You've got to backtrack to the first level, next to the bowling alley."

Duggan handed the notes to Swain. "Can you get us there?"

"I'm sure gonna try."

"Keep your deflector headsets on and shoot to kill," Duggan ordered. "JT, lock the door behind us and keep your phone handy."

Even with the headsets on, the blaring guitars were harsh and unnerving, as were the deep gouges and bullet holes perforating the walls. Swain took point with Duggan and the other men close behind. The hallway was deserted, but the spent shells on the floor and the blood smears on the walls told another story. Passing a window, Duggan looked out and saw combat helicopters and a column of armored personnel carriers taking positions around the north facade. He knew it wouldn't be long before the unprotected troops stormed the building. Ulrich's infiltration of the NSA security squad was unnerving enough, but the immediate emergency was to find and deactivate zeph.r. Ulrich's ultimate goal was more ambitious than Duggan had originally thought: he wasn't trying to punish the US government; he was trying to *erase* it.

"This way," Swain said, leading them down a stairway littered with debris and broken bodies. Duggan advanced with the group, trying to sidestep the pools of blood on the landing, gratefully gripping Mansfield's parting gift. At the far end of a red-carpeted corridor, a man in bespoke suit carrying a machine gun sprayed bullets in their direction. When Swain and his men returned fire, the man looked at his watch before moving on in search of easier prey. The shouts and screams were getting louder, mixing with the music and sputtering firearms, completing the macabre spectacle of the political epicenter of the world's most powerful country being overrun by gun-toting maniacs, a White House turned madhouse.

As they fought their way forward through ornate rooms of shattered Baccarat crystal and ruined national heirlooms, Duggan couldn't help wondering if this was the nightmare that the Founding Fathers envisioned when they had warned against "the tyranny of the majority." A disconcerting thought crossed Duggan's mind: wasn't technology, in its relentless march toward automation and software-enhanced efficiency, inevitably setting the stage for direct digital democracy? Wasn't the rusty machinery of representative government ripe for the same disruptive algorithms that had ruthlessly revamped and reformatted countless industries by replacing people with programs that did their jobs better and faster, emancipated from human error and cleansed of emotional congestion? Were the bio-emergent masses standing on the White House lawn, with their ability to think and act instantly and in concert, the last stand of government by and for the people—or the beginning of the end of it?

Swain halted at the intersection of two corridors and pointed to a door about thirty feet to the side. "That's it," he said as a machine gun rattled from a conference room in the other direction, pinning them down. As Swain's men returned fire, the captain waved for Duggan to keep moving. "Go on—we'll cover you."

The door to the audio control room was slightly ajar. Duggan discerned a figure leaning over a conglomeration of computer routers and monitors, turning dials and pressing buttons like a demented DJ. Somehow, the man sensed Duggan's presence and wheeled around. It was Ulrich, a specter in the flesh, fine-tuning his zeph.r playlist for a fresh batch of impressionable minds.

"Homeland Security!" Duggan shouted, raising his pistol. "Hands where I can see them. You're under arrest!"

The tear gas bomb exploded just outside the control room door, throwing Duggan to the floor. Dazed but still conscious, he spotted Ulrich's silhouette advancing toward him in the haze and squeezed off two rounds before the fumes blinded him. Duggan braced himself for the blow that never came, using his wadded shirt as a mask and managing to get to his feet and reenter the control room. He closed the door behind him and waited a few seconds for his vision to clear. Then he raised his gun and emptied the rest of his clip into the White House audio control panel. As he blasted away at the blinking components, Duggan knew this was the closest he would ever get to dispensing physical justice to zeph.r and every other amoral algorithm and errant equation that had no qualms or accountability, feeling visceral satisfaction as he took aim at the hard drive habitat of contagious worms and slave-bots, obliterating the outsourced operating systems of self-serving servers and microwave beams that festered in government labs and loud music, but not quite blotting out the knowing chuckle that Ulrich had made as he skittered away, confident he would escape and that their paths would cross again at some undetermined time and place because whatever the outcome of this particular skirmish, the vendetta between them was just getting started.

Duggan felt a hand on his shoulder.

"Are you okay?" Swain was staring at the bullet-riddled debris from Duggan's shooting spree.

"Yeah," Duggan said. "I never cared much for heavy metal."

"Me neither."

Duggan emerged a few minutes later on the south portico, disoriented and covered in dust. The South Lawn was still teeming with Swarm's blank-faced battalions—murmuring, yelping, watching, waiting. Duggan was positive that Swarm was out there somewhere in the crowd. He stared back into the mosaic of faces, trying to match one of them with the man he had shot at on the tower at X-ist. Did Swarm know that Ulrich's plot had been at least temporarily derailed? And if so, how would that affect his next move?

On a platform to Duggan's left, a team of workers was hastily setting up a holographic projector and loudspeakers. What Duggan didn't know was that during his pursuit of Ulrich inside the White House, a proposed constitutional amendment and the software plans for PHAROH had been anonymously released into the ether, where anyone and everyone could download them. Was it the work of Swarm or the Meta Militia? Time would tell. But what Duggan wanted more than anything right now was a drink.

A text from Eric told Duggan to look at the attached copy of the doctrine of freedom of mind:

Guy Garcia

All inhabitants of the United States, regardless of whether they were born in this country or not, regardless of age or economic status, in times of war or peace, are guaranteed the right for their minds to be free of interference, or coercion, or control by natural or artificial means, whether by radio waves, sounds, images, chemicals or any other device created to alter the thoughts of any person, without their knowledge or consent. This right is irrevocable and shall be protected and enforced as long as this nation is governed by the regulations and principles of the Constitution of the United States of America.

The document reminded Duggan of a college course he took on the drafting of the Constitution. He recalled a quote from the first essay of *The Federalist Papers*, in which Alexander Hamilton laid out the "important question" that was about to be decided, namely "whether societies of men are really capable or not of establishing good government from reflection and choice, or whether they are forever destined to depend, for their political constitutions, on accident and force." The very definition of democracy, Duggan knew, was based on the assumption of human reason, the God-given ability to think freely that was the essential requirement for civil reflection and choice. It followed that without the emancipation of mind, without the public recognition and protection of unfettered thought, there could be no liberty or democracy, only the tyranny of accident and force.

Moments later, a live apparition of the president materialized before a crowd that had swelled to several hundred thousand, with untold millions more watching on television and the Internet. The president's ashen face and humble posture showed a man who felt the weight of history in the making.

"My fellow Americans," he began. "What has happened here today will never be forgotten. I have heard you. And I give you my word that I will begin working at once to prepare a new amendment to the Constitution containing the words spoken here today and ensuring freedom of mind for all in this land. And I vow that before this Congress adjourns, I will submit the Twenty-Eighth Amendment to the states for speedy ratification. In the meantime, I am declaring an immediate suspension of further research or deployment of any device or weapon designed to alter, control, or otherwise infringe on brain activity, freedom of thought, or the independence of the human mind. Finally, my fellow Americans, I now ask you to leave here peaceably and go back to your homes so I can begin the important work that lies ahead."

The president's image flickered and faded, and the blue bracelets in the crowd also blinked off.

"It's over," Duggan said.

"You think the president will keep his promise?" Eric asked.

"I hope so—for everybody's sake."

As the crowd began to disperse, a lone figure in white stared up at the elevated platform where Duggan was standing. Eric pointed. "Look, Agent Duggan. Isn't that Swarm down there?"

Duggan braced himself for some sign or mental signal that the dark-haired young man below was the same person who had dared to hot-wire the genetic roadmap of the human race, fend off the US Army, and bring the federal government to a standstill. The man briefly locked eyes with Duggan and nodded before letting himself be swallowed by the receding human tide.

"Jake," Cara asked, "do you think it was him?"

Duggan took her hand and turned to go. "Plenty of people look like that," he said. "He could have been anybody."

Xander sat in his car and watched the house until Sonia emerged to make her monthly pilgrimage to her cousin's for the weekend. He approached the far side of the property, as he'd done so many times before, and let himself in through the window of Tom's room. It looked exactly the same, like an exhibit in a History of Human Evolution Museum. Except nobody would ever buy tickets to tour the house where Swarm was born, because Tom and his avatar alter ego had both vanished after the battle of Washington. Xander had followed the spectacle from a hospital bed in Philadelphia, wishing that he had the strength to catch a train and witness the spontaneous rebooting of the American experiment firsthand. It was a watershed event by any measure: eight hundred dead, two thousand wounded, millions of live video streams and no arrests. And a crowd-sourced Twenty-Eighth Amendment to the Constitution, protecting freedom of mind, added to all the other inalienable rights enshrined at the nation's founding and entrusted to succeeding generations charged with protecting and embellishing that vision.

Thanks to a global audience watching the president's speech, governments around the world were immediately besieged with demands for similar measures. But laws banning brain control experiments became redundant once the source code for PHAROH was released into the cloud, guaranteeing that no person, entity, or government would ever again be able to weaponize microwave brain research with impunity.

After an initial celebration and acknowledgment that the human race had taken a step forward, the inevitable cadre of doubters and detractors waded in to muddy the waters of history. Did the crowds in Washington really communicate in multiple languages and act as one, or were they reading the words from their phones? Was the X-ist rave Kickstarted, or secretly funded by Islamic extremists? Were the photos and video of Donald Westlake authentic or phony reenactments made with paid actors? For those who believed that the answer to all those questions was yes, for those who stoked uncertainty to keep consensus at bay, there would never be enough answers, only more questions.

The speculation on the fate of Swarm himself, at least among those who believed he actually existed, variously held that he was killed from the fall at X-ist, or that he was married and living in a small town in Nebraska, or that the government had secretly taken him prisoner and was trying to coerce him to help create a newer, better version of zeph.r. But savvier minds discounted the last possibility, mainly because those who sought covert control over others had already moved on to new methods that tapped the quintillions of bytes of public data to create predictive models of what people were going to do before they even knew it themselves. Instead of forcing anyone to behave one way or the other, it was much cheaper, and for the time being legal, to use prognosticative algorithms to pursue hidden agendas that appeared to be part of the random flow of day-to-day life. The inherent pattern in nature, machines, and human beings, if understood and parsed correctly, could turn seemingly random events into decisive factors in the fates of individuals, organizations, and entire nations. If the travel plans of a CEO ready to blow the whistle on his board and the explosion of a gas-processing plant near his office in New Jersey just happened to coincide, or if a typhoon leveled a guerrilla base in Malaysia days just before it launched a civil war, well, these things just happen, don't they? Already the mountains of personal data being compiled from the digitization of every possible action and device was being sifted to assemble a synthetic electorate, a prognostic primary where candidates could be vetted, pitted against each other, and projected to win or lose an election before they even decided to run.

For that matter, what were the odds that the window to Tom's room would be open when Xander arrived, a laptop plugged in and running, with a bottle of Patron and a single shot glass on the desk beside it? And how to explain the unpublished manuscript on the first screen, and the salient epigrams by Nietzsche, Darwin, and Radiohead to set the stage for the unlikely tale to follow?

Xander spent the rest of the afternoon and most of the night sipping tequila and reading the improbable tale of two guys from Austin who hitched a ride to the far end of possibility and never looked back. A postscript at the bottom of the last page explained why the file was prepackaged as an attachment addressed to hundreds of people he'd never heard of and didn't care to know.

Hey Xan,

I know that if anyone is reading this, it's you, my brother and unsuspecting partner in crime, if you can call unleashing the people from their chains and helping them reclaim their own minds a crime, as many, obviously, have already done. My actions and everything that has transpired because of them speak for themselves, but I'm not so naive as not to realize that the iterations and intentions of those who would rewrite history for their own purposes will eventually take their toll on the truth. So I decided it might be useful to record our own version from a third-person POV and relay the facts in a form that doesn't require verification, that can't be argued away or dismissed, because it isn't being presented as anything but a story, a fable, the unattributed product of an overactive imagination. Maybe sometimes the only way to communicate the veracity of certain events is through a fanciful meme, a swirl in the universal ether, as Tesla would say, that bypasses disclaimer or validation by using a more innocuous medium to deliver the message. If the truth is often stranger than fiction, then can't a novel be truer than the officially sanctioned reality?

I leave the decision in your hands, literally. If this book has only one reader, at least it will be you. If you decide it deserves a wider distribution, pick SEND *and this string will automatically upload to a global e-mail list. There will be no way to trace its origins or stop its widespread dissemination. If you choose to* DELETE, *it will be gone forever, The End. I've changed most of the names and some of the details, of course, to avoid unnecessary objections or embarrassment. Just remember: there is no right or wrong, no felt or unfelt, no said or unsaid, no written or unwritten, no lived or unlived, no done or undone.*

I trust you to act from a place that is sincere and pure, as always. You'll know where I am and what to do, even if you don't always know when or why.

Intrinsically yours,
Tom

Xander stared at the buttons marked SEND and DELETE, two possible actions with unpredictable outcomes, two paths with equally obscure destinations. Should he deliver the final message from his friend to those who would gladly receive it? Or erase his words to protect the shapeless entity that lives on in the chambers of the undiscovered mind?

His fingers trembled as they hovered over the keyboard.

a BRIEF HISTORY OF MIND CONTROL

··

Late 1800s–early 1900s

Serbian-born scientist and inventor Nicola Tesla conducts experiments using ELF (extremely low frequency) electromagnetic waves as part of his goal to create a global wireless communications system and a limitless power supply that uses the earth's atmosphere as a conductor. Tesla is credited as being one of the first scientists to explore how electromagnetic radiation can be used to produce altered states of consciousness in the human brain.

1945

The US Air Technical Command requests access to Tesla's personal papers, including documentation and drawings of his ELF beam experiments, for defense-related purposes. Government officials subsequently deny ever having had possession of Tesla's research materials.

1950s–1960s

Interest in the military applications of Tesla's ELF research spreads to the Soviet Union. Russian scientists, who have already been experimenting with mental telepathy and other nontraditional forms of communication, accelerate their own electromagnetic brain wave tests.

1975

A US congressional committee led by Senator Frank Church publicly reveals that the CIA and the Department of Defense have conducted experiments on American and foreign subjects as part of an extensive program to influence and control human behavior through psychoactive drugs, like LSD, and other chemical, biological, and psychological methods. A year later, President Gerald Ford issues an executive order prohibiting such experiments on unwitting human subjects.

1976

On July 4, the US embassy in Moscow is bombarded by ELF waves being transmitted through the earth and air. The microwave particle beam is dubbed the "Woodpecker" signal because of the persistent tapping noise it produces on shortwave radio bands in several countries. Woodpecker is comprised of as many as five different frequencies, including the 8Hz-to-10Hz range, which according to some reports is capable of inducing a hypnotic state in humans.

1980

In an article published in *Military Review,* "The New Mental Battlefield: Beam Me Up, Spock," Lieutenant Colonel John B. Alexander of the US Army openly depicts a brave new arena of brain-targeting "psychotronics," which he defines as "weapons systems that operate on the power of the mind and whose lethal capacity has already been tested." Mind-altering techniques, the lieutenant-colonel contends, are "well advanced" and include manipulation of human behavior through use of psychological weapons affecting sight, sound, smell, temperature, electromagnetic energy, or sensory deprivation.

1980–1990s

The US government continues research on electromagnetic devices with both defensive and offensive capabilities, including GWEN, the Ground Wave Emergency Network, a national network of radio towers, each capable of covering a three-hundred-mile radius with very low frequency (VLF) waves that hug the ground rather than flow through the air. Critics contend that VLF waves are harmful to humans and could be used to manipulate or disable brain functions on a national scale.

1998

The Institute of Noetic Sciences launches the Global Consciousness Project, which uses a geographically distributed network of computers and random number generators to detect and measure widespread emotional responses to natural disasters, social or political upheaval, football games, and other mass events. The project's goal is to measure and validate the possibility that large numbers of people thinking or feeling the same thing at the same time can generate a psychic wave or pulse that disrupts the function of random number generators around the planet.

2001

Work begins on the High Frequency Active Auroral Research Program (HAARP). Jointly funded by the US Air Force, US Navy, the University of Alaska, and the Defense Department's Advanced Research Projects Agency (DARPA), HAARP is an ionospheric research project based near Gakona, Alaska, that uses a high-energy beam to temporarily excite a portion of the uppermost layer of the atmosphere.

2006

The Media Freedom Foundation of Sonoma State University publishes a paper on US electromagnetic weapons and human rights. The authors warn about efforts by US-funded scientists to search for better means of controlling human behavior through "the use of wireless directed electromagnetic energy under the headings of Information Warfare and Non-Lethal Weapons." The foundation also says that the US military and intelligence agencies have at their disposal weapons that have likely already been covertly used and/or tested on humans, both here and abroad, and which could be directed at the public in the event of mass protests or disobedience.

2007

HAARP is completed and deployed. Its official purpose is to gather data on how the earth's atmosphere reacts to solar radiation and other cosmic phenomenon. According to DARPA, HAARP is also capable of generating ELF frequencies by heating portions of the auroral electrojet, an electrical current that travels around the earth's ionosphere. The main concern expressed by HAARP's detractors is its ability to bounce focused ELF beams off the upper atmosphere to almost any place on Earth, potentially making it the largest and most powerful electromagnetic weapon ever built.

2009

Nippon Telegraph & Telephone Company announces plans to develop an amusement park game that induces people to dance by wearing headphones connected to a galvanic vestibular stimulator (GVS), which transmits signals into the inner ear and brain. NTT scientists are considering mixing GVS signals into music in dance clubs to keep people dancing while another person remotely controls their movements with a wireless joystick. In the United States, patents are filed for devices that would use ELF and other radio waves to induce a receptive state in subjects and then expose them to images, words, and sounds that would transfer subconscious messages and emotions directly to the brain.

2013

Amol Sarva, an entrepreneur and cofounder of Virgin Mobile USA, announces his newest venture: a bio-tech start-up called Halo Neuroscience. The company plans to build and market a commercially available headset that uses electromagnetic waves, which he calls neurostimulation, to enhance human brain performance. Sarva claims that early testing has shown that neurostimulation can accelerate and improve a wide range of cognitive functions, from learning and creativity to memory and video game playing.

2013–2014

President Barack Obama seeks private and public partners for a one-hundred-million-dollar initiative to understand and map the inner workings of the human brain. Government agencies involved in the project include the National Science Foundation, the National Institute of Health, and the Defense Department's Advanced Research Projects Agency. A DARPA spokesperson says one of the agency's priorities will be to address the needs of combat veterans who suffer from mental and physical conditions, including PTSD. Listed among the initiative's key goals on the www.whitehouse.gov/share/brain-initiative website: "Understand how brain activity leads to perception, decision making, and ultimately action."

2015

After raising thirteen million dollars in funding for its brain-stimulating electrode headset and mobile phone app, Thync, a Boston-based start-up, continues testing a consumer mood-altering device that uses electromagnetic signals to make the wearer feel more focused, relaxed, or energetic. Thync uses neurosignaling via electronic or ultrasonic waveforms to activate and manipulate existing neural pathways in the human mind. The company's motto: "Shift your state of mind. Conquer more."

2016

A company called Nervana announces plans to market mood-enhancing headphones that generate electrical signals in tandem with music to trigger feelings of happiness and euphoria in the wearer. The headphones' music-enhanced signal stimulates the vagus nerve, which runs from the brainstem to the abdomen and triggers the release of dopamine, a chemical tied to the brain's pleasure centers and activities, including playing games, eating, and sex.

Chicago-based start-up Brain.fm releases beta of a product that uses 3-D audio technology and brain wave frequency protocols powered by a complex "Music-AI" engine to enhance beta waves in the brain and help the listener focus, relax, meditate, or sleep.

DARPA announces a new sixty-million-dollar initiative to develop an implantable neural interface the size of a small coin to allow unprecedented signal resolution and data-transfer bandwidth for improved communication between the human brain and digital devices, including computers, robots, and prosthetics. Among the goals of the Neural Engineering System Design (NESD) program is digitally accessing up to one million neurons in a human brain and feeding auditory and visual information into the minds of US military personnel.

ABOUT THE AUTHOR

Guy Garcia is an award-winning author, digital media entrepreneur, and expert on evolutionary social trends. His books include *The New Mainstream*, *The Decline of Men*, *Skin Deep*, and *Self Made* (with Nely Galan). A contributor to The New York Times, Time, The Huffington Post, and CNN, he is president of New Mainstream Initiatives for EthniFacts Inc. and a co-founder of the pioneering urban web site Total New York, where he lives.

Experience *Swarm* at ownyourmind.org

CPSIA information can be obtained
at www.ICGtesting.com
Printed in the USA
LVOW03s1654301017
554318LV00002B/168/P